Victoria Routledge is twenty-four, works in publishing and lives in London. This is her first novel.

Friends Like These is utterly unputdownable. Anyone who's ever blindly wanted their college mates to approve of them now, without knowing exactly *why*, will love this book. I adored it.

Cathy Kelly author of *She's The One*

friends
like these

VICTORIA ROUTLEDGE

WARNER BOOKS

A *Warner* Book

First published in Great Britain
by Warner Books in 1999

A CIP catalogue record for this book
is available from the British Library.

ISBN 0 7515 2712 2

Typeset in Berkeley by M Rules
Printed and bound in Great Britain by Clays Ltd, St Ives plc

Warner Books
A Division of
Little, Brown and Company (UK)
Brettenham House
Lancaster Place
London WC2E 7EN

acknowledgements

I'd like to say thank you to all the people who have comprehensively transformed my view of authors over the past year: to James Hale, special agent; to Imogen Taylor, Jill Foulston and Emma Gibb at Little, Brown, for all their help and enthusiasm; to Dan and Fiona Evans, for food and atmosphere beyond compare; to Shona Sutherland, and her Giant Smarties; to Ginny Clay and the Furters, for the soundtrack; to Liz, Daryl, Tom, Hulya, and all the college friends, who can stop 'just wondering . . .' now; and to Jeremy Maule, an inspiring and brilliant teacher, who shone lights on English literature.

But most of all, to Dillon Bryden, who transformed my view of love. Thank you very much.

For my mother, and my father,
with love and thanks

prologue

It was the hottest day of the year.

The punt floated unsecured under the shady branch of a weeping willow. The dark river, like the punt's indifferent pilots, was too idle to shift it anywhere. Trailing willow fronds bent over the hull, hiding the passengers from the glare of the shimmering afternoon. Sporadically, there was a gentle splash as a strawberry was systematically hulled, swallowed and the green core dropped into the water.

Behind the curtain of leaves, one of the girls, sprawling over the prow, turned the pages of a newspaper, reading out fragments of the *Varsity* review of the previous night's May Ball, while the others, hot-eyed behind big Jackie O sunglasses, fanned themselves with papers and ate strawberries from the three cardboard punnets balanced on the side, dripping juice onto their bare legs, trailing their fingers in the greenish water.

There was a long, heavy silence while the punt gently lifted and fell with the pulse of the river, the ripples from more energetically piloted craft farther downstream carrying into the backwater. Distant laughter and splashing drifted on the humid air from the packed beergarden of the Anchor pub, to be swallowed up in the close curtain of willows, where the girls lay in listless contemplation of the end of term and the life stretching out beyond next week's graduation ceremony.

One of the girls pulled off her straw hat and shook out her damp hair, matted to her head with sweat. Running her hands through it did not revive the tired curls. How appropriate, she thought. A week-long hangover had now merged into a general, unshakeable lethargy. She shifted miserably under her flat and nervous mood, now that the ball was over, the results were posted and only the unspoken uncertainty of an existence outside the comforting limits of grades, lectures, supervisions and vacations, was left hanging over them, like the blank white sky above her. Too hot to move. Too hot to speak. Everything already said. She felt the lassitude creeping through her arms and legs, pinning her to the flat boards of the punt.

She drifted back into her thoughts and closed her eyes against the brightness of the sky. No one could summon the energy to break the hushing silence of the river, and they lay there in the hot shade, letting the images of their time at Cambridge trickle unspoken through their minds; the same scenes from three different angles. The heavy summer silence descended on the river, and the newspaper was abandoned over the head of a dozing figure.

The sun began to sink and lose its warmth as the afternoon edged into evening. Far-off noises of a band, sound-checking raggedly before a ball, floated across the water. A gaggle of ducks, replete with stale bread, flew low through the trees, anticipating the rising current in the air.

And as the wind began to hush through the leaves of the willow branches, above the heads of the dreaming girls, rustling the sheets of the newspaper ever so slightly, the first distant rumble of thunder sounded, far away across the Fens.

chapter one

'Well, that's it then,' said Rachel, propping the card up against the teapot. 'We're all grown up. It's official.'

She went back to buttering the toast for the eggs, dropping a piece of crust surreptitiously under the table, where it disappeared with a crunch into a doleful-eyed basset hound.

Finlay nudged the dog out from under Rachel's chair with his foot, looked sarcastically at the boiled eggs in his hands and set them down in front of her. 'Would that be the grown-up who has just requested the soft-boiled eggy with buttery soldiers? In the Muppet eggcups?'

Rachel ignored him and began knocking the top off her soft-boiled eggy with the side of her spoon. 'Laura and Michael are getting married. No, I tell a lie,' she said, picking up the card again and showing it to him, 'they're Getting Engaged. I thought they *were* engaged. They have eight matching Habitat place settings, for God's sake. And four of those they bought together at college – I remember the dinner party they had to celebrate. Laura agonised for weeks about which design was most classic, for which read "easy to add to on a wedding list", and, if my memory serves me correctly, four people had to bring their own bowls and forks. Laura made a big point of giving the other two proper plates to Caroline and Alex.'

Rachel nursed a good grudge as other people nurse a fine wine. Fin opened his mouth to speak, but she carried on, 'Which would have been OK if Caroline hadn't made a big point of giving her the *rest* of the set as a "half-term present" and inviting all of us round for tea the following week to admire it. God knows how much it cost, but Laura had really saved up for the plates and stuff. Poor Laura. When she saw the matching milk jug and sugar bowl produced just like that, she looked as though she was about to burst into tears. Everyone else just said, "Oooh, Caroline, how generous you are!" I tell you, Caroline was the walking incarnation of whoever said that clever thing about the price of everything and the value of nothing. Was it Oscar Wilde? Probably.'

Rachel buttered a soldier too crossly and went through to the plate with the butter knife.

'Only at Cambridge. If we'd spent as much time in the University Library as we did in the home furnishings departments . . .' She didn't finish, and reached for the salt without looking up.

Fin never knew whether to enquire more actively what it was about these college gatherings that brought out an uncharacteristically fractious reaction in Rachel, or just be glad that she rarely went to them. He knew she didn't get on particularly well with some of the old group, yet she was still quick to pick up the latest gossip. Either way, she hadn't been to any of the regular reunions – despite cajoling phone calls from her best friend Alex – but had stayed at home, hoovering feverishly each time.

'So, is this the hen night invitation then?' he asked, carefully. Rachel put down her knife, looked up at him and smiled, her mood suddenly pushed away. Fin felt his heartbeat increase. She had the freshest smile he had ever seen in his six years as a press photographer and she never ever faked it. Fin had done enough politicians and their wives to spot the difference.

'No. It's so typical of them. "Laura and Michael invite you to their Pre-Marital Weekend." That, believe it or not, is their idea of a joke.' Rachel pulled a face. 'They're hauling everyone up to some cottage in the Lake District for the weekend. The Lake District! I ask you. In August! Just us and half of north Lancashire . . .'

The guest list implied by 'everyone' was understood. Finlay hoped guiltily that as an offcomer, he would be excluded from the gathering of what he mentally lumped together as the amorphous cluster of beaming smiles and long tanned legs from the photograph Rachel kept in the bathroom. Six people overloading a punt, having fun, laughing and careless, posing for the familiar camera that seemed to have logged their every step in Cambridge.

That picture was one of his favourites of Rachel, with her hair in damp curls underneath a big straw hat to shield her white skin from the sun, her arm round another girl in a rowing vest, who was lying across the knees of a dark-haired girl with hair like a black scarf, the sun making it gleam down her suntanned back. Alex and Laura. Mike, George and John. Familiar names, if not faces.

'Fin, you wouldn't *want* to come unless you were planning some kind of photographic study of Life in the Wild after University,' said Rachel, turning the teapot nearly upside down, dribbling the few dark brown drops of tea into her mug. 'Mike and John can't come to terms with the fact that the Bobbins Drinking Society isn't officially recognised by the outside world. They still think beer costs ninety pence a pint and has to be consumed within thirty seconds. I mean, even a woman like me knows that port isn't meant to be mixed with lager before consumption. And it's in August – I thought you had a steady weekend date with the paper's cricket team.'

'Oh, no, no, that can be rearranged,' Finlay assured her. 'If *you* want me to come, sweetheart, I'll be there. You know, for moral support and all that. If you want.'

Rachel handed him the toast she'd buttered and cut into a heart shape. 'Darling,' she said and smiled, with her eyes crinkling at the edges. Finlay liked the way Rachel called him 'darling'. No hint of the fashionable PR gush she put on at work, it was old-fashioned, pure Grace Kelly, revealing a little of the romantic beneath the professional exterior, like a glimpse of chiffon beneath bright enamel.

Sometimes, he thought, Rachel hid more than she should beneath the wise-cracking exterior. Her self-confidence was as fragile as the eggshell she was chipping with her spoon. He often wondered if these friends of hers ever saw that or whether they preferred the more straightforward, Dorothy Parker side of her. Finlay thought that this was exactly why he wanted to marry her, so he could draw out the chiffon, which was eternally fascinating, and which, he suspected, kept the bright enamel of her ready wit polished. He raised his eyebrows at his own spontaneous metaphor. Maybe this was what came of living with a copywriter.

He smiled at Rachel as she fiddled with the teapot and reached out to stroke her bare leg under the table with his foot. Unfortunately, through his sock he couldn't quite tell the difference between female calf and short-haired hound and was miffed as Rachel sailed on regardless, while Humpty their basset rolled over in ecstasy beneath his feet.

'Mmm,' said Rachel, thoughtfully chewing some toast. 'I mean, it'll be grim, obviously, but I haven't seen Laura since we moved in here and it'll be good to catch up with her and George and John, if he agrees to go. Mind you, the boys love getting together, they're bound to be there mob-handed. I wonder how long they've been planning this?'

She popped the last bit of toast soldier into her mouth and got up from the kitchen table. It looked full of sunshine, with its blue and yellow cloth and the jug of unseasonable tulips flopping in graceful arcs, despite Rachel's best efforts to keep them upright with a pin and the *Good Housekeeping Book of Household Hints*.

'Is the phone book still propping the study door open, do you know?' she shouted over her shoulder. Finlay heard Rachel wandering through the flat, then, leaning back on his chair to gaze down the hall to where the phone sat outside the sitting room, saw her dialling with a pen to save her freshly manicured nails. He knew that she'd probably seen Ava Gardner do something similar in a black and white film. Although Ava wouldn't have had the luxury of sapphire-blue metallic nail polish.

Fin looked at his watch and saw with some surprise that it was already nine o'clock.

'Shouldn't you be getting off to work, Rachel?' he called down the hall. Rachel was lying on her back with her legs up against the wall like a human set square, the card propped on her chest. 'You're not going to make it in for nine-thirty now. Do you want a lift?'

Rachel bent her head back and smiled at him upside down. 'No, it's Friday,' she said. 'Poppy never bothers to come in until she's been once down each side of Bond Street, so I'm safe until eleven, I reckon. But take me in anyway?'

'OK, but as soon as I've finished my tea. Some of us have work to do.' Fin poured some hot water on the tea leaves, glad for the extra thirty minutes in the post-rush hour London traffic listening to Rachel singing enthusiastically to the car radio. Humpty rubbed himself hopefully against his foot. Fin dropped him a piece of toast and stirred the contents of the teapot with the clean end of a butter knife.

This constant consumption of tea was a habit he'd picked up from Rachel. At art college, before he met her, he'd been a confirmed coffee bachelor, drinking it black with two spoons of instant per cup – or rather, per mug, slightly chipped. It kept him awake to finish printing projects and woke him up after all-night vigils outside politicians' houses, huddled with the rest of the press photographers. Then Rachel, with her beautiful 1950s mint-green china cups and packets of loose leaf English Breakfast tea, had waltzed giddily into his life at a party in a flat-share in Shepherd's Bush. In the morning she had introduced him to the ritual of teaspoons and her delicate biscuits baked in huge batches, and they moved out together the following month. Finlay took a fresh cup through to Rachel in the hallway, now the right way up, and she grinned happily as she took it from him, the phone cradled on her shoulder.

Rachel had drunk a lot of tea at university: in her rooms, in her friends' rooms, in Fitzbillies' with Chelsea buns, in Auntie's Tea Shop in the marketplace with a scrum of tourists (but only if none of the other options were open). It was probably the defining social activity of her girlfriends – they met up for tea as the boys met in the bar for a pint – and was one of the few pivots of their vague unscientific days, untrammelled by test-tubes or unidentifiable lumps of animal, reeking of formaldehyde.

Her experience of university, as Rachel confessed to Fin, had been an intensely painful one, an experience that tea had gone a long way to soothe. Rendered mentally frigid in awe of her surroundings, she read her way diffidently through the heaped piles of books in her rooms and went to the odd lecture if it interested her, producing at the end of this gestative process an essay that was mercilessly dismembered by the supervisor – although by the time the supervision came around she already knew that Henry James meant nothing to her and she shouldn't and didn't really care. This didn't toughen her thin skin against the mercilessness of the exercise.

But after the weekly ordeal, she would rush into the sympathetic kitchens of Laura or Caroline or Alex, who would brew a pot of steaming Assam and indulge her with guilty slices of chocolate cake and a stream of gossip about nontransferable lipsticks, men and the Femidoms that Laura, in her official capacity as Women's Officer, was sent to roadtest on a regular basis by the University Student Union. For these stolen hours in the warm chattiness around her, Rachel felt like a real woman and not a pretend student, which was what she feared she was becoming. And not even a convincing pretend student, at that.

After college, with the advent of taxable income, tea had sustained her social life too, as she couldn't afford to dine out on the pocket-money salary she earned as a press assistant for a PR company. Meeting at the weekend with friends at Bliss for sweet, deep lemon tarts and Darjeeling in tall glasses was a grown-up version of university, and that nostalgia in itself helped to prompt the conversation when it flagged.

More and more, as she became familiar with Laura's explanations of various legal loopholes in the cases she was assigned for training and George's earnest descriptions of liquidation procedures, Rachel felt that her natural flippancy was not in keeping with their Filofaxes. If there was one thing that kept her going – and about the only thing that made dealing with Sloaney PR bimbettes any fun – it was the seemingly infinite source of the ridiculous presented by office life. But when her initial wide-eyed question about the problems of accessorising with barristerial wiggage met with Laura's blank and newly contact-lensed stare, Rachel knew that while she was still a tea person, all her friends now seemed to be pretty much Long Island Iced Tea drinkers to a man.

Alex wasn't in when Rachel phoned her. And there was no reply at the shop either, which meant that Alex must be too busy with Friday morning customers to answer the telephone. Unlike Rachel's semi-hysterical publicity consultant, Poppy Bright, who regarded answering her own phone as an open sign of professional desperation, Alex didn't have an assistant to misspell names and mix up fax and phone numbers.

Rachel dialled Alex's flat again. Her very real reluctance to spend a weekend in the company of Caroline, after three years of conscious avoidance, was struggling with her curiosity to see what her friends would look like in their new 'affianced' personas. However, in spite of her high excitement, Rachel was loath to engage in what would probably be a significant and epic conversation on Alex's mobile phone, and so she waited impatiently until the procession of beeps stopped and left a message.

'Alex, it's Rachel and I *have* to talk to you about this *thing* right now, and you're not in. Damn! Damn! I'm going to keep on phoning until you are in and if you manage to sneak in between calls, phone me instantly. OK? I mean it, I'll keep phoning. It's all I do at work every day and I'm pretty hot on that redial button, *as you know* . . . Pick up, Alex! . . . It's the only thing stopping me running screaming from the window, to be honest, I mean, *can you believe this* . . .'

Click. Alex knew to keep her tape limited to thirty seconds.

At eight o'clock that evening, Alex Murphy kicked open the door of her flat, nearly squashing her black cat Otis, and staggered inside with four carrier bags, which were now nearly cutting through her throbbing fingers, and were filled to ripping point with records and cassettes she needed to sort through and price up. There was no room in the little kitchen, so, pushing open the door with her forehead, she dumped both bags in the bedroom, for want of anything nearer. It wasn't exactly a huge flat.

Alex had spent a long but rewarding day in her tiny Islington record shop, much frequented by Rachel and an increasing number of customers. She waved her hands above her head in an attempt to restore circulation, while the kettle boiled and Otis mewed pitifully for his evil-smelling cat food: Alex prudently kept this in a Tupperware box on her fourth-floor window sill. It was not a big enough flat to dissipate the noxious odours, and although it drove Otis mad to see the tin and not be able to put his greedy little head in it, since acquiring him and his pungent diet from the previous tenant, two too many hopeful invitations back for coffee had swivelled on their heels and departed on entering the kitchen.

When Alex pressed the play button on her flashing answering machine and heard Rachel's bubbling enthusiasm, she was surprised, then pleased, and then intrigued. Surprised because Rachel hadn't sounded so animated in ages. Pleased because it was about time she *was* bloody animated. What with her sexy boyfriend and that flat in Highbury and as many nail varnishes as she could carry home of an evening, the bucket in Alex's almost bottomless well of sympathy was frankly hitting the bottom. And intrigued because she had no idea what could have prompted it.

She tucked the cordless phone under her chin and dialled Rachel's number. There had been four messages showing on the machine, three consisting of only a heavy sigh and a click. Either the weird Goth that had been hanging round the shop had managed to get her phone number or Rachel must have phoned again at least once since she left that first message. This must be 18-carat gossip. Alex flicked through the post on the mat while the phone rang in Rachel's flat. A gas bill, a postcard from Caroline 'having a getaway break' in New York, her biannual Five Star fan club newsletter, two pizza delivery leaflets and, at the bottom, a pink envelope, probably a card, with two necking doves printed on the back with a rubber stamp. This must be the source of Rachel's excitement. She picked it up and turned it over thoughtfully.

After the fourth ring, Rachel's answering machine clicked on. Alex rolled her eyes. Those two were always too busy to come to the phone, one way or another.

'Hello, Rachel Sanderson and Finlay Moran are—' There was some muffled clunking and banging as Rachel picked up and tried to override the tape. Feedback squealed in Alex's ear. 'Hello, hello? Sorry about that . . .'

'Hi, Rach, it's me,' said Alex, leaning against the wall while she sorted through the post. 'Screening your calls again, I see. Thanks for your message. I take it you've managed to keep yourself from leaping into Highbury Fields?'

'Did you *see*? Can you *believe* it?' gurgled Rachel.

'Well, I'm holding "it" in my hands at the moment and, you know, I'm feeling a bit like Jonathan Ross actually.' Alex put on her best 'Caroline the serious act*ress*' voice and fumbled loudly with the pink envelope. 'And the winner is, ooh, I can't get it open, I really *do* hate this because they're all such darling, talented, wonderful friends of mine, but the winner is . . .' She stopped suddenly. Rachel was audibly holding her breath on the other end, making little squeaks of excitement in spite of herself.

'Oh my God. Well, there you go. Welcome to the grown-ups, girls and boys.' Alex turned the card over, in case there was a joke written on the back. There wasn't.

'Can you *believe* it?!?' squawked the voice on the other end of the line.

'Oh come on, Rachel, *Laura and Michael*? It's been on the cards since the end of the first year. I was always amazed that they didn't try to hijack our last May Ball and turn it into the biggest engagement party ever. I suppose the ceremony's going to be in the College Chapel, with an oyster reception in Great Court?' Alex picked up Otis, who was rubbing his head yearningly, pointlessly against the window and put him absent-mindedly on a bookshelf, where the tin of cat food was well out of his line of vision.

'Why do you think *I* know?' said Rachel sarcastically. 'I thought *you* would be the girl with the news. I haven't seen anyone for months. I mean, I was hardly going to be invited to that big do Caroline apparently had the other week, was I? Little Miss Persona Non Grata.' Rachel huffed to herself.

Hey, Rachel, easy on the self-pity, there, lady, thought Alex, but decided to let Rachel talk herself out of it. She usually did. It just sometimes took more than one pot of tea.

'Well, I know *ner*thing, as they say. I'll give Laura a call,' said Alex, stroking Otis under his chin. 'You know Caroline's in New York? I got a postcard of the Statue of Liberty this morning. You and I are in the wrong jobs, hon.' She turned the postcard over and decided to spare Rachel the gushing message, the gist of which was that Caroline was having a fabulous and extremely expensive time somewhere gorgeous.

'The flashy cow,' retorted Rachel, without missing a beat. 'How *is* my least favourite person in the world, then? Still networking for England and on the verge of a major pantomime engagement in Bournemouth? I'm surprised she has time to send postcards to a mere shopkeeper. Doesn't she have a secretary for that kind of thing?'

Alex pulled a face in the mirror above the phone and decided that it was time to play her trump card. It was never wise to rattle Rachel's cage on the topic of Caroline. 'Well, we are talking about the *mere shopkeeper* who, after much research and detective work on your behalf, is now the proud possessor of . . .' Alex raised her voice teasingly.

'Oh God! You *found* it?' Rachel's voice spiralled into a squeak with barely controlled excitement. 'Not *really*?'

Alex knew for a fact, even without the tell-tale thumping in the background, that Rachel was bouncing up and down on the spot with excitement. She was also thankful, in a practical sense, that aside from Fin, the great love of Rachel's life – and the usual destination of most of her wages – was pop music, of the bright and mindless variety that she sold in her shop, where Rachel did the odd day's cover. What had brought them together at college was now turning into a handy business arrangement. Alex pulled the prized double album out of her capacious record/handbag.

'Yes, Rachel Sanderson, *Now That's What I Call Music Six* is yours at long last. You haven't seen each other for over ten years, but surprise, surprise – tonight, The Real Roxanne and Hit Man Howie T—'

'*Bang zoom, baby let's go-go . . . Well, there's no-no way I'm gonna go-go easy, to the show-show, rock it to the beat . . .*'

Rachel was bouncing in time to a song which, Alex reflected, they were probably the only two people in London to remember. In its entirety, rap, bleeps, beatbox breaks and all. For this, thought Alex, we translated the *Complete Works of Chaucer* until five o'clock in the morning and then walked through the Backs of Cambridge, picking lilac with the dew still fresh on the leaves, thinking we were it. La la la.

'Hello? Hello! Rachel? Enough already,' Alex bellowed down the phone. 'I'll find out from George what the full story is. The boys must know something, they spend enough time together,' she said decisively. If the boys did know anything, it would almost certainly be by accident. But then they might just know everything worth finding out and simply not realise it.

'I wouldn't bank on it,' snorted Rachel.

'I'm seeing George tonight. Maybe autosuggestion will prompt some recollection. Maybe Mike has opened his heart to one of them.'

'More like they've kidnapped him and taken him on a Lads' Holiday to Marbella to bring him to his senses. You know what they're like about Commitment.' Rachel gave the word a disdainful capital letter and, affecting an air of frustrated memory loss, added, 'Now they have a useful phrase for it, don't they? Um, I can't quite . . .'

'I don't know what love *means*!' they wailed in unison.

'It is a *classic*,' said Rachel with feeling. 'One of these days, I'm going to write one of those epic songs for Meatloaf called "I Wanna Make Love To Ya Baby (But I Don't Know What Love Means)". With all five of them on backing vocals. Meatloaf and the Maybe Babies.' She began giggling.

'Oh come on Rachel, you have to stop this cynicism. They're all just a terrible memory for you, now you've encountered Islington Man. They just don't know any better. Go on, bugger off and wrap yourself round that gorgeous photographer of yours. Go on. Leave me to your desolate rejects. I'm meant to be all glamorous in All Bar One in—' Alex tucked the phone under her neck and twisted round to look at the wall clock and groaned. 'Oh arse and feck, in ten minutes.' Catching sight of her bemused-looking cat, she plucked Otis from his terrifyingly high perch and apologetically dropped the little cat into his basket. 'I don't have time for this, you dreadful woman, I'll report back tomorrow.'

'Tomorrow, hon. Come and meet me for a drink or something. I'd love to see you. And I want the full story. Price of ring, best man, honeymoon suite, the lot, OK?'

'OK, OK, look, I have to recreate my face and find something ironed. You know what George's like about Ladies in Jeans. I'd swear that he fell out of the Ark, if I didn't think that Noah would have rejected him on account of his reproductive capabilities.'

'Good*bye*, Alex.'

Alex hung up the phone and hopefully started to shake the creases out of the shirt hanging over the back of the chair in her bedroom. As it was Friday, George, she knew, would be all decked out in his slightly-less-formal-but-still-smart suit. As with many other aspects of his personality,

George's wardrobe was reliable and unfailingly correct. Alex and Rachel had often discussed the merits of opening a shop, with George as a consultant, naturally, selling one-stop clothes for bankers and City chaps, with firmly designated 'When to Wear and with What' sections – a much better financial prospect than Divinyl, 82a Cross Street. George would love that, thought Alex wryly, as she dug around in a drawer for a pair of tights to match the only clean skirt she could find; a much better all-round investment return.

After ten minutes of frustrated scrabbling through piles of clothes, all pending washing, Alex had managed to assemble something approaching reasonably smart and considerably less comfortable than the jeans and T-shirt she'd had on before. Crossly, she thought that she only kept a skirt in her tiny wardrobe for trips to the bank and drinks in City pubs with her friends from Cambridge. And the odd parental visit. Otis looked quizzically at her.

'Yes?' snapped Alex, displaying a level of annoyance unusual for her. As she said to the perpetually burbling Rachel, talking aloud to yourself is for the terminally disturbed and characters in ITV sitcoms only. As Rachel was starring in a widescreen musical adaptation of her own life, it didn't bother her much, but Alex, living on her own, in her own small flat, knew that it was one short step from talking to your cat to actually holding arguments with yourself in Sainsbury's about which colour loo roll to buy.

Otis looked back at her in an enigmatic cat manner. She looked down at her legs. There was a ladder running in a perfectly perpendicular line from her knee-cap to the toe of her navy court shoe. At the top of the ladder was a hasty smear of Chanel Rouge Noir nail varnish, an emergency repair job from the tights' last outing – with Caroline.

Oh bloody hell, thought Alex. Caroline, who never ever laddered her tights, could probably date the ladder from the Rouge Noir alone. She had munificently brought them all a bottle each over from Bloomingdale's at the high point of the *Pulp Fiction* fashion frenzy before it was even available in Britain, only to have her thunder stolen by Rachel, who had been working on a Chanel project in her office and had had fingernails like enamelled blackberries for at least a fortnight. It was striking on fingernails, but had the unfortunate effect of highlighting Alex's ladder like a big red arrow. Could she wear them backwards and hope for the best? Did she have a skirt long enough to hide the ladder if she did? Alex cursed inwardly, put on the record she'd bought for Rachel and resigned herself to being at least ten minutes late.

While Alex was arguing her way through her wardrobe with Otis, George was waiting at the bar of All Bar One with a Diet Coke. He flicked through his Psion organiser to see if there was anything he could be doing while he waited for Alex, who was inexplicably late and hadn't even phoned to let him know why she was delayed. He fished his phone out of his briefcase to check it was switched on. It was. Maybe she was stuck in traffic or couldn't find anywhere to park. At least she could ring.

George kept forgetting that Alex, and indeed Rachel, his erstwhile girlfriend, did not have a briefcase or a Psion organiser. Or a car. Rachel went everywhere by bus or in the passenger seat of Finlay's Golf. And though mainly out of defiance at her lowly position, she was the model of efficiency in her ridiculously casual office; outside work she was the proud non-owner of any diary of any kind, except the one hidden in her knicker drawer in which she wrote private poems and very bad lyrics. Alex had a diary of sorts, in which she wrote down the names of albums requested by regulars at Divinyl and the dates of record fairs in dodgy hotel dining rooms. Aside from these, both girls operated a complex Engagement Diary of un-sticky Post-it notes on phones and messages scribbled on the backs of old pizza delivery leaflets, stuck with magnets on fridge doors. For reasons such as these, Rachel and Alex were not deemed by the others to have yet come to terms with the demands of the Real World.

Something along these lines was running through George's head as Alex strode into the bar in what looked suspiciously like an ankle-length binbag. He decided not to mention it in the interests of their cautious relationship and instead rose gallantly to his feet and kissed her proffered cheek. Alex rather disturbed him by kissing his cheek back and he was glad to be able to turn to the bar and order her a . . . ?

'Laphroig, no ice, please, George, thank you.' She sat down gingerly on a barstool, trying not to let her skirt ride up to reveal the ladder. The only skirt long enough to hide the best part of the run was something she'd unwillingly accepted from Rachel and stowed at the back of her wardrobe as soon as Rachel had left the house, hoping Otis would relieve her of the burden by making a nest in it. It was from a Graduate Design Show and was apparently 'edgy'. Hmm. Alex crossed her feet demurely to hide the visible stretch of white ladder on her left foot. She had sacrificed ten precious minutes 'boosting her natural curl' with Velcro rollers in an attempt to minimise the impact of the skirt on George and it appeared to be working. Sort of. If Emmeline Pankhurst could see me now, she thought, she would slap my face. And she would be right.

George turned back with the drinks and smiled approvingly at her unusually ladylike posture. If she kept her bag on her knee, no one would be able to see that bizarre skirt and it looked as though she'd made an effort with her hair for a change. If only she had a proper job, she'd have more idea of how to dress for these places. There were three lads from J.P. Morgan in here, and he didn't want them to get the wrong idea about Alex and his relationship with her. God forbid! But those eyes, when they looked so sparkly, went a long way to excusing her rather spit and sawdust taste in drinks.

'So, Laura and *Mike*, hey?' He raised his glass and looked enigmatically over the top of it.

Typical George, thought Alex. What was that meant to mean? At least he'd mentioned it first. She returned his questioning look, to which he raised an eyebrow, and, despite herself and in direct contravention of what she'd agreed with Rachel in their last tearful pep talk, Alex felt her heart pound in an embarrassingly clichéd manner. She *knew* he was a trainee fund manager, she *knew* he liked girls who had an IQ roughly in proportion with their waist measurements, she *knew* his experience of women was based largely on the 'Girls in Pearls' activities of his sisters, but oh God, the way he looked in a business suit! Cupid was a malevolent little sod. She took a firm grip on herself and also the barstool for good measure.

'Well, yes! Laura and *Mike*!' She tried to look meaningful. He raised the other eyebrow. They both smiled, Alex sardonically, George suggestively. Facial expression deadlock.

The boys had whole evenings like this, except they didn't seem to see it as parrying. To them, this constituted conversation. They could go on for hours, gurning happily at each other, without exchanging a single coherent sentence and then stagger out of whatever tandoori house they'd met at, beerily congratulating themselves on what great mates they still were, even now they'd left college and had so much to talk about. Alex did not have the patience for this. Life was too short and this pre-wedding party business was too fascinating a source of gossip. So she plunged in recklessly with an opinion.

'Well, I'm thrilled for them!' she said with genuine affection. 'Really thrilled! Has Mike picked a best man yet?'

George poked at the ice in his glass nervously. 'Yes, he has, actually. Me. I'm the best man and John is the head usher. Hasn't Laura sorted out bridesmaids with you all?'

George, it had to be said, was the ideal best man. Alex could see the checklists forming in his head already: a) notify bridesmaids and identify universally popular outfit colours; b) defuse explosive potential confrontations between the chief bridesmaid and the matron of honour; c) pacify those not chosen to be bridesmaids with spurious ceremonial duties involving wedding cake/guest logistics.

'No, but I expect she'll announce it all on this weekend do next month. Engagement party in August, wedding in . . . ?'

'February.' George nodded unhappily. 'Laura has had what I hope is a temporary mental aberration and is talking about—'

'No!' said Alex. 'Not Valentine's Day?'

George nodded. They exchanged grimaces.

'The day they started going out. Oh dear. It all seems very advanced,' said Alex, 'but I suppose they've been planning it for a long time, haven't they?' This was indisputable. Mike's first anniversary present to Laura had been a subscription to *Brides and Setting Up Home*. She had got the special magazine storage files for her birthday. 'I mean, it's not as though we weren't expecting it. It's just that now it's actually going to happen . . .' Alex's voice trailed away as she found herself slipping into a George trance. She was suddenly aware that, quite without meaning to, on autopilot she sounded as though she were discussing the demise of a much-loved but elderly family pet.

'Still,' she went on, perhaps a shade over-brightly, 'what about this Lakeland cottage? Sounds like old times! Just the posse, all together again – we can rabbit on shamelessly about The Good Old Days all weekend! Photograph albums ahoy!' Alex gave George her best smile and to the delight of her churning stomach, he smiled back until a memory passed across his face like a cloud.

'As long as it's not like that riverboat holiday we had in the second year,' he grunted, poking more savagely at his ice. 'Who the hell suggested that? You girls cooked that one up, didn't you? Only God will ever know how close I came to hurling Mike overboard, bloody guitar and all.'

'Oh, come on, George – we had a *lovely* time. The weather was gorgeous! You loved it! Those afternoons listening to Wimbledon and sunbathing, the Pimms, those hilarious navigation charts you and Simon drew up . . .' Alex stopped while she could keep that enthusiasm in her voice.

George grunted again. 'Well, no one ever argued in Guadalajara, and we nearly got *deported*.'

According to George, the Lads' Trip to South America, painstakingly documented on camcorder by the relentless John, had been the official high point of their lives so far. For six weeks, George, Mike, John and their medic friend Andy had roved about the continent, drinking, picking up stomach bugs, climbing up freezing mountains and 'nearly seeing crocodiles'. They had been robbed three times but no Chilean bandit was able to prise the camcorder from John's hands: consequently, every mountain, seedy bar, bus depot, outdoor toilet and 'nearly' crocodile had been recorded for posterity and played back to the girls in full Technicolor over several evenings at John's parents' house in Chiswick. George's virulent and repetitive stomach upset was a regular highlight, as was the 'harmless' virus Mike picked up in a swamp, which had the unfortunate, if hilarious, effect of turning his urine – 'and, ah ha, *other* bodily fluids, ah ha ha' – black. Alex had vowed never, ever to go to Chile on the strength of this video alone. John was now a trainee travel researcher at Channel Five.

'But this will be the last time we'll all be together as, you know,' Alex could hardly believe she was stooping to this level to get information, '. . . the gang! After the wedding, that's it – grown-up! Goodbye, groovy May Balls and flaming sambuca evenings. Hello, Mr Mortgage and Mrs Support Tights.'

George looked at Alex's far from grown-up skirt and raised his eyebrow again – in much the same way as Otis had earlier. She dropped her enthusiastically raised hands and glared back, hating herself for finding him attractive when she knew she would smack most other men who gave her a look quite that patronising.

'It will be fun,' she said, holding his gaze steelily and laying a warning emphasis carefully on each word. 'I'm looking forward to it already. So's Rachel. She's looking into what PR Dunleary and Bright do in the mountain climbing fashion area. She's already got us both kitted out in funky Kangol ski-hats and fleeces. The Mountain Rescue won't see a better dressed climber in distress all year, or a hotter one.'

George knew them both better than to believe a word of it, and positively dreaded whatever Rachel would turn up in, but his impeccable politeness prevented him from commenting, particularly to Alex, whom he knew from experience to have a sharp tongue and an even sharper slap – the topic of college folklore amongst the boys, who secretly envied her merciless hand-eye coordination, even while tanked up on Laphroig. And they rather envied her capacity for that too.

George gave Alex a nervous smile, as he played with the ice in his glass. Was she trying to play footsie with him? She might just be shifting in her seat. He could never quite judge how keen she was on him, whether he was on the verge of being relegated to 'just a friend' again. Alex was so much cooler than the other girls he knew – and impossible to read. And as far as the weekend went, he intended to approach it with some caution too. On the whole, life seemed to present George with a series of suspended disasters, each only temporarily averted. Despite his suave and self-assured manner, he operated on the perpetual suspicion that something thoroughly illogical was lurking around each corner and he was rarely disappointed.

This was one consolation in the mutually dissatisfying relationship – if you were to stick your neck out and call it that – he and Alex were sort of conducting. When she could turn up to a City wine bar in practically any combination of random clothing, nearly all of it guaranteed to reveal, embarrass or bewilder, surely that, he reasoned, must be his quota of anxiety for the day – *more*, he thought, surreptitiously looking at her skirt again with a shudder. He had a table booked for nine-thirty at Coast and hoped that it would be one in a corner. Or maybe that was the thing to wear. He didn't mind admitting that he hadn't the faintest idea whether it was or not. He'd certainly never seen anything like it in the wardrobes of either of his sisters.

George violently fancied Alex when she made a room stop while she walked across it, and yet dreaded her arrival at his side in case she were wearing something advertising a thrash metal band or, his personal worst, something orange. That was the uneasy fulcrum of their troubled relationship. Alex really liked George for the way he would drive over London to pick her up if she got stranded in Hackney on the night bus, but hated the lecture she inevitably got on the way back. (She also dreaded having to listen to a selection from George's expensive in-car entertainment system, which usually meant at least one song by Bob Marley, Lenny Kravitz and/or Annie Lennox. These things hurt her. Rachel understood. George wouldn't.) Both were privately convinced that the other wasn't really right for them, despite the self-evident mutual attraction, but were too polite to think of a way of ending it on these grounds alone.

And so George and Alex had been meeting up for drinks and dinner on a studiedly casual but nevertheless regular basis for a year or so after leaving college, without making it public amongst their gossip-hungry friends. This was a tribute in itself to George's caution and Alex's pants dragging her famous pragmatism along kicking and screaming behind, even with his tendency to music-lite. Which is not to say, of course, that people didn't know.

'So, go on then, George,' said Alex, with a glint in her eye. 'What's really prompted this display of marital intention? And is it catching?' Now she raised her dark eyebrows and George's stomach lurched. Worryingly, he couldn't say exactly why.

George was, despite outward appearances, as big a gossip as anyone, but only Alex really knew the true extent of his insider knowledge. He was conscious of his reputation for scrupulous maturity amongst his friends and had honed a look which said, 'I can't believe you're giving credence to this terrible rumour about one of our friends by repeating it, but I'm too adult to stop you repeating it, so go ahead and I won't tell,' which had the happy effect of preserving his reputation *and* gaining him access to the best and most unrepeatable gossip. When Alex conveyed the story to Rachel, who either broadcast it or sat on it, depending on its value (a true PR at heart), it was absolutely impossible to trace it back to George.

George swallowed the last of his Diet Coke and furrowed his brow. 'Well, I'm not sure I should repeat this, but I was round at Mike's flat with the lads last Friday, while Laura was off on a training course in Guildford, and, you know, we'd got a couple of crates in from the offie, like at college, you know.' Alex knew. 'And we were a bit drunk, well, more to the point, John was a bit drunk.' John the notorious 'I love you' shandy lightweight, who belligerently claimed to speak fluent Czech when under the influence of tequila. 'And I took him up to the bathroom to, er, and, well, I was waiting outside, shall we say, when the phone rang. It was a bit noisy and you know how one girl's voice sounds the same when you're a bit pissed? Well, er, yes, they do, actually,' he added hastily, 'but anyway, I answered it and, I don't know, I said, "Hello" or something.'

George paused. Alex looked at him closely. He was waffling, trying to decide how much to tell her. This was evidently more important than she'd thought. There couldn't be that much to answering a phone, even for George. She made encouraging hmm-ing noises.

'And you know, Alex,' said George, dropping his voice to an unnecessary murmur, 'I could have sworn that it was *Caroline* on the other end.'

'But she's in New York, isn't she? I got a postcard from her saying she was out there for a break, maybe looking at drama schools, she said.'

'Well, that wouldn't stop her phoning Mike at home. If she had something . . . important to tell him.'

With a superhuman effort, Alex pulled herself up before she started speculating any further. 'Oh come on, George, what's so strange about Caroline calling Mike? What makes it more strange than Rachel calling John or me calling Andy? We are allowed to phone each other, aren't we?' Except, of course, that *we're* not, she thought. Not according to your Rough Guide to Clandestine Relationships.

'Well, that's just it, isn't it? There's nothing strange about it at all – so why did she hang up as soon as she heard my voice? Why didn't she just say, "Oh hi, George, can I speak to Mike, please?" and I'd have gone and got him, no problem, no questions, scraped John off the bathroom floor and thought no more about it. It was the way she sort of gasped and went, "Oh, er, no," then hung up. Almost . . . *deliberately*.'

George stared into his empty glass, the melting cubes of ice submerging the Coke-stained lemon slice. The bar was filling up now with herds of well-scrubbed young graduate bankers in suits. He was, for once, reluctant to share this gossip with Alex, but needed to hear it come out of his mouth in order to reassure himself of its irrelevance. Although he wouldn't admit as much to Alex, he was disconcerted.

'I mean,' he went on, 'I can't swear it was Caroline. She

didn't say enough to be certain, but the manner was hers, if you know what I mean.' Alex knew exactly what he meant – Caroline's 'manner' could transmit down far more intransigent media than a mere telephone wire. 'But where is she meant to be? You say she's in New York, I got a postcard from her in New York, but . . .' George paused and looked embarrassed. He'd clearly said more than he'd meant to.

'Come on, George,' prodded Alex, intrigued. 'You've gone too far now. But what?'

'Because,' said George slowly, 'I dialled 1471 to be sure and it was Caroline's number. I thought it would be something to tease him with, you know, who's your random bird in Chelsea, then, eh? But it was Caroline's number in Notting Hill. I suppose it could have been her flatmate, but . . .' He looked up to meet Alex's curious gaze. Caroline's flatmate was a student teacher from Newcastle. Not even a partially drunk George could mistake her broad Geordie accent for Caroline's glass-cutting Sloane drone.

'Even then,' George continued, 'I wouldn't have given it much thought – except for feeling guilty for being so nosy – if Mike hadn't acted so, you know, *touchy* all evening.'

Alex's eyes widened. This was more than even Rachel could have hoped for. It looked like Caroline was really going too far this time. But *Michael*?

'What do you mean? Wasn't it that evening when he broke the news of his defection from the Lads?' The bar was getting noisier by the minute. She signalled expertly to the barman for a bottle of wine, while George gazed blankly ahead into space.

She leaned in towards him. 'But George? What do you mean, touchy? I know what Mike's like when he's drunk and I'm surprised he was capable of any behaviour as specific as "touchy".' She didn't want to push this too far, in case the Code of Honour clanged down like a portcullis. It had been known to happen in the past and was frustrating in the extreme. But touchy? What was that meant to mean? Surely not as in 'touchy-feely'? No! Not Mike? Not George!

As the barman put the empty wine glasses down on the bar with a clink and a frankly unnecessary leer at the pair of them George seemed to come back to life.

'No, this is ridiculously melodramatic and I shouldn't have mentioned it at all. Mike was probably nervous – it's a big thing, getting married. God knows it gives me butterflies just thinking about it and it's not even my wedding.'

Alex tried not to look disappointed on a selection of different levels, while George poured her a glass of Rioja. At worst, she felt horrified. The boys were vituperatively homophobic to a man and if Mike really had . . . had *approached* George – George, her boyfriend! Well, clandestine boyfriend. Lover, even . . .

After a thrill of pure scandal, she abandoned the idea, reluctantly, as being improbable in the extreme. More likely, though, was this underhand possibility that Caroline and Mike were conducting some kind of last ditch fling, even while poor Laura was deliberating over whether to go for a short veil or a cathedral length one. Alex sizzled crossly and thought how best to tell Rachel, who tended to take gossip about Caroline with a 'Light the Blue Touch Paper and Retire' approach.

All this indignation was making her stomach rumble and she hoped that when the conversation level in the bar reached shouting point, and she was talking right into George's fragrant ear, he would suggest supper somewhere more peaceful. She knew he didn't really like the see-and-be-seen of this kind of place and to prompt the thought, she turned, deliberately, to the barman for a bowl of cashew nuts. Damn the calories.

George finished the wine in his glass and wondered how best to salvage this situation before Alex's battlewagon rolled into action and straight over to Mike's house. He could practically hear the cogs working, much to his horror. George looked up to say something to her, just as the barman, grinning goofily into Alex's wide blue eyes, unwittingly poured her an extra-large helping of salted cashews, reeling under the full effect of her charm. Admittedly, the barman wasn't in a position to witness the full horror of the skirt from Art Student Hell, but George felt a faint stirring that, in a mind not wearing a smart but subdued tie, might have come out as, 'Phwoar, that's my bird.' He looked casually at his watch and noted with quiet relief that it was nearly nine-fifteen.

'Come on, Alex, I've got a reservation for nine-thirty at Coast,' he shouted over the back of a futures trader he vaguely knew from work, who had unceremoniously barged in between his and Alex's barstools and was now gesturing impatiently to the barman, threatening Alex's precarious bowl of cashews. She turned and looked at him with such a shining smile that it was only when they were halfway there that George remembered exactly what she was wearing.

chapter two

Darling Molly, typed Rachel on auto-pilot, her eyes glazed over. *How thrilling it was to see you at Arabella's gallery opening last night!*

The first time Rachel had played the contents of her audio-typing tape to Alex, she had been met with a pair of incredulously narrowed blue eyes. 'No,' Alex had said slowly, in a sarcastic children-and-old-people voice, 'you're confusing *Absolutely Fabulous* and Real Life again, Rachel. I know it must be hard in your job, but please try to concentrate.' To which Rachel had replied, reasonably enough, that *Absolutely Fabulous* had only been written because there was a whole mine of inspiration out there, a large seam of which, in her opinion, ran straight through the feng shui designed offices of Dunleary & Bright Ltd.

I, and all the other girls in the press office, I might add! have done nothing but admire the wonderful little Prada creation you were wearing and we are simply green with envy!!

Rachel was simply nothing of the sort; though she could hardly have failed to know the fashion editor's dress was

Prada, having had it pointed out to her as such in dramatic stage whispers at regular intervals during the course of the open evening. However, unable to hoist her willing disbelief any higher than the normal day-to-day level necessary for working in the office, she had completely failed to work out why someone would pay quite so much for something quite so ordinary looking. Nice cut, nice material, er, nice shade of navy, even. But as far as she was concerned, it had a great big label hanging off the zip, reading '4 months' salary'. Not to mention a distinctly polyester look about it.

I do hope to be seeing you again on Wednesday at our own little open evening for Ffyona's new spring-summer collection – it truly is fabulous and we're having it catered by – guess who? Rafe's new company!! So, don't forget us, please, you must come, darling, and maybe we'll see what other lovely things you managed to snap up on that last Italian trip! Much, much love and many kisses, Poppy. Kiss, kiss. That's exes, Rachel, not the whole word, poppet. And do it on the good paper, sweetie – this woman knows John Morgan at GQ.

Rachel came to the last effusion feeling quite exhausted, having had to struggle between her natural reluctance to type such unpunctuated rubbish and her wry experience that anything less rubbishy would be suspiciously unPoppyesque. She printed off the letter on Dunleary & Bright's thick and creamy headed notepaper and read it through, grimacing slightly. It was still teetering on the edge of self-parody and this was after she had discreetly removed two more 'little's, three 'fabulous's and a 'darling'. Not to mention all the underlinings, at which frankly she had to draw the line. As it were. With a sigh for her lost standards, she pp'd it Rachel – *no surnames, darling, they're for civil servants* – with the first biro that came to hand. It was green.

Rachel looked at her curly green name with a vague feeling of horror and thought about redoing it. Would they care? Would they read it? Would they just assume that Poppy's feng shui consultant had insisted on green office stationery?

She folded the letter apathetically and slipped it into the envelope, for which it was half a centimetre too big. She tried, hopefully, to fold the flap round the sticking-out letter, but Dunleary & Bright's envelopes were of the superior thick paper that did not respond to negotiation of this kind. She resigned herself to printing it all off again.

This was not the kind of thing Rachel needed on a Monday morning. It was hard enough to drag herself unwillingly round the Underground as it was, reading the Media Section of the *Guardian* on the escalators and trying to keep her heavy gym bag tucked in front of her so more motivated people could jog up the left-hand side towards their open-plan office mazes. And this weekend had been so blissful – Saturday walking in Richmond Park with Fin and Humpty, followed by Sunday looking after Divinyl while Alex went off to a record fair – that a persistent voice in her head had demanded a reasonable explanation as to why she was reluctantly returning to the office that morning at all. Rachel tried not to think of reasons.

God, if only her tutors could see her now. She was glad they couldn't. After the first six months she'd had guilty office-hour visions, not unlike Ebenezer Scrooge's, as ghosts of supervisions past floated through the chrome-framed reception doors, some balefully waving copies of the *Riverside Shakespeare* at her, others brandishing enormous hourglasses, but all dressed in a very *now* black tunic style ensemble, none the less.

Rachel had given up trying to explain her job to her

parents, partly because she couldn't actually bring herself to reduce her office existence to its component parts. 'I file things.' 'I fax things.' 'I pop out for spare tights and champagne.' During the last conversation she'd had about work the previous month, her mother, a solicitor with twenty years' experience in cutting straight through legalese, had said very little, merely lifted an eyebrow and smiled wryly. Her father, wandering from his garage through to the kitchen in his oil-stained weekend jumper, had given her one of his reassuring hugs and reminded her – again – that as long as she was happy, they were happy. To be fair, by now they had stopped offering to pay for the law conversion course. But somehow this didn't make Rachel, with her CV full of A Level prizes and awards, feel any better about her wobbly approach to finding a more suitable occupation than the strangely random one she was in at the moment.

A thick waft of Angel perfume made its presence felt in the limited space that Rachel still called her desk, despite Poppy's protestations about 'cutting chi energies'. Four seconds later, resolutely studying her typing, she heard the voice of the body attached to it. She had got through to two o'clock without a visitation. It was only a matter of time.

'Rachel, have you done the press release for Sock It To Them yet? It's *incredibly* urgent.' The voice rolled plummily around the vowels like a well-bred spaniel. 'The courier has just dropped the pics off and I want it out to the papers in an hour. It's hot stuff, you know!'

Rachel looked up from the keyboard and attempted to disguise her contempt beneath a veil of stupidity. 'Sorry, Harriet, I missed that – when did Poppy say she wanted it by?'

Harriet Blythe bridled at this, all too predictably, thought

Rachel. As if I care about your job description. As if I could even describe your job.

'I said I wanted it *now* and if you really took an interest in our clients, Rachel, you would too! It's not every day we have an international role model, yet real-life working mum, wearing our socks.' Harriet dropped the courier package into Rachel's in-tray from an unnecessary height, turned on her heel and marched back into her office, where she proceeded to make a loud personal phone call to her friend Zinny, who was a permanent temp, floating like blond deadwood around the smarter offices of Knightsbridge.

Hello? Hello? thought Rachel, narrowing her eyes at the door. Anyone there? Angel lingered muggily in the air around her desk. She opened the envelope and shook out the photos. They were fairly typical 10 × 8's of Cherie Blair, leaving some City gym, brandishing a briefcase in front of her face – but not too obstructively as to spoil the photo – and striding towards her car.

Rachel squinted at the photograph. Princess Di used to do this a lot better, she thought. Cherie just doesn't look 'surprised' enough. Sweatshirt by Polo. Trainers by Reebok. Pretty good kit, though. She slid open a drawer and took out the magnifying loupe she used for mounting Finlay's transparencies when the office was quiet. Socks by Sock It To Them – or, as she called them in her head, Socks For Sloanes. No wonder Poppy had been holed up in her office on the phone since she wiggled in at half past eleven. At £10 per single sock and now featured on the lovely size 6's of Cherie B, these were obviously *the* socks to be seen in. She scribbled this useful piece of spontaneous gush down on her draft press release. Vintage Poppy. Rachel screwed up her face. God. She must actually be getting good at this.

Rachel turned the print to look for the byline and noticed with some surprise that it was Dan Wingate. Since when did he bother with Cherie? Dan was one of Finlay's photographer friends, an Action Man lookee-likee who prided himself on getting the pictures while the rest of the press photographers were still getting their instructions from the picture desk. The epitome of inscrutable commando cool on his all-terrain mountain bike. Rachel liked him, despite being more than a little wary of his covert radios and secret cameras. Even his bike had stealth tyres.

Harriet, who nursed aspirations as a 'media' type, since she lived in a loft conversion in Clerkenwell and had a school chum who worked on the diary page of the *Evening Standard*, had an enormous crush on Dan Wingate, despite having met him only once, at a private view of Tom Stoddart's Sarajevo photography, where Dan had arrived in semi-combat gear, straight from a weekend camped outside Balmoral, and had left after ten minutes, having mysteriously got word of Noel Gallagher's arrival at Heathrow with three unidentified young friends. Harriet had privately added Rachel's proximity to the James Bond of the tabloid press to her list of grievances against her: a list that began with Rachel's immaculate manicures and worked its way up to the powerful effect of her occasional sarcasm; as none of them, the fearsome Poppy Bright included, completely understood it, it gave Rachel what Harriet felt was an unfair advantage.

As she was picking out the best shot, with the Sock It To Them logo most prominent on the First Lady Ankle, Rachel blinked with surprise at the corner window, just behind Cherie's right ear. Was that Caroline's face in the gym café? She angled her desk lamp onto the picture. It was so hard to tell at that focus depth. How odd. It might very well be – she knew Caroline went to some pretty flashy places and liked to be seen at them. If it was her, the photo must have been taken before the trip to New York. There was no date on the back, but if Poppy was melting the phones talking up the pictures, they must be very recent. Rachel was intrigued, despite herself.

She picked up the phone and cradled it on her shoulder. As a decoy, should Harriet come out to check on her, Rachel began typing the outline of a press release on her screen as she dialled Alex's shop number.

Stepping out in style with Sock It To Them!! Sporty Cherie is holding court at her gym, kitted out in Sock It To Them's new Hurlingham range in super comfort cotton. It's 10 out of Number 10 for the Blairs' fitness fanatic, who'll brook no Opposition in these . . .

'Divinyl,' said Alex's voice, above a background of Doctor and The Medics.

'Alex, it's me.' Rachel propped the photograph against her computer. 'Look, don't read anything into this, but where, exactly, is Caroline at the moment?'

'It's not like you to take an interest in Caroline's where-abouts,' said Alex – a touch guardedly, Rachel noticed with surprise. 'She's in New York, as far as I know. You remember, I told you the other day when you phoned. At least she was on Friday, when she posted that postcard of Grand Central Station to me. She was "having a getaway break from the draining analytical sessions of her workshop course on 'The Inner Child of Ibsen'." And doing some shopping. Why?'

'Oh,' said Rachel, a little disappointed. 'Are you sure? I mean, she couldn't have got back today?'

'No, I don't think so. I've still got the spare set of keys she insisted on leaving with me before she jetted off. I was thinking of having a party in her flat but you'd have to glue everything down. If it's not glued down already.'

Harriet cruised past Rachel's desk en route to the coffee machine and looked pointedly at her watch. Rachel glared back and simultaneously typed some gibberish without looking at the keys.

'Yes, Dan, we've got your photos here and, really, they're *everything* we could have hoped for!' exclaimed Rachel loudly into the receiver, her eyes fixed on Harriet's back, which straightened suddenly over the coffee dispenser, introducing an unflattering series of wrinkles into her velvet trousers. On the other end of the line, Alex held the phone at arm's length, furrowed her brow at the receiver and resumed the conversation.

'Why do you want to know?'

Harriet was hovering around the desk, her eyes gleaming. Rachel frowned at her, covered the mouthpiece and stage-whispered, 'Please, Harriet, this is a *personal* call. You know Dan Wingate's a friend of Finlay's – he's promised me some prints.' She flapped her hands in a dismissive gesture and cooed into the phone, 'No, sorry, Dan, it's just a courier arriving.' Harriet scrawled '10 MINS!!!' in angry red pen on a Post-it note, slapped it on Rachel's computer screen and strode off.

In a normal, if hushed, tone, Rachel picked up where she'd left off. 'Because I've got some photos here from Socks For Sloanes – the lovely Cherie QC outside the Harbour Club or similar – and I'm positive that Caroline is in one of the windows. It looks just like her, all that hair, big shades on head, mouth wide open. But these are from yesterday morning so I suppose it can't be. What a shame. She'd be crushed if she knew what an opportunity she's missed for some vicarious swanking. Never mind. How's the shop? How're the muffins selling?'

She continued typing out her press release with the phone tucked under her right ear. Harriet opened her office door. Rachel raised her voice and smiled sweetly into the receiver whilst maintaining eye contact with Harriet. 'Oh, black and whites, please, Dan – we're just having the flat decorated and I'd simply hate anything to clash.' The door slammed.

There was a longish pause on the other end, long enough for a whole chorus of 'Spirit in the Sky'.

'Come for a pot of tea at Bliss this evening,' said Alex mysteriously, 'and bring a copy of that print with you.'

chapter three

It was ten minutes to seven and George had been at work since ten to eight that morning, trying to shift some of the paperwork from one end of his desk to the other. He'd taken fifteen minutes for lunch, to grab a sandwich and a Coke from the sandwich bar opposite the office, and by the time he got back to his desk, there was a priority e-mail from the group secretary, saying in as terse a fashion as e-mails can: 'Pls see MRB in his office before you leave re expenses.'

For years, George had imagined he was born for the cut and thrust of life in the world of financial markets – until he actually moved his laptop and silver fountain pen into one and then changed his mind before his first payslip arrived. Unlike most of the other graduate trainees on his floor, he didn't have the obligatory desk photo of a blond girlfriend grinning up from a fur headband, skis casually over one shoulder, and he knew that when he did, that really would be the end. Another reason to be glad for Alex: she was about as likely to go skiing, with or without him, as she was to take up night classes in Rudimentary Embalming.

He was just printing out his final spreadsheet of the day and shrugging his jacket on when the phone rang. George flicked it onto speaker phone and, looking through the paper coming out of the printer, said without thinking, 'Hello, George Warner,' then suddenly grabbed at the phone and tucked it under his chin. The last thing he needed this evening was the office getting a blast of Depeche Mode if it was Alex calling from the shop.

'Hey, George man! Er, are you OK?' It was Mike, obviously calling on his mobile from a bar, judging from the clinking and merry hubbub behind his voice. A wave of relief flowed through George, then promptly flowed back, as he remembered the last conversation he had conducted about Mike and his phone habits.

'Oh, yeah, yeah, fine, I just thought it might be – um, my mother. She's always ringing me at the office to check that I'm getting a proper hot supper. Or that I'm not, if you see what I mean. She doesn't know that if you stay until ten, they actually bring you one. I wouldn't know how to explain that to her.' George stabbed at his Psion organiser, which was stuck accusingly on Alex's address.

'Look, George, I need to have a chat about the wedding. Laura's got herself into a state about bridesmaids and things and I thought that you might be able to come over for supper and, you know, reasssure her. You know, convince her that Rachel won't go into a decline when she finds out she's not going to be one.'

George flinched involuntarily. That was a little beyond even his mighty diplomacy skills. The UN would be more appropriate for the worst case scenario which was now dawning on him. Especially if all his worst fears about Caroline turned out to be true.

'Oh, break it to me now, why don't you,' he sighed, sitting back down. 'Who are they going to be?'

'Well, my sister Kate, Alex, and, er, Caroline. Just three. Laura says she can't afford Paula Pryke headdresses for any more. You wouldn't *believe* the budget she's done. Asked her if she'd do some of my forecasts for me. I mean, typical women, I said, just get the bloody flowers somewhere else but no, apparently only Paula Pryke will do. She's got this book . . .' There was a commotion in the background, the sound of a fresh influx of bankers crashing through the doors of the bar and heading straight for chilled-beer oblivion. 'I can't hear you properly, what did you just say?'

George thought it wise not to repeat what he had just said verbatim.

'Come over for supper tonight?'

'Isn't it a bit late? I mean, won't Laura have already cooked something?' asked George, who was still surprised at the proprietorial assumptions Mike made about Laura's hospitality.

'Ah no,' said Mike, with the slightly smug air of a man whose Ready Meal for One days were already fading into the realms of distant memory. 'I know Laura's done a casserole in her slow-cooker and it's not going to be ready until after she comes back from aerobics anyway. Pick me up from outside Balls Brothers in about fifteen minutes? I'll get some wine.' And then his reception cut out.

George stared into space, listening to the disconnected tone, and then slowly replaced the receiver. He began to switch off the variety of hardware on his desk, letting out a big sigh as he did so. Only Mike could fail to anticipate the amateur dramatics that were poised in the wings when the wedding pecking order was announced. Women, reflected

George, cynically, tended to treat these things like a grown-up version of team picking for netball – not so much a joyful selection as an opportunity for pointed rejection. And only Mike would imagine that he had any power to defuse the situation without a big row and the gloomy possibility of tears, recriminations and a procession of tactical manoeuvres all the way up the aisle. George had a wry idea of his own diplomatic abilities, particularly with the girls, but this was pretty much beyond them. And yet, much to his annoyance, he was already involved.

As it was, his suspicions about Caroline, breeding daily like yeast ever since his conversation with Alex the previous Friday night, were now rising every time he spoke to Mike. In a wine bar, from his mother's (wasn't that in Stratford somewhere?) – Mike never seemed to call from home any-more. Or was that just ridiculous? And stupidly, he'd told Alex, who would no doubt tell Rachel – who would no doubt want to know *why* he'd told Alex, if she hadn't guessed already – and then he'd have another baleful session with Alex about the Future of their Relationship, and she might even tell Laura, or one of the others, and that would be it. Whatever revelation Alex decided to make, there was at least one wedding that wasn't going to happen. And as for Caroline, well, she was the last person he wanted to have a row with. Correction, the last person he'd want to be *seen* having a row with, because which one out of the whole lot of them, Alex included, wouldn't put their own spin on that?

With a silent groan, he pushed his glasses up onto his nose and squinted at the fingerprint which now obscured his field of vision. Looking down, George realised that he had doodled his way through two layers of his company desk pad in black biro. Row upon row of interlocking, angry black boxes, with Caroline's home number at the centre.

Laura was, of course, at home by the time George and Mike arrived at their brand new First Time Buyers' flat. Pink but neat in her grey gym kit, she was just lifting the lid off her slow-cooker and filling the small kitchen with the aroma of Delia Smith's Steak in Designer Beer, looking very much like an Oxo commercial behind the cloud of steam. Mike threw his briefcase on a chair, leaned over to drop a kiss on her head and opened the fridge, all in one fluid movement. George half expected him to call, 'Hi, honey, I'm home,' and then josh around a little with a scruffy but lovable dog and try to steal a taste of whatever was cooking on the stove, only to catch a teasing slap on the hand from Laura, while silent opening credits rolled in the background. They didn't have a dog as yet, but George was counting the days.

'Hello, George,' said Laura, with a wide smile. George bent to kiss her cheek and she pushed a loose curl back behind her ear. Laura had carefully removed all make-up and jewellery before aerobics and, flushed with exercise and her obvious quiet delight at seeing Mike home from work, looked about fifteen years old. George thoroughly approved.

'That stew smells fabulous, honey bunny,' said Mike, emerging from the fridge with a four-pack of beer. 'I've put the wine in to chill for a little while – do you want a beer? George?' He cracked open a can and drank about half of it, noisily.

'I've got some Volvic here, thanks. There are some clean glasses in the dishwasher, if you . . . Oh, OK. George, have you seen my socks?' Laura extended an ankle, on which the Sock It To Them logo was prominently embroidered. 'Rachel sent them to me a couple of weeks ago. She says her office is full of sports socks at the moment. Apparently, even Fergie has them. *Oh* yes.' She raised her eyebrows and laughed. 'Friends in high places, eh?'

Mike advanced towards her with his arms spread into a bear hug. 'They're the smartest ankles at Albany Fitness, aren't they?' he mumbled, nuzzling his face into her neck. Laura squealed happily. Then the pair of them broke off abruptly, remembering George, who was carefully pouring his beer into a glass from the dishwasher.

Living together had obviously given them even more time to practise their Terry and June impressions than college had, thought George. Mike was now fiddling with the stew, while Laura slapped his hands, playfully. George looked around in panic for the scruffy but lovable dog. Mike did not look like a man on the verge of an engagement-threatening affair with a known man-eater.

Maybe he'd got it all wrong, he thought distractedly. But as soon as the words 'innocent explanation' began to form in his head, experience rose up against them and forced him to dismiss the notion. God, he of all people should know that Caroline was about as capable of an innocent explanation for the whole thing as Gerry Adams was of admitting that the Canary Wharf bomb had been an exercise in deconstructionalist performance art. She knew what she was doing all right. But did Mike?

George looked up to see Mike put his arms round a wriggling Laura and squeeze her bottom lecherously, as she squealed like a happy little pig and tried to beat him with her wooden spoon. For heaven's sake, he thought, wasn't she elected by the massed female brains of the college to uphold the feminist rights of college womanhood?

'Are you my happy little piggie?' gurgled Mike. 'Oink, oink—'

Laura and George made embarrassed coughing noises. Mike seemed happily unaware and opened another can of beer, peering enthusiastically into the bubbling casserole. Poor sod, thought George. He has absolutely no idea.

After supper, Laura got out her wedding planner.

'I've been planning quite a bit in advance,' she said, laying an apologetic hand on George's knee, 'but there's so much to do. It's such a relief that you're going to be the best man, George – I had horrible visions of Michael being followed down the aisle by John, videoing him from ground level and making race car noises into his cravat.'

'Or making fart noises when the congregation sits down,' added George, recklessly, and immediately bit his tongue and looked apologetic. But Laura was either inured or oblivious.

'No, it's going to be a toughie persuading him not to do a panoramic overview suspended from the organ loft as it is,' agreed Mike. 'As soon as I mentioned the wedding he started asking me whether I thought Laura would let him put one of those micro-cameras in her bouquet, so he could get a bride's eye view of the service.'

Laura looked askance at Mike, who shrugged his shoulders.

'I don't think he's joking, Laura,' said George. 'John did try to hide the video camera in the bathroom when Mike was, erm, *ill* in Chile – it was on a time-lapse setting. He was watching a lot of *ER* at the time.' Laura stared at him. 'It was in a plastic bag,' George added quickly.

Laura blinked rapidly, as if flushing a particularly

unpleasant image from her mind, and then flipped open the section of her file marked 'Bridesmaids'.

'I've had to make some hard decisions about bridesmaids,' she said sadly, flicking through the filed pages from *Brides and Setting Up Home*, interspersed with quotations from shops and florists. 'It's not easy, you know. You have to work out who will look best in pistachio, who's going to look too tall in the line-up, who will be really upset if you don't ask—'

'How many headdresses Paula Pryke can make up for £200,' finished Mike, picking at the bowl of tortilla chips.

Laura ignored him and opened her file at a page of shiny satin Bo-Peep bridesmaids, each clutching a hoop of roses and beaming in the slightly sinister manner that comes from smiling continuously for a whole day. Laura wondered whether she too would be flaring her nostrils by the time the last guest had gushed down the receiving line. She thrust the open file at George. 'I mean, George, can you really see Alex in one of these?'

George wondered whether getting engaged meant surrendering all claim on rational thought.

'Well, I've never seen her in anything other than black, myself,' he offered without thinking. Laura looked at him more closely. 'Er, no . . . no! Why Alex? I mean, yeah, perhaps, she looks quite good in green, doesn't she?' he stuttered, turning a deep shade of pink not entirely dissimilar to the array of puff-sleeved lovelies on the page beneath his nose.

Laura opened her mouth to say something and George, having swiftly recovered, added smoothly, 'That *was* that colour she wore for the final May Ball, wasn't it? The one I took her to?' and crammed four tortilla chips in his mouth at once, with a definitive crunch, putting an end to the discussion. He raised his eyebrows at her. Laura regarded him thoughtfully with her head on one side, but before she could make any further comment Mike looked up from the wine catalogue he was examining with interest and said, 'God, George, you're worse than the girls. Did you have matching accessories?'

'Just my eyes,' said George camply. Mike snorted. Laura pulled the file back onto her knee and flicked through a couple more pages, pausing wistfully over a selection of *Pride and Prejudice*-themed bridesmaids from Angels and Bermans.

'So, let me get this straight,' said George. 'Who are the bridesmaids going to be?'

Laura put down the file heavily and Mike stopped crunching. Celine Dion could be heard clearly in the background. Laura fiddled with the lever arch on the file. It squeaked annoyingly.

'Mike's sister Kate, you know, the one who's still at college, Alex and . . . Caroline. Just the three. Any more is difficult for going up the aisle – you know, who holds the veil and who gets the bouquet and that sort of thing. It's only a little church, after all,' she said, and swiftly returned her gaze to the selection of floral garlands available from 'White Weddings'. She looked even more like a guilty fourth-former than ever.

George cracked his knuckles and looked straight at the pair of them. 'OK, as no one else is going to say it, I will. What about Rachel? Won't she be awfully upset? She's going to feel so left out if you have those three and not her. You were so close at college? Hello? Laura?' He leaned accusingly into her line of vision, as she wouldn't meet his eye.

'Oh God, I know,' said Laura, almost, George noticed,

wringing her hands, 'but what can I do? I haven't seen her that much since we left college and it's so hard, with her not going out when Caroline's around . . .' She petered off meaningfully.

'I mean, think how much damage Rachel and Caroline could inflict on each other with a floral hoop!' added Mike, with a bit of a laugh. George and Laura did not laugh. Mike busied himself with another bowl of tortilla chips.

George was feeling too tired to be his usual diplomatic self. It had been a long and tedious day in the office and he had had no time to do the crossword at lunchtime. Added to which, he wasn't used to going out unexpectedly on Mondays and he felt disrupted, especially as the realisation was now dawning that Mike and Laura expected him to sort out their bridesmaid problems. And it wouldn't just be a case of picking the headdresses.

'No, that's not fair,' he retorted. 'The reason she doesn't go out with the crowd *as a whole* is because she doesn't want to see Caroline but doesn't want to dictate who everyone else sees. Give her credit for that. I mean, if she wants to make a point about whatever it is that she feels so strongly about, let her. She's never asked the rest of us to take sides.' He ran his hand through his hair, which seemed of late to be thinning out alarmingly. 'But why one and not the other? Isn't that just being provocative?'

This was a fair point, all three had to concede privately. Ever since Mike, George, John, Laura, Caroline, Rachel and Alex had found a mutual escape route from the same tutor's drinks party during their interminable Freshers' Week, they had rarely done anything apart. Even after leaving – even after The Great Row between Caroline and Rachel – the invisible bonds of habit and familiarity had kept them together in London, more or less. It saved having to talk to people they didn't know at parties. They were just 'the gang'. They were all just there and always had been. Sort of like the cast of *The Mousetrap*.

So for Laura to miss out Rachel from the bridesmaids, as she sailed serenely into her new life, was an unusually political act. More to the point, it would be the first time ever she had actively taken sides in any dispute. Not that from where George was sitting, such wave-making was coming easily to her: Laura generally liked to keep things on the comatose side of peaceable and now she was looking positively uneasy. Pained, even.

'Caroline was my best friend at university,' said Laura, rather hotly. 'We shared a set together. She'd be really hurt if I didn't ask her. You know how she is about people not liking her – I was talking to her the other day and she says she's made a real breakthrough with her regression therapist. It turns out she had some kind of bad experience with her first au pair, or something; it inhibited her ability to make firm bonds as a child.'

George shut his eyes deliberately and Laura sighed. 'And I can't ask Rachel *and* Caroline – I mean, come on, George, what would happen when I tossed the bouquet? It would be like watching an England line-out, for God's sake! Rachel handing off Caroline like bloody Wade Dooley and Caroline elbowing Rachel in the uplift bodice. I'm really sorry, but it's just not going to happen. I couldn't bear the tension. It is my wedding, after all.'

'And with Rachel safely in a pew, all you have to worry about is her not stretching cheese-wire across the aisle,' added Mike, *sotto voce*, into his tortilla chips.

'Shut up, Mike,' snapped George and Laura simultaneously.

George gave Laura a searching look. 'Laura, are you saying that you'd rather have Rachel being hurt than Caroline being nasty?'

'Oh God, all right, OK, OK, so it might be easier to deal with Rachel, but that's not it—' said Laura, beginning to blush again.

'I want Caroline to be a bridesmaid,' said Mike unexpectedly. 'She's a laugh, especially when she does her luvvie routine about the Transcendental Meditation classes. She is hilarious.' He beamed the smile of someone who has just remembered a really good joke, complete with killer punchline.

'I think you'll find,' said Laura stonily, 'that Caroline considers her TM sessions essential to her creative process as an actress.'

'Right. I'll get some more drinks, shall I?' said Mike, collecting the glasses quickly and retreating to the kitchenette.

Laura relaxed across her chair and put her file down. 'I do love him, George, but he can be such a . . . *baboon*.' George smiled at her reassuringly. At least there weren't going to be any shock wedding-night revelations on that front. In the kitchen area, Mike was transferring ice from overloaded, intractable trays into drinks by sticking the freezing cubes to his fingers and dropping them into the Coke, sometimes with bits of frozen skin still attached.

'George, listen,' said Laura, leaning across once Mike was out of earshot, 'of course I would love to have Rachel too, but you know what Caroline's like. Having to tell her she wasn't going to be the preferred one would be horrific and it would ruin my whole day, waiting for the face-off over the wedding cake. Not to mention the dead cert that John would spend more time videoing them glaring at each other all the

way down the aisle than he would panning around my
family. I mean, you know I love them both dearly . . .
Caroline's a sweetheart, you know, George, really she is . . .'
Laura gave him a beseeching look but George had the bit
between his teeth and couldn't be parted from it that easily.
Besides, wasn't there some tradition about best men and
bridesmaids? He had his own back to cover here.

'So you're going to take advantage of Rachel because she's
too nice to make a big scene about it? Fine. Just don't make
me tell her about Caroline, that's all,' said George, wondering
neurotically if there was a hint of betrayal in Mike's last comment about Caroline and her TM.

'Well,' said Laura, 'between you and me—' She looked
round and saw Mike in the kitchen, shaking his hand wildly,
trying to dislodge a firmly adhered ice cube without losing a
layer of skin. 'Between you and me,' she repeated, lowering
her voice confidentially, 'Caroline told me that this trip to
New York might end up in a job offer for her and she might
be staying there for a few months, starting now-ish, coming
back late autumn. So she would miss the Lake District cottage and be back in time for the wedding.'

'So?'

'Well, that would mean that Rachel could come up for the
weekend of us all being together for the last time, without
Caroline around, and I'll be able to have some time with her
and explain about the bridesmaid thing. I know she'll understand. And,' she added more hopefully, 'I've been looking
through the list of best man's duties and I'm sure you can
find something for her to do that doesn't involve aisles and
trains and . . .'

'Mmm,' said George doubtfully. It was a compromise.
Laura had started flicking through her wedding file again.

George wondered uncharitably whether Caroline, with her come-to-bed eyes and just-been-to-bed hair, was a wise choice, if Laura was planning on being the centre of attention for the whole day. Laura, thinking much the same thing, was calculating how far this effect could be minimised by peach satin and a floral headdress.

'Mike seems rather keen to have Caroline in the starting line-up,' offered George, directed at her bent head.

'Does he?' said Laura, looking up with surprise. 'He was saying to me only last night that he and John are going to have a hell of a job keeping her out of every frame of the video. I mean, she knows Dad's a theatre director. Haven't I been reminded of *that* for the last eight years. Now John's got this Channel Five thing, she'll be all over him like a rash. John's quote, not mine,' she added, as George's eyebrows shot up.

In the kitchen, Mike's performance with the ice cubes was coming to a close. He dropped the last one on the floor, missing the glass by some way, just in time for Laura's warning glower to catch him before he picked it up and put it back in the glass.

'Laura, do you really need to upset Rachel like this?' asked George quietly.

With Laura's eye trained on him, Mike made to throw the ice cube in the sink. She turned back to George. Mike rinsed the cube and put it in George's Coke glass.

'Look, take it from a woman,' said Laura. 'When Rachel is in a bad mood, she is grumpy but hilarious. And it doesn't last long. When Caroline is in a bad mood, she is a liability. At least this way round, there will be sweetness and light from Caroline and some acid-drop comments to camera from Rach.'

'The alternative being?'

'Charm in abundance from Rachel, as usual . . . and the buffet being cancelled in the morning by an anonymous mobile phone-call to the caterers.'

George looked aghast. 'She wouldn't do that.' They both, rather uncomfortably, knew they couldn't completely rule it out. An uneasy silence prevailed as Laura and George dwelled on the unappetising prospect of exactly what a vengeful Caroline might do. Had she always been like this?

'Look, George,' said Laura, touching his arm, her eyes pleading, 'it's going to be enough of a circus as it is with my family thesping it up all over the place. I'm praying Dad won't try directing John's video. God knows what Mum will get up to once she sees the camera. Please don't make it any worse?'

Mike reappeared with three glasses of Diet Coke on a tray with two cuddling kittens embroidered beneath a layer of perspex.

'Coke, honey bunny?' he beamed at Laura.

'Oooh, yes please, muffin!' cooed Laura.

George began to gather his things together.

chapter four

By jogging up the escalators and smiling and apologising her way across streams of moving rush-hour traffic at the Angel, Rachel made it to Café Bliss just before seven o'clock and found Alex sitting at a table at the back with the crumbled remains of a lemon tart and a faraway expression on her face. She looked as though she'd been there for a good ten minutes and normally Alex had to be prised away from the shop before half seven if there was still a customer browsing through the racks.

'So, what's the big scandal?' she asked, dumping her bag onto a chair and gesturing to the waitress for a pot of tea for two and another lemon tart.

'Have you got those pictures?' asked Alex. She looked tense and peered anxiously into Rachel's handbag.

'Yeah, yeah,' said Rachel, rummaging through her bag. 'And here's a new trial size perfume for you from work. It's called Heroma — you know, *her aroma* — there's one for each of the Spice Girls.' She started squirting at Alex's arm. 'I think this must be Stinky Spice.' The tea arrived with the lemon tart and Rachel tucked in enthusiastically, mindful of her half-hour at the gym at lunchtime.

Alex lost patience and grabbed the hardbacked envelope marked 'Socks For S' out of the bag. Rachel mumbled an objection through a mouthful of pastry, but Alex had found what she wanted and held the print up to the light.

'Shit,' she said distinctly.

Rachel swallowed and peered at the photograph. 'It is her, isn't it?' she said. 'But I thought she was in New York?'

Alex let out an angry breath through her nose. 'Yes, well, that's what we're meant to think, isn't it? Bloody *cow*! The *bloody* . . . *cow*!' She huffed again for want of a better word.

'Look, Alex,' said Rachel, taking a sip of tea, 'you obviously know something I don't here. What's going on?'

'Our friend *Caroline*,' said Alex carefully, as if exerting precarious self-restraint, 'our *friend* Caroline . . . God! *Laura*'s friend Caroline—'

'Is having it away with our friend Mike?' finished Rachel, satirically, and cut herself another neat triangle of tart.

'Yes!' spluttered Alex, slamming her hand down on the table. 'How did you know? And how can you sit there and eat cake when this is going on just weeks before the wedding? Stop it and tell me what we're going to do. Now!' she added, banging the table, as Rachel showed no sign of rushing her lemon tart.

Rachel looked at her, enjoying the lemon cheese dissolving on her tongue, and eventually said, 'Alex. Listen to me. You know how much I dislike that ridiculous little slapper. That, believe it or not, was a lucky guess. You know exactly how I feel about her proclivity for bloke-poaching. But don't you see how this rules me out of any kind of interference? Who would believe it, coming from me? I don't know what's going on and I don't know what you know, but *nothing* she could do would surprise me.' Her voice suddenly turned icy-sharp. 'I wouldn't put *anything* past that trollop.' She looked up and out into St John's Street, her brow creased with the effort of not saying more, and Alex could see her eyes hardening and swimming suddenly to the colour of green bottle glass. She could have bitten her tongue. Alex stretched her hands across the table to take Rachel's.

'Oh Rach, I didn't mean to . . . You're so happy now, so much more *you*. It really doesn't matter anymore, I mean, look at what you have these days – look at Finlay and your house and your job . . . To be honest, sometimes I don't even associate you with all that, it seems like it happened to different people.'

'Well, let's just say that *I* haven't forgotten,' snapped Rachel. 'And I'm not going to, no matter how much everyone else brushes it under the collective carpet.' She opened her mouth to go on, but suddenly all the anger drained out of her and she let a long breath out through her nose. It was punctuated with a slight sniff. 'Sorry, sorry, it must be my raging hormones. I was crying all through the *EastEnders* omnibus last night. I don't know what's wrong with me at the moment.' She brushed at her eyes with the napkin. 'So, what have you uncovered, Miss Marple?' Rachel made an attempt at lightness. A heavy feeling had settled on her chest from nowhere.

Subdued, Alex turned her cup round and round in its saucer, staring into the swirling tea, as if some answer might float up in the leaves. 'You know I went out for a drink with George last Friday and – oh God, don't tell anyone this until we know what we're doing, Rachel – he said that he'd been round at Mike's with the lads one evening the previous week for a bit of a session while Laura was safely away on a course, and while he was, er, "looking after John", I think was the way he put it, the phone rang upstairs. He answered it and it was Caroline, but she acted all shocked and hung up. But not before he could be sure it was her. And when he dialled 1471, the call was from Notting Hill, not some fabulously expensive hotel in New York. And then when you told me about the socks thing, I—' Alex looked a little bit sheepish, 'I phoned her flat.'

Rachel tried to look disapproving but could only manage amused.

'Did you? What *did* you *say* to her? "Hello, Caroline, can I come over from Islington to borrow a cup of sugar?" Or did you go for something less suspicious, like "Hello, Miss Cox, this is the Samaritans calling on behalf of one of our customers . . ."?'

'No,' said Alex defensively, 'I didn't get her at all. I was hoping not to get her. I got The Lodger.'

The Lodger was Caroline's habitual name for the girl who lived in her spare room and whose rent paid the mortgage. Karen, the student teacher from Newcastle, was charming and, fortunately, good at washing up, but, as far as Caroline was concerned, her social connections were less *Harpers and Queen* than the *Morpeth Times and Star*, and so she paid no interest in Karen whatsoever, beyond sporadic hypocritical tirades about the state of the living room.

'Oh yes?' said Rachel, looking cynical. 'And I suppose Caroline had a prepared alibi sellotaped to the phone, in case of emergency?'

Alex allowed herself a big smile this time. 'No, I think poor Karen has been ignored once too often. I told her that Caroline had ordered a Katrina and the Waves album from the shop ages ago that I'd managed to get hold of,' – Rachel

wagged a finger at the fib and Alex shrugged it off happily –
'and should I hang on until she got back from New York or
drop it round this afternoon as a surprise? And Karen said
that she didn't know about any New York trip, as Caroline
usually leaves a list of things that need doing around the
house and the account number for ordering industrial size Jif
from Peter Jones when she goes gannin' off on holiday. And
aside from that, she was never generally party to such priv-
ileged information.'

She took a mouthful of cold tea, grimaced and ordered a
fresh cup. 'Poor girl. I don't know why she stays there – I bet
Caroline's charging her a heap of rent and it's not even as
though she needs it. I think she just likes having someone
she can hog the bathroom from. Anyway, Karen had no idea
she was dropping her in it at all but proceeded to tell me that
Caroline had gone out for supper with a man and had driven
into town to meet him about an hour ago. So I was a bit cunning and acted surprised and said, "Ooooh, that must be a
new one, is it anyone I know?" and Karen said she didn't
know anything at all because Caroline was being incredibly
secretive and coy. Apparently, she kept saying, "Please don't
ask me, because I really can't tell you," so Karen *hadn't* asked
and Caroline had gone into a mood.'

'Which would make sense if you were seeing your friend's
fiancé,' said Rachel drily. 'And I would think Karen is the
best person to show off to since she doesn't even know Mike
and Laura so she's hardly likely to phone them up and get
righteous about it.'

'So, put it all together. When did you say these pictures
are from?'

'This morning. I phoned Dan, you know, the photographer, to check and he actually remembered Caroline being

there. Well,' Rachel corrected herself, 'of course, he didn't *know* it was her, but he said that he'd had a tip-off from Labour Party HQ that Cherie was about to do a dramatic secret exit and a tall girl with a very loud voice, talking into a mobile phone, had been walking across the car park in a tight skirt and big Jackie O shades. Despite the completely overcast sky. He thought she might have been someone famous because she was doing all the "No, don't look at me" stuff with her hands, but when she strode up to the door, she couldn't get it open and stood there tugging away and stamping until the doorman opened it from inside. And then she left with a man who Dan said obviously wasn't her husband because he looked as though he was on his lunch break. And husbands like that try not to see their wives during daylight hours.'

'Or have lunch breaks, presumably. He saw all that? What was he doing?'

'It's his job. Fin's just the same. I ring them from work from under a mountain of filing, with bloody Harriet twining away to Skinny Zinny about the exorbitant price of Seabreezes in Fulham these days, and Fin and Dan are sitting outside the Dorchester with a tray of coffees and a great big bag of biscotti from the Seattle Coffee Company, waiting for Demi Moore to come trolling out so they can chase her across town in their covert Golf convoy. Thank God Fin only does it once in a blue moon – I think I'd pack in Dunleary and Bright and take up photography.'

Alex poured more tea and sat back. Rachel had touched on another of her excoriating list of personal grievances. 'But don't let me get onto the workings of photographers' minds. Let's pretend we're Laura. Let's be fair here. Forgiving. What exactly are we talking about? The evidence of an unwitting live-in housemaid, one alleged sighting of the pair of them at the Harbour Club—'

'During the day,' added Alex significantly. 'Not to mention Caroline's undercover sunglasses.'

'OK, and one overtly suspicious phone call to Mike's house, both when she made a very big point of being in New York. Those postcards *were* posted in New York, weren't they?'

'Mine definitely was, and I suppose George's was too,' mused Alex. Rachel raised an eyebrow and Alex shook her head. 'Let's not get into that now. He still thinks you don't know, you know.'

'Hmm,' Rachel said archly.

'But that's not to say that Caroline hasn't been in New York. She told us on the card that she was there for a little getaway. She didn't say how long, did she? She gets lots of Air Miles from her dad – she could have gone over for the weekend, done her Macy's thang, posted some cards so we'd think she was there for a week or so and then hopped on the Sunday night plane. And she made an even bigger point of coming over and dropping her spare set of keys off with me before she left. Karen was there anyway. She *wanted* me to know she was going away, just like she wanted George to know it was her on the phone.'

'Yeah, but she doesn't trust Karen to change the loo-roll without leaving a five-point plan for toilet-tissue replenishment procedure. As we now know from The Lodger herself. Oh Alex, I can't believe you were so restrained. Couldn't you have probed a little more, found out how they allocate shampoo space in the bathroom? And whether Caroline marks the gin bottle?' Rachel grinned mischievously.

'Stop it!' said Alex sternly. 'Unlike some, I have no *wish* to find out about Caroline's colour-coded knicker organiser!'

'But, Alex,' said Rachel, trying to purse her lips disapprovingly against a flood of giggles, 'Katrina and the Waves! As if!'

The waitress was now ostentatiously wiping down the other tables with emphatic strokes of the cloth. Rachel finished her tea and began to gather her things together.

'In summing up for the jury,' she began, 'I put it to you that Miss Cox, the defendant, is not only seeing Mr Craig, the defenceless, but is doing her level best to be *seen* seeing him. I would like to refer to Miss Cox's previous record of spotless behaviour without previous convictions, but I regret that I am unable to do so under oath. My client is shameless, ruthless and on at least one occasion, knickerless.'

'Objection! Hearsay!'

Rachel lifted an eloquent eyebrow. 'As I am unable to call my impeccable witness, please disregard the last comment and substitute "charmless". Or "pointless". Or—'

'Yes, yes, yes,' said Alex. 'I get the point. So who's going to tell Laura?' They stared hopefully at each other. 'OK, so we don't tell Laura then. I suppose that's what Caroline wants us to do. Straight to the centre of attention.'

'All this sneaking around – except she's not exactly bothering with the sneaking bit, is she?' Rachel said glumly. 'What can we do? I don't even know who the bridesmaids are yet. I suppose Laura will be keeping us in suspense until we get up to wherever this cottage is supposed to be.' She hoisted her bulging bag onto her shoulder with an effort to keep the contents inside. Her mobile phone wobbled precariously, tangled up in what looked like a sports sock. 'Where did you say it was?'

'Wasdale?' said Alex. 'Or it was the last time I heard.'

'Wasdale?' repeated Rachel, articulating each syllable with

horror. 'Now I can forgive you for not knowing where that is. But I'm not sure if I can forgive Laura for suggesting it as a weekend-break venue. I'm surprised she even knows where it is herself, come to that.'

'Where is it?'

'It's in the western bit of the Lake District, quite near where my gran lives, in Ambleside. Well, as near as anywhere is in Cumbria, anyway. Put it like this, Alex: if Caroline decides to throw one of her prima donna turns and storms out into the night, it's just going to be her, her wounded pride and forty sheep to keep her warm. I myself will be flouncing out in a huff purely as a last resort. Or to put it another way: if Caroline decides to create a scene, she's got a captive audience for at least two nights.'

'Oh hur*rah*,' growled Alex, mashing up the remains of her lemon tart with her fork. 'She might as well get some agents over. It's probably going to be the performance of her life – a real show-stopper. No Wedding and a Punch-Up.'

chapter five

Rachel hated the gym. If God had intended her to wear up-your-bum leotards, she reasoned, she would have come ready equipped with the kind of elasticated legs Sindy dolls used to have. Instead, not only had God generously provided her with sufficient fat storage for any famine that might befall Highbury Fields, but He had also fixed it that she worked next door to a very fashionable and exclusive gym, for which Poppy had negotiated discount corporate rates as a matter of course. Just to rub it in.

Some of the more honed PR girls actually held meetings with clients on adjacent StairMasters. Rachel had no intention of ever being recognised by anyone she knew on an acquaintance basis, let alone someone who might have to take her seriously in a professional capacity (a term which, she was prepared to concede, only barely covered the client/agency relationship of Dunleary & Bright). To this end, she dressed for her lunchtime exertions in a pair of grey M&S cycling shorts (slightly bulging), in which she had played three seasons of aggressive college hockey, and something from Fin's selection of T-shirts (greying and deodorant-stained), with a free pair of Sock It To Them socks, as a sop to gym chic. The irony of this attempt at disguise did not escape her: had she gritted her teeth and worn the cheesewire leotard uniform of the daytime gym regulars, she would have blended in like a slightly over-upholstered chameleon.

In fact, Rachel would happily have given up these routine humiliations altogether, had it not been for two factors. Firstly, Laura's wedding, at which, if she were asked to be a bridesmaid, she would have to look as good, if not better than, the others. And if she were *not* asked to be a bridesmaid, the gloves being well and truly off, Rachel intended to look better than the bride. Harsh, but from experience, it was the way she knew the rest would play it. And she was fed up with being the dumpy one.

Secondly, Fin had it from Dan, the self-styled 'investigative photographer', that someone famous, no names being mentioned, was a regular at O'Hare's Gym. And a sweaty snap on a StairMaster equalled a sizeable downpayment on a Highbury flat of their own. Quite aside from her personal concerns, as a woman, about the morality of exposing celebrity cellulite, the hidden cost of this flat, Rachel had worked out pretty quickly, was the likelihood of having to appear in the background herself, heaving away like a distressed porpoise, her dimply thighs and muscular calves exposed to the nation's breakfast tables, while Dan and Fin captured the lissom celebrity, mid-flex, on a long lens. Rachel remembered the takeaway caffe latte and brownie she'd picked up for the office for elevenses and stomped harder on the StairMaster.

She had been chewing over Alex's confession for a good

part of three days, in silence mainly, as she knew Finlay had little time for what he saw as incestuous bickering. In fact that was exactly what he called it, and Rachel knew from the tone of his voice that he didn't really know why she bothered to take part in it all, much less get upset by it.

'Darling,' he'd said on Monday night, stroking her hair into a curly ponytail after she'd walked home from Bliss in a foul Caroline-induced mood, 'why do you let Caroline get you so wound up? She's so . . . *nothing*. She's just a hopeless wannabe actress who thinks Method Acting is a form of Catholic birth control. For heaven's sake, Rachel, Caroline Cox probably spends more time in the Chelsea Arts Club talking about her colonic irrigation than she does at auditions. I know you had some big falling-out at college with her, but these people are meant to be your friends. Rachel, look at me,' he had said, swinging her into his arms on the sofa, 'look at this house, look at our dog, look at the . . . the . . . *life* we've made together. What has all this happiness we have here got to do with any of those people from college that you never really see these days? And what have they got to do with all this? When we're married—'

'When *we're* married, we will have a tiny, tiny wedding in a castle in Ireland and they will only find out through the college newsletter,' said Rachel defiantly into a cushion.

Finlay raised his eyebrows and shook his head at her.

'What? What's the problem with that?' asked Rachel, lifting her head off the arm of the sofa.

'Now is it that you don't want them to *know* or that you don't want them to *come*?' She met his gaze with a crooked smile, then rapped his knuckles with the remote control in pretend outrage. Humpty came waddling in and sank his head, with a reproachful sigh, on to Rachel's lap.

Undeterred, Finlay pulled her back into his arms and resumed the slow stroking of her hair, coiling it round his hand into a smooth golden bun. 'You're not the same girl you were at university, Rachel. You've changed even since I've known you. And I love you more with each new, mad thing you come out with. Even the PR bimbo thing, I love. You know what you're doing. Really. There's no pretence about you. Your confidence is nowhere near as high as you deserve, but whose is? So why do you revert to this wibbling neurotic every time you get a phone call from the Mime Queen of Notting Hill?'

'*About* her,' corrected Rachel, stroking the dog's ears on to the top of his patient head. 'I only have phone calls *about* her, I wouldn't actually *speak* to her, Fin. My bile would drown me and any innocent bystanders, if I were to be given an actual *audience* with her.'

'OK, what exactly is it that provokes these tides of bile, then?' he asked, cautiously taking his cue from her light response. 'I mean, is she in the "Male MPs who put VAT on Tampax" league or is it more along the lines of "Backpackers Who Stand on the Wrong Side of the Escalator at the Angel"?'

Rachel smiled and, lifting her chin, Fin was horrified to see a tear welling along her eyelashes.

'Darling!' he said quickly. 'What did I say? What is it?' He pulled her up into his arms and held her tightly. 'Tell me, Rachel. Properly. There's more to it than some squabble, isn't there? Oh Rach, why haven't you got this off your chest before now? You can tell me everything, you know that.'

She buried her head into his thick Arran jumper, which smelled reassuringly of Eau Savage and engine oil. Rachel hadn't ever unburdened the full story of the Big Fallout to anyone and was certain she never would now. Not even to Fin. She didn't want to give Caroline the satisfaction of having intruded into her life beyond college. But Fin would have to know some of it, and enough for him to realise how much she still ached inside for a period in her life she would never have over again to do differently. She couldn't bear it if Fin, who held her heart in his hands, gave her the same reaction as those friends who had seen the whole drama and remained firmly in the wings.

But she also knew she had to take the plunge sometime. It was the only part of her that she hadn't shared and, knowing he knew her as well as he did, Rachel realised, heavily, that she couldn't keep it from him for much longer. She didn't *want* to keep anything from Finlay. Better that he knew now, from her – now that there was a chance, with Caroline back on the scene and the wedding in progress, that he might hear it from the others, in their constant mission to share other people's secrets in the name of close friendship. Rachel took a deep breath.

'Caroline was one of the girls in the group I went around with at university,' she began, looking fixedly at the fireplace, with the invitations and postcards tucked behind the terracotta pots of ivy. 'We were this one big, happy family, supposedly still are – "the gang". Someone in my English set told me later that we used to be referred to as The Clique by everyone else.' She made the inverted commas gesture sarcastically with her fingers.

'If you ask me what we have in common, I could come up with a couple of vague things, but if we were all honest – on the whole, we prefer to be polite, as you know – I would have to say that the only common link we all have now is that we were at college together. And I'm afraid that that was much the same case then, too. We all met at the same party in the first week and didn't much break formation from then on.

'Anyway,' she went on, rubbing her eyes with the heel of her palms, 'I'm not going to be funny about this. Sorry. You remember George from the dinner party at Laura's? The merchant banker? Well, I went out with him for quite a long while – yes, I *know* you think the whole set-up was incestuous, before you say it *again*.' She stroked her hand down Finlay's jumper, without looking at his face. 'He was very sweet and I thought I was in love with him. My first boyfriend. Everyone told us what a lovely couple we made. We went punting, stayed in bed until lunchtime, ate entire packets of Jaffa Cakes, all the usual university stuff you do when you're let off the leash for the first time. My first year was pretty miserable, as you know, but with George, I was really, really happy – for the first time since I'd left home. I thought he was too.' She let out a deep breath and Finlay imperceptibly tightened his arm round her.

'Well, eventually our Finals term came round and I went up home to Manchester one weekend for a last-minute break. I had – I had some things I needed to think about, on my own, away from Cambridge. When I came back, very early on Monday morning, I thought I'd surprise George with breakfast. I'd picked up a bag of Danish pastries from an early opening deli and some orange juice, went round to his rooms, only—' Rachel bit her lip. 'Only to find him tucked up in bed with Caroline, my great friend and confidante.' Her voice was heavy with sarcasm, barely masking the hurt beneath.

Finlay, holding his breath, waited in hope for the acerbic

wisecrack, but none came. Rachel was fixing her gaze at the pots of ivy as though they were keeping her afloat and twisting her ring round and round her finger.

'I couldn't—' Her voice cracked and she coughed to hide it, bringing her sleeve up to her mouth. 'I couldn't *believe* that George would do something like that to me. I felt absolutely betrayed. I know it sounds stupid, but I never really got mad at *him*. More incredulous that he could be so . . . stupid. He's just a boy really, you know, but Caroline . . . She knew what she was doing all right. There had been little things that had made me think, "Er, hello?" earlier on, but boyfriend-snatching? It's so alien to the way I do things, I never thought she would really try it on. Not really. That was what hurt me most, deliberately stealing one of your friends' men like that. You never steal your friend's man. I thought it was an unspoken rule for everyone.' She exhaled deeply through her nose and slapped her forehead lightly.

'The way she looked at me when I waltzed in, all happy to be back, and drew the curtains and saw them in his bed together. Like it was some kind of game she'd just won. George just blinked and did that stupid sheepish look he has. But Caroline . . .' She tightened her grip on Finlay's jumper. The next bit hurt more.

'So I just ran out through college and down to the river. But when I got myself together and imagined stalking into the library and spilling out my tale of woe, it dawned on me that no one in the whole stupid group would take my side and tell Caroline what a shameless bitch she was, because we don't *do* confrontations, do we? They had seen all the flirting and no one had ever taken her aside and warned her off. They must have known something was going on. They even got me to the stage where I couldn't say anything, even when Caroline was draping herself all over my boyfriend, right in front of me in the bar. She used to get drunk and talk German to him, because they'd both had German au pairs and, of course, poor little parochial me, I couldn't understand. And because I spent all my time with these bloody *invertebrates*, when all this . . . *shit* came to a head, I had no one else I could run off and cry to.' She wiped the tears off her chin. 'I nearly went mad, Fin.'

Finlay kissed the top of her head tenderly, burying his nose in her hair while he tried to judge what to say, scared of breaking the delicate thread of her past Rachel was offering to him. 'What about Alex? She cares about you.'

'Yeah, Alex,' said Rachel with a sniff. 'She was there. She spent three days walking around Cambridge with me in almost complete silence. I think we must have gone everywhere. I couldn't face going back to college and seeing all of them, so I wandered around, not seeing anything, not saying anything, until night time and then crept in and never switched the lights on. I lived on pints of milk for a fortnight because I couldn't eat. Better than Slimfast, this shock business.'

A few moments passed and the lights came on outside in the street. Fin noticed the light catch on the trail of a tear down Rachel's cheek, like a snail track on her white skin. 'But did you give them a chance?' he said carefully. 'I mean, they might have been really embarrassed and not known what to say, how to deal with you. None of them are like you are. It's a *horrible* situation. It takes a lot of maturity to know how to handle it without making things worse. Not everyone would have the courage to speak up.' He stopped. 'Sorry. I don't mean to sound preachy.'

Rachel went very still and held his hand. 'Oh, Fin. I know it takes something to help, but Alex did. I thought that's what all friends did. She managed to find me, find out what was wrong. She's a great hugger. I'll always love her for what she did then.' She offered him a broken smile and Finlay felt his heart lurch towards her. 'But after three days of hiding and walking and crying without knowing why I was crying anymore, I'd decided I had to face it out some-time and I psyched myself up to go and see Laura in the morning. So I went back to my room that night and locked the door, not wanting anyone to know I was there. I just sat leaning against the door so no one could see me from the window. Part of me wanted them to come round, to worry about me, and the other part couldn't handle the whole idea of seeing them *not* say or act like anything was different.'

She shut her eyes and the dark corners of her study loomed up behind her eyelids. 'At about eleven o'clock, Mike – you know Mike, the one man who's meant to be so sensitive and relationship-orientated – came round with Laura and once they'd knocked on the door and bellowed in concerned voices, I heard Mike say, "Oh for God's sake, she's such a bloody drama queen, Laura – Caroline says it was only a drunken snog." And Laura said, "And from what she said George told her, it was only a matter of time before he dumped her anyway. Especially when Caroline told him about Rachel's test results."

'I sat there, rigid. I suppose it was my own fault for pre-tending not to be in, but honestly, Fin, I don't know, it was like they just started leaning on the door and conducted a complete dissection of all my inadequacies. Caroline hadn't wasted any time in those three days. Apparently, one of the reasons George had cheated on me was because I had some unspecified sexually transmitted disease.' Rachel snorted. 'Tragically, I will never know what I was *meant* to have been infecting George with as, at this point in the proceedings, Laura was suddenly afflicted by an attack of ladylike behaviour. You know, if I'd been watching it on television, I would have been in hysterics, but I was just slumped against the door, mouth wide open. Talk about two-faced. I felt like the room was spinning in the dark and all I could do was cry and cry and listen to how Mike thought that I was far too melodramatic for my own good and how Laura thought that Caroline had a point when she said I was still a bit too parochial for university life. She wanted him, she got him.'

Rachel made chopping gestures with her hands. 'Caroline let them make her defence up for her. She's had a very difficult childhood, you know,' she said, in a perfect imitation of Laura's best Esther Rantzen voice. 'I had no way of making them go away and no way to stop hearing what they were saying. I thought it had to be some kind of divine lesson to me. Too much Saint bloody Augustine, that's the problem.'

Finlay hugged her into his jumper, until he could feel her warm breath through the wool. The evening light had drained out of the room and they were sitting in the dark. He couldn't see that Rachel's expression had changed from a blank gaze to a contorted look of pure pain, while she bit down on her lower lip.

What happened next? She was still holding what happened next inside. He didn't need to know, not now, when it could be so wrong. It could ruin everything. Not when he loved her so much and for once it was all right. She curled her knees up towards her stomach.

They had sat on the sofa without speaking for some minutes but there was a gentle intimacy between them. Humpty's laborious breathing rose and fell. Finally Fin broke the silence.

'Rachel, forgive me if this is a stupid question, but if she was – is, such a bitch, why is everyone still friends with her?'

Rachel sighed. 'I don't know. It's just the way it is. Don't fall out with people once they're on your Christmas card list and if they do anything offensive or illegal, pretend it hasn't happened.' She thought for a few seconds, trying to be as fair as she possibly could. 'I mean, Caroline was good company and she was generous when it suited her and I used to think she was quite vulnerable underneath all the screeching, to begin with, anyway. She went very hard . . .' Her voice drifted away. 'I think the others just don't look at that side of her.'

Fin let her sit thinking for a moment, and said, 'Sorry, you didn't finish your story.'

'I die at the end of Act Three and Caroline falls on George's sword.' Rachel smiled to herself and looked up at him. The moment had passed, the door was slammed on the panicky void again. Houston, we have control. 'Oh, I know it must all seem melodramatic now. But, God, I was miles away from home, churned up by the way my course had gone, and maybe I was too naïve, but I just . . . crumpled up.' She shook her head at herself. 'I plunged myself into working for my Finals, saw everyone when I had to, but nowhere near as much as before and when I left, I left. Came straight down here. Got a job, found you. Life began properly. And that is it, Fin. I've never been back to Cambridge.' She stopped short. Fin raised his eyebrows, not wanting to break the silence with a question. Rachel let out a breath which might have been a small, rueful laugh, but her eyes were still sad. 'I've never wanted to. The weight of tradition, you know? The fact of it always being exactly the same just reminds you how much *you've* changed. Or haven't.' She met his eyes again and interlaced her fingers with his. 'I should have told you all this ages ago, but I just don't want it to be important to me. I want to get on, away from all this. But that is why Caroline Cox is the wicked fairy in my life. Cruella De Vil. And now it looks as though she wants to add Mike to her list of college conquests.'

'Except you're not at college anymore, Rachel,' said Finlay, holding her gently by the shoulders. For the first time, Rachel's celebrated smile touched the corners of her mouth and he kissed it.

Since Monday night, Rachel had been replaying this scene over and over in her head, wondering if the time had been right at any point to tell Fin the full story, to open up even the dark bits of her heart to him. But she shied away from those bits herself, afraid that he would stop loving her, think her less perfect and leave. He had hinted at marriage more than once recently and she knew that before she could accept, he would have to know everything. But to live without him would be impossible and she knew he felt the same. It was all more confusing than she had imagined it would be.

The flashing lights on the machine indicated that she had another three blocks of sixty seconds to go. Rachel cursed the fact that at her initiation session with Carla, the personal trainer allotted to Dunleary & Bright, she hadn't liked to ask in the face of toned instruction how to make the intervals shorter, and was subsequently always too embarrassed to give up and stagger off before the machine was finished with her. The popular myth that exercise allows time for deep thought didn't wash with Rachel either, and she found the process agonising unless loud music was pumped directly into her ears. Thinking generally made it worse. Her muscles were even now shrieking, 'Have you forgotten us?' and aching violently in retaliation.

Alex's prescription mix of exactly thirty-five minutes of appropriately frenetic disco music was nearing the end and, dripping with sweat, Rachel slowed down her pace until she was walking again. It wasn't even as though Fin minded her troublesome thighs. But then his interest in her gym membership was purely professional. She tried to reach normal breathing rate without slipping off the moving steps. Why did these places always have to have those horrendous wall-to-wall mirrors? Was that Helen Mirren on the bench press?

Alex had been right about Finlay. He made everything fresh. Rachel smiled inwardly as she towelled off her hair and thought of the way he had curled her ponytail around his hands as they talked in the dark. So gentle. How wonderful to be able to sit and say nothing for hours, absolutely peaceful in a communication without words. Particularly after a hard day faxing, phoning, e-mailing, couriering, post-carding millions of words, all deeply expressive, darling, on behalf of Sock It To Them or Detritus Cosmetics – all for no communication at all.

Stuffing her damp kit into her sports bag, Rachel resolved for the fourth time that month to start looking for something more . . . less mindless. Dunleary & Bright was easy and the only time she had to apply her brain was when the coffee machine needed descaling. But there was only so much free nail varnish a girl could nick before it started looking dangerously like a career. And Rachel only had to look at Poppy, with her rollercoaster blond flicks and her Gucci loafers, to know that she didn't want a career flogging sports socks to unseasonally tanned housewives.

chapter six

Alex, meanwhile, was having another very busy Friday in the shop. In addition to shifting the last of the dog-eared Genesis albums that she had recklessly agreed to buy as a job lot from an accountant friend of George, she had sold her entire stock of Human League albums to a pallid but thrilled young man, sporting possibly the only Phil Oakey wedge-cut in London. Not even Phil Oakey had a wedge-cut any more. Perhaps there were still one or two left in remote parts of Scotland, thought Alex, somewhere where perhaps you could still get Barry M kohl pencils like that, too.

Fridays were always good, particularly in Islington where, Alex guessed, all the self-employed writers, photographers, academics and dilettantes gave themselves the day off and took leisurely advantage of the area's superior range of coffeehouses and tiny specialist shops. If you liked handmade buttons and Viennoiseries, Upper Street was the place. For some reason Friday morning was, more specifically, a good day for early eighties' stuff like Bananarama and Adam Ant, Alex's pet theory here being that Friday morning Tumble Tots sessions at the sports centre freed up a lot of twenty-eight-year-old yummy mummies, desperate to remember a time when *they* were the ones with the face-paint stripes across their noses.

Friday was also one of Rachel's muffin days, which was bringing in increasing amounts of business, much to Alex's professional as well as personal satisfaction. She looked at the last apple and cinnamon muffin in the basket. There had been fifty muffins express delivered by Fin this morning – twenty apple and cinnamon, twenty chocolate and, for an experiment, ten carrot and nutmeg – and now, by twelve o'clock, only one remained, shining crisply on a bed of yellow and blue tissue paper. Crisply? Bed of tissue paper? Bloody hell, thought Alex, Rachel's PR-ese *is* contagious. I have to spring her from Dunleary & Bright before I call a customer *dahling* by mistake.

She dropped a pound in the till, took the muffin and made herself a cup of coffee. It all fitted rather nicely, she thought: the muffins, the coffee, the comfortingly familiar music. It was a browsy kind of shop, a few crumbs didn't matter and the sweet baking smell lasted all day. Much cheaper than flowers and a lot less corny than incense.

And, of course, it helped Rachel fund her escape plan. Fifty pounds for fifty muffins, of which Rachel kept forty and, with much protesting from Alex, gave her ten for hire of her counter space and customers. Two batches of muffins a week and two equally popular Biscuit Days on Mondays and Thursdays were selling out before lunch and helping a healthy number of records out of the door at the same time. Rachel said making a hundred and fifty ginger biscuits listening to the charts on Sunday nights took her mind off Poppy Bright's impending Monday tantrums at the absence of Dunleary & Bright's clients in the Sunday 'Must Have' pages. Then the Monday night muffins took her mind off the fact that she had to go back there for another four mornings before the weekend came round again.

Alex had brought her old coffee machine into work initially to keep her awake and alert at all times, as she was unable to afford an assistant to be bushy-tailed for her on the weary Monday mornings after the long journeys back from Sunday record fairs. Rachel, who lived very near, covered for her on the Sundays she was away, happily singing to Fin and advising customers on the much-heralded eighties' fashion revival which never quite seemed to take off. Now she made customers the odd cup of coffee while they munched Rachel's muffins and they happily paid for the pleasure. You couldn't discuss the finer moments of Ant Music at The Canadian Muffin Company down the road. (You couldn't actually sit down at Divinyl, but that didn't seem to deter Islingtonians with discerning taste in home baking.)

Yes, it was all going very well, thought Alex happily. Much better than predicted by George, Mike, Laura *et al*, who, with the benefit of three or four months as trainee paper-pushers and number-crunchers, had informed her that the whole scheme was financially suicidal. The money had come from a surprise bequest from a rebellious great-aunt, topped up with a small business loan from Barclays Bank, and it had saved her from teetering over the brink of despair and applying for the same law conversion course Rachel had been toying with. George, calling round with a portfolio of share options for her to invest her windfall in, did not even have an ironic response to hand when she informed him that she had bought a going concern in an Islington side-street – and it sold records. Vinyl ones. And that it was her vinyl decision. Ho, ho, ho.

Rachel, phoning from the office on the grand opening day, had told her that she was right to do something she was passionate about, but then had to terminate the call as a voice in the background beseeched her to run out to 'get some little strawberry tart thingies and a bottle of Lanson, Rachel poppet'. And Caroline had put in a personal appearance, accompanied by a strong and silent Italian in Versace jeans, and made a great show of buying five randomly selected LPs which she then gave back because her state-of-the-art music separates system didn't have a turntable.

Alex sniggered into her coffee mug and remembered how outraged Rachel had been at the big display and how horrified she was that Caroline didn't even have the . . . the *discrimination* to pick up five albums she might actually want. Alex didn't get so cross about Caroline because she had more important things to care about, and frankly, she found Caroline's constant performances rather sad, now her days as a captive audience in the next room down the staircase were well and truly over. Caroline never seemed to stop projecting, trying to be more than she really was, twisting her personality into ridiculous shapes, like someone's hands casting unconvincing farmyard animal shadows against a wall. It was rather pitiful and extremely wearing.

Alex, whose parents were both doctors working long hours in hospitals, suspected that Caroline had got into the habit of showing off for attention as a child, while she was being shunted around the world by her diplomat father and his diplomatic second wife. And she had simply never got out of the habit. It didn't excuse Caroline's crashing insensitivity and especially not her predatory instincts but, to Alex's kind heart, maybe it explained where they had come from.

But even as she thought this, Alex remembered Rachel's

blank, scared face the night she had found her crouched under the willow trees by the river, running away from Caroline and George. She couldn't ever forget the endless hours walking through the balmy Cambridge streets, talking consoling rubbish until Rachel emerged from her daze to tell her what had happened. She was like a rag. And the silence, so much worse than the tears . . . Alex had never in her life experienced someone *radiating* sorrow the way Rachel had that night. She bit her lip. No, actually, it would take a lot more than amateur psychology to excuse Caroline at all.

A customer coughed politely at the till and Alex realised that she had been staring like a zombie at one of the clip-framed *Melody Maker* covers on the far wall for some minutes. Her coffee was cold and the milk was starting to separate. She pushed the mug under the counter, next to the muffin she was saving for later.

'Er, hello?' began the young man, hopefully (probably a yummy daddy, thought Alex). 'Do you have any of those cakes left? My girlfriend sent me to get them. I'm not meant to come back without at least one of the apple ones.' He looked sadly at the empty basket. 'She's pregnant,' he added.

Alex's business mind was working quickly, but her stomach had the edge. 'No, sorry, all gone,' she said, 'but there'll be more on Sunday morning.' She offered a commiserating smile and shrug.

'Ah well,' said the customer with a wry grin in return, 'she'd better get here early on Sunday, then. Where do you keep early Wonder Stuff? On CD?'

Alex pointed him towards the corner of the shop where a cluster of glo-stars were still giving out a faint light and he began to flick happily through the racks of CDs, with which Alex had augmented the shop stock when she moved in.

Although she remained true to herself by playing her favourite music all day, any pretensions to vinyl-only purism had had to be abandoned at the start: Alex had decided that it was simply a business reality that if she were going to have a shop in an area full of Georges and Carolines, she ought to exploit the deficiencies of their stereos to the full. Some of them didn't even realise that it was an eighties-based shop. Some of them didn't know Peter Gabriel had left Genesis.

While Alex was admiring the man's 'caring father yet still stylish' cords, the old see-through phone rang under the counter. She retrieved it and her muffin at the same time.

'Hello, Alex, it's Laura,' said Laura. 'Look, are you free for a coffee? I need to have a word with you.'

I need to have a word with you. Why did that phrase strike fear into her heart? And why did it keep cropping up so regularly in her life at the moment? Alex closed her eyes slightly and leaned on her elbows so she could keep an eye on the three people now browsing round the racks. It wasn't a big shop.

'No, Laura, it's a Friday. I don't even have a lunch break on a Friday. Why don't you come here? Are you working at home today?'

'Yes, I suppose I could come over,' said Laura thoughtfully. 'Do you have any of Rachel's muffins left?'

'No, I just sold the last one,' said Alex, leaning on the counter to shield the offending plate from her Wonder Stuff man's line of vision.

'Oh, shame,' said Laura. 'They're about the only things worth breaking the diet for.'

'You've started on a wedding diet already?' gasped Alex, pulling in her flat stomach without thinking.

'Oh don't you start, Alex, you've never been on a diet in your life, you lucky cow. All I ever seem to spend my evenings doing is bloody step aerobics and Mike *still* calls me his little piggie.'

'Yeah, Laura, you really need to sort that out with him. Who'd blame you if you developed an eating disorder in time for the honeymoon?' said Alex, picking the sugar crust off her muffin. 'You're the lawyer – can't you get a mental cruelty plea for piggie jibes? If you ever got to the divorce courts, I mean?'

'*Alex*! We haven't even got married yet!' squeaked Laura. Sometimes, thought Alex, Laura was far too easy to wind up. More so now that the wedding had occupied the rational part of her brain like a Midwich Cuckoo with shepherdess sleeves and a sweetheart neckline.

'Oh, Laura, come over,' said Alex. 'It's a gorgeous day. The drive will do you good. I'll make some coffee for when you get here and you can pick up some sandwiches on your way. I might even close the shop for ten minutes.'

'Not on my account, Alex,' Laura retorted snippily. 'Not on a Friday.'

'Just get yourself over here.' Alex put the phone down to serve the woman in grey Ralph Lauren sweatpants who was hovering uncertainly with her friend near the counter. They were each clutching a couple of A-Ha tapes and kept looking around and giggling.

'Just those?' said Alex, wondering if Laura would be like this in a few years, given a couple of small kids and a two-day week at the office.

'Er, mmm,' said one, rummaging in her sports bag for her purse. She proffered a Switch card and, as the other one hissed, 'Morton Harket!' at her, she dissolved into giggles.

Two babies would be having a lovely Europop soundtrack to their evening bath tonight. Mummy might even get out her old leather Morton bracelets and denim waistcoat, if Daddy was working late.

The man in the cords had now plumped for a tape of *The Eight-Legged Groove Machine* and, queuing up behind the ladies, had spotted the muffin. Alex threw up her hands in defeat and, pulling off a chunk, offered him a bit. Smiling, he took it.

'Can I put my name down for six on Sunday morning?' he said decisively, spitting carrot crumbs and pulling out a leather Filofax. The ladies, out of habit, immediately began rummaging in their bags for business cards, too.

Ah, the power of positive advertising, thought Alex, as she took his name and address.

'How do you manage to keep this place going?' said Laura over the rim of her hot coffee mug. The sun was streaming in through the big windows – almost as good as being outside.

'Erm, our bullish economy? Our trendy location?' said Alex. 'I don't exactly know, to be honest. Oh, of course I can tell you all the figures,' she added quickly, in reply to Laura's shocked expression. 'I have picked up a *bit* of maths since I abandoned the wicked practices of literary criticism, Laura.' She sipped at the black coffee. 'The stock turns over more quickly than I thought it would, I still do regular DJing at the Eighties Nights at The Place which is a good advert, Rachel's muffins are something of a surprise crowd puller . . .'

'I'd be terrified working for myself,' admitted Laura. 'Don't you panic? Don't you lie in bed and see yourself being buried alive under huge piles of Kylie Minogue albums?'

'Sometimes,' said Alex truthfully. 'But it's not a permanent plan, this. I bought the shop fairly cheaply, as these things go, and it's making enough money to live off. And I love doing it. I worried more that I would end up hating pop music after three months but it seems fine so far. Still learning lyrics. My big plan is to persuade Rachel to leave Dunleary and Bright and come and bake muffins for me full-time. Have half the shop muffin-bar with big seats, and the other half record shop. With old-fashioned listening booths. Maybe.' She tilted her hands, looking for approval.

'Oh wow!' exclaimed Laura, putting down her coffee mug on a spare flyer. 'Now that I *would* come up to north London for! Do you think she ever would?'

'Who knows?' said Alex. 'If Finlay snaps Cliff Richard driving a Roller into Thora Hird's swimming pool at a hedonistic Songs of Praise Vicars and Traffic Wardens party, and makes Rachel a lady of leisure on the profits, then yeah, maybe. To live off your talents you have to trust them. And for that you either have to have the luxury of not having to live off them in the first place or a lot of chutzpah.'

'Well, I'd have thought that chutzpah would have been the one thing Dunleary and Bright would have taught her,' said Laura, slightly tartly. 'I've seen the sort of things she's taken to wearing to go out in. The first time I saw her with that black-red nail varnish on, I thought she'd trapped her fingers in the filing cabinet.'

'Don't tell her that,' said Alex. 'George once made the mistake of referring to her as a secretary and she nearly had his eye out with those very same nails. And to hell with the chips on the polish.'

Laura warmed her hands around her coffee mug carefully and her expression turned serious. Serious but still *caring*. So this is what you learn in your Legal Practice Year,

thought Alex. Laura's beautifully modulated gravity, however, did not fit happily with the Bananarama tape now
playing in the background.

'Alex,' said Laura, putting her hand on Alex's arm to
underline the concern in her voice, 'there's something I need
to discuss with you. It's about the wedding.'

Oh my God, oh my God, she's found out! thought Alex,
a wave of adrenalin running through her chest. In response
she managed a forced smile and inquisitive tilt of the head,
trying to disguise the wince as Bananarama's wobbly har-
monies boomed away in the background. What did George
tell her? Am I even meant to know? Will she put two and
two together? How many will she make? Laura looked suspiciously calm, no sign of her Rescue Remedy at all. Alex
struggled to keep her smile straight. She didn't normally let
herself be fazed by things like this. That was Rachel's territory – Emoting and Worse Case Scenario Construction.

'Er, right, mmm?' was the best she could come out with in
the circumstances.

If Laura noticed any nervousness in Alex's response, she
didn't show it. Another benefit of legal training, thought
Alex, scanning for any signs of 'My Boyfriend's About to
Dump Me at the Altar, Oprah' distress on Laura's tranquil
pink and white face.

'Alex,' said Laura, increasing the gentle pressure on Alex's
arm for emphasis, 'I'd like you to be my bridesmaid for the
wedding. I'd be really grateful if you could come with me
sometime next week to look at dress material at Liberty.
Maybe Saturday next?' She had her wedding planner out
and was running a highlighter pen down the countdown
calendar. 'Or one late-night shopping night this week? I
know you have the shop to look after.' Prompted by Alex's

unusual silence, she looked up. 'Sorry, is that a problem? Are you busy?'

Alex's face broke into a broad smile of relief, though not perhaps for reasons obvious to Laura. 'Oh, Laura,' she said, 'I'm thrilled, I'd *love* to be a bridesmaid. Will I have to wear one of those dreadful Bo Peep outfits? Can you fix the bouquet throwing?'

Laura had started to open the file at the bridesmaids' dresses section but now closed it abruptly, marking the place judiciously with her finger. 'Well, I still have to make the last decisions about the actual styles . . . But I'm pretty definite about pistachio green. I think it'll suit everybody.' She blinked nervously.

'And everybody is . . .?'

Laura had been preparing the answer to this into the rearview mirror all the way over and, after a display of expressive gurning that had unnerved the elderly woman driving the Vauxhall Corsa behind her, had settled on 'noncommittal' as the best facial option.

She drew in a deep breath and said casually, 'You, Kate and Caroline. You're all much the same height and size, it'll balance out nicely in the pictures. Don't you think?' Bravely, Laura took a deep swig of her now cold coffee.

Alex noted to herself that whenever her friends forced themselves to say something unpalatable – which wasn't that often – they almost always filled their mouths immediately with whatever foodstuff came to hand, so they couldn't be called upon to repeat the contentious remark. They even improvised if no crisps, wine or chocolate were available. Alex wistfully remembered one balmy night when she thought that George, in the throes of passion, had muttered something about loving her. What he had actually said was lost to history, as just as Alex was about to say 'Pardon?', he had availed himself of her gaping mouth and delivered an unusually lustful snog, leaving her mumbling excitedly into his thrashing tongue.

'Laura, are you mad?' said Alex, thinking she might as well take advantage of Laura's temporary silence. It would take a few moments for the coffee to go down. Judging by the pop-eyed look on Laura's face, it might already be going down several wrong ways. 'Are you sure about Caroline?' she modified carefully. Bloody George was meant to have prepared the way, wasn't he?

Laura flinched. 'You're the second person now to come out with that,' she complained. 'I don't understand what the problem is: I like Caroline, she's very generous and we've had some good times together. We've *all* had some good times together!'

Not as good a time as your Mike's having with her, from what I hear, thought Alex waspishly, but chose to say nothing. There was little point in arguing about this sort of thing with Laura, who was predisposed to see the best in everyone, regardless of glaring evidence to the contrary. Chain-burping Mike, for one, was a tribute to that facet of her character. Rachel was of the opinion that it all stemmed more from Laura's determination to take the path of least resistance than from any latent saintliness, but Alex interpreted this in light of Rachel's horrible behind-the-door experience of Laura's apparent concern. Her exact phrase had been, 'If you ask me, Laura's more Mother Superior than Mother Teresa', but knowing Rachel of old, Alex could separate the soundbites from the real venom, which rarely surfaced in public. So she didn't think she meant it, although like many of Rachel's acid drops it was beautifully delivered.

Laura, nervously turning her red Kit Kat coffee mug round and round in her hands, seemed on the verge of being really upset. Alex decided to leave it alone. There was no point introducing unnecessary stress into Laura's plans at this stage. Laura, she knew, would refuse to see any problem with Caroline's suitability as a bridesmaid, would have some handy excuse for avoiding telling Rachel and would be terminally wounded if she herself declined the honour out of solidarity. She couldn't see Rachel in a pistachio puffball anyway, and in a perfect world, this gesture of affection from Laura might just shock Caroline out of whatever it was that she was up to with Mike. Might. It might also give her a warped thrill. Alex sighed. Damn. This was probably exactly how it had gone with George.

Laura's brow was now creasing and her nose wrinkled prettily. Tears usually followed nose-wrinkling and that whole process took ages to clear up, as Alex knew only too well. Her mother the actress had taught her some useful tricks. Laura pulled her mouth down and pouted ominously.

'This coffee is foul, Alex, can I make some more?' she said.

'As long as I can open those doors again by two o'clock,' smiled Alex, pushing her the bag of Sainsbury's Premier blend and the filter papers, thinking that she had got off very lightly for the time being, all things considered.

chapter seven

Shortly after five o'clock, Laura drove home from Divinyl, after helping out with the Friday rush all afternoon and – to her surprise – really getting into it. Stuffed in her handbag she had a Simply Red album, an old Dire Straits tape for Mike and a booking slip for two Sunday blueberry muffins; in addition to making Alex a rotational diagram for the optimal spread of music for maximum daily sales, Laura was feeling rather pleased with the way she had instigated and organised the muffin bookings book. It occurred to her that maybe Rachel would reciprocate her business guidance in kind, and so, while Alex was serving a customer and explaining at length the line-up changes in the T'Pau tape currently playing on the shop stereo, Laura had surreptitiously scribbled 'Rachel – mini-muffins? Reception?' in her wedding planner.

She had done it under the cover of looking through a CD rack, since Mike wasn't convinced Alex would totally approve of her utilising her friends' businesses for their wedding, although it seemed perfectly straightforward to her. She was *utterly* willing for allowances to be made on the wedding list for those friends already making a behind-the-scenes contribution. The pages in the Liberty wedding book would have to be cunningly marked with blue spots. Or they could start a separate wedding list at Boots or Argos or somewhere.

Warned off by Mike (who had in truth been warned off by George), Laura hadn't got round to asking Alex about providing the music for the evening do yet. And anyway, she and Mike hadn't yet finalised their plans for the evening – the decision was oscillating uncomfortably between Mike's plans for a disco, to be not unlike the ones at university (dark, sweaty, lots of Madness songs, cheap beer in plastic glasses), Laura's plans for an elegant dance band playing Viennese waltz music and Laura's mother's plans for 'a jolly family evening', which, Laura thought miserably, might as well mean engraving 'Unwise Selections from *Les Mis* will be drunkenly improvised by the Cast of the Bride's Family. Dress: Thespian/Mutton as Lamb' on the invitations.

Laura had never fully come to terms with her parents' effusively theatrical lifestyle, insisting, at eleven, on Benenden over Bedales and downright refusing, at eighteen, a year off as an ASM with her father's company, touring *Tartuffe* round North Africa. In fact, up to the age of eleven, Laura's great year of rebellion, she had struggled under the burden of being christened Zuleika Tree Parker – not even in a hippy tribute to nature, she had confided to Mike, but after Max Beerbohm Tree, 'the last of the great actor-managers'. Which somehow made it worse. Her parents had accepted the new Laura Grace with amusement, thinking that one day she would long for the peacock brilliance of her old name, but at her graduation ceremony, even they had to admit that she had grown into her own chosen name far better than she would theirs.

Laura reached the Angel crossroads, weighing up the evening options with the air of a war minister. She might concede Mike the disco, but would use it as balance against the honeymoon, also in process of finalisation. As far as Laura was concerned, an aversion to garlic was insufficient reason to boycott Paris for a spring honeymoon. And, personally, she was determined not to agree to anywhere that would require a mosquito net and water purifiers as an essential part of her trousseau. On an impulse, seeing as she was almost in the City, Laura decided to go and pick Mike up from work. He usually finished at around this time and they could go out for dinner somewhere in town.

She turned left down City Road and wriggled in her seat slightly with excitement. There was something about driving through London in her own car during the early evening that made her feel as though she had really arrived in the adult world. Spending the day working from home. Going to meet her *fiancé*. Then going out for *dinner*. She turned up Capital Radio and sat happily in a traffic jam, the only smiling face in a line of snarling taxis, dreaming of a romantically dishevelled Mike agreeing to wear a Mr Darcy shirt in a Pride and Prejudice wedding.

While Laura was drumming her fingers on her steering wheel and conjuring up images of Empire-line bridesmaids' dresses, Mike was clicking away furiously at Minesweeper on his computer and talking equally furiously down his phone. To the untrained eye, particularly one that couldn't see his PC screen, Mike appeared to be absorbed in arguing the final details of some nailbiting US deal, making frenetic

calculations and shaving a crucial margin off whatever figures he was negotiating. The untrained eye couldn't possibly
know that he was discussing the previous night's cricket
nets and subsequent drinking session with John, the aftermath of which was still throbbing in his temples at 5.30
p.m.

'. . . no, John mate, that's where you are absolutely wrong,
it was a *gem* of a cover drive,' he was saying with an anima-
tion that belied his hangover. 'You can't just wimp out with
your shots just because you're in the nets and not on the
field . . . Well, how am I meant to "give you a bit of a warning"? You were meant to be fielding, for Christ's sake. No
one asked you to video the session . . . Well, yes, I know
things look much farther away on a wide lens, but you're the
bloody cameraman, John . . .'

Mike paused, grimaced, and rubbed his eye unconsciously.

'So . . .' he said, trying to stem the flow from the other end
of the line, 'no, so, John . . . John . . . look, John . . .' He inad-
vertently clicked on a square he had already flagged out as a
bomb and it blew up the game board. 'Oh shit. No, I wasn't
talking to you, I was just . . . yes, but John, as we both know,
cricket is a dangerous game . . . look at how Alex used to
play it at university. Talk about a fast right arm . . .' Mike's
dirty snigger was cut short by John's explosive reaction.
'Well, I didn't realise it was her *specifically* who broke your
nose . . .' He held the phone away from his ear and could still
hear John snarling.

Mike noticed that one of the new secretaries was getting
up to make coffee and he handed her his mug as she passed,
raising a finger to indicate one sugar, with what he imagined
was a winning smile. She took the proffered mug but with an

outraged stare. Women, thought Mike. She's old enough to be getting married – why hasn't she got a baby to look after, instead of spending her week typing faxes for the likes of Patterson and making sure her mascara doesn't smudge?

John was still in full flow and time was getting on. Almost the magic home-time hour. 'For God's sake, John,' Mike said ringingly, 'that three-legged cricket match against Alex's ladies' team was for Rag Week – it was in a good cause after all . . .' This seemed to provoke a fresh stream of invective and to Mike's relief, the call-waiting button started flashing on the phone console.

'John, mate,' said Mike, 'I have to go, I've got a call coming in from New York.' He had no idea where the call was coming in from, but had been told that this was a good way of making people get off the line in a hurry. He wasn't to know that this was standard practice for all his friends who worked in offices, to the extent that Rachel and Laura tended to use it as shorthand when demands from Higher Authorities forced them to cut short conversations in office time. And, as a last resort, he had picked up the handy phrase 'the switchboard girl must have cut us off' from his father, who had last said this with real authority in 1965 and clung to it ever since as a means of terminating impossible phone calls.

'Speak to you later, John . . . hello, Mike Craig,' he said, switching seamlessly from matey banter to deep and professional fund manager.

'Hi, Mike,' breathed a voice he recognised immediately. 'It's Caroline – I'm calling from New York.'

'Wow, now that is odd,' said Mike, 'because I just pretended I had a call coming in from New York!' His skin prickled at the sound of her voice, which always made him feel slightly undressed, although he would never have admitted it to anyone, least of all Laura.

'Ah, yaaaah, that is pretty spooky,' Caroline agreed huskily. The secretary woman returned and dumped his coffee on his desk. It slopped slightly over his reports.

'So, how are you, Caroline?' said Mike, ineffectually mopping up the mess with a Pret a Manger napkin from lunch and glaring over his shoulder. The napkin left red stains on the papers and a greasy mint and red onion mayonnaise stripe appeared across the company reports. 'How's the Big Apple?'

'Kind of lonely,' said Caroline, a little pensively. 'So much to do, you know, I hardly get a minute to myself with all the parties and dinners and things.'

'And auditions!'

'Mmm, yaah, auditions,' said Caroline. 'Actually, I'm thinking more about doing another course over here, maybe at the Strasberg Institute? I do see myself as a very *American* person, Mike, very open to ideas, and cosmopolitan, full of textual insight and yet deeply influenced by *people*, not tedious *traditions*, the way they are somewhere like, you know, *RADA* . . .'

She is purring, thought Mike. This is what they mean when they say a woman is purring.

'So, I was calling to say, what are you all doing?' she said.

'Er, well,' said Mike, a little surprised. 'You won't have got your invitation yet, I suppose, with being away—'

'Oh, don't tell me!' shrieked Caroline. 'You and Laura have announced your engagement!'

'Er, yes,' said Mike. He had forgotten how torrential Caroline's floods of effusion could be and how they tended to reduce his conversation in response to a series of 'er's. 'How did you know?'

'Ah, let's just say a little birdy told me that something was afoot. When is it to be?' she cooed.

'Well, we're all going up to the Lake District for a weekend, but Laura thinks that you'll—'

'When is it?' demanded Caroline, and Mike thought he heard a Filofax being ripped open.

'Er, the second weekend in August,' he said weakly.

'Hmm,' said Caroline. Flick, flick, flick. Pause. Flick, flick, flick. 'Aaaaah. Where are you staying, then?'

'Er, Laura has booked a little cottage through the National Trust,' said Mike, suddenly vaguely conscious that maybe there was a reason that Caroline didn't seem to know the details.

'Oh, honey, you don't want to be holding your engagement party in some *holiday cottage*,' she cried. 'I know someone who has the most beautiful "cot" you can imagine in Wasdale, right next to Wastwater Lake, apparently. I'll give him a ring and I'm sure if I ask him you can borrow it for the weekend.' More flicking.

'Er,' ventured Mike, 'will you, er, be coming back?'

Flick, flick, flick. 'Don't know, darling,' Caroline said airily. 'I'll have to see how things go in NY. I'm very fluid at the moment. How is everyone? Missing me?'

'Yes, very,' said Mike automatically. 'Laura's organising the wedding like a NATO summit, Alex is run off her feet at work and the shop's heaving with customers, George is, er . . . well, John got a black eye playing cricket for our work team last night . . .' He paused and decided not to mention Rachel. Laura had just about drummed into him the importance of not mentioning Rachel to Caroline, and although he thought the whole thing was bloody silly, something that lads would sort out with a few late tackles –

vengefully given, penitently received – on the rugby pitch, he went along with it for the sake of keeping the peace at home.

'And Rachel?' said Caroline sweetly. 'How is she?'

A woman's antennae would have tingled nervously at the saccharine tone in which this was delivered, but not Mike's. Seeing this as an invitation to cast aside Laura's warnings, he replied with some relief, 'Oh, she's very well, shacked up happily these days with her photographer bloke, you know, Finlay. Don't know if you met him. Decent chap. Irish. Plays cricket.'

'Oh?' said Caroline, still sweetly. 'I do hope she's looking after him. And herself. She does, aaaaah, *bloom* rather when she's in a relationship, doesn't she? And I've always found that being in love makes one *lose* one's appetite? Still, that's Rachel for you!' She laughed in a tinkly, actressy way.

When Caroline had begun talking, safe in the knowledge that she would go on for some time, Mike had taken a large swig of the coffee brought to him by the new secretary and now, finding it had been very liberally sugared indeed, he spluttered out about half of the mouthful all over his computer, which was bearing the 'full e-mail mailbox' message. Consequently, he missed the latter half of Caroline's immaculately delivered barb, but then, as Laura affectionately told people, Mike did honestly believe that an epigram was something the doctors called for on *ER*.

'Mike, hon, are you all right?' asked Caroline in a concerned voice. Honeyed, thought Mike, through his choking, that is a honeyed tone she's using. Has she turned into a Bond girl after however long she's been in New York or has she always been like this?

'Crkkrcrkk, yes, I'm fine, just some coffee gone down the

wrong way.' Mike glared over his shoulder again in the direction of the secretary but she'd disappeared. Probably ratting me up to the boss, he thought, coughing disconsolately.

'Darling, I have to run,' said Caroline. 'My mobile's ringing and it might be my agent?' Her old habit of flicking up the ends of her sentences into incongruous questions had returned with a vengeance

'So not much of a holiday after all, then?' said Mike.

'No, but then, that's life, isn't it? You know, Mike,' said Caroline, heaving a wistful sigh down the phone, 'between you and me, sometimes I just wish they'd leave me alone, but what can you do?'

'Indeed,' said Mike, as another message dropped into his e-mail box.

'Speak soon about the cottage, sweetie, and do give my love to Laura, won't you? Take care, lots of love. Big hugs – bye!' And Caroline clunked her phone down.

Mike rang off and tried half-heartedly to save some of the paperwork now covered with coffee. He clicked on the mailbox, and saw his first message was from **paula.cobb**, who he assumed was the secretary with the malicious line in coffee-making. Well, if it was to teach him a lesson, he wasn't going to be cracked as easily as that.

Mr Craig – I think your attitude to gender politics, on the whole, needs a little sweetening up. Can I take it you will be making the coffee next time? Paula Cobb

Mike laughed a 'hey little lady' laugh and began formulating his witty response. He wasn't above a little office flirtation, if that was what she was after. It wasn't as if Laura would ever find out and, anyway, it was harmless. He clicked on Reply and typed: **Well, honey, you might be just the artificial sweetener I need! Will you be coming down to the**

Foghorn & Firkin later? Mike. Feeling pleased with this spontaneous burst of wordplay, he sent it immediately and opened the next message, which was from Rachel's press office.

Heard about John's black eye. :-(!! Will you be meting out similar punishment to all photographers or is it safe to invite you round for supper on Thursday? Let me know later; I'll call Laura this evening. R

Mike preferred to leave all social arrangements to Laura, who kept a diary for both of them and declined or accepted invitations according to whether they fitted around Mike's cricket practice or work outings and her aerobics or Portuguese classes. Nights in together with a bottle of wine and a pizza were at a premium now, more so since they announced the engagement. He could have done with one night in this week, just to check he could still recognise Laura in her pyjamas. But dinner at Rachel's was always a good spread and, fortunately, hers was a home with copious cushions and duvets, since once past the main course and into the abundant wineage, there wasn't much point trying to get home. She may be a bit moody these days, thought Mike, but she knows how to cook a good meal, I'll give her that.

He looked at his watch and, seeing it really was time to go now, he started gathering his things together. One last message dropped in his box, and he opened it as he shrugged on his jacket.

It was a circular from Cathryn, the group secretary whom Mike had snogged on the photocopier at the last Christmas party. She had exacted her revenge when he confessed his attached status the following morning, by circulating the subsequent photocopy he had made of his buttocks, which she had countersigned for authenticity, to the entire division – including the directors. Whatever she wanted, thought Mike nastily, she could just piss off.

To all members of International Funds Division:

On behalf of Justin Patterson, I would like to welcome Paula Cobb, our new Deputy Managing Director, to the Division. Paula will be assuming responsibility for our Graduate Management Programme and can be found on extension 8749.

Thanx, Cathryn :-)

Helpfully, Cathryn had added **she's the one in the red suit with coffee stains on the skirt, sugar** to the bottom of Mike's e-mail.

Oh, fantastic, thought Mike, his face colouring. But how did Cathryn . . . He flicked back through his Sent Mail box. With a feeling of horror that spread rapidly down into his bowels, Mike realised that the message from Paula had also been a circular, addressed to his entire workgroup – a fact he hadn't registered at the time, preoccupied as he was by John's barely veiled threats and then Caroline's unexpected call. Could he . . . ? The Reply and Reply All buttons were practically identical, it had to be said. Arse!

Stuffing the rest of his papers into his briefcase and closing down his computer as fast as he could, he made a clumsy but swift exit.

Sadly, it was just Mike's luck that on escaping from the office without bumping into Cathryn (who was busy in the kitchen quoting his e-mail verbatim to all who would listen), the only person waiting for the lift in the lobby was Paula Cobb herself. And indeed she did have coffee stains on the skirt, which even Mike could see now was probably part of a Joseph suit.

'Er, er, er,' mumbled Mike, his customary casualness evaporating under her coolly amused glance. He tried looking straight ahead in the lift but all he saw was a hundred coolly amused glances in the mirrored sides, each answered by a blushing, shuffling figure next to the bright red suit. Why was the lift taking so long? Why was no one getting in? Erk, erk, erk, thought Mike, floundering in a million *GQ* ways of laughing off the situation, none of which seemed to fit.

The lift pinged and reached the ground floor foyer. Mike remembered at the last minute to let Paula Cobb step out of the lift before him, but had to turn his instinctive lurch to be first out of the doors into a rather overdramatic sweep of the hand, which he didn't think he quite carried off.

She turned as she stepped out, her heels making an executive clicking noise on the foyer floor. She seemed OK; she hadn't slapped him, she hadn't given him a Laura Freeze-Out stare. Maybe his boyish charm could still win her over. He thought about trying a cheeky grin, but she held up a finger.

'Two words of advice, Mike,' said Paula Cobb, with a shiny red smile. 'Always check the address list on an e-mail and don't click Reply on a circular. Unless you want to include the whole division in your after-hours invitations?'

As she waved him a coolly amused goodbye, the lift doors closed again and Mike found himself being swished back up to the twenty-first floor, slowly thumping the sides of the lift with his forehead as he went.

chapter eight

Laura's traffic jam outlasted her good mood by exactly five minutes. By the time she had found a parking space outside Mike's office, he was already on the Tube home, wedged between two unpleasantly perspiring Spanish tourists. However, she was not to know this, having left her mobile phone on the kitchen table, and Mike, in his blue fit to get home without meeting anyone else from work, had not thought to call her anyway, imagining that she was at that same kitchen table, knocking up a steak and kidney pie.

'Hello,' smiled Laura to the girl at the front desk, in her best 'I'm more important than my youth belies' voice. After several expensive seminars on presentation and client relations, you could *hear* that smile. 'Could you see if Michael Craig is free, please?'

The woman looked up at her from behind an expensive cloud of lilies and straw foliage and smiled vacantly, tapping out Mike's extension with very shiny nails. Laura tightened her lips imperceptibly. Shiny nails suggested a lack of housework and too much time alone with an emery board. Rachel had shiny nails. Alex didn't. That was the difference. She stared fixedly at the receptionist's chocolate brown nails clicking on the receiver as she waited for a response. Caroline had a manicure once every ten days. But then she had to have that, since she had made a feature of her nails in her Spotlight entry. She had once done a hand advert for Mappin & Webb through a business associate of her father's. Huge diamond rings and a chunky identity bracelet. The most fantastic jewellery. Actually, now she thought of it ... .

'Mr Craig left the building earlier this evening,' the receptionist broke in. 'They're not sure when. Sorry about that. Can I page him for you?'

'No, that won't be necessary,' said Laura graciously. Mike did not yet have a pager, but the receptionist didn't need to know that. Bestowing one last smile, she swung her briefcase back on her shoulder and swept out of the air-conditioned building, feeling slightly cheated.

The cool black marble of the office foyer had not prepared her for the sudden blast of dry July air which almost stopped her in her tracks outside the revolving door. It hung around her nose, as though it had gone through several people already before meeting her lungs, and not, Laura felt, particularly clean people at that. Not the kind of people she wished to share the limited supply of oxygen in London with, at any rate. Thank God she wasn't going back on the Tube.

The car was very, very hot inside, which justified an ice-cream from the nearest petrol station. And that justified stopping to buy Mike something nice for his supper and by the time she was turning into their road, bags all over the back seat of the car, Laura was more like her old self. If Mike had gone out for a drink with his friends from the office, it would give her half an hour or so in the garden with her Factor 10 on and her top off, before the sun went down completely; Laura had mentally transferred the money from the sunbed sessions she *could* have had to the flower budget, which was burgeoning rapidly since she had been shown what could be achieved with white roses and out-of-season orchids.

An hour later Laura was stretched out on the balcony with the curtains discreetly pulled to behind her and the miniature topiary bushes discreetly arranged in front of her for maximum nipple concealment. Mike was still perspiring crossly in an overcrowded carriage somewhere between St Paul's and Chancery Lane.

He had no particular love of his fellow Europeans at the best of times, equipped as he was with a sound education from the Walter Raleigh school of foreign policy, and the permanently yapping group of French exchange students, brandishing yellow rucksacks and exuding ferocious body odour, were, in his opinion, largely to blame for the rapidly increasing carbon dioxide level in the carriage. Having been stuck in the dark for over ten minutes, with no explanation from the driver, Mike thought Jean-Marie and Co could at least join in the mild sense of polite panic now emanating from the other passengers. If he had known how long he was going to be there . . . but then, he reflected irritably, it was never a great idea to think too hard about the London Underground.. Particularly on a strangely motionless train. After a distinctly clammy day in the office. In complete polite silence. With gritted teeth,

Mike stared at the rapidly spreading dark patch under the armpit of the person hanging on to the rail next to him and was surprised to find himself looking forward to the weekend in Cumbria.

Laura's phone rang, and, remembering that Mike's mother was due to phone that evening with his sister Kate's dress measurements, she levered herself off the balcony, trying not to boot any of the miniature topiary bushes into the street below, and ran inside, clutching her discarded blouse to her chest.

She got to the phone on the fourth ring, just before the answering machine clicked on, and answered it breathlessly. The voice on the other end of the line was equally breathy, but in a more professional manner.

'Hello, Laura sweetie – Caroline.'

Laura gripped the blouse tighter round herself. She hadn't spoken to Caroline for a little while, not since they had last discussed Caroline's plans for staying on in New York. It had seemed easier not to. And she *really* didn't want her to have changed her mind in the meantime. 'Caroline, what a lovely surprise! Are you calling from New York?'

'*Er-huh*,' said Caroline, as if she were being interviewed. 'Listen, darlin', I'll come straight to the point here – Mike tells me you're planning a little party?'

Laura felt a variety of emotions at these words, but noticed mainly that Caroline could now say *darling* like both Liz Hurley, with audible Gucci shades, and Dolly Parton, with an audible apostrophe. She was very versatile. Maybe you had to do all this to get auditions in the States.

'Yes, we are, but I think it will be while you're still in New York – didn't you tell me you'd be there until the middle of September with this new agent?' said Laura, wondering why Caroline didn't seem to be mad that she hadn't been informed. Well, it wasn't as though she'd deliberately not told her . . .

'Listen, Laura, I have a little gift for you, sort of,' cooed Caroline, ignoring Laura's question altogether. 'Now, I can't have my friend and her fiancé staying in some dreadful little hire cottage, can I? So I've had a word with a friend of mine, Inigo Aikin-Rose – you might have heard of him, he's a big property developer? We were at boarding school together and he's very, very sweet, you'd absolutely adore him. I think, to be honest, Laura,' and here her voice dropped to a deliciously furtive purr, 'I think he has a bit of a *thing* for me, you know. I mean, if Inigo didn't have such dreadful teeth, I would be more than happy to go out for dinner with him; his father's opening a really fabulous restaurant in Notting Hill, you know, but anyway,' her voice resumed its previous level of breezy authority, 'he has a tiny, weeny little cottage – what Wordsworth would have called a "cot", you know, *rustic* – which he is more than happy for you to borrow for the weekend, as a favour to me. It's right on the lake so all the boys can do boy-things, like, you know, sail . . .' Caroline trailed off, as though she were not entirely certain what boy-things might be, beyond general strenuous, preferably mindless activity.

'Oh, Caroline,' exclaimed Laura, 'that's really *most* generous of you. How kind!' Frantic thoughts raced across her mind: how far was it from the cottage she'd booked? Could she cancel and still get the deposit back at this stage? How many people did Caroline think were invited beyond her and Mike? Did Caroline assume she would be coming too? Should she know Inigo Aikin-Rose? 'Where is it, exactly?'

'Aaaaaarh . . .' murmured Caroline. Laura could hear the

rustling of Filofax pages. Caroline liked to hold her Filofax quite close to the telephone receiver. 'It's in a place called Wastwater? Near somewhere called Gosfroth? In the middle of lots of mountains apparently. Very dramatic and inspiring, according to Inigo. He's gutted because the locals won't sell him their barns for making sweet little conversions.'

'Yes,' agreed Laura, 'Mike and I would love a place somewhere like that, eventually. A bolt-hole from the city, you know . . .'

'But you do know they're *dreadfully* expensive, Laura, sweetheart. Still,' sighed Caroline, 'I have to dash, I have a million things to do before I catch some lunch with my new man – *please* don't ask me where he's going to take me because I simply don't know. Different places every day, you know?'

Laura curled her toes enviously. 'Oh, you do lead a glamorous life, you lucky woman,' she said. 'And here am I just sunbathing on my little balcony.' Caroline hadn't seen the flat. She wasn't to know the exact dimensions of the balcony.

Caroline did her tinkly actress laugh, which Mike had admired so much. 'A balcony! I had no idea you and Mike were installed in a pied à terre with a balcony! A bit like our NY fire escape!' And as Laura had failed to pick it up the first time, she added, with a faintly pointed emphasis, 'His balcony overlooks almost all the city on a clear night. The nice bits, obviously. Very romantic!'

'Now who is this mysterious new man?' asked Laura. 'I haven't heard his name before, you dark horse.' In her head, she already had it down to one of three possibilities: the mysterious new agent, an older man/influential producer type her dad had introduced her to or a dark, moody and non-English-speaking toyboy, not unlike Pierpaolo, the Italian dreamboat she had towed along to the opening of Alex's shop.

'A-ha, ha, ha!' Caroline tinkled infuriatingly. 'No details yet! Early days, early days!'

'Oh, go on, Caroline,' wheedled Laura. 'Who is he?'

'Let's just say,' drawled Caroline, 'that he's someone who can do a lot for me and we're not talking about a season at the Cambridge ADC, OK?'

'Ooooooh,' said Laura.

This was evidently the response Caroline wanted, because she became very businesslike and refused to give any more information beyond that snippet and rustled her Filofax again, as if to indicate the number of other pressing engagements she really had to sort out that morning.

'Look, Laura, I've given Inigo your number and if there are, like, any problems, you know, I'm sure he'll be in touch, otherwise I just know you're going to love it. I know Mike will – it's *just* his kind of place.'

'You mean uncivilised?' Laura joked affectionately. Well, if she had to pick up Caroline's cues, why shouldn't she have her turn?

Caroline made no reply to that and instead went into a cascade of tinkly laughter – a little too freely, in Laura's opinion.

'. . . yaaaaah, ha, ha, ah, dear, Laura, you are sweet. *Anyway*, I have to fly, I can see his Merc outside and he's just like really stressed about parking, you know? I'll call soon, love to Mike, yes? Take care, take care, 'bye now.'

''Bye, Caroline,' said Laura over this stream of gush, and once she was sure Caroline had finished, she put the phone down. Laura remembered one epic phone conversation which began ostensibly with Caroline's indecision about which drama school to go to and her simultaneous trauma about having to dump Elsdon, her tennis coach/boyfriend. After a couple of dramatic and Kleenex-filled hours, the naked truth emerged that *in fact* Caroline was actually paralysed with shame, darling, having been rejected by nearly all her college choices and having been dumped by Elsdon for someone who was meant to be an It-Girl because she had once held a party that Tiggy Legge-Bourke had gone to for ten minutes by mistake – or *something*. Laura couldn't remember details. Her rôle, as usual, was to agree for ten minutes, disagree for the next ten, and so on and so on, until Caroline stopped.

But she had made the fatal error of assuming that Caroline had terminated their conversation when in fact she hadn't quite finished her tearful farewells. As soon as Laura had replaced the receiver on the cradle with a sigh of relief, it rang again, and Caroline was still talking away on the other end. Laura hadn't been awake enough to disguise the hanging-up noise as a fault on the line – which was only to be expected, as Caroline had called at half past two on a Thursday morning, having spent the entire evening drowning her sorrows in 192 – and consequently she had had to endure another forty minutes on how all Caroline's friends still hated her after *all* she gave them *of herself*. Laura sometimes hated being the professional plastic ear. She heard more of Caroline's angst than her therapist. But, as Laura sighed to herself, if it helped a friend . . .

Caroline had definitely gone. Laura listened to the dialling tone for a couple of seconds to be sure, then hung up. With a small sigh, she picked up her blouse, now thoroughly creased, and went into the bathroom.

The bathroom was one of the first projects for refurbishment after the wedding, thought Laura, as she ran herself a calming aromatherapy bath. Although the evening was quite sticky, she felt in the kind of self-indulgent mood a shower wasn't going to satisfy and besides, she could think more clearly immersed in the steamy lavender water. You had to start moisturising properly to develop a lasting tan. Mike wasn't here and the flat was unusually tranquil. Caroline had arranged a luxury cottage by a lake – and if she knew Caroline's other school friends, it *would* be a luxury cottage – and she hadn't had to go into her practised spiel about not telling Caroline about—

Shit! thought Laura suddenly, almost dropping the bottle of aromatherapy oils in the running water. How did Caroline know about the cottage? She remembered that she'd said Mike had told her. Which meant what *else* had he told her? And when had he been speaking to Caroline on his own? Caroline hadn't mentioned the wedding or the bridesmaids and Laura had been so surprised to hear her voice, standing in her kitchen feeling vulnerably underclothed, that she hadn't thought to mention it herself. Should she phone Caroline back? The bath foamed extravagantly.

No, thought Laura, trying hard to retrieve her previous calmness. I will lie in this bath with the new copy of *Wedding Bliss* and I will wash the grime of London away. I have only six months until my wedding and I will not allow stress to affect my complexion.

But as Rachel would have put it, Laura did no more good until Mike got back from the Tube station, grubby, xenophobic and carrying a bottle of toxin-rich Merlot, which they proceeded to enjoy over pasta salad and Friday night television. There is, thought Mike, with Laura's bare legs stretched over his knees, nothing nicer than watching the box after a hard day at work, with a woman of your own, who can make a proper meal in under ten minutes with just a can of tuna fish and an onion. Marvellous.

Laura, on the other hand, was otherwise preoccupied.

chapter nine

Alex's bedroom windows were wide open to catch any passing breeze that might freshen the muggy night air in her bedroom, but only the sounds of late Friday, early Saturday morning were floating through the curtains. The distant shouts and the thrumming bass of car stereos faded in and out as the traffic drove by. A police siren wailed down to Archway, or was it a fire engine? She couldn't sleep in heat like this; it made her eyes feel sticky. It was too hot for pyjamas, yet her bare skin was even more uncomfortable with a sheen of sweat. The sheets had been on the floor, then knotted round her legs, then kicked off again. She couldn't make her pillow soft and the sheets felt clammy.

And then of course having an extra body in the bed made a difference.

George was asleep. He has a great talent for that, Alex thought ruefully as she went into the kitchen for a glass of water. No matter how passionate I am or he is, gales, thunderstorms, heatwaves or snow, I am willing to bet that George will be asleep in under ten minutes. She suspected he had a precision timing switch that ensured optimum amount of sleep hours per night, regardless of individual circumstances, in order to leave him bright-eyed and bushy-tailed to rustle up his morning cooked breakfast. Apparently he always had a cooked breakfast.

Although, Alex silently conceded, manners being his middle name, he was always polite enough not to fall asleep immediately after sex. That had to be said. Sometimes, if she hadn't obviously scaled the same heights of discreetly muted pleasure as he had, George would initiate a polite (why did she always come back to that word?) if abbreviated exchange along the lines of, 'Did you . . .?' 'Er, not really . . .' 'Can I . . ..?' 'Er, if you don't mind . . .' Alex was a bit worried that she might become as inhibited by euphemism as him – if not actually getting as specific as mentioning nouns could count as euphemism – and forget all the technical jargon she had spent the last six years acquiring, resorting instead to covering all eventualities with a raised eyebrow and a blush.

Sometimes, especially on water retention days, she even preferred to decline his second round advances altogether, feeling as though she had suddenly been thrust into the bedroom spotlight and was expected to perform accordingly. Sometimes, she blushed to admit, she feigned exhausted slumber. And that was like *Cosmo* Woman had never happened. Something had to be done in that department if the wistful thoughts of a long-term sleeping-over arrangement, occurring to her more and more these days, were ever to come to fruition.

With a small effort, Alex put her feet up on her kitchen table. She was wearing a pair of monster-feet slippers that she'd had since school, not to keep her feet warm but because Otis had a habit of dragging his catfood round the kitchen before he ate it and she had already had one bad midnight experience, treading barefoot on what she thought was cat poo. That it turned out to be Science Diet was only just a relief.

The tabletop was cool on her legs and she held the glass of water against her forehead. It misted up immediately, the tiny beads of moisture catching the streetlight's yellow reflection outside. It was only the third time George had stayed over at her flat in the year or so that they had mutually acknowledged their relationship. He hadn't been happy about the idea at all, until one evening the previous month, after an enormous and delicious supper (secretly prepared by Rachel in exchange for another gym-mix tape) and a thrilling bout of passionate albeit fairly drunken sex, they had fallen asleep on Alex's bed. By the time they awoke, it was morning and George was forced to concede that, no, Alex hadn't produced a tray of engagement rings or designated a drawer for him in her wardrobe with three shirts and a pack of M&S shorts.

Last Friday had been the first time he had just driven straight back from the restaurant to her flat without asking her first; George had stared at her revolting skirt all through supper and then rushed her home, his eyes flicking all round the dining room as he helped her into the coat it had been too hot to need. But tonight . . . Alex smiled and sipped at her water. It was a bit disconcerting having him sleep over, but she thought she could get used to it.

At the time, she had tried not to look too pleased by this new advance, but inside she had been delighted. Alex's theory was that George could be persuaded into a relationship – albeit a temporary one until her long-haired fantasy drummer materialised – as long as he wasn't frightened by overt displays of hormone-lashed womanhood. And that wasn't her thing anyway. That was Rachel's speciality. But to be fair, thought Alex, recrossing her legs, even Rachel didn't lash her hormones on behalf of men that much these days. She'd looked a bit teary in Bliss when they'd talked about Caroline, but that could just be her period. Or an intensive day with Poppy Bright in the office and no lunch appointments for respite. Or a little dog looking lonely in a car. Rachel, by her own admission, cried at 'the brave horses in the Lord Mayor's Parade'. But not so much had been heard about her broken heart of late. Maybe artists were good for the soul. Fin seemed to keep her happy – he certainly improved her muffin production rate.

George began breathing stertorously in the bedroom. Oh God, thought Alex, biting her lip, what if he turns out to be a night-time yodeller? Can I ever truly love a man who snores? She couldn't decide if she really wanted to hear the evidence. Listening to a man snore embarrassed Alex. It made her feel that she had just rolled around in ecstasy with a twenty-something lover, and then woken up with a horrible premonition of their fifty-something future. Mouth open, double chin ahoy, pungent smell of dormant male hanging heavy on the air: staying over opened the door for all manner of horrors of the unintentional farts/revealing sleeptalking variety.

Alex was suddenly struck by a mental image of Rachel lying curled up next to George's slumbering back. She found it strange now to imagine them together. What had precise and career-planned George found in Rachel's occasionally inspired if incomprehensible observations about poetry – and vice versa? What had they talked about, at night, in bed, when all the others had left them alone? They must have talked about something in the year or so they were together – I mean, thought Alex, you can't dissect the personality flaws of your friends for ever. And even with that charming capacity Rachel has for listening raptly to male witterings, there are only so many hilarious accountancy anecdotes a girl can take. As we know.

Alex poured another glass of water from the cool filter jug and contemplated her evening conversations with George. It occurred to her that he hadn't mentioned anything to do with the office at all in the course of last night. They had talked about music, the film they'd been out to Leicester Square to see, the window box Alex had planted, Caroline and Mike, Mike and Laura, the chilling prospect of Laura's trip to Liberty for bridesmaids' dress material, and, briefly, the possibility of a weekend in Paris together in the autumn. This was touched on so briefly that Alex barely had time to register it and George had quickly followed up with something about using his allocated AirMiles before Christmas, but hey . . .

Like a garlic aftertaste, George and Rachel popped up again in Alex's mind. She sometimes wondered why Rachel had been quite so upset for so long about George and then seemed to have wiped everything from her memory. Rachel had admitted to Alex, later, that she had known he wasn't the great love of her life, but that in itself was very unlike her – Rachel usually treated everything and everyone as potentially the most exciting thing ever to happen to her. But immediately afterwards, for months, refusing to see people, hiding herself away, then emerging as if nothing had happened. She had behaved very oddly, to Alex's mind, very oddly indeed.

In private, Alex had various theories, none of which had

ever been aired. She had often suspected there was a lot more in the background than Rachel had told her; she didn't believe that such an obviously nasty trick, albeit spectacular, could hurt her for so long, and then seemingly disappear. But then Rachel was like that: she could confess everything in a torrent of confidences and keep other things to herself, until she almost made herself ill with the secrets.

As far as she remembered, George and Rachel had been a very sweet romance that had gone unpleasantly wrong and if Rachel had made a big scene at the time, Caroline might not have got away with it the way she seemed to have done. That was when the Rachel-as-hormone-lashed-female image had gathered speed, Alex realised with a stab of guilt. Mainly because of what Caroline had told everyone. Why was it that she honestly couldn't remember George's part in all the aftermath? Didn't anyone say anything about George? He had certainly never talked about it – or even been asked.

Otis glided in through the open kitchen window like a black Slinky stairclimber and looked mildly surprised to see Alex up and awake in the dark. Ever opportunistic, he leaped onto her bare knees and curled his tail into his 'feed me' question mark, which always got results since Alex was so impressed with the stylishness of his greed.

'I *cannot stomach* the smell of cat food at this time of night,' she whispered to him, in case George wasn't as soundly asleep as she thought. 'You can have some milk but that's it.' The green eyes blinked. Alex swung her feet down from the table and padded across to the fridge, picking up Otis's milk bowl – a white china bowl decorated with orange stencilled fishes, which Rachel had painted in a creative burst when she was off work with tonsillitis. She gave it a quick swill out in the sink, letting the cold water run over her wrists.

Otis mewed impatiently and rubbed himself around her ankles, in danger of being trodden on or fallen over. 'For God's sake, Otis!' hissed Alex and pulled the fridge door open, nearly braining him in the process.

The fridge let a wedge of yellow light into the dark kitchen. Well, there's a lot more food in here than I remember, thought Alex, trying to recall when she had had time to go to the supermarket in the last few frenetic days, submerged as she was by the shop's welcome rush of summer popularity. She got on her hands and knees and looked more closely at the brown paper bags, obviously from a delicatessen and not the chill cabinet of her local 7-11. There were smoked salmon slices, pain au chocolat, pots of kedgeree and a wrapped slab of pale creamy butter. Normandy butter for croissants.

Otis was now nearly in the fridge with her. 'Bloody hell, cat!' Alex batted him away and reached for the milk in the door compartment. She was pouring it into the bowl when she noticed that it was full cream, not the semi-skimmed she had been trained into drinking by her fat-unit-manic girlfriends. She stood up and frowned at the plastic container.

I am standing in the kitchen in the middle of the night, thought Alex, wearing a pair of monster slippers and talking – aloud – to a cat, while someone has infiltrated my fridge. Either I have been shopping whilst under the spirit possession of the last Viceroy of India or I really have to start shutting these windows, fourth-floor flat or not.

Otis was making loud and appreciative lapping noises, flicking tiny spheres of milk all over his black chest. Alex shut the fridge door thoughtfully. The only light now falling into the kitchen came from the streetlight opposite. She thought about closing the kitchen window, to be on the safe side, but leaned out instead, trying to catch some fresh air on her face, too lethargic to do anything except listen to the splashing of Otis's tongue and the rumble of cars on the road. She was too tired to sleep. Suddenly too wary of what was happening to the plans she'd laid for her bachelor-girl lifestyle. What if she followed her instincts back to her sleep-warmed bedroom, to watch George breathing heavily, wrapped in her sheets, with his handsome head buried in her pillows? Where did that leave her plans for living as the heroine Nick Hornby never wrote – record shop, groovy flat upstairs, fed-on-demand cat? And when was the last time she had skimmed her horoscope *without* her eye skidding across from Aquarius to Capricorn, just 'out of interest'?

'Please don't jump – I don't know how to work the coffee machine,' said a low voice, smelling of sleep, into her ear. Alex felt a pair of hairy arms wrap around her waist and she realised how cool her skin must have become, compared to their solid warmth. 'And who said anything about wearing my T-shirts?' George began to nibble her ear.

'Did you put all that stuff in the fridge?' asked Alex. Her voice was wobbling slightly, despite her best intentions. The nocturnal George was a very different animal from his day-time self. Why did he bring out her best intentions, when most men delighted in her worst? Why did she end up behaving like the Singing Nun when inside she was churning with unbridled desire? Why couldn't she just be like Rachel and go with the flow, no matter how Niagaraesque the flow might be?

'Yes, I have to confess it was me,' George murmured into her ear. 'You never have proper food for breakfast in your fridge, Alex my dear. You are the only woman I know who scrambles one egg on half a bagel and calls it lunch. So I stopped by a deli on the way over. Is that all right?'

'Oh, yes, yes, that's quite all right,' said Alex. 'I've put the cooked meat into the cooked meat drawer – it stops it affecting the dairy stuff.' This was a remark straight from the *Laura Parker Big Book of Hints for a Happy House* and Alex, mentally slapping her forehead, wondered how it had come out of her mouth at such an inopportune time. Hot summer night, minimal clothing, encounter in a darkened kitchen, double cream within easy reach – ah, yes, *obviously* the time for fridge hygiene tips. Catch her on a normal day in Tesco's and she couldn't give you a single one. Laura must have slipped that one into her subconscious mind when she wasn't concentrating.

There was a slight silence, although Alex wasn't to know that far from being revolted by this uncharacteristic show of domesticity, George was actually rather touched that she was taking more of an interest in her house. To her relief, he tightened his grip on her waist.

'Why don't you come back to the bedroom, Alex?' he said. 'I've remade the bed.'

Surprisingly enough, this sounded very tempting. More tempting than the premise behind it, on closer inspection.

'Can we just sit here for a little bit first?' said Alex. 'I like sitting in the dark on nights like this, when it's too hot to sleep. You can hear all sorts of things going on outside. And it's not sweaty like lying in bed. Sorry,' she added quickly, as George's face dropped, 'I'm not saying you're sweaty. I just don't like lying in bed all awake when I should be asleep. I prefer to ditch the pretence completely and sit up.'

George led her gently over to the big sofa next to the window which had been left there, near the door, when she moved in and never moved since. John, in particular, still claimed to bear the scars on his lumbar system from the three flights of stairs. They knelt in its squashy cushions, looking out into the street, where a few people still roamed about in monotone beneath the streetlamps.

'Is that a prostitute, do you think?' asked Alex, pointing to a discussion taking place next to a parked BMW. 'Do women really wear those fishnet tights non-professionally? I mean, apart from Sigue Sigue Sputnik. Not that they were women.' This last observation was more to herself.

'Why are you asking me?' replied George, with a good semblance of outrage. 'Do you honestly expect me to answer that? Do you honestly want me to be *able* to answer that?' He stared across the road at the vision in fishnets, now joined by someone who appeared to be having trouble digesting his kebab. 'Now call me an old traditionalist, but I can recognise an Adam's apple when I see one. And I don't remember that being fitted as a standard feature on your average woman, even in my limited experience.'

He pulled Alex away from the window and on to his knee. The sudden contact of warm skin again made her stomach tighten with pleasure. There was something very sexy about seeing the body hair of a man who rarely even loosened his collar during daylight hours. If this is the psychological side effect of all that predictable office dressing, thought Alex, I am prepared to iron blue Pink shirts for all eternity. *What do you mean, iron shirts*!?! yelled a disquieting voice in her head. *What is going on*??

'Why are you being so romantic?' she asked, temporarily thrown as George's hands ran up and down her back. 'You're not like this in the cold light of day.' Her voice wobbled as he pulled her back into a horizontal Hollywood clinch and deposited a kiss on her throat.

'Maybe I can only show you my dark side when we're all

alone and awake on hot nights when we should be sleeping.' With that, George pulled her up to his chest for another kiss, which began quietly and ended with Alex making low groaning noises. Quite spontaneously, George lifted her up into his arms and carried her back into the bedroom, something that had never ever happened to Alex before – or at least, not without one party being raging drunk or the other making comments like, 'Bloody hell, Alex, have you got lead knickers on or what?'

George dropped Alex on the freshly straightened duvet which now seemed meltingly cool and soft. She stretched out on her side, her arms reaching out to the pillows above her head, unselfconsciously, like a long white cat, watching George, who gazed at her smooth white legs with undisguised lust. She peeled off the T-shirt she was wearing and wriggled.

George was about to pull his shorts off and climb onto the bed, but stopped and bit his lip. 'Let me put on some music.'

Oh, this is exactly what Rachel has been wittering on about all this time, thought Alex deliriously. This is the luxury of passion! He wants it to be just perfect too! What kind of music would he choose from the selection by her bedroom stereo? They were all relax-y, sexy sounds, nothing that could go horribly wrong. Portishead? Massive Attack? She shut her eyes and ran her fingers across the cool duvet.

George couldn't see where she kept her CD rack in the half-darkness of the room and didn't want to do anything embarrassing like knock over a lamp or try to pull a phantom CD out of some wacky art school photo frame. It was bad enough with the benefit of natural light. Quite by chance, and almost despairing of finding anything before Alex had to put the lamp on and offer to help look, he trod on a plastic bag by the door, which felt from the resultant crunch as though it might be full of plastic cases. Gratefully – George was more conscious than most of the exquisite importance of timing – he picked up the first one that came to hand, *The Greatest Love Album Ever*. Can't go far wrong with that, he thought with some relief, loading it into the player with an expert touch.

Shorts now removed, George slid onto the bed, looking unusually sexy and unshaven in the faint morning light, and began covering Alex's flat, downy stomach with little kisses. Alex wondered deliriously if he'd bought a guide book.

'*You're once . . .twice . . .three times a laaadeeee . . .*'

George felt all the muscles in Alex's stomach contract as though she'd been punched. He sat up abruptly.

'What's the matter? Am I being too . . .?' He couldn't think what he might have been 'too' – it wasn't as though this stomach was virgin territory to him.

As the syrupy tones of Lionel Richie oozed through the room, Alex lay rigidly on the bed, able to think only one thing. Where seconds before her mind had been full of George and what she intended to do with him once he had covered her stomach entirely, she could now only think, '*Laaaddeee*.' Lionel Richie and his *ladeeez*, his *very special ladeeez*. Flares and open neck jumpsuits. Glitter on those pointy lapels. Having sex with this in the background would be like having her parents at the end of the bed. And at the thought of George actually liking this embarrassing rubbish, of him wanting to make *lurrrrvvvve* to her, she felt her toes curling under until her feet stung. He *chose* this. He chose this as a soundtrack to *makin' luuurve*. Alex felt slightly sick. Erk. What was wrong with her?

'Alex, what's the matter?' said George, who could now

only imagine that perhaps she was in the throes of some strange Women's Thing. Her eyes were fixed on the ceiling and she was blushing furiously.

'It's this song, George,' mumbled Alex. There was no point in lying. She hoped that she wouldn't be called upon to explain further.

George's heart sank. Oh God. This was what he had had at the back of his mind all along. He sat on the bed with his back to Alex. He had known from the start that she had had other boyfriends before him, but had hoped that she felt that their relationship, perhaps, given time . . . But obviously this song had some connection with some other bloke who might as well be in the room with them, for all the immediate effect he had had on George's ardour. Ardour, snorted George to himself, talk about dampened ardour. He looked miserably at his discarded boxer shorts and pulled them back on.

The Commodores continued to croon oleaginously in the background.

And it had been going so bloody well, thought George. He had followed Rachel's advice to the letter – the breakfast, the romantic evening, the kisses on non-genital areas, the romantic music. (He had drawn the line at candles, on account of not being able to keep a close eye on them while otherwise engaged, and the danger of falling asleep afterwards.) What did he have to do to cross these lines Alex put up for him?

Sadly, he turned back to the bed, where Alex lay with her eyes closed, mentally screaming 'For fuck's sake!' at her prone state, trying to will five minutes back and cursing her messiness in not getting all that sodding bag of dreadful compilation albums into the shop when she'd fetched them home from the record fair. What the hell was she playing at? It had been *perfect*. How could you tell a man prepared to feed you chocolate croissants and nibble your stomach that Lionel Richie rendered you frigid? What the hell could she say? It was too ridiculous to sound like anything other than a cack-handed brush-off – even though it was true. How the hell could she haul the situation back now? Alex, hating herself violently, couldn't bring herself to say anything at all.

It was just wrong. She didn't know how to explain. It had been perfect and now it was . . .wrong. The silence was hypnotic and the longer it filled the hot room, the more it weighed down Alex's tongue. For the duration of 'Three Times A Lady', which is to say, until her brain made the connection with the remote control for the stereo by her side of the bed, Alex tortured herself imagining the whole situation with George slipping out of her hands for ever, after all these months of trying and nudging, and all because the 1970s embarrassed her sense of nuance.

But George, still picturing the softness of her stomach and the white curve of her hip in the pale light, just imagined a history he was too gentlemanly to enquire about, but which evidently still threw a shadow on their future. He sighed eloquently and turned himself under the duvet, as the true morning noises began in the street outside and Alex agonised silently, wakefully, beside him.

chapter ten

By four o'clock on Wednesday afternoon there was not an empty seat in the faded chintz-covered lounge of Brown's Hotel. Waiters weaving in and out of the deep chairs, swinging tiered cake trays and teapots, took care not to tread on the elegant paper carrier bags, discreetly but distinctively embossed, which were piled carelessly by the tables. Long slim legs were crossed and uncrossed at the knees and at the ankles, as the ladies discussed their shopping and their friends, punctuating each morsel of gossip with the tiniest, most delicate *petit four* from the top layer of their silver cake stands. The waiters hovered solicitously at the nod of a black velvet Alice band, proffering fruit cake, extra raspberry jam, with just the right note of ingratiation. They were elegantly ignored.

A trio of American women from Middletown, Connecticut, appeared at the door and enquired whether a table for tea might be found for them. They looked ready to drop in the afternoon heat and were loaded down with several bags each, including a selection from the better shops of

Bond Street. The *maître d'* flipped unnecessarily through the booking volume on the lectern and scanned his practised eye across the room, while the two elder ladies shifted their weight from one leg to another, and the very slightly younger, more hungry-looking one discreetly tugged at her girdle.

His glance fell upon a solitary young woman sitting in a large wing chair by the window. Rachel was gazing distantly around the room, her eyes flicking distractedly from one group to another, then resting blankly in close contemplation of the untouched cakes on her table. Amidst the sociable chatter, she looked rather lonely, although the *maître d'*s discreet tilt of the head towards the spare chairs next to her table drew a look that made it clear that she would prefer to remain alone. However, Brown's *was* a popular place for the English tea in London and these *were* the only spaces left, so with an apologetic shrug he led the wilting Americans across the tea room to the heavily padded sofa.

Oh, God, thought Rachel forlornly. They look like talkers.

The three ladies, glad to get out of the heavy summer heat and into an authentically cool English drawing room, sank gratefully into the cushions, smiling in a friendly way at their young neighbour, who gave them a weak smile in return, bit her lip and suddenly bent down to rearrange her handbag underneath her chair.

Rachel was in no mood to make small talk. One of the reasons she was here in the first place was that there would be no one she knew and certainly no obligation to talk to anyone she didn't. The elegantly arranged chairs were just far enough apart to prevent conversation spreading; however, she realised with a sinking heart, short of going, 'La, la, la, I can't hear you!' with her fingers in her ears, there was no way of avoiding overhearing the Americans' barely muted comments. Rachel wished she had brought a book to offer a cover, then remembered with a pang how her mind had skittered across the grid of the *Telegraph* crossword that morning while she was waiting, her thoughts unable to connect with the clues for the first time since the Sixth Form common room.

'Just like Lady Di,' hissed one of the women to her friend, a stout lady wearing a lot of tweed despite the heat. 'Beautiful . . . but tragic!' Out of the corner of her eye, Rachel saw her nod none too subtly in her direction. She wished she could close her ears, but couldn't.

'What do you mean, Kit?' the tweedy lady hissed back, turning her shoulder on the girl and glaring warningly at her friend. Her younger sister was no help, poring as she was over the menu, her lips moving slightly as she read through the different types of tea.

'Just look at that lovely porcelain skin! What else would she be doing here, in Brown's, at four o'clock on a Wednesday, with a complexion like that if she wasn't an Honourable? She'd be out in an office somewhere!'

Well, thought Rachel, who had heard all of this exchange, though manners had prevented her from showing that she had, right on almost no counts there. She should indeed be in the office. In fact, she should at this moment be talking to Dinah Spell of Detritus about the brochure shoot for the next season's catalogue. And as it was nearly four o'clock, and if Poppy had made it into the office, she should be heading out to Cullens about now for some pastries to resuscitate her flagging employer. She looked forlornly at the top tier of glossy *petits fours* and for the first time in her life found she had no desire at all to eat them.

Was this a symptom? she wondered. The urgently whispered discussions of the American ladies abruptly ceased and she looked up. All three were smiling at her in a 'we know who you are' way, their hands folded on identical ample laps. Automatically, because she was a nicely brought-up young lady, Rachel smiled back and the whispers started up again, more fervently than before.

Who do they think I am? she thought. Even Rachel was having problems working out who she was today. From the instant she had woken up that morning, the sense that all was not going according to plan, a feeling that had been creeping up on her now for several days, had become a fixed certainty in her mind. And – she checked her watch – as of two-thirty, things were officially so out of kilter that she was seriously wondering whether this was a dream. Or whether this wasn't actually her life at all. She certainly felt as though she were taking no active part in it.

Had promising herself a tea at Brown's, a plush hotel afternoon tea dangling like a carrot if she got herself through this morning, been a way of pretending this wasn't happening? she thought with a dispassion that surprised her. Tea at Bliss would have been normal. Tea at Brown's meant that she was trying subconsciously to be someone else, someone for whom these new and frankly unreal developments would be more manageable. And now she was here, she couldn't eat anything and – she wasn't sure if this was a figment of her imagination – even the tea tasted funny. Was that a *sub*-subconscious reflection?

Rachel had to blink back a lump in her throat and swallowed a mouthful of hot Assam tea. The teacups were beautiful, almost transparent. She sat hers in the palm of her hand. Treating this situation as a piece of real life

Practical Criticism wasn't going to be much use, even if it had made her initial reactions of confusion, followed by panic, subside into the background. Alex would probably say being a cool observer would point her in the right direction, but cool observation had never been Rachel's strong suit and this weird feeling of numb detachment, so *pleasantly* numb at first, was becoming unsettling.

So easy to pretend that this was happening outside her, to push it to the back of her mind and note the polished, authentically weathered surface of her silver tea service, the heavy chintz of the curtains in the bay windows, the genteel selection of light Mozart from the hotel pianist. It had been easy all day: shower, catch the Tube, ten minutes early for the appointment, listen carefully throughout, then tea at Brown's for three-thirty – she had been meaning to come to Brown's for a proper tea since she moved to London – then home, supper, meet Fin for a film at the NFT. No need for talking, bed, alarm clock, Tube, office. Easy.

Fin. So much a part of her that it was hard to consider him separately. Hard to keep anything from him. Rachel was sure he knew anyway, that he had an inkling of what had been behind her confused manner for the past week or so; their minds were so used to running together that any secret felt like a division. She put her lips to the rim of the cup and felt the hot liquid touch her mouth, using the sensation as a diversion from her elusive thoughts.

If coming here for tea had been an attempt to drag this troublesome day back onto a recognisable schedule, the rarefied atmosphere of indulgent leisure was pushing Rachel out into greater depths. Especially as the twittering trio of Americans was now, to her consternation, trying to decide amongst themselves whether she could be 'one of those titled interior designers', whilst hushing one another extravagantly every time Rachel lifted her heavy eyes their way.

She poured herself another cup of tea. The silver strainer was choked with dark leaves and, attracting the attention of the waitress, Rachel asked for a fresh pot of Assam. She was in need of deep strong tea. Here the tea ritual was at its height – the silver pot and hot water jug, the fresh full cream milk, the sugar and tongs and the beautiful, delicate cup, which gave a genteel tinkle as Rachel replaced it in its saucer. Each stage required a measured action, nothing rushed.

'Meredith,' she heard one of the ladies – the younger, more carefully coiffed one – murmur to her companion, 'we've been doing the tea wrong!'

'What, what?' replied the other fearfully, through a mouthful of warm scone and Devonshire clotted cream.

Rachel suppressed a rueful smile and gazed into her teacup as if deep in thought.

The distressed American matron looked askance at her teacup, as if she expected it to reprimand her, then shot a quick glance at Rachel, who was serenely adding a drop more milk and observing her reflection – and theirs – in the big picture mirror above the fireplace. 'The tea goes in first! Not the milk! Oh, *darn*!' She glanced about quickly to see if anyone had noticed her *faux pas*. Rachel dropped her eyes. The light chatter and surreptitious piggery continued around the room, the tea-takers unaware of her imagined clanger. She blushed to the roots of her white roller-set nevertheless.

Everything comes down to order, thought Rachel, with a composure that amazed her. It's not ladylike to do things out of order, is it? Milk, tea, sugar. I've got this all wrong. Proper job, marriage, baby. And it's not even as though I have the proper job.

There. She'd said it in her head. It had a pleasant, imaginary status in her head. Unspoken, the word vanished again. If only she could make herself *panic*. Instead she was floating around in exactly the same way she used to when she had an essay to do for two days' time and still pushed her panic away until tomorrow. Sliding over the surface of it all. Nothing engaging.

Rachel poured herself a cup of tea from the fresh pot and let her eyes drift back to the American ladies, who were fidgeting and whispering snappishly amongst themselves. One had *Fodor's London* discreetly open between her knee and the side of the chair; another, ignoring the discussion raging next to her, was tucking into the last of the egg and cress sandwich fingers, holding it delicately between thumb and forefinger.

Rachel was reminded of her grandmother up in Ambleside, knobbly gardener's hands cutting and mixing floury pastry in the bowl, snipping roses from the sheltered cottage garden for Rachel to take home to Manchester, stripping the thorns expertly from the red stems. 'A little piece of Westmoreland for your room, pet,' she used to say, deliberately ignoring the newfangled change in county boundary lines. The summer holidays, long before her grandmother grew frail and faded, when she would bake ham and egg pies and take Rachel out riding, while her parents worked through the week in the dusty city, then came up at the weekends for the cool, bright air of the lakes.

What was her mother going to say? How would her father react, the source of so much comfort in the past for failed tests and unworthy boyfriends? Not that there had been many of either, she thought ruefully. But his solid arms had never questioned or reproached. But then she had never given them cause. She slipped it to the back of her mind with the rest of the difficult questions.

The two ladies finished their little quarrel and noticed that all the sandwiches had gone. Rachel gave them her best smile. They simpered back happily, seemingly pleased with her approval, and fiddled with their china.

Let them think I'm an Honourable interior decorator, thought Rachel, disengaging herself once more and floating loose from her thoughts. I might as well be for this afternoon.

chapter eleven

George got out of the car, slammed the door and strode up the steps to John's front door, muttering darkly. August had come round very quickly, with hot, sticky weather and even more heated discussions and clandestine theories. Needless to say, the topic had not been raised before Mike or Laura, and, in the circumstances, Caroline's subsequent silence had remained gratefully unchallenged by any of the others.

In the car, Alex turned up the stereo and winced. It was Bob Marley, singing 'No Woman, No Cry'. She winced again and turned it onto the radio. Atlantic Starr, 'Secret Lovers'. She turned it off. It was very hot inside, even with all the windows open.

'John! For God's sake!' bellowed George into the intercom. 'It's nearly bloody four o'clock!' The intercom crackled unhelpfully in response. He leaned his head against the wall. The normally tranquil George was coming close to breaking into a sweat, something Alex hadn't seen him do since video footage of the boys' spoof 'arrest' in Guadalajara.

The red door to the flat swung open and John staggered

out under the weight of one tiny sports holdall and three hefty camera bags. George sprang back from his praying position on the intercom and grabbed a bag, hustling John towards the car.

'. . . breakfast on *Mars*, George, mate,' panted John, as they opened the boot and squeezed his luggage into the tiny available space. Alex thought that this might have made more sense as part of a sentence but from the black look on George's face she didn't think it was the best time to ask him to repeat it.

'Alex, have you got the Routemaster printout?' asked George, still polite, but now with a discernibly metallic edge in his voice.

'Eh, George, is that wise? Letting one of the little ladies navigate?' bellowed John good-naturedly from the back seat. 'We'll be parallel parked at Brent Cross Shopping Centre and into Ikea before we know it!' With her teeth on edge, Alex smelled the opening of a packet of dry-roasted peanuts and hoped George, ever concerned for the state of his back seat, hadn't. Not that the back seat was ever likely to see much action, she thought ruefully. Peanuts or otherwise.

She rummaged in her bag and came up with the plastic folder George had given her when they left her flat. In it was a map of Cumbria, a list of phone numbers in case they should break down in the Wilds of the North and the Routemaster plan George had prepared on his computer the night before, showing the quickest and the shortest ways to get from London, England to Wastwater, The Middle of Nowhere. He was recharging his spare mobile phone battery as they spoke. Alex suspected that there was even Kendal Mint Cake in the glove compartment, but didn't want to look in case there was. She was glad that Rachel wasn't travelling with them, since this kind of 'The North is a foreign country' talk habitually sent her into sarcasm overdrive.

'I'm OK until we have to turn off the M1,' said George, as they approached the North Circular and the first traffic delay of the journey. 'But I'll need guiding into the wilderness, so it might be a good idea to have a look at the map now, Alex.'

Alex abruptly stopped fiddling with the ominous bag of tapes. Every single tape seemed to have some reproachful selection of titles: 'If He Knew What He Wants (He'd Be Giving It To Her)', 'My Best Friend's Girl Friend', 'Stuck in the Middle With You' – even 'Sweet Little Lies' was taking on sinister new overtones in her current state of anxiety. Was it merely her professional oversensitivity to lyrics or was it the onset of paranoia? Alex was beginning to feel like the embodiment of the Tense, Nervous Headache. And now she would have to stew away nicely for the five hours it would take to get there, lest a chance remark be captured on videotape (oh, she had her suspicions!) by John. She didn't put it past him to be doing a little scene-setting right now, comedy footage to be used later of her with her head in the glove compartment, searching for Fox's Glacier Fruits and George snarling uncharacteristically at a school minibus trying to change lanes by using apologetic hand gestures instead of the traditional indicating lights.

'Pringle, Alex?' A tube of salt and vinegar flavoured Pringles was poked between the front seats, closely followed by a cassette. 'It's Roxette's *Greatest Hits*. God, you loved this tape in South America, didn't you, George? It's on nearly all the video.' Alex had thought at the time that there was something mildly sadistic about the way that footage of George's colourful stomach upset was inevitably drowned out by the strains of 'It Must Have Been Love'. *Almost* drowned out.

She waved away the Pringles with a shudder and a polite smile for the benefit of the camera, which John was now pointing at her.

This journey was going to feel much longer than five hours.

Laura stirred at the pheasant soup that was bubbling away on the Aga, and gazed out at the clear sky. Her mobile phone was propped up against the kettle, in case Mike should call her when his conference was over to let her know he'd set off. She had asked him to call, but didn't really like him using his mobile and driving at the same time, so she was afflicted with mixed feelings. And a part of her doubted that he would remember to ring anyway.

It was a good job she'd taken the day off and come up here early, Laura thought to herself. Even though the cottage seemed to have been very recently cleaned, with big bunches of lilacs in the double bedroom and on the side of the bath, she hadn't felt happy until she'd aired all the rooms, to be on the fresh side. When that thought had gone through her head, Laura had been acutely aware that it was something her grandmother might have thought. Was this a good sign for her impending marriage? Or just another indication that she had already begun to think like someone with fifty years of matrimony under their belt – in which case, why was she bothering with the logistical nightmare that would transform her from cohabitee girlfriend to cohabitee spouse?

Laura sighed and decided that those kinds of questions were best kept to herself. Particularly this weekend. Her girlfriends, much as she loved their gossipy evenings, had a habit of turning private advice sessions into a full-blown *Kilroy* in her own home. And she didn't want to give Mike an excuse for wriggling out of wearing morning suits at this late stage of play.

The capacious fridge was full of local bacon, sausage and eggs, not to mention a bottle of champagne. There was also a greaseproof package of something that could easily be black pudding. Maybe Rachel would be able to confirm its exact constituents. Laura had left that for Mike and the boys. Even on a hot day like today, she liked to have some proper food made for supper. It hadn't taken long to get the soup going and make a cake and now the cottage smelled welcoming and homely, ready for the arrivals from London. When they arrived. Satisfied, Laura made herself a pot of tea and settled down with the file of tax cases she'd brought with her.

Hawk Cottage was at the foot of Yewbarrow, a fell hunched behind Wastwater like a sleeping diplodocus. It was down a concealed drive that hid it from the road and looked out on to the lake, some rocks and the neighbouring farmer's flock of Herdwicks. The front door, confusingly, was unused, and access was via the back, where Laura had tentatively parked her car. No one had told her this and she'd had to go through every key on the huge bunch left for her at the local post office before giving up and going round to the back door, which swung open easily, leading past a bootroom and a pantry to a big, cheerful kitchen. Fully equipped by Caroline's friend Inigo to accommodate the every whim of the discerning London fell-walker, the white-washed, slate-roofed cottage even had an Aga, which kept the place snug on chilly March afternoons and perpetuated the happy conviction that all rural folks ate round a scrubbed deal table and had sheep roaming in the back garden. The cottage sat beautifully positioned in the valley, with the Screes rising over the lake in front of it and the fells looming behind and, to Laura's mind, simply screamed, 'Paint me'. Or it would have done, if she had enough time for such things.

Once fortified by a good cup of tea, Laura thought that the view alone was worth every jolted minute of the uncomfortable train journey it had taken to get here. As far as she could make out, this particular weekend was some kind of Glaswegian migratory thing and she'd certainly picked up some unorthodox childcare tips from her fellow passengers. It had never even crossed her mind to allow children near McEwan's Export, let alone bribe them with it. And *certainly* not in the middle of the day.

On arriving with some relief at Carlisle station, she collected the Fiat Punto she'd hired for the weekend and began the complicated car journey down the coast, Mike's advance enquiries about public transport having been met with a wry explanation of the two daily buses which went within four miles of the cottage. The drive to Wasdale had been a real test of her simultaneous road-holding and map-holding skills, but she'd made it in a much shorter time than anticipated by Mike, who, with much gnashing of teeth and stabbings at a calculator, had finally put to use the fiddly device for measuring map mileage that he'd been sent as an introductory gift from the RAC. Laura could tell after a cursory glance at the map that Carlisle to Wastwater was hardly going to take her three hours, but hadn't liked to say anything.

She had taken care to put a couple of audio book tapes in her handbag, so she wouldn't feel too lonely on her long drive; she had listened to the best part of *Wuthering Heights* with the conclusion saved for the drive back. No one had honked at her, tried to cut her up or made obscene 'lady-driver' hand gestures and the only delay had come from a herd of Friesian cows being led across to the opposite field for milking. By that stage of her journey Laura was so sedated by the country air that, instead of feeling the usual London impatience at the delay, she merely gazed beatifically at the cows, their heavy udders swinging as they swayed their way into the field like forty bovine Marilyn Monroes, and had to prod herself to restart the engine once they'd passed.

And now, for another blissful hour or so, this gorgeous Chelsea-in-Cumbria cottage was all hers. Every detail was perfect, she thought, looking round happily. It could have been fitted out by the General Trading Company yesterday. Even the heavy curtains in the sitting room had matching pelmets and white shutters behind them. And there was a proper larder. With those really old-looking stone jars – she'd seen some very similar in After Noah on Upper Street, but much cleaner.

Maybe when Mike starts earning a bit more and I become a partner at Morris Dunlop, we can get a little place like this, thought Laura. Not so long a drive from London, though. Maybe in Scotland, nearer the motorway, much quicker. We can pack the car full of food, get a labrador, some tweedy things, maybe go shooting. Laura didn't know anyone who went shooting and she was fairly sure Mike didn't either, but she knew from reading her *Tatler* that shooting and Chelsea-in-the-Country cottages went together like port and Stilton. In fact, she thought she might have spotted a gun cupboard while searching for the freezer, and a little frisson ran through her.

Laura rocked back and forth on the heavy rocking-chair, admiring the stone flags which held a glow of warmth from the Aga. The afternoon had been very hot with little breeze. Now, at the beginning of the evening, it was still mild outside but soon, Laura thought fondly, the sky over the lake would be shot through with ripples of orange and purple from the setting sun. Perfect for her welcoming pot of soup (someone must shoot, she thought, to account for the two plucked pheasants waiting in the fridge) and the deep cream cushions of the three-people-sitting, four-people-flopping sofa. Yes, once she'd got over the initial panic at having her plans disrupted, she was grateful to Caroline for arranging this. She must write and thank this Inigo chap for giving her such a perfect setting for her party. How romantic. How perfectly un-London.

Watching the stout sheep graze in the field behind the house, she thought it was remarkable how easily the strains of the city fell away from her shoulders. For the first time since she had begun her law course, Laura felt as though she were really on holiday. Better than that, with a heady rush of sensation unusual for her, she felt as though, for this afternoon, she were completely absolved from any responsibility whatsoever and, much to the delight of her rusty poetic sensibilities, her heart actually lifted, just like . . . Wordsworth? Laura put away her tax files, unable to summon up any real concern for the button and toggle fastenings company she had been assigned to shuffle neatly into order, and started to doodle sheep on her legal pad, rocking back and forth in what she happily supposed was a country-wife manner.

Mike had always expressed surprise that she hadn't gone in for family law, given that she was so compassionate and good with people. He had, he once told her, misty-eyed, a mental image of His Laura, dressed in a stylish but feminine suit, holding the hand of some snivelling tug-of-love child in a divorce court, gently coaxing the parents into an amicable settlement (possibly an emotional courtroom reconciliation in the retiring room) and moving even the cynical court usher to bring out his handkerchief with her kind words to the defendants and wise direction to the judge.

Laura had smiled sweetly and said nothing, as was her wont. Despite what Mike might think, the idea of aiding and abetting wrangling parents in their own power games, unpleasantly flavoured as these trials normally were with the florid language of made-for-TV movies, appealed about as much as having her wisdom teeth out without anaesthetic. In describing this vision of judicial gorgeousness – sort of Solomon crossed with Princess Diana – Mike hadn't actually used the phrase 'the mother of my children' but she could sense it hovering in the background. Laura privately doubted that she had the patience to put up with those kinds of shenanigans: it was bad enough always having to spring to the defence of one of her friends when another had an axe to grind. And, as she demurred modestly to Mike, the thought of having someone's future resting on her abilities to speak in court was a dreadful burden. He had taken this as proof of yet another womanly virtue and had gone away happy.

Button and toggle fastening companies might be dull but they were not life-threatening, thought Laura. And she only intended to carry on at Morris Dunlop until she and Mike wanted to start a family. Or 'try for a baby', as her mother had put it. At the moment, not to put too fine a point on it, they were trying very hard *not* to have a baby. She could think of nothing more embarrassing than to arrange the wedding, marquees and bridal favours and all, and then discover with a month to go that you were two months gone. And have everyone assume that the whole thing was a rush job.

Laura added a fence around the four fluffy sheep she had

doodled. At least no one could say that this wedding was a rush job, not with the amount of planning it had taken. It was all pretty much done now. Just the hat to pick for the going-away outfit and as far as that went, she thought Rachel might have some PR connection with David Shilling or one of those milliners, and could rustle up some press stock. It was going to be a pretty big wedding and she knew her mother wouldn't turn up without some dreadful friends in tow – it wouldn't be without some PR in it for Rachel. And Finlay – she'd had various extortionate quotes from wedding photographers, but maybe he could do it as a wedding present? She scribbled 'Fin – Wed Phot?' and drew a box around it, so she'd remember to bring the matter up tactfully with Rachel when they had a quiet moment. These things had to be done carefully.

Laura settled back in the rocking chair and balanced the legal pad on her knees. She had a sudden craving for chocolate rich tea biscuits and remembered that she had a low-fat cereal bar in her bag for such emergencies. Some women bought 'inspirational' size 10 dresses then left them hanging for ever in their wardrobes; Laura had much more riding on her size 10 wedding dress. Her iron will tended to bend at fortnightly intervals, though, but with the steely determination of one whose life was now ruled by the countdown calendar of *Debrett's Wedding Guide*, she was gradually inching towards the crinoline of her dreams. With a rush of satisfaction, and a mouthful of cereal, Laura began another stumpy-legged sheep.

chapter twelve

Rachel looked up at the office clock and let out a tetchy sigh. Only half an hour left in order to catch the last practicable train from Euston that would allow her to meet up with George and Alex, as prearranged and confirmed by fax from George (map included). She was having to leave early as it was. Her in-tray was still towering and she had a pathological fear of leaving anything incriminating for Harriet to find on Monday, when she had booked the day off. Harriet, she knew, was not above having a quick trawl through her desk, should the opportunity present itself. And as she would have to cover reception while Rachel was away – reception being something usually beneath Harriet, who did after all have a Diploma in Press Relations – she would consider it well within her rights.

The office phone rang and Rachel answered it, scrolling through a letter template at the same time.

'Good afternoon, Dunleary and Bright,' she said, opening the Detritus Cosmetics file on-screen.

'Er, hi, Rachel, Dan here.' No wonder there was no

number on the display, thought Rachel, it's a covert call. 'Do you know where Fin is?'

'He was doing a job for the *Standard* this afternoon. In Highgate, I think,' said Rachel. 'Although, having said that, he's probably finished by now. Have you tried The Anglesea Arms?'

'Er, right,' said Dan mysteriously. 'I need to borrow him for a job this weekend, that's all. One of Our Friends, y'know, *Marvin*.' Rachel heard a shifty cough at the other end.

Dan and Fin had a bizarre series of codenames for people who might qualify for a spot of hot pursuit by the Golf Convoy and Rachel didn't ask and wasn't told. Except when her connections might be useful. Harriet Blythe dreamed of achieving sufficient fame as a PR It-Girl for Dan Wingate to give her a codename and follow her out of Heathrow at 110 miles an hour.

'Well, borrow away, Dan,' said Rachel, 'I'm going up to the Lake District for the weekend. He's all yours. Try his other mobile – I don't think he tries very hard to be reachable after lunchtime on a Friday. Especially not if he's settled in with a pint and a salt beef stovey.'

She gave him the number, he thanked her and, with sounds of excitement now clearly audible in the background, he rang off. Harriet came slinking round the corner just as Rachel put the phone down.

'Sorry, Harriet, you just missed Dan on the phone,' she said sweetly. And because it was Friday and she would be out of the office for seventy-two whole hours, added, 'He says hello.' Harriet blushed visibly and diverted the sheaf of filing she was obviously about to dump in Rachel's in-tray to that of the emaciated work-experience girl from the London College of Fashion, who rolled her eyes heavenwards *à la* Kate Moss.

Rachel began typing her covering letter to Miranda at Detritus, to be despatched by bike with the copy she'd written for their promo brochure. It had taken her ages, mainly because she'd had to rewrite Harriet's original draft completely. Detritus produced make-up at the cutting-edge, the edgey-edge, the so-grim-it-has-to-be-in-edge, and, Rachel felt, describing their latest range as '*simply super colours for all slinky ladies*' wasn't going to make it walk into a *Vogue* spread.

Dear Miranda, she typed – none of this *darling* stuff if the letter was officially coming from her – *I am delighted to enclose the proof of your Spring/Summer promo brochure.* Oh God, could it really be twenty to four already? *We are thrilled with the finished version and hope that you will love it as much as we do. Everyone here at Dunleary & Bright* – 'Rachel, sweetheart, don't forget to remind the client who's doing all the hard work for them!' (Yeah, right) – *is sure that this will be the breakthrough season for Detritus and that this dynamic promo will be the clinching factor in securing excellent magazine and TV coverage.*

I would be amazed if you could be bothered to cast your eye over this proof and let me have any of the myriad and pointless corrections you might like to make. I will need to pass this on to the printers by August 31st, so I won't expect to get any indication from your office that you have actually received this until it is far too late to do anything, that is to say, late September.

When your directionless and inarticulate PA does get round to it, I will, of course, be here on 0171 873 6092, my direct line, for personal abuse and blame-apportioning. Please do contact me if there are any further questions I can answer, or more likely, if you require the whole thing explained to you, with diagrams. All best wishes, Rachel Sanderson, Dunleary & Bright.

Rachel sent the letter to print, and just as she realised with a groan that she had actually been typing what she was thinking, the phone rang again. This time it was Fin. She checked her watch against the office wall clock. What if she ran up *all* the escalators? Like the gym, but with no music? George hated lateness and would remind her from London to Lancaster about careless time-keeping costing money.

'Darling, how would you like me to drive you up to the Lakes, instead of taking the train?' Fin asked urgently, dispensing with formalities.

'I take it that this has something to do with the encoded phone call I've just had from Dan?' said Rachel. 'Because if it is, I need to go in the next ten minutes and I really don't need to know anything else about it. I don't even want to know who Marvin is.'

'Dan has a lead that he needs me to help him with. We have to go in the next *five* minutes and I'll pick you up from the sidestreet by the office. If you can pick up some coffee.'

'OK, Finlay One, over and out,' said Rachel and began to salvage her covering letter.

It was remarkable even to Rachel how much she could get done in five minutes under pressure, when whole days could sail serenely by without her doing anything more taxing than playing Patience with the computer. Before Fin's Golf appeared in the street below, she had printed the letter off and finished the package, deleted all her unofficial e-mails, changed the password on her computer and removed her emergency make-up bag from her top drawer and therefore out of Harriet's reach. She just had time to make a quick sweep of the press box for last-minute presents for people (a good job she'd had first pick on all those Detritus samples that had come in for the photo shoot – what would Laura make of silver nails?) before she made her exit at speed, calling, 'See you on Tuesday, Poppy' in the rough direction of Poppy Bright's office and blowing an unseen and sarcastic kiss towards Harriet's.

Seeing Fin come round the corner through the glass door of the outside lift, Rachel dived into the coffee bar next to Dunleary & Bright's – the side that wasn't O'Hare's Gym – and picked up the enormous bag of chocolate biscotti and two almond steamers she'd ordered from her desk. What a lovely ironic PR location for D&B, she thought – between heaven and hell. Fin hooted his horn at her and she waved through the glass, making 'coming, coming' gestures. He smiled suggestively and she nearly dropped her change in her haste to get out.

Fin was waiting on a yellow line, engine running, with cars already lining up behind. Rachel pulled open the passenger door of the car, preparing to dump her overnight bag and presents on the seat, only to find that no seat was visible, covered as it was with a tied bunch of milky white roses. She gasped with pleasure and Fin's smile broadened.

'For you,' he said, a little unnecessarily.

'Oh, Fin,' breathed Rachel, 'I don't know what to say, they're so beautiful! And you know white roses are my favourites.'

'Well, I knew you weren't looking forward to this weekend and I thought these might give you a bit of a boost. Something to remind you that I'm thinking of you,' he said, putting her bags in the back of the car. 'A bit of romance. I was going to give them to you at the station, but now I've the pleasure of your company all the way up the M1, you can have them right here.'

A taxi honked crossly behind them, but Rachel took no notice of it. She slid into the passenger seat, leaned over the gear stick and kissed him gently. 'You *are* the centre of my world,' she said. 'And I *always* want to be with you.' The scent of the roses filled the car. To the annoyance of the street-full of cars, it was a couple of minutes before they set off.

After they had driven through the centre of town and had Ikea Brent Park safely behind them, Rachel became conscious of a soft snoring sound in the back of the car. Now the windows were wound down to make the most of an Indian summery afternoon, the sweet smell of the roses was being permeated by a less sweet smell of sleepy dog.

'Fin, tell me the truth,' said Rachel. 'Do we have company?'

Fin nodded. 'I took him with me on the Highgate job and then Dan called me and said we had to leave immediately. There wasn't time to take him round to my mum's and I didn't know when either of us would be back. Do you want to take him up to Cumbria, for company?'

Rachel leaned into the back of the car where the basset hound was spread langorously across the back seat and ruffled Humpty's floppy ears. 'I don't think you're much of a covert doggy, are you, Humpty? Would you like to come with Mummy?' Humpty lifted his melting brown eyes to hers and licked her face affectionately. 'He can look after me. One false move, Caroline, and my dog will slobber all over your Armani countrywear.' Humpty looked lovingly at Rachel and snuffled.

'What is this job Dan's got on?' she asked, turning back to admire Fin's profile as he concentrated on the road ahead. 'Seems a bit off the beaten celebrity track.'

'It's a tip-off he's got from one of his contacts. Some big unnamed media figure on a morality mission who's going to be up to something he shouldn't be this weekend. And, apparently, it's somewhere up North. Dan said, and I quote, just drive up and as soon as I get some more details, I'll phone you with the directions.' Fin looked in his mirror and changed lanes. 'You know what he's like. If you see a green Golf travelling at the speed of light up the fast lane behind a Porsche with blacked-out windows, we're in business.'

'So who is it?' asked Rachel. 'Film star? MP? TV personality? Celebrity chef?'

'You know as much as I do,' said Fin, but she guessed that he must have a good idea. Not even Dan made up code-names to keep himself in the dark. Marvin. She couldn't think of anyone it might be, especially since the Peter Mandelson thing had fallen through last month, and she didn't feel like asking now. He would tell her when he was able to and until then she was happy to imagine that it was somebody famous enough to be worth a Highbury Fields flat and full legal protection.

As if he could read her mind, Fin added earnestly, 'Look, Rachel, in case you're worrying, it's not a "snap and run" job – I'm really not interested in that. You can get clobbered by the Press Complaints people these days – seriously. I wouldn't risk our future together on a flash of Kate Winslet's pants. Dan knows that's not my thing, he just wants an extra pair of hands. OK?'

He squeezed her hand reassuringly and rested it on his thigh as he drove. Rachel settled back into her seat and let out a long contented breath. She wondered whether this was a good time to broach the Big Topic, which still floated in and out of her consciousness with an unnerving lack of bite.

Once the words came out of her mouth though, like the old tree falling in the forest, it would be something else entirely.

Rachel thought it was quite a giddying feeling to be able to control the reality of something just by keeping her mouth shut.

The very second the final chord of the final song on the final side of *The Greatest Driving Songs in the World Ever Part III* faded away, Alex had snapped the tape out of the tape deck before you could say Robert Palmer. Or rather, just before John could say, 'I love that song, wasn't it one of the Levi's commercials, you know that one on the beach where the guy takes his jeans off and goes into the sea, no, hang on, that was the one that went, gdang, gdang-ga-ga-gang-gang-gang with those foxy mermaids, what am I thinking of, I mean . . .'

It was a shame, or maybe a blessing in disguise, thought Alex, that a camcorder had not yet been invented to pick up thoughtwaves as well as the spoken word. On the one hand, the combined subliminal messages from her and George would have been enough to buckle John's camcorder equipment; on the other, those messages were not the sort of language she would like others to hear coming from her subconscious. And given that the unspoken undercurrents circulating whenever her friends got together were complex enough already, it would make a tape John could sell directly to BBC2.

Before either of the men could make a suggestion, Alex shoved in one of her own cassettes, the calming music from *Twin Peaks* that she used as a musical tranquilliser, and folded her arms defensively. This was meant to have been a lovely romantic journey, during which, as a direct result of having to converse for at least half of the five-hour drive, out of politeness if nothing else, she and George would finally get to discuss the direction of their feelings for one another, as the summer sun set over the distant mountains of the north. Hence the romantic music in her travel bag. Hence the wicked Belgian chocolates in the glove compartment. Hence her chic but uncomfortable choice of travel outfit.

How was she to know, as she wiggled into her silky wide-leg pants in the stockroom of Divinyl, that even then John was phoning George at work to cadge a lift? Damn and blast George's bloody politeness! Alex felt like a fifth-former done out of a slow dance at a school disco by the ebullient arrival of the Ents Committee Chairman. It was scant compensation that George looked as though he was pissed off, too – maybe he was thinking along the same lines. Maybe a declaration of fondness had been in the offing, nipped in the bud by bloody John and his bloody camcorder.

Alex stirred away masochistically at the frustration building inside her stomach and snapped another large piece off the Kendal Mint Cake bar that she had, as predicted, come across in the glove compartment, while looking for the 'other' map. George was too busy simmering at the wheel and John was too fascinated by the running commentary he was making of the journey. Alex's blood was now thick with minty sugar and they had only just passed Birmingham.

The music at least was soothing, if only because, on George's powerful car stereo, it helped to drown out John's cheerful laddish inanities, and Alex could feel her pulse slowing to an irritable trot. Broadcasting incessantly to an inattentive audience must come naturally to a Channel Five employee. Glancing across at George, at his long nose and strong jaw, she allowed a small ripple to run down her spine. He was handsome, in a shirt-sleeves-rolled-up, five-o'clock-shadow, I've-been-on-the-trading-floor-since-seven sort of way, no matter what Rachel muttered about his surgical approach to personal hygiene.

Alex reached out to adjust the volume control and her hand brushed George's as he changed gear. Imperceptibly, his little finger stroked the underside of her palm, before it returned to the steering wheel. The small ripples turned into waves crashing down Alex's spine. The hairs on the back of her arms stood up and she let out an involuntary sigh, which was fortunately covered by the swelling music. Their eyes met briefly in the rearview mirror and, to her confusion, Alex saw herself blush. Blush! Swelling! Crashing waves! This would all have to come out of the thought-transmitting video, said the voice of her conscience, sounding somewhat desperate and a long way off.

George gave her a cryptic smile and one of his ambiguous eyebrow twitches. *Does he know how much like Roger Moore he looks when he does that?* Alex thought. Caught offguard, she wrinkled her nose back at him in an uncharacteristically cute gesture. *Does she know that she goes from Jessica Rabbit to a little bunny rabbit when she blushes?* thought George, and realised immediately that although this was undoubtedly A Good Thing as far as he was concerned, it would in all probability be too close to Laura-and-Mike-fluffy-bunnydom for Alex. The thought must have registered in his face because Alex's face returned to its normal amused if enigmatic state, and she ran a quick hand through her hair.

John caught the finger touch, the blush, the look, the wrinkle and the flick of the fringe, all on superzoom and all perfectly in focus. He lingered for a moment on the lovely curve of Alex's jawline. That was on Tape A, which would stay very, very quiet for the time being. Tape B, on the other hand, with Alex pulling faces in her rearview mirror at him, her face smeared with crystals of Kendal Mint Cake, and George swearing at the coach from St Agnes Nunnery, Godalming, was rapidly building into exactly the kind of tape that would go down a storm at the wedding reception.

'Oh, for *fuck*'s sake!' shouted George, smacking the horn on the centre of the steering wheel with the flat of his hand.

Why do pukka people make 'fuck' sound so polite, Alex wondered. Do they teach them to swear in prep school elecution lessons?

One second later, a black Porsche with blacked out windows and a minimalist personalised number plate (white on black) shot down the fast lane just as George managed to swing his car into the middle. Alex let out an involuntary moan and heard a clunk from the back as John's 'steady hand' was thrown against the window.

'For fucking hell's fucking sake! Who the fuck does he think he is, fucking Damon Hill? I can't believe these people, give them a fucking Carrera and they think they're bloody James Bond,' snarled George through gasps.

'Except he would have had an Aston Martin, George. And you can go as fast as you like in one of those. Licence to thrill and all that,' said Alex, trying to stop the hammering in her chest showing in her voice.

John zoomed in on George's sweating brow. 'Alex,' said George, very quietly (John had to turn up the microphone control), 'we were almost in a motorway pile-up then.' He let out a discreetly shuddering breath. 'If I had taken my eye off the rearview mirror for a second longer, I . . .' He looked at her for an intense moment and then fixed his eyes firmly on the road. The black Porsche was nowhere in sight.

Alex's heart was still thumping. Only now, to the distant, very distant, wailing of her conscience, she was hearing the theme tune to *Top Gun* in the back of her mind. Desperately, she tried to regain control of the situation, before the regression to adolescence took hold completely and she started doing anagrams of their names. She had never really noticed this car fetish thing before now but it really was startling. Suddenly she understood what Rachel had been raving on about Finlay's Golf for. It was the *driving* thing. So *this* is what it felt like before feminism then, she thought. What is happening to me? Is it the silk trousers? This was the last time she let Rachel lend her anything at all.

With John editing silently and seamlessly between video tapes in the back, she smiled at George, who smiled back.

'Let's have some proper music, eh?' said John. 'Please?'

Alex twisted around underneath her seatbelt and scowled at him from the front.

John stared back at her unrepentantly. 'There is such a thing as too much relaxation, Alex,' he said. 'I don't want George falling asleep at the wheel.' He pushed a tape at her. 'Here, put this on, it's a tape I made myself. There's something for everyone, honestly.'

Alex narrowed her eyes. For a moment it had been so romantic. And all at once she was about to be subjected to another round of Mariah Carey.

'No Mariah Carey,' said John, putting the hand that wasn't holding the camcorder on his chest. 'Or Celine Dion. It's an old tape.' He tried the winning smile that had broken a hundred hearts at hockey dinners. John was blessed with the kind of blond good looks and gappy smile that had made him hard to resist when he was really trying at college – and provided him with a stream of dinner party invitations as a reliable 'unattached bloke' now. After one such baptism of fire very early on in her colourful college hockey career, Alex was resistant to his charms, but for the sake of peace – and so as not to appear a whinger in front of George – she took the tape and pushed it into the radio. John slid back in his seat and gave her a knowing nod.

'*You're once . . . twice . . . three times a laadeee . . .*'

Suddenly, Alex felt positively ill as the scene in her bedroom with George flashed before her eyes. Oh God, oh God, oh God, she thought over and over and over again to prevent herself thinking anything more specific. She longed to rip the tape out but knew she couldn't, without acknowledging her chronic embarrassment to George, and then having to cover it up for John. Oh God, oh God, oh God, oh God, oh God . . .

It might have come as some consolation to Alex that George, whose knuckles had discreetly whitened during the introduction to the song, spent the following three and a half minutes studiously counting the number of red cars passing down the opposite carriageway.

Laura prided herself on memorising all the key recipes in Prue Leith's *Cookery Bible*, and had armed herself with an apposite menu for all occasions. Now she regarded the pound cake she had just taken out of the oven with justifiable pride. It steamed gently in its pristine baking tin. During her inspection of the pantry she had noticed that there was some lemon curd that would go very well with that. Not that she would be eating any, but it did make the house smell nice and she knew how much Mike liked his home-cooking. Possibly a physical reaction to teenage years of Pot Noodles and takeaway curries – a habit she had more or less broken with compulsory green vegetable intakes.

She gave her mobile phone, sitting silently by the kettle, a hard look. It had not rung. Mike had not phoned. The seeds of worry were now firmly planted in her head. More than once she had been tempted to call, in case there was some fault with reception here, but he had told her not to – she knew herself how embarrassing it was when phones went off in meetings or on the bus, so she had resisted the growing temptation. But where was he?

It occurred to Laura that she didn't actually know where he was. Or, in fact, what kind of a conference he was attending. This unusual lack of information about Mike, who normally hovered comfortingly around the edges of her peripheral vision, suddenly made her feel disorientated and, for reasons that slipped out of her grasp when she tried to pin them down, she felt uneasy.

Laura thumped down into one of the easy chairs by the Aga and curled her legs under her. Why did her instinct make her feel uneasy? She didn't like too much self-examination: you ended up like Rachel, believing in the healing powers of putting your wastepaper bin in the 'problems' corner of the room.

Fortunately the phone rang before she could explore the logic of this and she galloped across the stone floor, almost skidding into the butcher's block.

'Hello, bunny!' she said happily.

There was a crackle of motorway interference. Or it could have been a snort.

'Hello, Laura, it's Alex here.'

'Oh,' said Laura, her face falling. She picked up the cake-mix spoon and began to lick it disconsolately.

If Alex was surprised at this less than enthusiastic response, she didn't show it. 'I'm calling on George's mobile – he won't drive and call at the same time. It's illegal apparently.' More snorting.

'Where are you?'

'Where are we, George? Yes, I know I'm supposed to be navigating but how can I when I'm on the phone? *You* can't drive and talk at the same time . . . Well, every time I look at the map, we've gone through the place, they're so tiny . . . No, I'm from *Yorkshire*, it's a very different place entirely . . . Well, try saying that to one of the locals and see if they agree with you.'

The phone sounded as though it had been dropped and grappled over. There was a distinct clunk, a distinct 'Sod off!' and then John came on the line.

'We're just past Penny Bridge, Laura. I hope you've got a pot of tea on!'

'Where's that?' asked Laura. 'I drove down from Carlisle.'

'Er . . . we'll be with you in about an hour if George goes round the coast or maybe a bit less if he goes the straight way. Bit of a last-minute change of plan – Rachel's just called us to say that Finlay's dropping her off, so we don't have to go via the station anymore to get her. How do people cope without mobiles, eh? We were going to race them but George wouldn't—' There was an indecipherable comment from a grumpy-sounding Alex. 'Oh, apparently, we're going the straight way. Alex has got the map and she says it's loads quicker. What, George? George says, are we late?'

'No, you're not late,' said Laura, 'it's just me here so far.'

'Doh!' John said jovially. 'I'd have thought that Mike would be there, making the most of an empty lovenest!'

'Yes, I'd have thought so too,' said Laura, 'but he's

attending a conference in London. I'm not expecting him until later.' It all came out rather more formal than she intended. Still, it was only John. John couldn't spot an atmosphere if it came in and spilled his pint.

It sounded as though Alex had wrested the phone back, with some unintelligible hisses in the background.

'So we'll see you soon, OK, Laura? We're all *really* looking forward to seeing you and the cottage soon. I can't wait to get there!'

She sounds quite hysterical, thought Laura.

'Take care, Alex. Tell George to take care over the passes! They're a bit hairy!' said Laura, but then the reception broke up. Or maybe the phone was dropped in one last tussle, she couldn't tell.

An hour before they arrived. As the evening sky began to lose the warmth and light of the sun, the kitchen seemed less cosy than it had done when she had sketched her sheep and rocked in the chair. Laura propped the phone back up against the kettle thoughtfully, then dropped it into her handbag and put the kettle on. She considered going for a walk along the lake shore, but with a long, exhaled breath pulled her button and toggle fastenings file towards her again.

chapter thirteen

'Biscuit,' said Finlay, without taking his eyes off the road. He moved smoothly into the fast lane, bypassing a precariously swaying caravan, destination Grange-over-Sands, and held out his hand as he slotted neatly back into the thinning stream of traffic. They were almost about to turn off for the Lakes, outside Sizergh.

Rachel dug into the bag of biscuits. 'You've got through these quickly enough,' she said with mock disapproval.

Finlay looked aggrieved. 'If you didn't keep feeding them to that slobbering hound of yours . . .'

'Of *yours*,' retorted Rachel indignantly. 'Who was it taught him to beg for biscuits in the first place?'

'Well, I think it was you who gave him his refined taste for Italian coffee biscotti,' said Fin, frowning in his mirror to see that the caravan was now tailgating him, the driver glaring over the wheel in a bellicose fashion. 'Anyway, didn't you get some more when we stopped at that service station? You know I need feeding on long drives.'

Humpty woofed reproachfully from the back seat.

'No, Humpster, we've moved on from you now,' said Rachel.

'So?' said Finlay again. 'Can I have a biscuit, please?'

With a pretend sigh, Rachel reached into the greased paper bag and her fingers closed on something that was definitely not a chocolate and almond biscotti. It felt more like a small round box.

Rachel's heart started racing. Could this be . . .? She had imagined this moment in her head since she was about ten. What should she say? What if the ring was too big? How could she make the defining decision of her life while travelling up the M1? Her heart really was beating much faster than it had done at the gym for some time.

Rachel realised that she had been frozen with her hand in the biscuit bag for about twenty seconds. Fin must be waiting too, she thought in a flash. And he's willing to make the defining offer of his life while trying not to get run off the road by a geriatric flat cap towing a Sprite Sprinter. What a hero.

She slowly removed her hand from the bag and indeed it was a small green ring box. Rachel discreetly flicked off a couple of crumbs from the glossy exterior and looked at Fin for some direction but he was staring steadfastly in his rearview mirror. With a deep breath, she opened the tiny catch and let out an instinctive sigh. It was perfect. Absolutely perfect. One perfect round emerald, British Racing Green, surrounded by eight sparkling diamonds, like a little glittering flower.

'Oh – My – God,' breathed Rachel, hardly knowing what to say. Now that the moment had actually come, she was suddenly overwhelmed by the significance of the gesture. This was it. She had known it would happen at some point, but events of recent days had rather dominated her immediate thoughts. Which was funny, now she thought of it, because shouldn't Fin's making an honest woman of her have been the first thing that should have sprung to mind? Of course he had been an essential part of the equation, but . . .

'Rachel,' said Fin, pulling off at Junction 36, 'Rachel, didn't I tell you to keep an eye out for the junctions, by the way? I don't want you to say *anything* now. I didn't mean to surprise you with the ring like that, I mean, I didn't expect to have finished those biscuits until we'd got near your dramatic exit point at Wastwater for a start, but you know how I feel about you and how I want to be with you for ever.'

Rachel gazed across at him, her eyes filling up with tears. Fin changed down his gears expertly to negotiate the roundabout, flashing '*Come* on' at a dithering Fiesta and continued, 'I don't feel that there's any point in us being apart and I don't think we ever will be. But I've felt something's been up with you recently – I don't know what exactly but I know there's been something – and maybe the time's right to make this kind of commitment. If you want to, too. I absolutely love you, Rachel. You know that.'

'I love you too, Fin,' said Rachel, her voice wobbling. 'And I—'

'Darling, the last thing I want to do is force you into such a big decision on the bloody M1,' said Finlay, laying his hand gently on her thigh. 'Please think about it over the weekend, make sure in your heart of hearts that you want to be married as much as I do, and then give me your answer when I come to get you on Sunday night. If you think that it's too soon, or you'd rather wait and sort out whatever it is that's weighing on your mind—'

Rachel opened her mouth again and Finlay put a hand over it, steering expertly with his knees for half a mile, Rachel noted, impressed.

'No, don't tell me, darling, *if* you decide that you want to wait, then please keep the ring and we'll call it a friendship ring or an eternity ring or whatever trendy singletons like to term these things. I wanted to give you something special in any case. It was my grandmother's.'

Rachel thought her heart was going to burst. Either that or she was. What a complete hero. No pressure, no emotional blackmail, no tacky heart-shaped diamond pyramid clusters. Was this man really and truly hers?

She tried to say something to this effect but found that for one of the few times in her life, she couldn't speak. Which was lucky, perhaps, as she wasn't sure what would come tumbling out first. Her mind was bubbling away like the Lottery ball selector.

'Oh, Fin,' she murmured, wringing everything she needed out of one syllable.

Fin stretched an arm around her shoulders, gave her a squeeze, and reached into his camera bag on the back seat for the emergency Homewheats he'd packed earlier.

'The parson's cat is a lard-arsed cat and her name is Loretta,' said John, with the air of someone whose vocabulary can only be admired. 'OK, your go, Alex.'

Alex took several deep breaths to stop herself from screaming. Every single muscle in her body wanted to get out of the car and she didn't think it could be blamed entirely on the dangerous amount of Kendal Mint Cake she had now consumed. She could have survived for a week on the side of Ben Nevis on the amount she had eaten in the last hour alone. The thought of Rachel's company from Lancaster on had been some consolation when things started to get bad after breaking past the M25, but even that small hope was dashed by a joyful phone call somewhere around Northampton. And all this was in addition to the increasingly mindless games John had insisted on playing in order to while away the eon they had spent so far, a substantial part of which had been spent crawling along the Birmingham ring road at several miles below the recommended speed limit.

George, of course, had said nothing at all, except to give stylishly succinct responses to the various inane word games. He had also managed to guess all five of Alex's very cunning I-Spy's without taking his eyes off the steep, winding and ominously single-track roads, which were rapidly becoming steeper and windier as they drove on towards Wasdale.

In fact the only sign that he hadn't glazed over completely was his response when Alex had spied with her little eye something beginning with C; George had muttered, under his breath, 'cuckold'. And it was clear from that what he was chewing over in the long silences between his contributions.

'I hope you're not taping this, John,' said Alex over her shoulder, in what she hoped was a slightly menacing voice. It had occurred to her that a rather cool tape could be made of people reciting Parson's Cats over a jungle backing. '*Critical, critical, cr-cr-cr-cr-critical, etc.*'

'Nope!' lied John.

'Well, OK, the parson's cat is a Jehovah's Witness and her name is Jezebel.' '*Jezebel, her name, her name was Jezebel.*'

'Would a parson's cat actually be allowed to be a Jehovah's Witness, Alex?'

'And would they necessarily be allowed to have an Old Testament name, anyway?' George wondered drily. 'We're on M now, incidentally. Do try to keep up.'

Alex could not believe this. 'Oh, for God's sake! This isn't a bloody supervision! OK, OK.' She struggled wildly for an alternative, trying to ignore John's irritating 'tick-tock' noises.

'Come on, come on,' said John. 'You're meant to be the English student!'

Out of the corner of her eye, Alex could see George allow himself a slight smirk and she clenched her teeth together, her mind a complete blank. All she could think was 'sheep' and, understandably, 'mint'.

'Oh God, I don't know!' snapped Alex and said the first thing that came into her head. 'The parson's cat is a mendacious cat and his name is Mike!'

There was an immediate silence.

'If I see that on whatever tape you're making, John,' said George, 'I will make sure your steady hand is permanently less than steady.'

Alex sat on her balled-up fists, sweating. That was possibly one of the least tactful things she had ever said. It was also one of the most unintentionally true.

John sat silently in the back weighing up this surprising new information. Mendacious? Mike? Why? Who? And why the unusually violent reaction from George? Something was definitely going on, and not just in the front seats.

George drove on, feeling more and more burdened, and not just by the driving conditions.

chapter fourteen

Finlay pulled up with a scrunch of gravel outside the white-washed cottage, just as the sun was beginning to set over the Screes. He put on the handbrake and he and Rachel sat in silence for a moment before she leaned over and kissed him.

'Thank you, Fin,' she said. 'You're too good for me.'

He touched her nose with his lips. 'Hardly. Before I met you I had no idea what to do with a tea strainer. Look at me now – an Earl Grey convert.'

The final rays of the setting sun cast a warm flush of red light into the car.

'You've got my mobile number,' he said. 'Call me if things get too stroppy or you want to come home – I can soon have an urgent picture desk crisis that means we have to leave instantaneously.'

'And you be careful with Dan,' Rachel said seriously. 'The roads round here really are dreadful. I don't want you wrapping yourself around a sheep at ninety miles an hour.'

He lifted his eyebrows suggestively. 'Not even if they ask me?'

Rachel laughed. 'And don't do anything you think my mother might be ashamed of. I know how persuasive Dan can be. Mind you, I can't think who on earth he thinks he's got a lead on round here. Cumbria's leading celebrity is Melvyn Bragg and God help us if that's the best scandal Dan can get these days.'

'Well, you may be wrong there. Dan doesn't come this far north for any old—'

Fin's mobile phone rang and he answered it on the second ring. There were times together when Fin's 'other life' appeared like a phantom on the sidelines – as he drove with his knees (handy for loading film on the move) or tore round the shortest cuts to Whitehall (essential for reaching recently disgraced ministers before everyone else) – and it sent a vicarious shiver through Rachel. She had wanted to keep their working lives their own domain, but it was only when these little echoes struck her that she felt this strange mixture of pride and nervousness and admiration. Her stomach leaped now because she knew it must be Dan.

'OK, I'm in Wastwater. Wastwater. It's near Gosforth . . . Oh. Oh, OK, fine, well, I'll see you in half an hour then. Yes, I've got it in the back. A 500 mil and an 800 mil, with a convertor. Well, that was lucky, wasn't it? No, she doesn't. Yes, I'll tell her. Right. Bye.'

Finlay flipped the phone off. 'Dan sends his love and says not to worry about me.'

'I bet he said "I won't let him near anything important", didn't he?' said Rachel.

Fin blushed and pushed his dark fringe off his face. 'How did you know that's what Dan said?'

'Because he always says that,' said Rachel. 'I think he thinks it reassures me. Now am I taking this floppy old

Bagpuss with me?' She leaned into the back of the Golf and stroked Humpty's ears. The patient dog made a doggy smile and pushed his nose into her hand. 'Thank God you haven't ruined my lovely roses, you old slobberer.'

She turned back to Finlay and hugged him tightly, feeling her arm muscles squeeze against his solid frame. 'I won't make a big thing of the flowers,' she said. 'I'm sure Mike won't have brought anything so gorgeous up for Laura.'

'And don't mention the ring,' he said slowly. 'It's got nothing to do with them and I don't want them to influence you in any way at all.'

'As if.' She looked into Fin's eyes, normally so sparkly and alive, now more serious than she had ever seen them. She realised with a pang of sadness that he must really be suspicious of her college friends.

Fin replied immediately to the thought passing across her mind. There were times when Rachel felt that her belief in astropsychology wasn't as misplaced as cynics made out. What could she ever hide from this man?

'It's not that I don't like them, Rachel,' he said now. 'They're sweet, some of them, but I feel that they upset you. I can't help worrying that whatever's been bothering you recently has got something to do with this whole kerfuffle about Laura's wedding.' He cupped her chin in his hands. 'I *worry* about you, darling. I feel as though I'm letting you into some . . . *lion's den*. They turn you into something, someone, I feel you're not anymore. If that makes sense.'

Rachel was painfully aware of what he was getting at and, as usual, found herself in the strained position of defending the very people she herself privately raged about.

'I know,' she said as cheerfully as she could. 'Of *course*

it's our thing. You know I wouldn't upstage Laura on her engagement weekend of all times, anyway! I mean, I wouldn't put it past Caroline, but I think Laura's taken the precautionary measure of not inviting her. So that's all right. I think.'

Finlay looked unconvinced, but time was pressing on. He reluctantly uncoiled his arm from around her shoulders and gave her a final squeeze. 'Remember, phone me if you want out. Code word: Fontella.'

Rachel looked blank.

'Fontella Bass, "Rescue Me"!' crowed Fin triumphantly. 'At last! You have no idea how long I have waited to do that! Score one against the Pop Queen!' He ducked as Rachel aimed a playful punch at his head and Humpty began to bark in a concerned way.

'And that is my cue to leave, I think,' she said, undoing her seat belt. 'I know when I'm beaten.' She opened the door and, pulling her seat forward, let Humpty waddle out, his splayed front paws hitting the gravel with a heavy crunch. The luxuriant bunch of creamy roses had indeed been scrupulously untouched by dog dribble.

Fin helped Rachel drag her overnight bag out of the car and carried it up to the back door of the cottage for her.

'I can't believe Laura didn't hear us arrive,' said Rachel. 'Not with all that barking from the Humpster there.' She banged on the red door. There was no immediate response from inside.

From the outside, Hawk Cottage looked perfect, with a handcarved sign and an old bootscraper at the door, a thick covering of purple heather in the little border around the path. Whoever this Inigo Aikin-Rose was, thought Rachel, he must have pots of money and a surprising amount of taste in proportion to it. This was a prime example of how Lakeland cottages looked through the eyes of *Vogue*'s property section. If Hawk Cottage were in Wales it would have a severe case of scorchmarks by now.

Rachel was just about to ask Fin if he had come across one Inigo Aikin-Rose, perhaps in the more covert side of his job, when the door swung open and there was Laura, looking radiant and rosy-cheeked.

'My God, Laura, but don't you make the perfect farmer's wife!' exclaimed Rachel as she leaned to kiss Laura's cheek.

'I know, it's absolutely *divine*,' said Laura, brushing her cheek against Rachel's. 'In fact, the only teensy thing I would do to it if it were mine would be to take off this awful stone roof and have it thatched, but there you go. I don't suppose you could get people to come and do it round here.'

Out of the corner of her eye, Rachel could see Fin cringe imperceptibly at this but she suppressed her own instinct to give Laura a lecture on slate roofing. She wished Laura wouldn't do this sub-Caroline twittering. She never used to.

'Can you stay for a quick coffee?' Laura asked Fin with a big smile. She had flour on her face – albeit in a very neat patch – and Rachel suspected that, given a couple of hours in a cottage like this, Laura must have come up with a battery of produce. A pleasantly vanilla-y smell wafted through from the kitchen.

Fin held up his hands apologetically. 'Laura, I would love to, but I don't know if Rachel said – I'm up here to do a job with someone and I have to get going. I'm sorry to miss whatever that delicious smell is, though.'

'I bet you are,' said Rachel, playfully poking him in the tummy. 'You would not *believe* the amount this man has eaten on the way up, Laura.'

'Oh, don't tell me about it. Have you noticed the way Mike tucks back his grub?' said Laura, looking a bit wry. 'And he calls *me* little piggie. It's all right for men . . .'

As he turned to go, Rachel gave Fin one last lingering look, trying as she always did to commit the curve of his nose, the set of his brow to memory. Reluctantly, she hugged him and he kissed the top of her head tenderly.

'Take care, darling,' she murmured into his jumper.

'And you. I'll be thinking about you all the time.'

Laura thought what a lovely couple the two of them made and wondered if this might be a good moment to ask Finlay about the wedding photos. Sadly, as she was about to frame her tentative question, he lifted Rachel up in a bear hug, put her down and leaned forward to kiss Laura's cheek.

'Bye, Laura, have a lovely weekend, don't let Mike do anything I wouldn't,' he said.

'I think that's the whole point of having a joint party, isn't it, Laura?' Rachel said mischievously.

Laura just smiled brightly. 'No, that's the whole point of *marriage*, Rachel, doing everything together.'

And for that, read 'keeping a suspiciously close eye on each other', thought Fin, who picked up rather negative feelings about neat and tidy Laura.

'Ah,' he said, 'but I don't need to be with you to know what you're up to, do I, Rachel?'

'No, you have Humpty,' she replied, elaborating for Laura. 'He's sent the dog with me to keep an eye on what I get up to. Dog's reporting back in detail with covert pictures. Hidden camera in the collar. Nudge, nudge, wink, wink, say no more.'

Laura laughed uncertainly. You could never tell with

Rachel whether she was joking or not. She had heard some very strange things about photographers.

'Right, I'm off,' said Fin. 'If I don't make a move now, I will never go.' And with a wave, he crunched back to the car and swept off with a professional flourish.

chapter fifteen

As the Golf disappeared round the first bend in the road, Rachel felt the sudden pang of Fin's absence and the million things she had meant to say before he left sprang into her mouth. She put a friendly arm around Laura's shoulder.

'It's so nice so see you, Laura. I can't remember the last time I saw you for a decent chat. Not since Fin and I moved into the new Highbury flat, anyway.'

Laura returned her hug warmly. 'I know, I know. We've all been so busy, it's ridiculous. If I'd known how much stress getting married would involve, I don't know whether I'd have agreed it all when Mike proposed!' She laughed.

Rachel thought this was extremely unlikely, given Laura's lengthy college discourses about the importance of natural confetti, but said nothing.

They walked through into the cool kitchen which was almost exactly as Rachel would have made it herself. Stone flags, scrubbed pine table, red checked window seats – in ten years' time, this little cottage would be perfect. As it was at the moment, the Heal's price tags were virtually visible under the fiddleback chairs.

'There was the sweetest message on the answering machine from Inigo Aikin-Rose, who owns this place,' said Laura. 'He sounds awfully nice. He said he hopes we have a lovely time and to help ourselves from the freezer.'

'He's a friend of Caroline's, then?' said Rachel, pouring herself a cup of tea from the big brown teapot sitting on the Aga hotplate.

'Mmm,' said Laura. She creased her brow prettily. 'He said something a bit funny, actually, I couldn't tell whether he was joking or not – he sort of laughed and said something like "Don't let Caroline do anything I wouldn't!" I hope he doesn't mind that she's not actually coming.'

'Were they at school together?' asked Rachel, sipping her tea. Caroline's school had been notoriously strange, particularly given her own completely incident-free experience at Manchester Girls' Grammar.

'Mmm,' nodded Laura. 'She said he used to have a big crush on her. But then according to her, most people did. It's *extremely* kind of him to let us come for the weekend when he hardly knows us.'

'Yes, well,' said Rachel, trying to be light. 'When are the rest going to be here?' It was hardly subtle but she was damned if she was going to let Laura make the inevitable 'It was *so* kind of Caroline to think of asking for us' comment. Rachel was pretty sure there had to be something in it somewhere for Caroline herself. Going on past form, it was not like her to go to so much bother otherwise, although perhaps for her best friend's wedding . . .

'They shouldn't be that much longer now,' said Laura. 'I had a call from George about an hour ago – they were at

Penny Bridge, with Alex navigating them over the passes, which is very brave of George, I must say, and poor Mike is stuck in a conference in town and thinks he's going to wait until rush hour is over before he drives up.' She looked a bit worried.

'What kind of conference is it?' asked Rachel. 'I didn't know graduate trainees went on conferences at this stage.'

'Well, conference, meeting – Mike didn't tell me exactly. To be honest, I don't know what it is,' Laura confessed, fiddling with a teaspoon. In a moment, she had gone from confident proto-country cottage owner to nervous school-leaver, just as she had been when she had first arrived at college. And she looked on the verge of a major confession, thought Rachel, surprised. Erk, it was only meant to be a joke. Five minutes into the party and Laura was already warming up for some soul-searching.

Tentatively, Rachel put a hand over Laura's and tried to peek up under her straight-cut blond fringe.

'Laura?' she said. 'Are you all right there? Is there something wrong?' There was no response. 'Look, if there's something you want to get off your chest before the others come steaming in . . . Laura?'

Rachel reached across the table to Laura, who immediately looked up with a wide smile balanced precariously on her face. Back to Lucie Clayton summer-school manners, thought Rachel. I suppose it's marginally more useful in polite society than being able to walk around drawing rooms with a book on your head. Or perhaps inheriting maternal genes from a woman who wore little else but a broad smile in endless *Carry On* films has its advantages after all – something else Laura didn't like to discuss.

'No, nothing's the matter,' said Laura. 'I'm just a little bit nervous about him driving up here on his own so late at night. You know what Mike's driving's like and these roads are just dreadful. There's some decrepit tractor or herd of sheep round every corner.'

'Oh, I know,' said Rachel, not entirely convinced at the sudden change in mood but relieved, in a guilty way, not to have Laura's premarital burden spilled onto her shoulders at such short notice. 'I used to go on D of E expeditions round here. Followed the wiggly line all the way round Devoke Water before the group leader sussed it was a contour line and not actually a footpath, as we had originally thought.'

'*No*,' said Laura, aghast. 'Did they fail you?'

Rachel smiled and helped herself to another cup of tea. 'Couldn't. We were the assessing teacher's passport to a boozy weekend away. There were a few raised eyebrows in the staffroom at the fact that all our meeting places were local pubs, but . . .'

Laura wondered afresh at the educational vagaries of northern schools. Rachel meanwhile was beginning to relish her school nightmares from a safe distance.

'You see the Screes out there?' she said, pointing to the sheer curtain of loose rocks, framing the shimmering water of the lake. 'On my last fell walk, when I was about seventeen, we walked across there almost in the dark. I think we were late setting off, or something, but we were an hour or so behind schedule when we started to cross the Screes – the campsite for the night was on the other side of the lake. Quite near the Wasdale Head Inn, surprisingly enough.

'There is a path, I don't think you can see it from here, but in places you literally have to walk on the rocks and on a choppy day, as you can imagine, they're all wet with the water splashing from the lake. One rock, loosened from the top, can bounce all the way down. Well, we set off when dusk was about to fall and were about there' – she pointed to a wretched-looking tree at the far end of the Screes – 'when we had to put our torches on. Can you imagine a line of six girls, all in horrible blue cagoules and rucksacks, on a weekend trip from Manchester, creeping across the wet stones, just waiting for a disaster to happen?'

Rachel paused dramatically to take a sip of tea, and predictably Laura shuddered, her mind immediately crowded with worst case scenarios.

'What happened? Did someone drown?' Inigo Aikin-Rose's idyllic cottage was feeling slightly less idyllic all of a sudden. Visions of dead and drowned fell walkers, *à la Under Milk Wood* but just across the road, flitted across her mind's eye. Laura was generally acknowledged by the rest to be the Queen of Bathos – whenever they all went out to see a film, she liked to know what the worst thing that happened in it was, so she could steel herself appropriately all the way through.

Rachel ignored her nervous outburst, her motto being: Never let audience participation get in the way of a good tale.

'Well, of course the last thing the teacher in charge said before we all piled into the minibus was, don't forget to check that your torches are in full working order. And of course they were fine for the first twenty minutes, but that stretch of rock is a lot longer than it looks, you know. Added to which we had to keep waiting for Cal at the back to keep up every ten minutes, and to cut a long story short, by the time we were halfway across, we had one vaguely operational torch between us. I would have given anything to have seen the Duracell bunny at that point, the little bugger.

'Three of us slipped on the path and nearly went in – the water's only a foot away in some places. Being that close to the lake suddenly makes you see it as it really is – a natural force, a huge expanse of freezing water. Hardly the picture-postcard stuff at all. The sheer fall of those screes continues down into the lake, you know. Straight down, whoomph. I had to cling on to the girl in front's rucksack at one point to stop her sliding down the bank when she lost her footing. Bloody frightening in the dark.'

Rachel made an effort not to get too carried away by Laura's appreciatively widening eyes, and pulled herself up short before she embroidered Catherine Scot's grazed shin into a full-scale broken leg and hypothermia.

'And of course we were winding ourselves up something ridiculous,' she admitted. 'I couldn't see the girl two places in front of me, but I could hear her making these little snuffling noises like a scared puppy. I think we were all doing *Emergency 999* acting. You know, "Don't worry, Margery, the helicopter will be here soon!" and making splints out of old copies of *Just Seventeen*.'

'Did you make it?' asked Laura, agog with vicarious thrills. Her D of E expeditions had been in a big field on the Isle of Wight. She had taken a travel hairdryer.

Rachel gave her a serious look over her steepled hands. 'We arrived at the Wasdale Head Inn only half an hour after our estimated time, in a state of complete nervous exhaustion. It only occurred to us later in the tents that we'd actually caught up half an hour going across. The good old adrenalin, bad weather and weak bladder combo. Not that I'd recommend it,' she added hastily.

'No, for God's sake, don't tell the boys,' said Laura. 'They'll have us all out in formation tomorrow night, only we'll be *starting* without torches.'

They both drank their tea in silence for a few moments, staring out at the pewter-coloured lake, rippling very slightly under a gentle breeze. Framed by Inigo Aikin-Rose's crisp new curtains and freshly painted window seats, it looked dramatic but far from life-threatening.

'It's so beautiful,' Laura said at last. 'I'd love to live here all the time. Get out of London.'

'It's very pretty, the Lake District,' said Rachel thoughtfully, testing the fineness of the china teacup with her teeth, 'but it's also wild. That's why I like this area of it, the western Lakes. It's not chocolate-boxy, like Windermere or somewhere, where you can't move for coach parties of forty-five-year-old grannies from Salford with terracotta hair and ossified husbands. My mum's family come from near Ambleside. All very pretty. But you can see the danger of *those* rocks out of this window.'

Laura saw a very nice view, albeit now overlaid with Rachel's second-hand panic.

'You have to be so careful. One minute it's beautiful, the next it's savage.' Rachel fell silent again, thinking of the summers she had spent around Wasdale with her family, watching the purple hillsides turn a blazing orange as the autumn bracken obscured the heather. 'But that's all part of it, don't you think, that danger informing the beauty? Part of that sense of awe, of something bigger than you? Something that will outsee mankind at either end of its allotted time?' Rachel put the last remark in quotes in case Laura thought she was being pretentious.

Laura wasn't sure what Rachel meant. She herself couldn't

love something she was scared of, nor could she relish the idea of setting herself in the midst of such violent unpredictability in the same way that Rachel seemed to. She made a vague agreeing noise and wondered if Rachel was quoting from *Lyrical Ballads*.

'I'm sometimes glad that I wasn't blessed with great imagination,' said Rachel rather sadly, drinking in the imperious sweep of the Screes, 'because I think I'd be a lot more scared of things than I am already.'

Laura seized on the comment and she lifted her gaze from her teacup. 'Do you ever worry that if you're not truthful with yourself, no one will ever be truthful with you?' she asked, her eyes more serious than her voice.

'I'm never really truthful with myself,' said Rachel ruefully. 'That's why I need Fin so desperately. He is relentlessly truthful for me. Why? Is that what's bothering you?' She knew not to push for confidences from Laura. If there was a problem, the confessions would come in a gush to either her or Alex; Laura, like the rest of them, never felt reassured by fewer than three rounds of advice.

The two women sat in fairly companionable silence for a minute, one waiting, the other weighing up. The big wall clock ticked on the chimneypiece. It was quite a long time, thought Rachel, since she had supplied a psychiatrist's couch for Laura. Caroline, as set mate for her second year at university, should have provided the permanent in-house counselling, as Rachel had effectively done, three floors down, for Alex. But though Caroline's company was never less than entertaining, according to Laura at least, that year was the time in which Mike and Laura had grown inseparable and had begun nesting in Mike's set, Laura flitting back and forth for bits and pieces to furnish it from hers. Or was putting that migration down to Caroline's own nocturnal 'socialising' too uncharitable an interpretation on it? Rachel wondered, picking the chocolate carefully off a Jaffa Cake.

'Rachel,' Laura began hesistantly. 'What you were saying about Finlay earlier – do you always know where he is?'

Rachel looked at her, waiting for her to expand a bit, but Laura just looked back hopefully, as if Rachel could guess whatever it was that lay behind the question. Rachel *could* guess and thought it was a pretty miserable question to have to be hedging around six months before getting married, never mind so soon into your engagement party. But Laura looked so serious that she couldn't be flippant.

'Well, not always,' said Rachel. 'He phones me at the office during the day to see how I am – I usually leave the house threatening to be back with my P45 by lunchtime, so he likes to know how things are progressing in that direction. I know more or less what his jobs are for the day, who he'll be doing, if not where exactly. But, no, I don't know where he's going now, for instance. I didn't ask.'

'And you don't mind?'

'No, I suppose not. He's a grown boy. He's with Dan, a friend of ours. There's a limit to how much trouble the pair of them can get up to.' She hoped, anyway.

'You never worry that he's . . . *with someone*?' Laura was looking really tormented now. She hadn't imagined how horribly compelling this line of confessional hypothesis would be; she didn't know whether she could stop now she'd begun. She certainly hadn't realised how worried she was until the words had come into her mouth. Rachel was such a good listener and who knew when she would have another quiet moment like this?

'No,' said Rachel, very slowly, as she tried to gauge the

right reaction to give. All that debate with Alex about whether Caroline and Mike's illicit romance was a figment of their imagination and here it was, straight from the horse's mouth!

Or was it? Maybe she was talking about something completely different – a poker-with-the-boys-after-hours habit, perhaps, or an addiction to scratchcards. She didn't want to put anything into Laura's head that wasn't already there. But what on earth could be wrong between Mike and Laura otherwise? If Laura really was onto something herself, it gave the whole proceedings a new, scary edge of reality.

'No, it's obvious how Finlay feels about you,' Laura said before Rachel could go on, a note of sadness creeping into her voice. She stared out of window at the swirls of gravel where Fin's car had been parked. It had been seeing that bear hug, Rachel lifted squealing off the ground, that had shot this sudden rush of nervous misery through her. They were so close, with no secrets or unaccounted space between them, and yet they seemed to thrive on the intimacy, not feel stifled by it.

'I really do love Mike, Rachel,' she whispered. 'But sometimes I wonder if he really knows me – the *real* me . . .'

Tea now stone cold, Rachel sprang up and knelt by Laura's chair, stroking her knees with comforting hands. Laura gave no reaction to Rachel's comforting caresses.

'Oh, Laura, what's happened? Are you having second thoughts? Any *one* of us could have told you how much Mike adores you!' she said, rubbing Laura's arms. 'You poor thing, making yourself all worried about nothing! What makes you think that anyone could ever come between you two? You're made for each other, Laura!'

Oh my God, oh my God, thought Rachel, desperately

trying to fill up the difficult silence with comforting noises, what can have happened? Surely Caroline hasn't done something appalling with this cottage? The word 'lovenest' flashed across her mind in *Sun* banner headlines. No! She couldn't have. *He* couldn't have! Surely Mike didn't have it in him?

Humpty's claws skittered on the stone flags as he waddled in from the garden. He gave Rachel's knee a nudge with his nose and she bent down to fondle his long brown ears gratefully.

'Oh, he was so good on the journey, wasn't he? I don't know where I would be without my Humpty to keep me company!'

For once, Humpty lived up to all Rachel's hopes and, shuffling round the table, laid his head balefully on Laura's lap, his eyes watering affectionately. She smiled at him despite herself and her normal aversion to dribbly dogs.

'What a clever dog you are, Humpty! I suppose you'll be wanting a bowl of water?' Laura got up and began opening and shutting cupboard doors in an attempt to find a big enough receptacle. Finding none, she wandered into the hallway, where there were several large wall cupboards.

'He really is more like a human than a dog,' said Rachel proudly. 'He sat in the back all the way and didn't dribble once on— Oh God! The flowers!' Rachel straightened up with a jerk. 'Finlay's driven off with a wreath of roses on his roof! He'll look like a hearse!'

'Do you mean these?' Laura called from the hall. She walked in with the huge tied bunch of roses, an uncertain but hopeful look playing across her face.

'They're for you,' said Rachel immediately, smiling. What the hell, she thought. Laura looks happier already. 'Why don't I put them in some water while you find that bowl,' she continued, taking the bouquet from her and surreptitiously rummaging through the arrangement to make sure Fin hadn't put a card in with them. Rachel even inspected the cellophane – nothing. He must have collected them from the florist himself when he knew he would be driving up, instead of having them delivered to the office.

There was a big blue glass vase standing on the window sill, glowing in the last reflections of the setting sun. Carefully, Rachel picked it up and carried it to the sink to fill it with water.

'Pop some sugar in the bottom – makes the flowers last longer,' called Laura automatically. She had decided that the hall was the best place to contain Humpty's potential mess.

And don't forget to crush the stems, mouthed Rachel to herself.

'Oh, and don't forget to crush the stems – roses are a woody plant!' yelled Laura from the hall.

Selecting a drawer at random, Rachel pulled out a well-equipped kitchen armoury, and began cutting neat horizontal ends off the long stems with a Sabatier kitchen knife. Well, I'll still have the pleasure of them, she thought, and Fin would have wanted me to do it. Gestures are easy enough. The emerald ring in her pocket sprang into her mind, and the strange lightness in her stomach she had felt in the car coursed through her again, the way it had on the few occasions she had been persuaded to dive from the high board at school. The paralysing moment of decision when suddenly it's too late, when the only decision left is how to hit the water . . .

'There you go, Humpty,' said Laura, loudly enough for Rachel to hear, so she wouldn't come in. She put a protective newspaper down so the basset wouldn't splash too much. To her narrowed eyes, he looked like a splashy dog. Humpty began slobbering happily over the bowl.

In her hand Laura held the card from the flowers, which she had eagerly plucked from the heart of the bunch in case Mike had sent them up with Rachel as an apology for being late. A message to dispel the unsettling feelings she had been experiencing since she had driven up, something reassuring to set it all back in place.

The card read simply: *Darling, with this ring? You're the one who's good with words! All my love – always.*

Although her heart grappled valiantly with the logical possibility, Laura knew instinctively that it couldn't be from Mike – he tended to give her extravagantly foliated tropical plants that she could add to her 'jungle' in the house and these were long-stemmed white roses from one of the most elegant florists in London. There was a Prince of Wales crest on the card. And although she longed to believe that the florist's writing disguised Mike's intention, the message wasn't really him, much as she would like to believe it was. Fin must have given them to Rachel as a present for working over the weekend. Or something more.

But it wasn't as though Mike never gave her flowers and it wasn't as though this sort of gesture was *completely* out of character for him (Laura felt a slight squeeze on her conscience at this). But these weren't from him and he was late and all these worries had made her make her friend hand over a spectacular bunch of flowers out of *sympathy*. On her big weekend! She couldn't give Rachel the card now – Rachel would know she'd read it and would realise that she had wanted the flowers to be from Mike and . . .

There was the sound of a car engine at the end of the track and George's blue Audi pulled up outside.

'I'll get the door!' called Laura, pushing the card into the corner of a pinboard. She could pretend later that it fell out of the cellophane. Wishing with all her heart that Mike were here to put her back to normal, Laura once again hoisted the big smile she had learned at home on to her face, and flung wide the door.

chapter sixteen

The second the car stopped on the drive, Alex sprang out with more than her usual enthusiasm at seeing Laura.

'Oh my God, I thought we'd never get here, Laura!' she said, flinging her arms around her friend. The last few rounds of Parson's Cat had been particularly testing, with John using it as an interrogation technique to probe the obvious intrigue about Mike. George maintained a steely silence and, to Alex's growing frustration, kept his hands very much to himself for the rest of the journey. Although to be fair, with the roads like something out of Alton Towers, she had conceded that his hands should be on the wheel at all times.

But he hadn't exactly reignited the spark that had flared on the motorway. Like it was *her* fault John brought out the worst in her subconscious. Bloody Lighthouse Family for long stretches of the M1, irksome kids' games, the sneaking feeling that everything she said could end up on *You've Been Framed*! What else was her subconscious meant to do to register its distress? Alex made a vow to detune Channel Five in protest as soon as she got home.

Rachel came out of the cottage at the sound of the car and waved happily at George. Alex wasn't the only one to be relieved. Traumas on the scale she suspected Laura was winding up to demanded reinforcements. Humpty bounded out from behind her and began sniffing all the new arrivals.

'Do you want a hand, there, George?' she called, as he unloaded the bags from the boot. Chivalry struggled briefly with practicality but he graciously waved her away. George marvelled again that Alex was the only woman he knew who could pack less than he did for a weekend trip. She had one small rucksack, procured from a fashionable source by Rachel, and she'd assured him that she'd got all the vitals. The rather dubious advantage of wash 'n' go hairstyles, he supposed.

John had got all his stuff out of the car in minutes and immediately panned the video camera round the cottage.

'I see John has come prepared,' said Laura, reflex-smiling as she came into the viewfinder range.

'Yes,' said Alex, through gritted teeth and a similar wide smile, 'you could say that he's already got a good background built up to the weekend.'

'Here's a big hint from a snapper's girlfriend,' murmured Rachel into her ear, creeping up behind them both. 'Always make sure you're *behind* the man with the camera.' She gave John her best grin and thumbs-up sign.

'Don't think I'm going to forgive you that easily for abandoning me with King Zoom there, Sanderson,' muttered Alex in a tone that belied her beaming expression. 'You owe me.'

'Nice group shot now!' shouted John, inching backwards on a projecting rock. The three girls grinned broadly. It was a picture taken many times before on punts, at parties and in pubs. The end-of-the-day light caught Rachel's hair and made it shine round her head like a halo. Trying to catch the effect, John fiddled with his lens and, despite his frantic arm wavings, the girls took their chances and escaped to the cottage, leaving him to do some background footage of some uninterested Herdwick sheep.

'Hello, Laura,' said George, slamming down the boot of the car. He leaned forward to kiss her politely on each cheek. Ah, thought Laura. What perfect manners he has. And what subtle aftershave.

'Hello, George, I'm amazed you survived the journey over the pass,' she said. 'I looked at that route and thought, "Er, no".'

'God, yes, it can be a nightmare if you're not ready for all the bends and cattle grids,' added Rachel, slipping an arm around him in greeting. 'You must be shattered.'

George's manners hid any evidence to the contrary. 'No, I had a first-class navigator.' Alex had the grace to blush, having spent the last hour gripping her seat with the map in the hands of John in the back.

'So, any sign of the blushing bridegroom yet?' asked George as he hoisted the last of the bags onto his shoulder and they walked to the door.

Laura's broad smile wavered and Rachel leapt in.

'No, he's driving up from London – he's going to call when he gets nearby.'

She pulled her face into a warning grimace, which didn't quite come off. Alex and George exchanged glances behind Laura's back.

'Well, guess what I've brought for a weekend of last ditch reminiscing?' said Rachel, cheerfully shepherding them all into the kitchen.

'I really can't imagine,' said George. 'A selection of your old boyfriends? Oh, here we all are.'

Alex pinched him sharply just above the waistband and he raised his eyes beatifically to the cottage beams. There was not a lot of flesh to pinch, she thought, with frustrated desire.

'Everyone take their shoes off!' Laura called anxiously.

'Photo albums!' Rachel picked up a heavy bag and dumped it triumphantly on the table.

'Oh, excellent!' said Alex. 'I haven't seen any photos at all since we graduated! Have you brought *all* your albums?' She made a move to unbuckle the bag, drawing up a chair to the table with a squeal of wood on flagstones. George flinched.

'Or maybe we should wait until Mike gets here?' Rachel looked to Laura, who was absently stroking one of the silky roses, flamboyantly displayed in the centre of the scrubbed pine table. 'Laura?'

'Er, well, I did think we might have some tea first . . .' she began. Again, despite herself, she felt unsettled. It showed on her face.

'OK, tea!' Rachel leapt in, somehow feeling responsible for Laura's uncharacteristically vague behaviour. 'In which case, I brought some muffins with me. If I can remember which bag they're in.' She disappeared from view as she rummaged in her luggage with unnecessary brio.

'How am I meant to reconcile this with the fact that I was turning customers away muffinless all yesterday due to an unforeseen hitch on the Highbury muffin production line?' asked Alex, hands on hips.

'Yes, and why are you acting like Brown Owl?' asked George. 'Have you made an itinerary for us? Are we actually camping in the grounds and not sleeping in this house at all?'

'Why are you getting at Rachel?' John looked from Alex to George and back again.

'I'll put the kettle on,' said Laura.

She seemed to be in another world, which was fortunate, because a more observant person would have concluded that the International Gurning Championships were going on in that very room. Alex and Rachel rolled meaningful eyes at John. George gave him a conspiratorial wink. John looked blankly at the three of them.

'Can we have a look around the place while you're sorting out the tea, Laura?' asked George at last. 'John can help me with the bags.'

John began, 'No, I can't, I've just arri—' but Alex was quick enough to scrape her chair back again, making another loud and painful noise, and Rachel chipped in with, 'Yes, I'll show you where to go,' leaving Alex to offer to help with the cakes and George to down load John with two rucksacks and an overnight bag, like a 'Double or Drop' contestant on *Crackerjack* with seven cabbages and no hope of a Scalextric.

'What's going on with Laura?' George asked as they climbed the narrow stone staircase. 'She looks as though she's been Mogadoned.'

'She's been very funny since I got here,' said Rachel in a low voice. She pushed open the door of the first room she came to at the head of the stairs. 'Come in here.'

George kicked the door shut, leaned on it briefly and walked over to the window.

'What a wonderful place,' he said. 'Worth every minute of

the most tooth-wrenching drive I have ever had the endurance to complete.' He turned back to Rachel.

'Sorry, I just had to have one moment to make it all worthwhile. Hell is officially "The Ten Best Guitar Solos for Background Music for Goal of the Day". And now, on top of trial by Parson's bloody Cat, Laura looks pained in her own very special and very unique way. The Catholic Church have really missed out on something there. She could have been a twentieth-century martyr of our time. Has that pillock Mike missed their anniversary or something? Or has he double-booked this weekend with the cricket club?'

Rachel's eyebrows shot up involuntarily at this unusual display of pique from the normally wipe-clean George.

Before she could say anything, the bedroom door crashed open and John dumped his bags on the nearest bed.

'OK, chaps,' he said, 'will someone please tell me what's going on? Has someone taken Mike to Paris and tied him to a *gendarme* for a stag-night prank? Is that why Laura's got a face on her like a robber's dog?'

'Where do you use phrases like that on a day-to-day basis?' asked Rachel. 'Is that how they talk at Channel Five? Or are you now living at Sun Hill Police Station?'

'Got to keep up with the word on the street, Rachel.'

She rolled her eyes and turned her attentions back to George who, she could sense, was clenching his buttocks.

'She was rather quiet when I got here. I got the impression that she'd been brooding about something, probably to do with Mike. Don't mention Mike again, John,' she said, prodding him emphatically. 'Can't you tell that there's something up?'

'Er, not really,' John replied sarcastically.

'And don't mention the flowers either. They're a present

from me. Well, actually, they're a present from Fin for me, but when Laura saw them, I think she thought they were from Mike, you know, as an apology, so I said I'd brought them up as a present for her from me. But I think she might know they're from Fin for me, because that's when she went all funny, just before you arrived. And started talking about trust and honesty and did I know where Fin was going and all that kind of business.'

George and John stared at her.

'Which is ironic,' Rachel went on, 'because I *don't* actually know where Fin is going this weekend – he's on a job with Dan Wingate. And it could be anyone, so really I'm trusting him not to get into serious trouble.' She suddenly stopped.

She looked at George, then at John, and George shook his head quickly. There were things that John didn't need to know. Even if he were the only person in the dark this weekend, it wouldn't make much odds to the standard of his contribution.

'Oh, John, by the way, how's the eye now?' asked Rachel.

John put a tentative finger up to his right eye, where the faintest yellow shadow of a bruise could still be seen. 'More or less healed up, thanks. Bloody dangerous, the way Mike plays. He wants to watch out next time I'm in the nets, and I won't give a shit about the subsequent working order of his wedding tackle.'

'So, where do you think Mike is?' she asked George.

'Well, it's the first I've heard of a conference,' he admitted. 'Could be he's planning a surprise for Laura. Picking something up for the weekend? Lady C is still . . . *en étrange*, I take it?' he added delicately.

'As far as I know.'

There was a pause.

'So what's the problem?'

Rachel let out a sigh and, swinging her legs up on to the bed, stretched out and stared at the ceiling. 'Maybe she's just having last-minute nerves. It's very stressful getting engaged, probably more so than getting married, I would have thought. I mean, once you're down the aisle, it's all out of your hands, isn't it? But this period now, when your mum suddenly waves a cutting from *The Times* under your nose and, printed in final black and white, you and every other single person you know sees your name and your boyfriend's name, announcing that you are Going Out in the most permanent way possible . . . There's no going back, not without maximum embarrassment. I sometimes think I'd rather bite the bullet and get married than call it all off once it had been in the Happy Ads section of the *Salford Advertiser*.'

The three of them dwelled miserably on the embarrassment factor of placing the It's All Off notice in the paper.

'Someone my sister knows had to call off her engagement,' said John. 'Really pukka couple – she was in the Civil Service fast stream and he was a researcher at Millbank. They had the wedding list half finished at Peter Jones, curtains ordered, headed notepaper bought and everything.'

Rachel pulled a face of horror. 'So why was it called off?'

'Apparently, the groom got lashed to a lamppost in Chelsea on his stag do. Very embarrassing repercussions with the management of a certain restaurant and a reporter from the *Mirror*. Francesca was furious and pulled the plug. Can't blame her, really. Or him.' John looked pensive. 'She was a real *moose*.'

'What a sparkling range of friends you have, John,' said Rachel. 'You really should do a documentary about them for television.'

'Hmm,' said John. An indecipherable expression crossed his face. 'So, what's the plan with Laura, then? Lots of positive chat about mimosa and Teasmaids?'

'Maybe we should keep off that. This is meant to be a reunion weekend, isn't it? I expect she's bored to tears talking about wedding things, isn't she, Rachel?' asked George hopefully.

The memory of his evening spent negotiating the bridesmaid minefield round at Mike and Laura's was still reasonably fresh – not knowing what, or how much other people knew was proving very wearing already. It was a bit like playing Cluedo all the time, throwing out bluffs and double bluffs and sneaking secret looks at other people's cards until you weren't quite sure what you were supposed to know in the first place.

'Oh God, I don't know,' said Rachel. 'I'm just looking forward to a weekend of seeing everyone, out of London, away from work and all those boring conversations that go with it, just being together the way we used to.'

'Without Caroline, you mean,' John said helpfully.

'Yes, thank you, John, I think that was taken as read,' she replied, swinging her legs off the bed. 'Now, we have an option with the bed situation.'

'Wahey!' said John and was quelled instantly by a look from George.

'I've had a quick scout round and as far as I can see, there are two double rooms, a sofabed in the sitting room and a spare mattress which can go in the kitchen by the Aga – quite cosy – or in the hall. Either we sort it out now and bag the best beds for ourselves or we leave it till later.'

'Leave it till later,' said George, just as John said, 'Bags I the sofabed.'

George glared at John again, who shrugged his shoulders.

'Come on,' said John. 'Presumably our lovebirds will want one double bed since it's a bit late for them to start saving it for their wedding night at this stage of play, and I'm not sharing a double bed with you, mate, much as I think you're a great bloke. And my chances of sharing with either the lovely Alexandra or Milady here are, regrettably, equally low. So it looks like it's the mattress or the sofa and I do have this dreadful sports injury that requires a comfy bed.'

Rachel looked admiringly at him. 'You should talk to Laura about law,' she said. 'For a chronically tactless man you've got a very quick mind, when it's working on your side.'

chapter seventeen

They bounded noisily down the stone stairs, John out of natural clunkiness and George and Rachel in order to give Alex ten seconds to dry up any tears Laura might have spilt in their absence before they reached the kitchen.

As it turned out, Alex's calmness had worked its usual spell and she and Laura were sitting at the big scrubbed pine table, talking earnestly about BSE. There was a heaped plate of chocolate muffins and a glossy cake next to the tea set and Alex had flung the windows open, letting in a welcome fresh breeze. Laura's nerves were nowhere to be seen and, although she was wielding a large knife for the cake, she looked a picture of domesticity.

John sniffed the air appreciatively. 'For a couple of academics, you two cook very well,' he said, ignoring the howls of protest from Alex and Rachel.

'For a complete bimbo, you just about managed to fool the examining board into giving you a degree,' said Alex. 'Get a plate and shut up.'

Rachel cuffed him playfully about the head and pushed him into a chair. 'Even if it was in Geography.'

Laura's equanimity had obviously been more than restored by whatever Alex had said to her. She was wearing her familar air of serenity as she began serving up her perfectly risen, no-cracks cake.

'Rachel, are you going to be Mother?' she said, gesturing towards the teapot and the six blue and white cups.

Rachel's attention sprang away from admiring the authentically stripped Welsh dresser and fixed itself on Laura, much to their mutual discomfort.

'Can you not reach the pot, Rachel?' said Alex, sensing something in Rachel's suddenly tense posture.

'Er, yes, if I stretch,' said Rachel quickly, leaning over John and pretending to bat his hands away. Blood continued to pound in her ears and she knew she must be blushing. The truth coming out of her own mouth would be shocking enough. Out of someone else's, even unintentionally, it was a jolt. Get a grip, for God's sake, she shouted at herself, and even as she thought the words, she realised that she'd mentally turned away from them.

John took a large mouthful of pound cake and made a happy mmm-ing noise. He smiled at Laura, dropping a few crumbs. Laura thought affectionately that he looked about seven years old.

'This is just as good as the ones you used to make at college, Laura,' he said. He leaned across the table and patted her hand. 'You know, I'm so glad you and Mike are getting married. You're the one thing we can depend on not to change now we've all left college.'

Laura flushed at this spontaneous display of tenderness and knitted her fingers around his, with a happy smile.

George looked a little surprised. 'And what's that supposed to mean?'

'Well,' said John, leaning back in his chair and holding his cup the wrong way round, 'we've all changed a bit, got new ideas and, you know, *mellowed* . . .' He put an ironic accent on the word.

'Speak for yourself!' interrupted Alex. Rachel just looked pointedly at John's Mr Men socks which, since he'd put his feet up on the window seat, were in full view.

'But you and Mike,' John went on, 'you were sickeningly in love at college and you're sickeningly in love still and you can put me down right now for the four matching egg cups, please.'

'Oh, that's so sweet,' said Laura.

'Sweet but true,' said Alex. 'And I think you can sting him for a bit more than four egg cups when the time comes.'

'Yes, means-tested wedding lists are the way forward,' said George. 'Travel cameraman equals Dualit toaster, at least.'

'Well, I'll tell you all now, spoil the surprise,' said Rachel, 'you're all getting Christmas tree decorations from me. All of you, whether the list's at Peter Jones or Argos. Sorry.' In response to the four blank looks, she added, 'It's something you wouldn't think of splashing out on, is it? And it's always festive.'

'And you can get them in the January sales every year!' joked Alex.

Laura tutted at her and put her head on one side in a gesture that Rachel had seen many times before.

'Ahh, Rachel, that's a lovely idea, hon. And we'd always remember you at Christmas, wherever we all were.'

'Ah yes, poor Rachel,' teased George, in a dreadful Oirish

accent. 'All snowed in alone in that lovely Irish castle with the wild man of Moher and a cask of Guinness.'

'Why are we talking about Christmas at the height of summer?' said John. 'Do you remember that summer in Chile? Filming crocodiles, eating off the roadside, living the lives of young, free single men riding on the edge of oblivion, with a couple of bottles of tequila in life's rucksack . . .'

He poured himself more tea and hacked off a generous slice of cake. Two hundred and thirty calories, Rachel thought automatically. Twenty minutes StairMaster. As if John needed to work out, with his effortlessly long legs and flat stomach. Life was so much easier for men, even if you just counted the things they didn't need to know.

'Well, while you lot were playing at being Indiana Jones, I was working as a camp counsellor at Camp Columbine in Massachusetts,' said Laura. She offered the teapot to George, who politely refused it.

Bloody hell, thought Alex, it's Parson's Cat all over again.

'I didn't know you did that, Laura,' said John. 'Why didn't I know that?'

'Because you didn't ask?'

'Well, I'm asking now. Was it fun? Did you learn a lot?'

'Put it like this: it was either get out of the country or join some godawful touring production of the *Orestia* that my dad was putting on. They're always on at me to go to these dreadful drama festivals with them – it's so embarrassing, you can't imagine. So, I had to get the whole camp thing organised before the end of term; caught the first plane out and I had a wonderful time. A couple of the teenagers I looked after still write to me,' she said fondly. 'They were a good age to be with, not too young and not so old that you couldn't control them. Mind you, the camp principal still managed to find out about Dad and put me in charge of drama. I produced a version of *Joseph* with rollerskates. We had to be quite sensitive about the more religious aspects of it.'

'*Roller*skates . . .?' murmured George.

'Suppose you had to have something to keep you busy while Mike was out of the country!' said John. 'Bet you didn't miss him for a minute, did you?'

Laura looked pensive at the thought of the long separation which had been a real trial for her. She had written a letter every other night and had had one postcard back – three lines from each of the boys, mostly about toilet facilities.

'OK, when *I* was nineteen, I was staying in London with my cousin writing record reviews for a Riot Grrrl fanzine in the evening and working in a bookshop during the day!' said Alex, banging the table with the flat of her hand. 'Beat that for groovy studentness!'

'Fine!' said George. 'When I was nineteen I had a summer job working as a political reporter for the *Standard* and spent the evenings learning Russian at night classes at the City Lit.'

'Wooooh!' shouted John, doing a drumroll of appreciation with his teaspoon.

'John, you have been working at Channel Five for too long,' said Rachel. 'Your sense of irony has healed up.'

Alex and Laura looked hopefully at George, wondering at this side of him that he'd kept so quiet, Alex perhaps a little more hopefully than Laura.

George maintained a straight face for a whole minute and then cracked under the pressure of expectation. 'Oh, you know I didn't,' he spluttered. 'I had an internship at BZW.'

Rachel felt happier in the wave of laughter that swept across the table than she had done with her college friends for a long time. She suddenly remembered what those long evenings on the Backs, with bottles of cheap – and sometimes not so cheap – sparkling wine and the bleeding punnets of strawberries, had felt like. All the photos she had reminded her of the way the evenings had looked: the backdrop of weeping willows, the flowing scarves and long button-through skirts that had been the only thing anyone had worn that summer, the scoop necklines of the rowing vests sun-burned onto John, Laura and Mike's chests, Alex's long brown legs in her cricket shorts, omnipresent tubes of sunblock. But this warm feeling of comfortable bantering with people was something diaries and cameras couldn't record. And the next summer had been so shatteringly different . . .

'You know, I've really missed you lot,' she said warmly.

George and Alex looked up and smiled at her. Laura seemed delighted at the fairly instant testimonial to her engagement weekend and John, getting up to put the kettle on again, gave her a hug from behind in passing. He could be quite sweet when he tried, thought Rachel.

'You're right,' said John. 'It's lovely to have all the gang back again, even if it is to celebrate Mike's expulsion from The Lads.'

'Group hug! Group hug!' called Laura, using one of Caroline's cast-off favourite expressions.

'Well, I'll pass on that,' said George tactfully, getting up from his seat and out of range of Laura's widespread arms, 'but why don't we bring those photograph albums into the sitting room and dig up some ghosts?'

'Great idea,' said Alex. She linked her arm round Laura and steered her into the mozzarella-white sitting room, com-plete with linen throws, bolster-sized cushions and a large arrangement of dried flowers in the unused fireplace.

Between the five of them, there were more than enough albums to go round and Inigo Aikin-Rose's soft furnishings lent themselves perfectly to lounging. Laura settled herself very comfortably next to Alex on the sofa, with one of John's legs across her knee, from which vantage point she could keep a watchful eye on the leisurely comings and goings of Humpty.

By nine-thirty they had still only looked through three albums. As soon as one person went into hysterics, pointing dumbly with tears of laughter streaming down their cheeks at yet another picture of John in drag, the album had to be passed round, compared and the events of the evening ticked off. George, cursing, protested that he had never shaved his legs for a party, until Laura passed him evidence to the contrary. Very close-up evidence.

It was the first time since leaving college that Rachel had really looked closely at the pictures. She had shown them to Finlay once, when he had expressed curiosity about her time at Cambridge and she had flicked through them then, skating her eyes over some of the more painful images. She had tried to pass off her discomfort as embarrassment at showing her photographs to a professional, but the sensation was more like the vicarious revulsion she had felt when she flipped squeamishly past the gory dissections in her GCSE Biology textbooks: she knew she would feel sick if she looked, but had to fight a morbid impulse to peer round the page, knowing they were there.

Looking at her shyly smiling university self now, rounder and curlier, somehow protected by an objective interest in Caroline's proximity to Mike, Rachel felt more of a twinge of sadness than distress. She had deliberately chosen to look through an album from one of the happier periods of her college life, still unwilling to look closely at those of the last summer. Although the happy, celebrating faces changed in line-up, all the backgrounds were relentlessly the same, every year, every event. Why had she needed to take three sets of pictures of Great Court in the snow? Was it to prove that she had really been there? It was hard to conjure up the feeling of living in that stage-set Oxbridge court, even now, so soon afterwards. But ageless Cambridge remained the same, unmarked by their presence or their passing.

'Well, you can tell by that line on the wall how pissed Alex was!' said John, pointing to a particularly dishevelled picture of Alex, clutching on to the men's hockey captain and very much the worse for wear at a hockey dinner. The photo had been taken some time before she discovered the bonuses of wearing contact lenses to functions instead of going without her glasses and hoping for the best.

'Er, John, if you look closely, you'll see that that line is actually the skirting board,' Rachel pointed out, turning the album around helpfully, and clapped her hand over her mouth in pretend horror at the indiscretion. Everyone howled and crowded round the picture.

Alex raised her eyebrows. 'Not so fast, Mary Whitehouse,' she said, 'because the next page is . . . the Rocky Horror Picture Show cocktail party night!'

Rachel pretended to die with embarrassment on the floor. 'No! Not the black basque and suspenders!' she whined.

George lingered over a picture of Rachel in her basque and suspenders, a faint hint of nostalgia twitching at his heart. He could remember her buying that at Robert Sayle department store. He vividly remembered her trying it on for him, shyly walking into his room, the light from his bedside lamp lighting her from behind. George smiled at such a forgotten feeling bubbling to the surface and turned the page, only to see himself, Mike and John, grinning drunkenly in a line, dressed as rent boys in Lycra cycling shorts and braces. He blanched, turning over three pages at once, and wondered how much that picture would be worth in ten years' time to the chartered accountant, management consultant and film producer respectively.

Laura leapt up suddenly, thinking she could hear her mobile phone ringing. It was nearly ten already – she couldn't wait much longer before she started supper. She padded through to the kitchen and wondered for the third time that day why seagrass was meant to be so great when it looked and felt as though you hadn't had the carpet delivered yet.

'Where did Laura go?' asked Rachel, noticing the door closing.

'Kitchen,' said Alex.

'Well, I hope she's putting some supper on because I could eat a hippo,' said John, who was lying on his back and trying to work out with George who all the girls were perched on Mike's birthday-party drinks table.

'We're waiting for Mike, you oaf,' said George. 'Didn't you go out with her? You *must* know what she was called.' They both squinted at the picture. John had gone out with many girls who had fallen for his floppy blond fringe and Blues scarf, but then, as now, there had never been anyone special. Drunken tussles early on with first Alex and then Laura, after which he had chivalrously kept their secrets, fixed John's place in their own memories of college as something more than his role as Jack the Lad with the boys. Whatever he was looking for evidently still hadn't arrived or wasn't available.

'Not necessarily,' said John, turning his head to look from

a different angle. 'I know she was at New Hall. Definitely New Hall. Definitely not within walking distance, anyway.'

Rachel looked at Alex and said, 'Bugger.'

Laura came back in, looking tired.

'Was that Mike?' asked Alex.

'No, I think it was Rachel's mobile but it stopped ringing before I could find it,' she said. 'I wish Mike would call. I don't want to start supper without him and I'm getting worried, you know. You hear such dreadful things on the news about motorists going over the side of these roads in the dark . . .'

'Oh, come on, Laura!' said George, hoisting himself out of his seat. 'Mike's a great driver. The reception for mobiles is pretty bad round here. He's probably trying to call you even now and can't get through. Look, who fancies a gin and tonic before supper?'

'What a great idea,' said Alex, shepherding Laura into the kitchen. 'I bet Inigo Aikin-Rose has got a well-stocked booze cabinet. We can get the supper going and it'll all be ready when he does turn up. Eh, Laura?'

Laura protested a little, but once in the scrubbed pine splendour of the kitchen, she seemed to rally. George started rummaging in the cupboards and found the glasses. Red wine, white wine, champagne flutes, beer tankards, shot glasses, water glasses, tumblers. Rachel came in from the boot room, carrying a bottle of Bombay Sapphire and a bottle of Gordon's, with a full silver ice-bucket balanced in the crook of her arm.

'Can you check the fridge, Alex?' she said. 'I would imagine our Inigo keeps his tonic well chilled.'

Alex retrieved a couple of half-empty bottles of tonic water from the fridge and put them on the table in front of

George, who was slicing up a lemon into exactly the right dimensions.

'Er, Diet Spar tonic?' he said incredulously. 'I don't think so.' He wiped the lemon juice meticulously off his hands with a tea towel.

'Oh, come on, George!' said Alex. 'Is there a local shop that'll be open at this time? And what's wrong with Spar tonic? It's just a mixer!'

'You wouldn't use Chaumet in a Black Velvet, would you?' said George, who was now hunting for his car keys. 'And a gin and tonic on a night like this should be perfect. We'll find some proper tonic, even if I have to drive to Kendal to get it. Where are my keys?'

'In the bowl in the hall,' Laura said automatically.

'Are you going to mark the gin?' asked John, who had come in from the sitting room in search of early food.

'*What*?' asked George and Rachel in unison.

'Well,' said John, stuffing some stray cake in his mouth, 'are we going to replace it? And if so, how much of the new bottle can we have ourselves? Just a thought.'

George ignored him and shrugged on his jacket.

'You go with George, Alex,' said Rachel helpfully. 'You can translate for him in the shop. I'll help Laura with supper and John can . . . assess the drinks cabinet.'

Alex threw her a grateful look and followed George outside. The latch clicked shut behind them.

'So, supper!' said Laura.

Rachel emptied a bag of potatoes into the sink and handed John a peeler.

chapter eighteen

Dusk had fallen and George was relying on his sense of direction to steer him around the high-hedged roads near the lake. Alex had reached for the map in the glove compartment when she got in, but George made some gallant noises about the scale being too small to make much difference, not fancying a repeat of Alex's last 'shortcut' over Corney Fell, which had felt more like a sequence from *Top Gear Motorsport*. He would have to have a word with her sometime about map-reading gradients.

The car was stuffy with the trapped heat of the day. Alex slid the sunroof open to let in some fresh air and slipped a tape into the player. After a brief whirr, the otherworldly sounds of the opening track filled the car, the bass notes throbbing tangibly through the speakers. It was Portishead, a Christmas present from her last year – part of a move to introduce selective listening to a man who tended to bulk buy *Best of*s. It had evidently found enough favour to be in the car itself. She wondered why she hadn't found it earlier. Or had George just put it there?

Alex shivered pleasurably. 'Ooooohmmmm,' she murmured. 'Perfect for driving in the dark.' Her fingers clicked and slapped to the pulse of the music.

As they drove away from the lake, George could feel the pull of the engine as he came out of the corners and the power of the brakes balancing the car. He'd only had the Audi for a couple of weeks and it hadn't had a proper run out yet, cooped up as he had been in west London. He didn't count the journey up as driving. It had been more like a mobile form of Chinese water torture.

But he was beginning to enjoy driving through the empty narrow lanes, now that it was just him and Alex. And the music in the background was giving him a *Top Gear* feeling again, but this time definitely more Jeremy Clarkson in a TVR than Tiff Needell in a RallyCross Cosworth.

He took in a deep breath of the cool evening air rushing through the sunroof and smelt Alex's perfume, mixed with the heavy night air. *Eau d'Issey.* Well-tutored by his two elder sisters, George never forgot a perfume. To his credit, he never confused them either.

'You know, Portishead has such an instant effect on me,' murmured Alex. 'I'm just like Pavlov's dog – as soon as I hear "Wandering Star", I just . . . melt.' She slid down in her seat, with her eyes closed. 'You might want to write that down for future reference,' she added, flicking one eye at him.

George smiled and slid his hands round the steering wheel. He bounced his head gently to the music and pressed his back into the car seat.

Actually, he didn't need to write it down. He remembered the effects of 'Wandering Star' vividly from one particularly sexy night which had begun with supper at a restaurant in Chiswick and had ended in a bath in his house. Against his protestations and despite the fact that she had downed at least one bottle of wine, Alex had brought his stereo into the bathroom and surrounded the bath with white candles. This ethereal music, with its threads of sound fading in and out, had fitted perfectly with the surreal feeling of drinking chilled wine in the warm water. And the rest.

Alex was giving him that same look again now, he could see out of the corner of his eye. She looked irresistible and slightly dangerous.

'Are those your trousers?' he asked. 'I don't remember seeing them before.'

'Do you like them?'

'Mmm.'

He slipped a hand on to her knee. 'Change gear for me.'

Alex laughed. 'I don't know how!'

'Well, I'm not moving my hand.' He stroked the length of her thigh and the warmth of his hand through the silky material made her muscles contract. 'How many driving lessons have you had now, Murphy? Into fourth.'

Alex obediently pulled the gear stick down into fourth. Why couldn't he be like this all the time? she thought. Not that she approved of male domination, but with the voice *and* the car *and* the music . . .

The Audi was gliding round the lanes like a cat, the headlights carving out yellow arcs in the dusk, picking out sheep and rocks unmoving in the fields. As George's hand moved slowly up her leg, Alex fervently hoped that the nearest shop supplying up-to-standard tonic would be a good hour away each way.

'George, pull over.'

'No.'

'Come on, George, pull over. A strange feeling's coming over me.' Alex wriggled luxuriantly to the music.

'No. Down to second.' George accelerated into a corner and swung round it. 'Third and . . . fourth.'

'Oh, why not, for God's sake?' moaned Alex in frustration, crashing the gears. 'We're never going to get a minute to ourselves in that cottage without someone drawing their own conclusions and sharing them with the others and— Fucking hell!'

George stood on the brakes as a large sheep the size of a small horse appeared in the headlights, right in the middle of the road and staring straight at them. Its eyes glowed yellow in the dark. With a satisfying if not exactly bucolic screech, the Audi came to a beautifully judged halt. Both George and the sheep were pleasantly surprised. *Vorsprung durch Technic* indeed. George and Alex sat rigid in their seats as the sheep continued to stare at them – slightly malevolently, Alex thought. Then it ambled off into the dark.

They breathed out in unison.

'I feel as though I'm on some kind of advanced driving test today,' said George. 'Tell me if you see any slalom cones for reversing round, won't you?'

'Where's the nearest village?' asked Alex heavily. 'Because at this rate we might as well just go there, get the bloody tonic and get back. I won't give them the satisfaction of drawing any conclusions we haven't had a chance to reach.' She let out a big sigh and slumped back into the seat. 'It's just one thing after another. If it's not John being an arsehole with that bloody video, it's Laura on the verge of some unexplained wobbly and if it's not Laura, it's sodding *sheep*.'

Without saying anything, George put the car into gear and it purred off, rounding the next corner with insouciant ease. All the lights in the isolated cottage opposite the bend, which had come on suddenly a few moments ago, were switched off again.

'I take it Laura's found out something untoward about her husband-to-be?' he asked.

'Er, no, I don't think so,' said Alex. 'While you lot were upstairs – very subtle, by the way, I don't think – she muttered something about having just come off the Pill and her hormones being mad and that kind of thing. Wiped her eyes on a tea towel – which is *most* unhygienic, as you know – and said something else about having no secrets from her husband. Then went all faux chirpy and started talking about vacuum cleaners.'

George raised his James Bond eyebrow without taking his eyes off the road ahead.

Alex shrugged in response. 'I think it's just one of those traditional pre-wedding nerves things. I'm sure it's in *Debrett's Guide*. You know, "Should I? Shouldn't I? Oh, go on, tell me again how Mike is the most domesticated man since Fred Flintstone." Once she'd got that off her chest, she proceeded to tell me that I really should think about getting a Dyson cleaner because Caroline had recommended them to her and do you know, they've changed her life.'

'Oh,' said George. 'Is that a village shop I see before me?'

Lewthwaite's Stores was the only shop in the village and by strange and fortunate coincidence, not only was it open at half past ten, it also stocked the appropriate tonic water. George picked up five bottles.

The shop was empty apart from them. The dazzling strip lighting and an eerie absence of background music reminded Alex of an alien spaceship. She and George skulked round the shelves, followed by the eagle eye of Mrs J.E. Lewthwaite, the proprietor. If the shop was disconcertingly modern, she at least fulfilled George's expectations of rural shopkeepers by wearing a furry hat, despite the heaviness of the evening.

'Tunnocks Teacakes!' hissed Alex out of the corner of her mouth, waving a packet of cakes surreptitiously at him.

'What?' hissed back George.

'I can't get these where I'm living,' she said excitedly. 'How much money have you got on you?'

George rolled his eyes. 'How can you *think* of buying whatever those things are when we both know that Rach and Laura will be furiously out-caking each other all weekend? Do you have any idea how many muffins there are in that tin she's brought?'

There was an emphatic cough from the direction of the till. Alex soberly put the Tunnocks Teacakes in George's basket.

'And anyway,' said George, straightening up, 'more to the point, did you see any Pimms in the cupboard?'

Alex looked blank. 'I can't remember. There was a lot of fizz.'

'Doh!' said George. 'Get a couple of lemons and some oranges and a cucumber – you know, Pimms equipment. I'll see if they've got any.'

Alex gratefully went to the back of the shop and fiddled with a couple of wizened lemons in a wicker basket, hoping fervently that she wouldn't be able to hear the exchange between George and the ferocious looking Mrs Lewthwaite. The last thing she wanted was to be labelled as one of the 'City Offcomers from That Holiday Cottage Who Asked for Garlic Paste' – she'd seen plenty of those drifting in and out of the Yorkshire village where she'd grown up. There had been a village bet on how long it would take their local shop to sell out of the sun-dried tomatoes ordered by one gourmet cottage. She suspected that they were still buying the same carefully-dusted consignment on their return the following year.

She could hear George's voice drifting back over the rows of processed peas. 'It's a vodka. Based. Mixer,' he was saying, very slowly.

Alex cringed.

'We don't get much call for that kind of thing,' said Mrs Lewthwaite, equally slowly, pursing her lips as though she'd been asked where she kept her amyl nitrate poppers. 'You could. Try. In Whitehaven.'

Mint, she thought, suddenly. Please God don't let George ask for fresh mint for Pimms. She could hear him umm-ing and ahh-ing his way to another polite assault on the shop's various deficiencies. Her high embarrassment factor took over.

Striding quickly to the front of the shop, Alex said briskly, 'That'll be grand, then, just the tonic water and the Tunnocks Teacakes, please.'

Both stared at her, Mrs Lewthwaite more specifically at her right hand.

'Oh yes and these two, er, lemons,' added Alex lamely, putting them on the counter.

'You're not a very good shoplifter,' said George. 'I could see them the whole time.'

'Shut up, George,' said Alex under her breath.

'I'd have expected better from a *soi-disant* shopkeeper,' he continued jovially.

'You'll be stayin' up at t'cottage by Wastwater?' asked Mrs

Lewthwaite, as she rang the prices up on a very high-tech electronic till. She rhymed Wastwater with MastMatter. And it wasn't really framed as a question.

'Yes, we are,' George said politely.

'Ahhh, *well* then,' she replied in the manner of someone sharing an understanding. A very knowing smile cracked the frosty veneer. A full-on cackle was surely only moments away.

Uncertain as to how she was meant to respond to this, Alex tried a weak smile at the lady and nudged George in the back, towards the door. He picked up the bag with the tonic waters in and raised his hand in a country-style greeting.

'Bye, now.'

'Bye, lad.'

As they shut the door behind them, Alex was sure she could hear a giggle stifled by the clanging bell.

By the time they found their way back to the cottage, it was definitely dark and the roads seemed to have changed completely. It was a good job Hawk Cottage was the only place in the area – even Alex could hardly fail to navigate towards it.

The kitchen lights shone out on to the gravel drive. Inside, Rachel was reluctantly scattering some herbs on to a chicken, while professional cooking pots bubbled and hissed around her.

'We got the tonic water,' said George, dumping the bags on the table.

Rachel did a pantomime of double-taking at her watch and widening her eyes. 'And the rest,' she said.

'Yes, we got some lemons too,' said George, deadpan, 'although apparently we have to go farther for Pimms.'

'Where's Laura?' asked Alex. She twisted a fresh tray of ice cubes over the glasses.

'Well, just before you got in, she finally had a call on the Piggie Wiggie phone and she ran off upstairs to take it.' Rachel did her 'But I said nothing' face.

'And John?'

'Retuning the television. He says anyone can find Channel Five if they try hard enough.'

'And Cinderella?'

'In the kitchen, trying to salvage a chicken who may well have died in vain. Not to mention this carcass stew.'

Laura's feet in Alex's big monster slippers came clumping down the stairs and she pushed open the kitchen door.

'Mike says to start without him. He's going to be a bit late.' She pushed down the aerial of the phone with the flat of her hand and looked worried.

'Ah, come on, Laura,' said George, handing her a gin and tonic. 'He'll be making a detour by the only florist in the North he can find that's still open at this time of night.'

'Absolutely!' said Rachel. 'He'll have left it until the last minute to phone, in the hope that he could have got here sooner. I bet you the instant the food's on the table, Mike will walk in. With a bottle of wine.'

This was undeniably true.

'And besides,' said Alex practically, 'you can't keep supper hanging on for ever.'

'No, certainly not,' said Laura, 'I've done a special recipe from my Prue Leith book – stuffed chicken with sage and fennel. Did you see there's even a little herb garden in the back? So lovely.'

Rachel caught Alex's eye and nodded at the chicken in the casserole dish. Surrounded by onions and whole cloves of garlic, it looked like Frankenstein's Chicken, having been stuffed and then stitched up again, with thick black cotton crosses running angrily across each breast.

Alex swallowed.

'I'm going to do some garlic and pesto mash and some veggies,' said Rachel, 'and there's some very nice ice-cream in the fridge. If John hasn't found it first.'

'Excellent,' said George. 'Just enough time for a couple of G and T's before supper and we'll all muck in with the washing up afterwards.' He clinked the ice in his glass. 'To a splendid weekend!'

The others raised their glasses and individually hoped for the best.

John had never seen anyone spin out a starter as long as Laura. She moved the slivers of trout round her plate, into piles, to the side, to the other side, deboning it as if it were radioactive, all the time staring at the door. Her conversation veered erratically from the effusive to the plain vacant.

Eventually, with the candles burning down and beginning to make solid puddles of wax on the table, John was moved to say, 'If you don't want that trout, Laura, I'll have it,' and was instantly quelled with a warning shush from Rachel. He made a 'What did I say?' gesture with his hands, appealing incredulously to an invisible referee.

'I think we really ought to be starting the chicken, Laura,' said Alex. 'There is a limit to how long it can stay in the oven without drying out.'

Laura pouted and put her knife and fork together over the shredded fillets. 'I did put those strips of bacon over the breasts, if you noticed,' she said. 'It's a very handy tip for keeping them moist.'

Laura gave Alex a withering look that would have not been out of place marching across Miss Jean Brodie's patrician features. It's all down to the expression, thought Rachel wonderingly. A year's intimate contact with Caroline Cox and her wide range of meaningful glares had had some effect on Laura after all.

'Don't get short with me because Mike's late,' said Alex affably. 'I just don't think we should spoil the chicken when we already know he's going to be delayed. We've already finished four bottles of wine. And John's about to eat his placemat.'

The suggestion of being anything less than sweet-tempered had a spontaneous effect on Laura.

'OK,' she said, managing to blend hospitable indulgence with just the right amount of disappointment and self-sacrifice, 'I'll get it out of the oven – if you could clear a space on the table.'

'I'll give you a hand with the vegetables,' said Rachel, getting up and gathering in the side plates. Alex slapped John's hand as he tried to pick the trout off Laura's plate, but he managed to snatch it anyway when she took some dishes to the sink.

Laura peered into a pan. 'I thought we decided we were having *boiled* new potatoes and carrots,' she said.

'Er, yes,' said Rachel, 'but the potatoes couldn't hang around for that long, so I mashed them after all. With olive oil and some pesto I found in the fridge. Is that OK?' she asked the table in general.

There was a murmur of approval.

Laura brought the slightly crinkled chicken out of the oven, with a 'ta-da!' gesture.

There was a politer murmur of approval.

George had been sharpening the carving knife on a steel and privately marvelling at how well equipped a kitchen could be when it was left to a man to equip it. Now he flourished the razor-sharp knife at the bird and found he had to flick off several shrivelled layers of bacon before he could make contact with any flesh. In addition to this, his carving action was immediately impeded by the thick hanks of black cotton with which Laura had secured the stuffing.

'Wine,' Rachel mouthed at John and mimed a drinking action, which John pretended to misinterpret in a comedy manner. Alex coughed, to indicate that Laura, who would not find it amusing, was coming back with a casserole dish of mystery vegetables, cooked to a 'particularly good Prue recipe'. John went off in search of yet more wine and came back to the table with a chilled bottle of champagne, beads of condensation running enticingly down the neck.

'Some folk have milk in the fridge and others have Moët,' he said. 'You've got to hand it to this Inigo chap – he knows how to kit out a country getaway.'

Laura enthusiastically nodded her agreement. 'Oh yes, he's been so thoughtful. I went up to unpack my bags earlier and found that someone had even put a vase of lilac in the bedroom. Even some nice soft towels. Caroline must have told him it was an engagement celebration party. That's probably what the champagne's for.' This broad hint did not stop John peeling off the foil.

'John, hang on until everyone's got something to eat,' said Rachel, dishing up the surprise sprouts, which, she guessed, had had some kind of unspecified vine fruit garnish. Although a warm sense of well-being had settled on her over the course of the evening as she relaxed into the reassuringly familiar company, she hadn't really been feeling that well.

The drive up had been emotionally charged, to say the least, and she had been downing George's generous G and T's with convivial abandon. And now she wasn't sure if she was up to eating Laura-cuisine.

Laura was the kind of cook who saw stuffing sprouts as a challenge – not even cranberries were too small for her to tackle. And although her cooking was decidedly grown-up, she did still demand a chorus of enthusiastic 'yum-yum's from her guests or else a sulk would descend before the elaborate dessert. Rachel thought she saw something move in the dish and felt her stomach twitch. Had she read something about evening sickness or was she just making excuses?

Laura was passing round the plates very slowly.

'I'm going to give Mike one last call before we eat,' she said suddenly. 'Hold on there for a minute.' She went into the hall and they could hear her dialling on the old black Bakelite phone.

'Oh, I'm *so* glad we all came up,' said Alex, stretching her long legs under the table. 'It feels just like old times.'

'But with cars,' said George.

'And better booze,' said John, holding his glass up to the light.

'And no work,' said Rachel.

George snorted. 'Speak for yourself.'

Alex leaned back in her chair and gathered her long black hair into a high ponytail on top of her head. It fell in glossy strands through her fingers. 'It's so weird,' she said, 'how much it feels like being back at college. Shame we can't ever get this kind of atmosphere in London.'

It wasn't that weird, Rachel thought. The strangely companionable mood could be directly attributed to a) not having any background traffic noise; b) everyone trying hard, for once, not to use their jobs as a topic of conversation – which usually led to point-scoring and tears before bedtime; and c) talking about other people when the photograph albums came out – always a top comforter. She decided that, out of politeness, she should keep b) and c) to herself, although she was sure they must have occurred to the rest. They weren't that stupid. Even after d) a bottle of wine each.

'No, I'm really going to enjoy this weekend,' she said, meaning it.

'Brilliant!' exclaimed John. 'Can you say that again for the camera, please?' He whipped the camcorder out from under the table.

Rachel picked up her champagne glass and said, with a big smile, 'I'm so pleased to be here with my favourite people on this momentous occasion of Laura and Mike's engagement.' She toasted her glass at the camera.

'George, is that Laura in the hall squawking at Mike on the phone? You're nearest the door,' said John, panning out to the doorway.

George looked askance for the camera and kicked the door open with his foot, out of sight of the viewfinder range.

The door swung open to reveal Laura clutching the phone and looking sacrificial.

'But darling,' she was saying, 'I've waited ages and I *miss* you, rabbit. Where are you— Oh my God! John, put that away! I'm talking to Mike on the . . . No, sweetheart, it's just John, he's got that stupid— OK, OK,' she covered the mouthpiece with her hand and glared at John, 'Mike says hello and he'll be with us shortly and— What? I can't say that! Not on camera! He says to start the booze flowing without him. And hopes that your eye is feeling better.'

'Wife as tactful translator,' murmured George to Alex.

Laura gestured to shut the door. George pushed it closed, but not so hard that it wouldn't swing open again in a few moments.

'Ah me,' said John. 'I feel five years younger already.'

'. . . well, how long is soon?' Laura was whining down the phone. 'We've got dinner on the table . . .'

John brandished his knife and fork in front of the camera lens. 'Hurry up, Mike mate,' he yelled, 'your lovely wife's cooked a platypus for us and it's going cold!'

'There's just one thing missing,' said Rachel.

'What's that?' asked Alex, picking a crispy piece of skin off the chicken breast while Laura wasn't looking.

'I *am* waiting!' wailed Laura in the hall. 'And, frankly, Mike, I can't imagine what surprise could *possibly* be worth . . .'

The kitchen was suddenly illuminated by a very bright light as headlights swept up the drive.

'Ah,' said George.

'About time,' said Alex, hastily serving up another portion of spicy vegetables and crinkly chicken. Rachel got a wine glass out and filled it with champagne. They settled themselves back at the table, fixed expressions of surprise and pleasure at the ready. George ran his hand through his hair nervously.

In the hall, Laura was still speaking to Mike, but now her voice sounded positively voluptuous. She was making funny cooing noises. Rachel peered round the door and saw Laura leaning against the wall, her face shining and her fingers clutching the stair rods. 'Yes, I'm waiting, rabbit,' she said.

Boots sounded in the hall and Mike's voice called out, 'Hi, honey, I'm home!' Everyone laughed in a sit-com manner and George and John got up, ready to administer the Blokes' Hug. Rachel pushed her chair back and picked up the glass of champagne to offer him, blowing airkisses first for Alex, who had snatched up John's discarded camera.

A cool draught of air rushed into the room as Mike kicked the door open. He had to kick it open as both hands were full – one was clutching a battered bunch of service-station chrysanthemums and a bottle of Pimms and the other was wrapped firmly around the shoulders of Caroline, who was creaselessly attired in a white Bianca Jagger trouser suit and a pair of Gucci shades, which she now pushed onto the top of her head. Rachel numbly identified this as a courtesy. Caroline did not look as though she removed her shades for just anyone these days.

She projected effortlessly into the stunned vacuum.

'Oh, look!' she carolled, in what might have been a parody of a bad actress. 'Fizz and cameras! My *favourites*!' She accepted the glass from Rachel's unresisting fingers and waved at Alex for the camera. Mike grinned.

There was a clunk from the hall, which sounded like a phone being dropped.

chapter nineteen

Fin was woken by the screeching of his mobile phone.

Trying to dig it out of his bag, he found that although his mind was just about working, the rest of his body was still very much asleep and those few bits able to bend were protesting hard about spending the night cramped into an unnatural position on the back seat of his Golf, a back seat that he was sharing with quite a lot of equipment – lights and reflectors left over from the job he'd been doing before Dan had summoned him. All of which were long, sharp and expensive to replace.

He winced and pulled up the aerial.

'Hello?'

'Hey, Fin!'

'Dan,' groaned Finlay. 'Where the hell are you?'

He rubbed the small of his back which was aching violently and pulled a film canister out of his rucked-up jumper.

'I'm calling from a hotel, of course. The, er, Royal

Lakeland, according to the paper napkins. Just about to have some breakfast, actually. You're not still at the house?'

'Yes, I bloody well am, you bastard. I take it you lost her?' Fin threw the canister out into the hedge.

'Yeah. Look, Fin, when I said watch Marvin's house, I didn't necessarily mean all night.'

The signal was breaking up in the hills where Fin was parked, but he thought he heard Dan put in his breakfast order and it made his stomach rumble.

'Dan, I've been here all bloody night and no one has come in or out. You haven't even told me what I should be looking for.' Fin reached out and flipped open the glove compartment where he thought he might have stored an emergency Mars bar. It was empty and his stomach protested. Rachel must have eaten it. 'I mean, will he be in his own car?'

'Let's just say that you might want to keep an eye out for a black Porsche, OK?'

'Marvin or Margery?'

'Marvin.'

'Dan, I'm not staying here to wait for a car I don't even recognise—'

'How many Porsches can there be in this place? I have never *seen* so many Austin Marinas still on the road! And they're the boy racers!' said Dan, incredulity bringing his voice rather above his normal covert level.

'I'm coming to you for breakfast,' continued Fin regardless. 'There's no point doing this unless I've got a radio – the reception's crap up here – and I want to know exactly what's going on before I start chasing random punters around the Lakes. And as you obviously won't tell me over the phone, I'll have to come to you. Order me a full English, please.'

Before Dan could argue, Fin snapped his phone off and

got out of the car to stretch his long legs out. He was a big lad, with strong shoulders from carrying camera bags around, and a solid tum from snatched lunches of cappuccinos and crisps. The car smelled doggy compared to the clean fresh air of the hillside and he wondered how Humpty was getting on with Rachel. He would have loved a run up here, barking and dribbling at the sheep, rolling in the sheep shit.

Fin took in a deep breath of the early morning air, still soft before the heat of the day, and stretched his arms above his head. His joints cracked with the effort. He hated mornings waking up without Rachel. There had been very few since they had met and moved in together. But from the first time he had woken to find her curled up against his back, all warm and yielding, it was as though he had suddenly found the other side of him, the part he'd felt was missing all his life. Now the thought of living without her was ridiculous, even if she did snore like a very small cow.

Rachel was behind all his best work; she was more supportive of what he did than anyone he knew, because she seemed to understand the peculiar risk and reward that went with living off creative ability. Fin was a very gifted photographer, and in his own modest way he knew it, but even after all the hundreds and thousands of films he'd sent to the lab, the chill of potential rejection still hovered each time he sent the contact sheets in to the picture editor. Rachel saw the skill but also the thin skin so necessary to his work. She always knew the right thing to say, even when it was something he didn't want to hear, and he was grateful.

But he tried to keep her separate from this kind of work. Not that there was anything glamorous or dangerous about sleeping out all night in a car, he thought ruefully. She said she didn't care what he did as long as he was happy with it –

he believed her. He'd tried to explain that it was the challenge of the planning, the coordination, the Mission: Impossible radio drops, that he enjoyed, not the hubristic snapping of *in flagrante* pop stars and footballers. She had just smiled and told him that he never needed to justify himself to her, as long as he stopped nagging her about promoting witless cosmetics at Dunleary & Bright.

Dan knew not to ask him too often and then only when he needed a Golf convoy and had a very good story. There had to be at least one use of the phrase, 'abuse of privilege', which Dan heard in his head, in Fin's lovely Irish tones, as 'ungentlemanly behaviour'. And, Fin couldn't deny it, the money was good, if it all came off. The shiny new contents of Dan's garage was a testament to that. Very tempting. TVRs do not have consciences about their roots. And Fin so wanted to make a nest for himself and Rachel, before they got married . . .

He mentally chided himself. *If* they got married. He knew he shouldn't tempt fate or seem to push her. Especially at the moment. Fin ran his hand over a scratchy chin. Whatever it was that was weighing her down, holding her back, he hoped she'd work it out this weekend. He had an instinct that it might be something to do with her friends from university, but he didn't want to pass judgement on a group of people he knew very little about. Even though he had seen them all in their underwear at various points in Rachel's photo albums. She should be working for Dan, not him.

Well, this would probably be the last time, he thought as he painfully folded himself back into the driver's seat. All he knew about this job was that he was looking for a black Porsche containing some media personality 'with a strong family profile' and a mystery companion. Neither had made an appearance at the Cumbrian retreat of the former and apparently Dan had lost the red MGF of the latter. A great start to the weekend.

Fin started the engine and put the radio on, hoping for something to make him feel human again. The radio tuned automatically to Radio Cumbria, which was playing 'The Night Has a Thousand Eyes'. He tried to find something else, but it stubbornly refused to tune to any other station. His stomach rumbled as he pulled out of the concealed passing place and at the thought of a full English breakfast, and with the road map open on the empty passenger seat, Fin roared off to Bassenthwaite.

chapter twenty

Rachel woke sweating at eight o'clock in the morning. She'd been having her college nightmare again.

In the year since she had last had it, she had more or less forgotten how much it scared her. In the dream she was punting down the Cam on her own, lying on her back in the punt, watching the sunlight flicker through the overhanging willows and leafy trees. The water was green and very quiet and she could feel the light playing on her closed eyes. She felt happy, like the swans floating serenely past her in an escort.

But the farther she went downstream, the darker it became and when she opened her eyes, all the daylight had gone, and a strangely dusky evening had fallen. She floated past the college and saw her friends on the Backs, having a picnic in broad daylight, Laura in a flowery dress, sitting with Mike's head in her lap, George in his chinos, Alex in her white rowing vest, black hair plaited down her back, John with a knotted hanky on his head. In the dream Rachel thought she could see herself sitting with them, but before she could look properly the punt had swept her past them and when she called and waved, they stared through her to the other bank.

Then, without knowing why, she always began to panic, knowing somehow that the punt was being punted to the Rollers, down by The Anchor, where the punts have to be dragged up to carry on up to Grantchester. But the Rollers have changed to Niagara Falls, from *Niagara* with Marilyn Monroe, and she can't stop the punt and when she turns to tell the punter to stop, when she twists round and sees how choppy the water has become, she sees that it is Caroline punting her, wearing the red ballgown Marilyn wears to sing 'Diamonds Are a Girl's Best Friend' and laughing like—

But sometimes, when Rachel turns round in her dream, clutching the sides of the rocking boat, she sees herself furiously punting, wearing Kim Novak's neat grey suit from *Vertigo*, her blond hair scraped into a glossy whorl at the back of her head, and these are the truly nightmarish nights. There are waves on the river and the boat is going to overturn and Rachel's mind fills with panic, nausea grips her stomach and all she can think is: 'I can't get the suit wet', even though she is still the one in the punt . . .

As soon as she opened her eyes wide, to try to push the dream back into the night, Rachel realised that she still felt sick. The nausea obviously wasn't a new feature. It was morning sickness.

Stumbling across the landing in her pyjamas, she almost fell across George, cocooned in a sleeping bag. In the absence of a spare mattress, he was sleeping on a collection of Inigo Aikin-Rose's walking jumpers and even in repose, backache was written all over his face.

Caroline, of course, was sleeping on the comfy sofa in the

sitting room. Her arrival had added another dimension to the bed negotiations: Mike and Laura still kept the double bed, Rachel and Alex hung on to the twin room only because Rachel had gone to bed first, soon after the plates had been cleared, pleading a headache – after Caroline's entrance, no one sought to dissuade her or even disbelieve the excuse. Alex had come up soon after to check she was OK and, hearing Caroline's voice floating up the stairs, informing the rest that she had been diagnosed by a New York reflexologist as having sensitive discs, the pair of them tactically changed for bed, before Laura could take pity on Caroline's spine and turf one of them out.

Sadly for John, his alleged back problems were no match for Caroline's and she got the soft white sofa with practically all the cushions, except for those he snatched and carried, in high dudgeon, to his place in the kitchen next to the Aga. That he had to share this with Humpty, already ensconced in a cardboard box provided by Laura, made him grumble vociferously until she offered to make warm drinks for everyone and he was quelled with a milky Ovaltine.

And George, the gentleman, had to sleep in the only place left – the landing between the double and twin rooms. He offered to do this with such perfectly judged resignation that only Rachel second-guessed the hidden conveniences of his choice. And she said nothing but smiled privately to herself.

Fortunately, George didn't wake up as she stumbled past and Rachel made it to the bathroom with her hand pressed over her mouth, locked the door and stuffed some loo roll into the bowl to muffle the sound of the splashing. An old trick. No hangover or stomach bug could ever compare with this, she thought. I will never complain about either again ever, God, if you make this stop. I get the point, OK? I've had the tests done, I've seen the doctor and very soon, I promise, I will work out how to discuss this with my boyfriend. Once I've come to terms with it myself. Or are you trying to remind me?

The bouts of nausea had proved a very good means of focusing her mind on the situation. Rachel had spent the night flitting queasily back and forth between various scenarios, like a low-attention-span teenager with a remote control and cable television. And now, with Caroline making her appearance – a cross between the Wicked Fairy turning up at Sleeping Beauty's christening and Joan Collins opening the Harrods Sale – it wasn't just her own problems she was channel-surfing. Scenes of Caroline clasping Mike to her suspiciously increased bosom, Laura weeping into her flaky pastry, her own inability to shriek out her festering grievances, filled her head.

Fucking Caroline. Rachel gripped the bowl as another lurch of sickness ran through her, but there was nothing left. Fresh air, she thought shakily. Get out of the house. Get some food for Humpty. Yes. Clothes. Village shop. Each thought was abbreviated so as not to interrupt it with sickness.

Gently she stood up. The house was silent. There was a funny house-party feeling of uncertainty as to when people should be up and about. Rachel imagined they were waiting for Laura's lead, but given the events of last night she wasn't sure when that would be. Would she wake them if she flushed the loo? The bowl looked like something from a summer festival. Rachel took a deep breath and flushed it, watching the evidence disappear, accompanied by a series of mechanical clanks and gushing.

She walked gingerly back to her room, feeling light-headed. George was no longer on his mattress of jumpers but there was a big lump of duvet on Alex's bed, which she did not stop to examine. Rachel pulled her overnight bag off the chair and took it downstairs, pausing only to make a few token 'George' bulges under his covers outside, in case anyone should notice he was sleeping elsewhere.

Humpty was more than ready for a walk when she peered into the kitchen. The resonant snoring coming from John's sleeping bag was quite unbelievable. Rachel picked up the camcorder from the table and zoomed in on John's half-open mouth, adding into the microphone, 'It is very rare for a warthog to be found so far from its natural surroundings, yet our bristly friend is clearly enjoying his northern vacation,' panning to a pile of crumbs and four discarded paper muffin cases. She zoomed in on the lurid cover of *Amateur Photographer* next to the sleeping bag for good measure.

The zoom action made her feel ill again and, taking the camcorder with her, she slipped Humpty's lead on to his collar and let herself out into the dazzling morning.

Upstairs, Laura was lying wide awake with her eyes shut and a serene expression of peaceful slumber playing on her face. Inside she was seething.

She loved Mike. Everyone knew how much she loved Mike and had loved him ever since they'd met. And, yes, she'd say she trusted him, even in extreme circumstances like last night. Not every bride-to-be would believe her fiancé when he explains that he is five hours late for their engagement party because he has had to detour via Manchester to collect the bride's glamorous best friend who just happens to have flown in from New York as a surprise. And of course the long journey has made the fiancé look thoroughly ruffled yet strangely pleased with himself while the best friend is spotless.

Mike's snoring began again – a snuffling intake of breath which, in Laura's experience, presaged greater things. She jabbed him irritably with her elbow.

And everyone knew how much she loved Caroline, too. I mean, how wonderful of her to have gone to all the bother and expense of flying in to be with them. All the way from New York, just for her weekend party. Just like her to have done it as a surprise. It had been a little bit awkward re-arranging the sleeping situation and Rachel had looked a bit piqued when she arrived, but Caroline wasn't the sort of person who quibbled about the small things. And the cottage itself. That was so sweet of her to organise in the first place. No, she wouldn't hear it said that Caroline was thoughtless.

Laura had almost platituded herself out of her bad mood when she began to imagine Mike's drive up from London. At what point had the crease-free Caroline got in? Had she changed before she arrived at the cottage? She was the sort of person who would do that. Laura wished that she'd changed for supper, or at least taken off those ridiculous slippers of Alex's. What had she been wearing, for God's sake? Some comfy old cords and a loose cotton shirt that she thought looked 'country casual' at the time. She wondered what Mike had said about her to Caroline. What had Caroline said to him? What things about the wedding had they discussed? She hoped that Mike hadn't ploughed through all the bridesmaid problems with Caroline. A grumpy mood settled on her again.

Mike's snuffling turned into a kind of drilling noise.

'Oh, for God's sake!' said Laura theatrically, and swung herself out of bed. 'Do I have to listen to this for the next fifty years?' There was no response from Mike. Laura muttered darkly about laser surgery and found her own slippers, placed neatly together under the bed. Out of instinctive concern for Mike, she did not wrench open the curtains to let the morning sun flood in, as she had fondly imagined herself doing whilst cooped up on the train journey, but picked up her dressing gown and stumped downstairs. Breakfast would need to be started.

To her surprise, Alex and George were already at the pine table, buttering toast. John was propping himself up on his elbow, still in his sleeping bag.

'Morning, Laura,' said Alex. 'Tea's in the pot if you want it, or you could be like George and insist on waiting for the kettle to boil on the Aga for some coffee.'

'Oh,' said Laura. 'I didn't realise you'd be up. Both of you,' she added.

'It's such a lovely day, I couldn't wait to be up and about. Best part of the morning. I was just about to bring a cup of tea up for you and Mike, actually.'

'Against my advice,' murmured George into his toast.

Laura felt inexplicably put out by this.

'Would anyone like an English breakfast?' she asked. 'George? There's all the bits in the fridge, won't take me a moment.'

'If it's not too much trouble, Laura,' said George politely. 'I'm sure Alex can make something while you get dressed. It's your weekend after all.'

'No, no,' said Laura, 'that's what hostesses are for.'

'Practising for married life already, eh? Keeping the old man's strength up, eh?' gurgled John. 'Jolly good.'

Laura smiled indulgently at him. 'Have you been fed yet, John?'

'Count me in,' he said, 'especially if it's good local tuck. Can't beat a nice bit of black pudding.'

'I don't know how you can eat all that,' said Alex, as Laura pulled one greaseproof paper package after another out and scraped some dripping into the frying pan. 'On a day like this as well. It's going to be another scorcher, according to the papers.'

'Have you been out?' said Laura.

'Yes,' George said drily. 'It turns out that if we'd gone the other way out of the lane last night we would have found a village shop in about five minutes.'

So, thought Alex, there's that excuse blown, thanks George. No more 'nipping out to Gosforth to get some eggs' and indulging in some roadside passion for *us*. God, if only there were some consistency to his moral rectitude stances.

She was feeling a little more appeased than she had done last night, when after driving back in a swollen state of mutual frustration only to be thrust into the Caroline Cox experience, she had been forced to stake her claim on a decent bed at the ridiculous hour of half eleven. This had not been the plan. Alex had been banking on Mike and Laura retiring early in a sickly manner, Rachel crashing out with a book, John spending the evening retuning the TV, so she and George could get pleasantly pissed with the case of Cabernet Sauvignon he had brought as a present, followed by a couple of erotic hours in the garden, looking up at the stars. Or at least *she* intended to be looking up at the stars.

As it was, once Rachel disappeared in the morning, George had discreetly shared her duvet for a bit, but uncertain of the movements of the rest of the house, it had all been rather nervous. And although George apparently got off on near-death scenarios involving her driving his brand-new car, his capacity for arousal in a house full of pathologically nosy friends was minimal.

Alex munched her toast contemplatively and tried not to think about the amount of money she wouldn't be making in the shop this weekend.

'I said, fried egg for you, Alex?' repeated Laura, fish slice aloft.

'Er, no thank you, Laura. Can I put some music on?'

'I'll do it,' said Laura, leaning over to the yellow radio on the window sill. It was tuned to Radio Cumbria, which was playing 'Feels Like I'm in Love' by Kelly Marie.

'Oooh, I haven't heard this since I was at dancing lessons!' she said happily. 'Ballet, tap and modern. This was the modern bit.' She made window-cleaning circles with her hands in the air, in what might have been her old routine.

'Laura, is my bag in here? I've got a present for you,' asked Alex.

'No, I moved it into the sitting room,' said George.

'I don't think Caroline will be up yet,' said Laura, now making one potato, two potato movements with her fists in time to the music. 'And we don't want to wake her. She must be terribly jet-lagged.'

'Didn't look very jet-lagged when she came in last night,' said John through a mouthful of fried-egg sandwich. 'I'm always *todally* zoned when I come back from the States. Three times this year, too.'

George raised his eyebrow. Alex let it pass, although Laura did permit herself a quick rhythmic seethe, bearing in mind the size of her office and travel perks in relation to the quality of *her* degree.

The kitchen door swung open. Caroline stood framed in the doorway and stifled a yawn. She was wearing a silky wrap, trimmed at the wrists with white marabou feathers and a pair of white silk pyjamas. Despite the dramatic yawn, she looked as though she had managed to brush her hair and wash her face.

'What time is it?' she asked sleepily. 'I thought I could smell cooking and didn't want to hold the rest of you back from breakfast. You know, if you were waiting for me.'

Laura froze in mid-gyration and immediately began bustling about, laying another place for Caroline at the table. 'No, I was just about to dish up. What would you like?' She suddenly felt very matronly in her tartan dressing gown, which covered a pair of cotton pyjamas decorated with Scotty dogs.

'Oh, an egg-white omelette will do for me,' said Caroline airily. 'It's OK, Laura, I'll make it. You know, now I've said I'm a hundred and twenty pounds in *Spotlight*, I have to stick to it somehow!'

Egg-white omelettes, thought Alex. And George thought she was bad making scrambled eggs with one egg.

Laura put down heaped plates of fried breakfast in front of George and on a spare placemat. 'Everyone eats at the table in this house!' she said, half-jokingly, to John.

'You might want to put on my jumper,' said George in a warning tone, as John emerged from his sleeping bag, clad only in a pair of Bart Simpson boxer shorts, the bagginess of which only served to emphasise the improbable tanned length of his legs.

'Yeah, right. Is there any brown sauce?' He poked enthusiastically at his fried egg with a piece of toast.

'Well, I'll just go upstairs and get dressed,' said Laura to no one in particular. 'You can manage if anyone wants anything more to eat?'

'Yes, Laura,' said Alex. 'Just about.'

Laura pulled her dressing gown tightly around her and scuttled up the stairs, wondering what on earth she'd brought with her that could compete with white marabou feathers.

A slightly strained silence fell on the kitchen. Caroline stood at the work surface separating eggs into two Denbyware mugs. She transferred the whites to another bowl and began whisking. The marabou fluffed up around her wrists like the feathers on Ginger Rogers' frock.

'What are the plans for the day?' asked Alex, suddenly aware of the noise she was making chewing her muesli.

George carried on cutting his egg into uniform sunburst slices. 'I don't know what Laura has planned. All she said last night was that she wanted to relax and enjoy the scenery.'

'Mike was up for a bit of a walk, he said to me,' put in John. 'Bit of a Lads' Hike. You on for that, George, mate? Bit of a trekster?'

'Er, yes,' said George. 'Do you think the girls are on for that? Alex?'

'Well, I didn't bring my walking boots, but there are some trainers in the car,' said Alex slowly, unwilling to commit herself to what could be an epic trek. 'And Rachel has brought some very nice fleeces and ski hats, although by all accounts it's going to be thirty degrees . . .'

Outside the sun was already heating up the sky and the lake was shimmering invitingly. There was a pair of fluorescent windsurf sails darting about, then splashing out of sight as the breeze dropped and fell.

'How about you, Caro?' asked John heartily. 'Fancy a little run up Yewbarrow?'

Caroline turned from the Aga, where she was now

simmering her egg whites in a pan with no fat. It was a tricky operation and one that evidently required a lot of bowls. Alex hoped that she would not be roped into washing up and wondered if she should do some token cooking now while there was still time to foist the entire sinkful on to the lads.

'Oh, I don't know!' she said with a laugh. 'Power walking is the new big thing, but I don't know if I've got the right boots, either.' She gave her egg whites a flip and added, 'I do think these mountains are so inspiring, though. It's so easy to see how Wordsworth and Coleridge were so intoxicated by them.'

'And *on* them, from what I've read,' said Alex. 'Do you want to hear the one thing I learned about the Romantic Poets?' she added, as John's interest pricked up. 'They decided to celebrate the Battle of Waterloo up on Skiddaw by carting a cask of gin up – well, they got some servants to do the carting, I imagine – and then while Wordsworth was poncing about in a big velvet cloak or similar, he knocked the boiling water over so they had to drink it neat. As you do. And it wasn't just the daffodils that were dancing by the end of the evening.' Alex put a finger to her nose and frowned. 'I think there's a punchline but I've forgotten.'

'And you say geography is a non-subject,' said John.

'Oh, but so *romantic*,' cooed Caroline, bringing her omelette to the table. 'Midnight revelling. Don't you feel that you can be so much *freer* up there? I'm hoping that when the big-screen version of *Maid of Buttermere* gets beyond the drawing-board, there might be something there for me. I see myself as a free spirit, naked-on-the-mountains type.' She lifted a meagre forkful of egg to her lips. Alex thought it looked like stir-fried phlegm.

'Is that meant to be good for you?' she asked.

Caroline rolled her eyes enthusiastically. 'Oh yes. Definitely. It's all I ever have for breakfast and sometimes for lunch too if I have a casting. New York is so much more geared towards a low-fat life-style than London.' She looked askance at George's swimming plate. 'I'm surprised people live beyond their twenties up here.'

Laura's feet could be heard coming back down the stairs, accompanied by another, less enthusiastic pair. She bounced in, Mike shuffling behind her, waving his hand in response to the cheery greetings.

'What you need, mate, is a good breath of fresh air,' said John, pointing with his fork. 'That'll have you up and raring to go in no time.'

'Oh, that's right,' said George mildly. 'Spend three hours flogging up a mountain to re-energise yourself. That's logical.'

Laura looked pained. 'But the whole point of this weekend is that we do things together. Like we used to.'

'Well, what did you have in mind?' asked George, ever keen to bail out the hostess.

Laura was floundering for an answer when the front door opened and the skittering of claws became audible in the hall.

'You've covered me in sheep shit, you little bugger,' laughed Rachel's voice in the bootroom. 'Don't lick me! Get *off* me! Oh my God, Hump, get off Laura's coat! Have you no respect for labels?'

Laura turned white. Alex prayed silently that it *was* Laura's coat and not Caroline's.

Humpty bounced barking in to the kitchen. He was indeed covered in sheep shit. His tongue was hanging out happily from the exertion of the walk and he seemed to be grinning. 'Heel!' bellowed Rachel from the bootroom. Humpty clumsily did an about turn, tail wagging furiously, and Laura began breathing again.

'Phoooo-war!' said John, holding his nose.

Rachel came in, looking apologetic. 'Sorry, it's what bassets do, apparently. See shit, roll in it. And he was a model of good behaviour until then,' she said, waving the camcorder. John gave her a black glare and she handed it over.

As she straightened up and took in the whole room, Rachel was horrified to feel the old panic spread through her stomach again. A tremendous sense of isolation gripped her: all of them together, her on her own. For a spinning second she was back in her college nightmare, imagining them all like this, ranged against her in silence, even Alex and George, not seeing her. And she was liberally smeared in sheep shit – though that had not been part of the nightmare. Caroline was in white, looking as if butter wouldn't melt in her mouth, sitting there in the middle, her eyebrow raised in a silent-movie challenge. Rachel put her hand out to the work surface to balance.

'Good walk?' asked Alex, signalling concern with her eyebrows. She looks just like George, thought Rachel. The language of eyebrows.

'Wonderful,' she said dazedly, 'it's a beautiful day outside.'

No one moved. Rachel dragged up all her self-control and managed a casual smile. 'Do you think Inigo Aikin-Rose has such a thing as a high-pressure hose for cleaning up dogs?' She made herself look at Caroline and thought of Fin. I have a man who loves me, I have a man who loves me, I am going to clean up the dog of the man who loves me, she thought fiercely, and felt marginally better.

'I'll come and help you scrub him down.' Alex pushed back her chair and looked about for her shoes.

Don't let her chase you out, don't let her chase you out, thought Rachel as her nerve began to waver. She tried to fill her mind with blocks of positive sentences, allowing no space for other thoughts to creep between. All she wanted to do was to run out, run away, be swept out by the physical compulsion gripping her. She felt that the hand hanging on to the work surface was the only thing holding her in. Silence made the seconds pass like treacle, as Alex looked for her shoes. Typically, no one else was brave enough to break it. They simply sat with their eyes trained expectantly on her. Rachel could hear her heart beating.

Had it been so agonising when Caroline had joined their suddenly sober table last night? She didn't remember speaking at all until she went to bed, just adding her voice into general agreements, so it wouldn't look as though she were sulking in silence. Rachel concentrated on breathing, horrified at the physical reaction her tension was creating. *What are you scared of?* One of the last things Fin had said to her in the car came back to her: 'You can't run away from things if you know what they are.'

Alex was pushing her gently in the small of her back. Rachel swallowed and her mouth tasted foul. Still she smiled at Laura, who was sitting next to Caroline – near enough for anyone to think her smile was all-encompassing – and said, 'We can use the washing machine, can't we?'

Laura nodded, eager to leap into the now broken silence. 'Yes, of course—' Her brow puckered and she turned to Caroline. 'You don't think Inigo would mind, do you?'

Caroline shook her mane of hair dismissively. 'Oh no, rather that than have filthy carpets, any time. Seagrass is so practical. I suppose country people are rather more relaxed about . . . country smells. No,' she flashed a toothy smile up at Rachel, 'go ahead. That's what it's there for.'

Rachel managed a twisted smile in return and turned to leave, prising off her trainers on the step down. In the hall, Alex clapped her hands to her cheeks in her Munch scream and gave Rachel a hug, without saying anything. They untied a frisky and smelly Humpty from his place of safety in the bootroom.

'What a good job for Rachel that she was wearing her old clothes,' said Caroline to Laura in a concerned tone, just loud enough for Rachel to hear on her way out. 'I wonder if anything of mine would fit her to borrow?'

Alex listened, scowling, and whispered to Rachel, 'Is that meant to be thoughtful?'

'There's bound to be a punchline.'

'No,' said Caroline, a fraction louder than before, presumably to compensate for their walking farther away, 'you're right, Laura. And I don't know if anything would be quite big enough. What a shame.'

Alex caught her breath and looked about to storm back in, but Rachel just rolled her eyes and put her hand on her friend's brown arm.

'Best eaten cold, Alex.' She was shivering inside.

chapter twenty-one

'What do you mean, you're "off out"?' said Laura, looking up from the table, where, for want of something communal to do, she had brought Rachel's photo albums. The heavily ketchuped remains of breakfast lay around her.

Mike, George and John stood by the door with their boots in their hands, looking sheepish. George had a small rucksack over his shoulder – Alex's trendy backpack – packed with water and apples and his mobile phone. All the modern Boy Scout essentials.

'We're off for a Lads' Hike, darling,' said Mike. 'We did offer, but none of you wanted to come, so we'll leave you to the tea and gossip and be back later.'

'For more food, I suppose,' purred Caroline. 'Well, boys will be boys.'

'But what about the washing-up?' wailed Laura. Even career domesticity had its limits.

Mike, George and John looked at the table, piled-up sink and gungy work surfaces as if for the first time.

'Oh, leave it and we'll do it when we get back,' said John.

'Yes, leave the boys to go off hiking,' said Caroline, who had about as much intention of doing the washing up as John had.

'Oh no you don't!' said Laura. 'That's very cunning, but you forget how long I've been living with Mike now. Translated, that means "I know you won't be able to bear looking at that congealing plate with the beans running into the gristle and ketchup, so eventually you'll wash it up and once you've done one you'll do the lot and put the pans on to soak".' She looked at all three sarcastically. 'I suppose you intend to be out long enough for me to get sick of looking at soaking frying pans?'

Caroline laughed her tinkly laugh and waved them out. 'Off you go, quickly, before she gets her rolling pin out!'

They took this as their cue to go and clattered out, thankfully, into the sunshine.

'Have you got a map, George?' asked Mike.

'Oh damn,' said George. 'It's in my car and the keys are inside.'

He knew that going back inside would be fatal. Laura's plans could only be slipped once.

'Don't worry, I think there's an Ordnance Survey one in my glove compartment.' Mike beeped his car open and emerged with map, compass and Kendal Mint Cake. Laura flung open the kitchen window and, leaning out, shouted, 'Mike! Mike! Don't forget your sunscreen! All of you!' and shut the window with a slam.

'That's my girl,' said Mike proudly.

John adjusted the floppy brim of his cricket hat. 'So, off we go!' he said, marching in the direction of the fell. 'Our last hike as fellow singletons. Shall we sing?' And he embarked on the first of many rugby songs he and Mike knew off by heart and George didn't, but could easily guess the words to.

Behind the house, Alex and Rachel had hosed much of the slime off Humpty and then Alex hosed Rachel. Humpty had seen the whole exercise as a complete hoot and was barking and wobbling his ears in uproarious dog laughter.

'That's the trouble,' said Rachel, ruefully shaking her hair dry. 'It's so much fun that he can't wait to do it all over again.'

'I know,' said Alex. 'Blokes, eh?'

The day was warming up nicely and Rachel's blond hair was drying into ringlets. She ran her fingers through them distractedly, tugging as they twisted into knots.

'Leave them, they're sweet.'

Flapping her hands at Alex, Rachel sat down on a rock and gazed towards the house. The white walls were coming alive in the sun, gleaming ivy trails picked out against the stones. Behind them rose the fells, purple and green, necklaced with dry-stone walls. Rachel filled her lungs with the sharp, clean air and expelled it slowly.

'Why has she come?'

Alex threw a stick for the dog, who looked quizzical and then reluctantly loped after it. 'You don't believe this Mike thing?'

'No, I don't now I've seen them together. I don't get the right feeling about it. They don't look . . . innocent enough.'

'Irish logic.'

'No, I mean, if Caroline was leading Mike astray, she would hardly have arrived with him.'

'Unless it was to make Laura jealous.'

Rachel swished some grass with a twig. 'OK, put it like this: if Mike were shagging Caroline, he wouldn't arrive with her. Mike's not up to double bluffing. And he would be making far more effort to appear innocent of anything he was up to.'

'And he would have told George by now.'

'Who would have sworn not to tell a soul and then told you.'

'Hmm,' said Alex, wondering exactly how much George would tell her. 'Have you remembered to put some suncream on? I've never seen anyone burn so fast.' She gripped Rachel's soft upper arm gently and let go. Three finger marks stood out, whiter against the freckly cream of Rachel's skin. 'See? Little china doll.'

Rachel smiled and laughed softly. 'Thanks, Mum. Do you remember all those summers on the Backs? Going out to sunbathe and revise and you lasting all afternoon—'

'—while you had to go and sit in the library after ten minutes? Oh, yes. The only person I've ever known to get in a foul mood when the sun comes out.'

Humpty returned with the stick and dropped it at Rachel's feet, opening his floppy mouth in a dribbly pant. She bent and stroked his dangling ears. 'Poor Hump. We walked all the way for breakfast and you still haven't been fed.'

Rachel picked up the carrier bag with the dog food and bananas in it. 'The woman in the shop knew I was from the cottage as soon as I picked up the bottle of fizzy mineral water. I had to make small talk about Wastwater for nearly twenty minutes before she believed I wasn't a soft southerner.'

'Yeah, sorry. I think George is to blame for that one.'

'They have got Pimms in that shop, you know.'

'Really?'

'It's with the mixers . . .'

They walked slowly over the rough grass towards the house. Rachel lingered by the door, leaning with her back on the wall, staring up at the mountains rising behind. She looked lost, Alex thought, her pale face peculiarly fragile, bleached out by the direct sun bouncing off it. It must be hard for her, seeing Caroline here like this, after she'd seemed so happy before dinner. It dawned on Alex that she had been expecting a collapse that hadn't come.

'But there is *something* going on,' said Rachel, out of nowhere. 'It's this weather, like that last summer we had at college. It's oppressive, this heat.' She shook her head, running her fingers through her cherub curls one more time and straightening her back. She pulled herself up like a puppet and marched into the house.

Maybe not so fragile, thought Alex, following with Humpty waddling at her heels.

In the kitchen, Laura was systematically scraping and piling dishes into separate consignments, in order of washing priority: glasses, cups, cutlery, plates and pans.

'I don't know how boys can just walk off and *leave* things,' she was saying to Caroline, who was flicking through her Filofax, a tea towel hung over a shoulder in a token way. She had evidently got dressed once the boys had left and had easily trumped Laura's duck-egg blue cotton twinset and check Capri pants with a cream linen dress and devoré scarf.

'I mean, you can be sitting watching television after a perfectly good meal that you've spent an hour cooking and they'll bring in crisps and biscuits – which they'll put in bowls to soften you up, of course – and then you come down in the morning and not only is the sink full of dishes from the meal, but the sitting room is full of dirty plates, milk bottles and flat Coke! I tell Mike every time, but I don't think he realises how *upset* it makes me . . .'

Laura tied her neat blond bob out of her eyes with a scrunchie. Caroline's hair was curling down her back in a loosely tied plait, leaving tendrils around her little ears.

Laura sighed to herself and pulled on the rubber gloves, rather like a vet about to perform an unpleasant examination. She began running hot water into the big stone sink.

Rachel popped her head round the door and deliberately looked in the direction of the monologue, not knowing where Caroline might be lurking in the kitchen, but assuming it wouldn't be by the sink.

'Laura, do you have a big bowl I could use for feeding Humpty? I'll put it in the hall with the water dish. He doesn't make a mess.'

This last detail was a blatant lie – Humpty was a typical basset and a real trougher. However, she wasn't going to let Caroline think her dog was anything less than charming. And with luck, Caroline might tread in some of it.

Laura fiddled around under the sink and came out with a brown earthenware bowl. Caroline opened her mouth to say something and then changed her mind.

'Ta,' said Rachel and disappeared round the door again. There was the sound of excited barking in the bootroom.

Laura looked at the pile of greasy plates with a sinking stomach and forced herself to ask Caroline to help directly. She might be angry with her, but there was something about Caroline that made that kind of request difficult. Possibly the manicure that she kept touching up. Laura had similar problems ringing in sick to work – she simply couldn't face the idea of resistance and hated herself for crumbling.

'Caroline, could you give me a hand, please?' asked Laura in her sweetest tone.

Caroline gave a slight shrug of surprise and closed her Filofax. She pushed her hair back with her hand, a nervous gesture she'd always had, but one that, with her thicker, fuller hair, now looked very elegant and almost Jane Seymourish.

'Of course,' she said. 'You should have mentioned it sooner. I'll have a scout around the house and see if there are any wine glasses left anywhere.' And she padded out of the room in her mules, taking her handbag and phone with her.

Once Caroline was safely out of earshot, Laura gave a *tsk* of irritation and aggressively squirted an overgenerous dollop of washing up liquid into the sink. It foamed titanically in the soft water.

Oh, come on, Laura, she said to herself. You should know what she's like by now. But she did, and somehow it wasn't good enough. She felt guilty at the thought at once. But, said a traitorous voice in her head, we're all meant to be doing things *together*! Everyone said they wanted to – it's not as though I'm forcing them!

Unlike Rachel (and increasingly, Alex), Laura wasn't given to internal discussions. As she slipped the glasses into the soapy water and carefully wiped the rims and insides, her mind went back to college. She was forever washing up in their set then, but it was fun. The dinner parties she and Caroline used to have, all the theatre people from other colleges, the writers and the debaters. That was when she had started learning her recipes, for those three-course meals. Borrowing Rachel and Alex's ovens, deciding, with the delicacy of diplomats, whom to invite, what to cook, when to have it . . .

'Do you want a hand with the drying, Laura?' asked Rachel, suddenly at her elbow. She and Alex stood there with tea towels in hand. Nice tea towels, noticed Laura. Proper Irish linen. She smiled. This was better. Nice communal drying up, with the radio, and then tea, as the sunshine streamed into the kitchen. Despite everything, Laura didn't ask for much.

Rachel turned up the radio, which George had turned down, and began singing along with the music. The wine glasses went quite quickly, Laura washing, Alex rinsing, Rachel drying.

'Oooh,' said Rachel, turning up the radio, 'I love this game. They had it on the radio when I used to stay with my gran in Ambleside. It's brilliant. You'll be good at this, Alex.'

Laura and Alex stared at the radio. The DJ was saying, 'I'm thinking of a tune, and the clue is . . . it's a city. If you think you've got the answer, ring us up on Carlisle 68484 and we'll see if you're right. And now a lovely tune for Millom Young Farmers, who are having a ceilidh tonight in the village hall.' And then he segued in to 'Saturday Night's Alright for Fighting'.

Laura was looking blank. 'Is it "Rotterdam" by the Beautiful South?'

Alex and Rachel were laughing uproariously. 'It could be *anything*, Laura! That's what's so brilliant about it,' gurgled Rachel. 'Don't you get it?'

Laura still looked blank. 'No. I don't get it. Is this a northerners' thing? It's a quiz, isn't it? What do you win?'

'Laura, it's like saying, "I've got a piece of string here in t'studio" and you have to ring in and guess what length it is. Don't you see?' said Alex.

'No, actually,' said Rachel, making her face straight, 'to be fair, it is usually "(Are You Going to) San Francisco".' She did the brackets with her hands in the air, an old in-joke from Divinyl. 'Or sometimes, if they're feeling racy, "New York, New York" by Frank Sinatra.'

'Ring in if you know the answer!' said Laura. 'Go on! If you tell them you've come up from London, they might give you a prize anyway! Go on, we'll listen to you on the radio! You can do a dedication for me and Mike!'

'Noooooo!' said Rachel, gurgling.

'And she's not from London, Laura Parker, she's a Mancunian. They eat her lot for breakfast up here!' said Alex.

'Well, you then!' said Laura, clearly excited by the thought of a mystery prize.

'Laura, do you know how many songs there are in the world with cities in them?' said Rachel. 'And there's a long history of bad feeling between the Cumbrians and the Yorkists. Why don't you phone in? The answer's bound to be "San Francisco", I promise you. You don't get anything later than 1982 on this show. It's for deaf grannies – everyone else is out at the rugby.'

'Oh . . . oh . . .' Laura wavered. Nobody knew her round here. And Rachel and Alex always seemed to make her do mad things.

'*Go on then.*'

They ran through to the hall, almost pushing each other through the door frame in their haste to get Laura to the phone before she changed her mind.

'Take the phone into the sitting room, so we don't get feedback from the kitchen radio,' said Rachel.

Alex gave her a close look. 'You've done this before, haven't you?'

Rachel shrugged. 'Did you never wonder where all my Radio Manchester mug trees came from?'

Laura was dialling the Radio Cumbria number on the heavy black phone. 'You can get these in London,' she observed. 'They cost about eighty pounds. I was going to get one for Mike last Christmas, but he said it wouldn't have direct dial for, I don't know, pizza and things . . . No one's answering . . . oh, hello!' She reverted to the telephone voice, as taught on the Legal Practice Course.

'I bet they don't get the Queen ringing in that often,' said Alex.

Rachel rolled her eyes. 'First time lucky too!'

Laura covered the mouthpiece with her hand and stage-whispered, 'There's someone called Betty before me and then I'm on!' She pulled an excited face and sat, ramrod straight, on the sofa.

Rachel and Alex ran through to the kitchen, ignoring Laura's frantic 'Come back! Come back!' hand gestures. Turning up the radio, they were just in time to hear Betty from Drigg incorrectly guess 'The Streets of London' by Ralph McTell.

'Never mind, pet,' the DJ was saying, 'no one goes away empty-handed, as you know, so if you stay on the line, Margaret will take your name and pop a totally exclusive BBC Radio Cumbria tea towel, as used by the lovely Val Armstrong herself' (a deep voice intoned 'oooh, cheeky!' in the background) 'to wing its way down to Drigg. What do you say to that, Betty?'

'Ta,' grunted an unimpressed-sounding Betty, who had clearly had designs on a BBC Radio Cumbria travel alarm clock.

'And good luck with that wallpapering, love,' he ran on

seamlessly, as Betty was cut off and Laura was put on. 'Now, who've we got here?'

'It's Laura from Chiswick,' came Laura's voice from the radio. She sounded positively regal. Alex was bent over with silent laughter.

'By 'eck, you're not from round here are you, love? Was it Keswick, you said you were in?'

'Go through and help her,' said Rachel, overcome with a sudden sense of duty. Alex looked reluctant. 'Go on,' said Rachel, 'God knows what she'll say otherwise.' Alex disappeared and Rachel leaned her elbows on the work surface, staring at the radio with a big smile on her face.

'Em, well, no, Chiswick in London, but I'm not in London at the moment, I'm in . . .' There was a pause and a muffled sound, like someone putting their hand over the receiver and desperately flicking through an address book. 'I'm ectually calling from Wasdale, near Gosfroth!' said Laura's voice, triumphantly, and then, with Alex's hissing audible in the background, added hastily, 'Er, *Gosforth*!'

Rachel heard Alex come out of the sitting room into the hall, shut the sitting room door and moan, 'Oh my God!' and then go back in again.

The DJ, who could evidently see mileage in this, was playing it deadpan. And you have to respect him for that, thought Rachel. 'So, *Laura*, I didn't think you were from round here with a name like that! Am I right in thinking that you're on holiday up in Gosfroth?'

'Yes, I am, I'm having an engagement party for some friends—' Oh, Laura, *stop*, thought Rachel, before you say something dreadful, like 'Cambridge University', and it would seem that Alex had had the same thought, because there was an almost imperceptible thud on the line and Laura went on, 'and we're having a great time.'

'Are you now? That's wonderful, Laura. Now, we're asking everyone today, what with it being a Cup final – who do you fancy then for the game this afternoon? Are you a Wath Brow Hornets girl?'

Get out of that, Laura, thought Rachel, smiling to herself, and went over to the kettle to make the tea. She would need it by the time she'd finished. Betty from Drigg had had the wallpaper for her front room discussed in infinite detail before they'd finally got round to her guess.

As she spooned the tea into the pot, out of the corner of her eye Rachel noticed the kitchen door being slowly pushed open. She held her body tense, knowing who it was before she saw and resisted the temptation to turn round; a moment later, Caroline slipped round the door into the kitchen. She crossed the floor in two quick steps, heading for the front door. Her soft leather mules didn't make a sound on the stone flags. When she saw Rachel at the sink, she stopped short and Rachel was forced to turn round and acknowledge her presence.

Caroline had her shades back on and she didn't lift them for Rachel, even though they were both indoors. Rachel gripped the handle of the kettle and focused on Caroline's receding chin. Like a hen looking down a bottle, as her mother had put it. She obviously hadn't got round to fixing that yet. Dispassionately, Rachel noticed that on her own and without an audience, Caroline was not as intimidating as she had been in her mind's eye. She tried to remember that Caroline was the sort of person who bought Detritus cosmetics on the strength of their advertising.

'I'm just going outside for a walk,' said Caroline, waving

her hand airily in the direction of 'outside'. 'I thought I might catch up with the boys, maybe.'

On the radio, Laura was still struggling politely with the complexities of local amateur rugby league, unaware of the small-scale drama in the kitchen and the further collapse of her plan 'to do things together'.

'Really?' said Rachel. 'Well, I wouldn't go too far in those shoes, Caroline, if I were you. There's a lot of sheep out there.'

Caroline laughed, a precise social laugh of about four syllables. 'Well, I have my mobile phone. I can always call the Mountain Rescue to come and get me in their helicopter if I get stuck. But I'm sure the boys would carry me down. I'm just a little thing, really. Mike could just pop me over his shoulder.'

Rachel noted that Caroline was fidgeting. No! Not Caroline nervous of her? What did she think she would do? Advance on her with slapping gloves at the ready? She stood firm, aware of her moral stance near the still piled-up sink of washing up.

'When will you be back? I don't know what Laura has planned.'

'I'll be back when I land. Whenever the boys said they would be back,' said Caroline, turning for the door before Rachel could ask any more. She heard Humpty barking as Caroline left and hoped that he had landed at least one wet paw on her linen dress. She couldn't really be going walking in that? Maybe she just fancied an hour floating about, absorbing whatever actressy vibes she was wittering on about last night. Rachel's feeling of relief that Caroline had gone submerged her feeling of foreboding. The problem had been taken out of her hands.

'. . . so, anyway, Laura, anyway, enough of all that, let's get round to the matter in hand, shall we?'

'Yes, absolutely!'

'I'm thinking of a song and the clue is, it's a city and the answer, Laura Parker from Chiswick, is . . .'

'"(Are You Going to) San Francisco"!'

'Eeeeh, what do we think, Chief Invigilator? Right, I think I'm going a bit deaf there, Laura pet, could you say that for me again?'

'I said, "Are you—" there was some muffled whispering and Rachel could hear Alex's voice hissing, 'Just *say* it, Laura!'

'Er, is it, um, "Show me the way to Amarillo"?'

Taped cheering broke out on the radio. 'Show me the way to Amarillo, I've been crying on to my pillow,' recited the DJ.

'Oooooh!' Laura's squeal of triumph almost threw the studio sound levels. 'What have I won?' she shrieked.

'By 'eck, I haven't heard that kind of noise since I were last at Cockermouth Livestock Market. You get to the point, you London lasses, don't you? Well, Laura Parker, or should I say, soon to be Laura Craig, you have won,' (taped trumpets) 'a Radio Cumbria travel alarm clock and key ring set!'

'Yesssssss!' This was clearly Alex. Laura had suddenly gone quiet.

'Can I make a dedication, please?' she piped up.

'If you're quick there.'

'OK, I'd like to dedicate this next record to Mike, my fiancé, and my friends, Alex, Rachel, George, John and especially Caroline!' said Laura breathlessly.

'Aaaah! Isn't that nice, eh? And specially for Laura, here's "It's My Party" by Lesley Gore!'

Rachel cringed in the kitchen, but consoled herself with the thought that Laura wouldn't notice the words.

While Laura was giving her details to the switchboard girl, Alex came in, waving her hands above her head like a football supporter.

'Well *done*,' said Rachel, and, nodding towards the radio, pulled a face of horror.

Alex returned her cringe. 'I know. Still, Laura would probably have requested it anyway, given a choice. No, it was an inspired guess, that Amarillo thing. Did Caroline hear the "Big shout to my mates the Wasdale Wrecking Posse"?'

'Hardly, since she legged it to catch up with the lads about ten minutes ago.'

'Nooooo!' Alex rolled her eyes. She nodded at the washing up. 'Want to make a start on the sink from hell and see if it helps pacify Laura when she finds out?'

Rachel pulled on Laura's discarded rubber gloves and began swishing at the cooling water.

'God, I can't believe it,' said Alex, drying off a plate. 'Did she change into a designer speed-walking outfit?'

'No, she was wearing that linen dress, a long devoré scarf and her shades. And a pair of white leather mules. Not what I would choose for shimmying up a fell, but what would I know? Anyway, one has to give the Mountain Rescue boys something to look at on the way down.'

Laura bounced in beaming. She tucked her bob behind her ears and gave Alex a hug from behind. 'Thank you!' she said. 'I promise I will come in to Divinyl on Monday and buy three records! Oh, *and* you're washing up! Should I get Caroline to help?' A frown creased her forehead.

'You'll have a job, Laura. She's decided to go walking with the boys,' said Alex, as cheerfully as she could. 'Still, I'm dying to hear all about the wedding plans and— Oh! I haven't given you my present!'

'Oooh! Me neither!' said Rachel. What was this like? Kindergarten bribery or what? Laura's face fell and lit up with transparent speed at the mention of presents.

'Oooh, you shouldn't have!' she said. 'But maybe we should finish the dishes . . .' She paused and dried a cereal bowl, picked up another, inspected it closely and slipped it back into the sink. Rachel held her tongue.

'I suppose it's good that Caroline wanted to go out with the boys,' mused Laura, opening a window to let in some air. 'It's *sort* of doing things together . . .' She was rather quiet, until Rachel asked her about her wedding list.

chapter twenty-two

Fin wiped his plate clean with a piece of toast in the Little Chef near Lindale, just off the A590. He hadn't realised how ravenous he was until the waitress had put the full English breakfast down in front of him about seven minutes ago.

Dan, skinny as a whippet, looked at him over the rim of a black coffee.

'I don't see why you couldn't just meet me at whatever hotel you were staying at,' complained Fin. 'All this chasing about.' He stuffed the bread in his mouth.

'There are people at hotels, and people notice things,' said Dan. 'I don't want us to be seen together near Marvin's place.'

Fin saw the logic in this. Dan was always several steps ahead of him, but then, in general, Fin's subjects tended to stay in one place while he photographed them, and Dan's were usually doing about eighty miles an hour.

Fin finished his last mouthful and said, in a covert whisper, 'So fill me in.'

'Right. You say you watched Marvin's place last night.'

'Right. No one. Nothing.'

'OK. Well, after I lost Margery, I went to the other place I thought Marvin might be this morning and there he was. I saw him getting into his car – black Carrera, blacked-out windows, et cetera, et cetera. OK. Can't miss it. It'll stand out like a pork pie at a bar mitzvah round here. Land of the Alpine bleeding Sunbeam.' Dan sipped his coffee. He could have been discussing the road works on the M6. 'So I am willing to bet you a full-on supper at the Anglesea Arms that by this evening, Marvin will be safely installed in his Lakeland Love Nest with our friend Margery. We're waiting up the road, they pop out for a bit of moonlight nookie, bang, bang, bang and that'll be the deposit on your very own love nest. No need to leave the car.'

Dan made a round 'sorted' sign with his fingers and leaned back in his chair. He winked at the waitress. 'Two more coffees over here? Thanks, love.'

'Look, Dan, we're not actually going to . . .' Fin was wrestling with his conscience. 'This isn't going to end up . . .'

Dan ran a hand through his curly hair and wrinkled his nose. He leaned forward and whispered confidentially. 'Fin, you would not believe who we are talking about here. I wouldn't have asked you to help me out if I thought you were going to go soft on me when it came down to it. Seriously, this one's worth too much to me. And I am telling you,' he prodded the table for emphasis, 'when you see who this is, the only thing stopping your jaw hitting the floor will be the Nikon round your neck.' He added, 'I tell you, mate, if Rachel saw this little lot, even she'd be snapping away like a pro.'

The coffees arrived. Dan grinned cheekily at the girl and said, 'Thanks, love.' In his leather jacket and combat trousers, he could have been a lorry driver like the others scattered around the Little Chef. The chirpy Cockney accent gave him away a bit, but he'd learned to blur it, just as he never washed his car, so it didn't stand out. The waitress took one look at Dan's sexy morning stubble and simpered her way back to the kitchens, swinging her hips a little too obviously – Dan's attention, alas, was elsewhere.

'Tell me who it is,' said Fin.

Dan pretended to consider, tapping one finger against his cheekbone, and then leaned forward, still grinning, to whisper in Fin's ear.

Fin's jaw dropped open and he narrowed his eyes incredulously. That *had* to be an impossibility. Just that morning there'd been a page five *Express* spread with Marvin (was that really the best codename Dan could come up with?) and his wife, outlining the secrets of a happy and healthy . . .

'No!' he said.

Dan raised his eyebrows and smirked.

'Who did you get this one off?' said Fin, still unable to believe what he'd just heard.

'Sources in the BBC,' said Dan mysteriously.

'But he was in the *Express* this morning, talking about porridge!'

'Don't believe everything you read in the papers, Finlay.'

'Bloody hell,' said Fin, stirring his coffee. 'The dirty old dog. I can't believe it! What a sod! And what about Margery?'

'Half his age. Goes like a train, from what I hear. Or, rather, from what he's been telling certain people.'

Fin was still shaking his head.

'Just goes to show,' said Dan, waving off the last drops of coffee from his spoon. 'What a man says in the privacy of the Groucho toilets can no longer be regarded as sacred. It's a hard world and no mistake.'

They sat and drank their coffee in silence for a few moments.

'So what's the plan?' asked Fin, draining his cup.

'Don't think they'll do much today,' said Dan. 'We might catch them unawares, but if they're out and about, they could be anywhere. And given Marvin's recent profile, I very much doubt that they'll be having a cream tea at Wordsworth's birthplace. Don't know about you, but I don't fancy running up and down mountains in this weather trying to find them.'

Fin nodded. It was already hot enough to make him wish he'd brought some shorts. 'Are you not roasted in those?' he said, nodding at Dan's multi-pocketed trousers.

'Nah,' said Dan. 'You get used to them, they're handy for films and stuff. Anyway, I reckon they'll head home about tea time, OK, so we should aim to be at Marvin's place about five, well out of sight, and see if we can't get something on a long lens. Wouldn't put it past him to suggest a bit of alfresco romping, what with his background.'

Fin agreed that this would indeed be more than likely. He wondered privately if this was something Rachel, with her outdoor background, might be on for.

'So, drink up,' said Dan.

'What for?' said Fin, startled out of his vision of Rachel in walking boots, reclining Lara Croft-esque on a rock.

'Well, I've never been up here,' said Dan. 'I might fancy a bit of culture.'

Fin looked incredulous. 'Yeah, *right*.'

'No, straight up. I've done all the recceing. You know where Marvin's place is. All you have to do is follow me.' Dan tapped Fin's forehead with the coffee spoon. 'I don't want some local Neighbourhood Watch reporting two out-of-town cars hanging about their secret celebrity's hide-away house.'

'Got you,' said Fin.

Dan tossed some coins on the saucer for a tip and pushed his chair back. 'Want to take my car for a spin? I've just had the suspension redone.'

'Yeah, and about time,' said Fin. 'You have no idea how to look after that car.'

Dan put an arm around Fin's shoulders as they walked out into the car park and resigned himself to a lecture about Golf care. Fin was a good snapper and a better driver. He was also a good mate. What more could he ask for? All in all, lectures on window seals were a small price to pay for what looked like being this year's rollover legover jackpot.

chapter twenty-three

George had thought he was quite fit, at the bottom of the hill. He played squash once a week at work. He used the company gym in the basement. And wasn't Alex always going on about how there was nothing on him? He held that particular thought close to his heart as he sweated and staggered up to where John was standing, staring out at the view, camcorder in hand. George looked up, sweat trickling down his red face, and saw that the camcorder was, in fact, more specifically aimed than that.

'Don't look at me, look at Mike,' he gasped with the last of his available breath, covering his face with one hand and pointing downhill with the other.

A year of living in with Laura and Prue Leith has obviously taken its toll on Mike, who was ascending Yewbarrow almost on his knees. His green T-shirt was adorned with black rings of perspiration around the neck and armpits and the chirpy rugby songs had long since been replaced with a surly and increasingly breathless refrain of '(For fuck's sake) Slow down, John (you bastard)'.

'Knees up, fatso!' John yelled cheerfully, zooming in on Mike's halfmast v-sign. George staggered up to the rock where John was standing and crawled to safety behind the camera.

'Gor,' said John, in his new-found and strange TV dialect, zooming out to demonstrate the pathetic gradient that they had climbed, 'this is just like being at work!'

George screwed the top off a bottle of water and glugged it down gratefully. Before he had quenched his raging thirst, Mike made a lunge for the bottle, having just made it to the top, and they fell in an undignified heap, taking care to keep the bottle upright. Mike was the colour of a bad chicken tandoori masala. George saw a greater need and gave him the bottle.

They sat leaning against the rock and regained their breath. The view was stunning, sweeping down to the lake, which shivered and shone in the bright sun, and around the valley basin. George shut his eyes and all he could hear, apart from Mike panting in his ear, was the distant baa of a wandering sheep and birdsong. Once the immediate pain in his lungs eased, he could enjoy the dull ache beginning in his legs. The three men sat in companionable silence for a while, thinking their own thoughts and not feeling the need to share them, or to ask what the others were thinking.

John broke the silence. 'What have you got in that rucksack, George? Any chocolate?'

George rummaged around and threw him an apple, then reclined again on the heather.

Mike was lying with his eyes closed, tracing circles on the grass with his outstretched fingers. 'It's great, isn't it, the quiet?' he said.

George murmured his agreement. He could guess what

Mike was thinking. He too was relieved to be out of the house. Not just the Caroline/Rachel thing, which was bad enough, but the Caroline/Mike thing, which was, in his opinion, outrageous. He hadn't had a chance to ask Alex properly how Rachel was taking it, but he had looked for signs of tears or panic and, to his surprise, he hadn't seen them, at least, not last night or this morning. George's conscience gave a twinge and he probed it to try to work out whether he was pleased or disappointed. It was tricky.

The whole thing was tricky. For one thing – not that he would dream of saying anything – it was bringing back some very dark memories, memories that he had firmly stashed at the back of his mind. He put his hands behind his head. No one ever seemed to mention his part in the Caroline/Rachel explosion. He had faded into the background there, not coincidentally, he had to admit. Not that he was proud of that. It had been a mistake, a drunken mistake on his part, and he had learned a lifetime of manners from the one whole minute that Rachel had stared at him that morning. As though her heart were about to break. A cliché, George thought impatiently. He still couldn't describe the pain he saw in her eyes which, he had noticed then for the first time, were an incredible deep green – he'd always thought they were blue, to go with her blond curls. And that, rather than the screams, the rows, the reported tears which came later, was when the shame had cut into him and he had felt like a complete shit. When he realised that he hadn't even noticed what colour her bloody eyes were.

The hot remorse washed over him for the first time in ages and he realised that it had been lurking again at the back of his mind since last night. It had been so glib, when Rachel had disappeared for the rest of the summer, to pretend that it hadn't happened. That wasn't just him – everyone else had too. But in all sorts of ways it had affected him, more than he'd been allowed to say. George let out a breath and pressed one arm over his eyes to block out the sun. It was why he wasn't letting Alex know how he felt about her. Why he always ended up being the grown-up. Why he couldn't completely trust Mike about this Caroline business now.

George probed some more. How did he feel about Rachel now? He really hadn't thought about this for ages. She was a friend from college. *Just* a friend from college? He tried to make his conscience sting but it wouldn't. He reflected with some shame on how easy it had been to set up a more convenient arrangement of relationships and just accept what was there. The Rachel he had eaten Chelsea buns with outside the Fitzwilliam Museum was an echo from another part of his life – one that was growing more distant by each day spent in the office or on the Tube.

He rolled on to his side and opened his eyes, staring at the sparse grass of the hillside. That wasn't something to feel guilty about, it was just the way things were.

John's voice cut through his self-examination. 'So, Mike, you jammy bastard, what's all this with Caroline?' George propped himself up on his elbow in surprise and looked at Mike, who was flat out, still trying to get his breathing down to a normal rate.

'What's wha'?' mumbled Mike.

'Oh, come on,' said John, 'don't tell me there's nothing going on there.'

George swivelled round and stared hard at John. He must have been putting two and two together very quickly to go from blithering ignorance in the car to broaching questions he himself had been considering part of the way up the side of the mountain. Or at least, had been considering until more pressing matters took over, like establishing a sensible breathing pattern. And not letting himself stop. He looked expectantly at Mike, who had now opened his eyes.

'I told you, it was a surprise for Laura. Caroline called me from the States a couple of weeks ago to say that she might be able to get back to England for the party, but not to tell Laura or anyone because it was a surprise.' Mike paused to get his breath back after what had been a longer sentence than originally planned. He went on, 'She said she didn't want people to know because she couldn't stay long enough to see all the people who would expect her to see them.'

'Ra-*hah*,' said John incredulously. 'And the rest.'

'Straight up!' protested Mike. 'She called me at work on Thursday, said she would be arriving at Manchester Airport at six o'clock and could I pick her up on my way up to Cumbria. I mean, OK, it wasn't exactly on my way . . .'

'But you don't say no to Caroline,' said George sardonically.

'Not when she's flown over from New York specially,' replied Mike, a little more reprovingly than George thought he had a right to be.

'But come on, Mike,' said John, in an 'All Lads Together' way, 'are you really telling us that nothing's going on?'

'Yes!'

'No!'

'John!' said George in a warning tone, having suddenly had a vision of where this might be going.

'OK, OK, if you say so, but do you not think she's being rather . . . you know?' John wiggled his eyebrows.

'A bit what?' said Mike, sitting up, his interest now inevitably whetted.

'Well,' said John, 'turning up in that skin-tight trouser suit, giving you the old eye all evening over supper . . .'

Mike looked more interested, but unconvincingly feigned some token disbelief.

'. . . all those little jokes about how fast Mike goes on the motorway and how good he is on dangerous curves . . .'

'Caroline did not say that!' interrupted George. 'Stop stirring, for God's sake!'

But his words were falling on stony ground. George saw the look of smug pleasure spread over Mike's face and slumped back on to the grass. Where had John got all this from? Had Rachel said something? That was the thing about John – once he got hold of an idea he liked to milk it as much as he could. More to the point, he knew this was a conversation he'd hoped to be leading himself and as it was, John was steering it in exactly the opposite direction. Furthermore, Mike wasn't exactly being evasive or guilty.

'For God's sake, John,' said George, leaning up on his elbow and fixing John with what he hoped would be a warning death look. 'This whole weekend is meant to be celebrating Mike's engagement! He's getting married in six months! Why on earth would he be interested in Caroline? Don't be so bloody stupid.' He flopped back, as if to end the conversation.

But John was not to be so easily deterred from what was the only potential bit of Lads' Behaviour in a weekend full of baking, cosy chats around the table and seating plans.

'She's looking very good these days,' said John. 'Can't say I wouldn't be tempted myself.'

George rolled his eyes behind his eyelids. *Is your wife a goer, is she? You into photography? Nudge, nudge, wink, wink* . . .

'Well . . .' said Mike in a verbal leer, 'I suppose, speaking objectively . . .'

Which of course he's *not*, thought George, as we know. Oh bollocks, how am I meant to broach this now?

'Speaking *objectively*,' gurgled John.

George could hear John and Mike giggling like a pair of schoolboys with their first *Playboy* calendar. Mike said something under his breath about Caroline, which George missed, but wasn't difficult to guess.

'Oh for crying out loud!' snapped George, forgetting about being discreet. 'She's a bloody troublemaker and you're being bloody stupid messing around with her when you have a beautiful and intelligent girl like Laura, who's been generous enough to agree to spend the rest of her life with you! Fuck knows why!'

Mike stared at George.

'I thought we'd agreed that there was nothing going on with Mike and Caroline,' John said innocently.

George gritted his teeth. This was obviously Parson's Cat payback time. 'Well, if there were anything going on, then Mike would be very stupid to risk a wonderful relationship on such a trivial woman.'

'I don't know why you're being so sanctimonious, George,' said Mike, who much preferred John telling him how much Caroline fancied him to George telling him it couldn't happen anyway. 'You did it.'

They sat in silence. Already the conversation was treading on more home truths than was usual. There were so many givens between the boys and girls, topics that were understood but never mentioned, that conversations like these could skate on several years' worth of subtext in as many sentences. The silences were more eloquent than the comments in between.

Mike was confused by John *and* George. Were they arguing from the same side of the fence? They both seemed to be
saying that Caroline fancied him, which couldn't be a bad
thing, but, if he was following this correctly, George seemed
to think that there was something going on already. He
couldn't in all honesty say he'd noticed.

He lay back on the grass thoughtfully. George was always
the one to know what was going on, probably because the
girls told him things. Maybe Caroline had told Alex, and
Alex had told George. Of course, Caroline wouldn't have
told Laura, so maybe Alex was the next best confidante.
That would make sense. Mike allowed himself the indulgent
fantasy of Caroline sitting in white silk pyjamas in her New
York flat, confessing her secret passion over the phone to
Alex. He had to adapt his experience of Alex in reality to fit
the image, but she was only background.

The more he thought about it, Caroline *had* been insistent
on him taking her up to the cottage. And she had been insistent on buying him an early supper in that flashy
Manchester restaurant . . . Hey, what could be more attractive to a woman who had everything than a man she couldn't
have? Or, at least, couldn't have after 14 February next year?
Mike, usually on a tight leash at home, had found great
solace in the private world of fantasy. It didn't let him down
now.

'You've been going out with Laura for a very long time,
haven't you, Mike?' said John. 'What is it now, three years?'
George leaned over and thumped him. But John only needed
to plant the idea. Mike's imagination could never be accused
of infertility.

'Longer. Since the second year at college,' he murmured
automatically, but he was thinking of Caroline's long legs and

trying to remember the last time he had had sex with someone other than Laura.

'I remember that,' said George grimly. 'Didn't you start
going out on Rag Blind Date night? You were set up with
someone from New Hall but she ended up snogging John in
the Curry Centre. And then you and Laura went out for an
ice-cream instead, didn't you? I remember seeing you in the
college bar afterwards, all covered in vermicelli. We thought
you two were never going to accept the inevitable and get
together.'

'Mmm,' said Mike, miles and miles away.

'Because we knew you were made for each other,' said
George emphatically. He nudged John to get him to agree.

'Oh, er, what?' said John. 'Oh, er, yeah, absolutely, look at
you now, bloody welded together! Not so much joined at the
hip as, well, one body between two!'

'Mmm,' said Mike, with a touch of wistfulness in his
voice.

The birds wheeled overhead and the sun beat down.
George wondered what he could say to salvage the situation.
If he gave Mike his 'Pack this thing in with Caroline' lecture,
Mike could pretend he thought George was referring to
John's hints and deny the whole thing. On the other hand,
he didn't want to confirm John's hints by telling Mike what
he already knew and make him explain or deny. For once he
understood what Alex had been saying about the impossibility of being subtle with men.

But, most of all, George felt a crushing sense of responsibility. He really didn't want to see two good friends destroy
their relationship for nothing. Because that's what it would
be. He was sure that Caroline was only interested in Mike
because he was a challenge – not just someone's husband

afflicted with the seven-year itch, or someone's boyfriend with no knots tied, but a man still meant to be starry-eyed and besotted with his lover. He knew he had to do or say something to stop this going on. But what?

John hauled himself to his feet. 'OK, chaps, only a few more feet to the top! Hup, hup, hup!'

George and Mike groaned. George because his knees were aching almost as much as his conscience and Mike because he was only beginning a very pleasant mental encounter with a desperate Caroline.

George got up and stretched out a hand to help Mike up. He saw the camera trained on them and made a V-sign at it. John returned it and began hiking up the mountain, the toned calf muscles of his brown legs glinting in the sunshine. A rude version of 'Hi ho, hi ho,' came floating down the hill. George marvelled at how women, bedazzled by the floppy fringe and the gauche charm, never got to see the sadistic bastard side of John. But then, they usually didn't manage to stay on the relationship pitch after half-time.

Mike wobbled to his feet like a new-born calf. 'Cheers,' he said, hauling himself upright with George's arm. The sun was shining in his eyes and he shaded them with his hand.

'Mike, whatever you think about Caroline, she's not worth losing Laura for,' said George softly. 'Believe me.'

The two men looked very seriously at each other. George felt that this might be the only sensible exchange he'd had with Mike in the six years he'd known him. Mike stuck out his lower lip thoughtfully.

'I know,' he said.

George clapped him on the arm and they started walking.

chapter twenty-four

Rachel was reclining on the sofa in the sitting room, doing the *Telegraph* crossword from the previous day's paper, which she had found in her bag, while Laura and Alex went over Laura's plans for bridesmaids' dresses again. A jug of Pimms, the remainder of Rachel's muffins and a box of Belgian chocolate biscuits – a present from Alex – were on the coffee table, and Laura had one of her cereal bars on a plate next to her, cut into ten small pieces. She had also found coasters from somewhere for the Pimms glasses.

Terminal glaze was spreading over Alex's face. Rachel paused to chew over a clue, her pen at her lips, and caught Alex aiming a 'Help me!' expression in her direction. She wondered how long Alex had had to fix her mouth in that position without Laura noticing.

Rachel unclicked her pen and folded her paper. She was about to open her mouth to suggest a walk along the lake before everyone got back, when Laura caught her looking over the file, currently open at a display of Edwardian-themed page boys loitering pastily by the Serpentine. An expression of guilt crossed Laura's face.

'Look, Rachel, you would tell me if you were upset about not being a bridesmaid, wouldn't you?'

Rachel was relieved that she could laugh and reply with complete sincerity, 'Really, Laura, I quite understand. I'm perfectly happy being a lady usher. It was a brilliant idea of George's.'

Laura looked doubtful. 'Well, it's not in the *Guide*, but I suppose if George says he's seen it done . . .'

'Put it like this,' said Rachel. 'If I were a bridesmaid, could I wear a hat?'

'No,' said Laura decisively.

'Well, there you go. I have a wonderful Philip Treacy hat that I've been saving for something exactly like this. And Alex wouldn't wear a hat if you paid her, so she's more than happy with a Paula Pryke coronet, aren't you?'

'Yeah, cheers,' muttered Alex, turning the pages of Laura's section of bridesmaids' dresses with growing despair. Everything was neatly cut out from a selection of wedding magazines, prices and stockists annotated in Laura's small and rounded handwriting. Alex and Rachel had quietly agreed the previous night that Laura was to be encouraged in all aspects of wedding planning, just so long as she was thinking positively about it. Her mood seemed to be swinging from wildly enthusiastic to worryingly contemplative, but she hadn't tried to unburden herself again to either of them. And after Caroline's arrival, she seemed to have become more of a party planner than before.

'Laura,' said Alex, 'what does Mike's sister look like? Will she suit this kind of thing?' She held up a selection of column dresses in stiff moiré satin which seemed impossible to walk in. 'Because I'm sure I won't.'

Laura chewed her pen thoughtfully. 'She's a redhead, so

I'm steering clear of pink, obviously. And tangerine. But you know, I keep coming back to pistachio green, which I think will be flattering for everyone. Don't you like those dresses?'

'Yes,' said Rachel, at the same time as Alex said, 'No.'

Laura frowned and, reaching for the file, she flicked through to the wedding dresses section. 'But I want it to go with what I'm wearing, which at the moment, looks like . . . that.' She handed the file back to Alex. Rachel peered over her shoulder.

It was a long, tight-waisted dress in brilliant white, with lacing all the way down the back and a train. The model wearing it also looked very white, probably, thought Rachel, because there was no blood going past those corsets to her head. In addition, she was about six feet tall, with striking pre-Raphaelite black curls. Rachel looked at Laura's neat ash-blond bob. She caught the very faintest sarcastic exhalation from Alex.

'Here, let me see,' said Rachel. Alex was more than happy to relinquish her impending nightmare in white satin. She flicked through the plastic pages until she came to a collection of film-star-style dresses, the models in creamy Audrey Hepburn suits and pill box hats with veils, posing with tiny tied bunches on the bonnets of white Jaguars.

'Oooh, that's more like it!' she said, pointing to a fitted sheath dress in oyster coloured silk. The model was gazing in a most unmaidenly way at a fizzing pyramid of champagne bowls and holding her cascading veil over one gloved arm, while a well-scrubbed line of morning-suited young men, arranged down a convenient staircase, looked admiringly at the large bow on her behind.

'She's wearing gloves!' squeaked Laura.

'Yes, I know,' said Rachel. 'I once read somewhere that if

you wear gloves to your wedding, the groom has to rip the finger off to put your wedding ring on. I kind of like that. It's rather . . . symbolic.'

Alex rolled her eyes. 'I didn't realise you'd put so much thought into it.'

'Oh, but I have. I've had the whole thing planned in several different permutations since I was fifteen,' said Rachel seriously. 'It's all we ever talked about at school. I mean, it was only when I went to college that I realised that it's not something you're meant to discuss seriously. If you're an intelligent woman, with a career and all that, obviously you're not going to want to get married. Why, that's for people on checkouts and Geography graduates! Not for young ambitious career women like us! Graduate training schemes – much better! I don't know why the lads used to get so aereated about it – it wasn't as though there was any danger of us marching any of *them* down the aisle.'

'I found the girls the worst,' said Laura glumly. 'Especially the historians. I had Sophie and Meg over for supper one night at college; they saw a copy of *Brides and Setting Up Home* in the magazine rack and I got a three-hour lecture on the Suffragette Movement and the Cat and Mouse Act.'

She reached out her hand automatically for a Viennese shortbread and had put it whole into her mouth before she noticed. Alex thought the very fact of Laura having a magazine rack disturbing enough.

'Mind you,' said Rachel, 'most of my ideas have completely changed. I used to want a full-length meringue-skirt shepherdess number, in one of the side chapels in St Paul's Cathedral – you know, when I had that thing with an old Pauline – with full choir, singing "I Vow to Thee My Country". Now I'm more on for a column dress in a little church with maybe "For Those in Peril on the Sea" and "Guide Me, O Thou Great Redeemer". Because everyone knows it,' she added, in answer to Laura's surprised look. 'I can't be doing with those mealy-mouthed wedding hymns that only the vicar can sing along to.'

Alex hadn't realised that Rachel was so advanced in her plans for Fin. She felt rather behind these two, given that George wouldn't even snog her in public. 'I had no idea you'd got so much arranged,' she said. 'I haven't seen the ring and you two are picking hymns already.'

'Are you getting married, Rachel?' asked Laura, suddenly anxious that her weekend was about to be eclipsed by a rival announcement.

Rachel thought of the emerald ring still in its box in her bag and of the tentative life bubbling and sprouting inside her. She couldn't think of it yet as a child, wouldn't let herself yet. The question of order niggled in her mind, but the longer she eased herself into the situation, the calmer she felt about it all. Or that might be the Pimms. She really wasn't sure. But she had surreptitiously watered down her drink with lemonade when Laura and Alex were bent over the floral headdresses.

'No, not yet,' she said. 'That's the funny thing – before I met Fin, I used to imagine myself at my wedding and it was the most consoling thought in the world – you know, that I might be miserable now, whatever, but somewhere, someone in the future will want to marry me and this is what it will be like, white roses, blah, blah, blah, wedding list at Liberty, blah, blah, blah. But now . . .' She smiled up at them. 'Now, it's not quite so necessary. I know he loves me and isn't going to leave me and, well . . . we'll get married one day, I'm sure of it, so I'm not in a desperate hurry.'

'But that's the wonderful thing,' said Laura passionately. 'The security!' She bit her lip and looked up from under her neat fringe. 'Don't repeat this,' she said, 'but sometimes I come home from work and think, "God, my job might be driving me up the wall, but at least Mike loves me enough to marry me." And if I'm making him happy, then I'm succeeding at something!' She looked slightly ashamed. 'Oh dear, can I unsay that, please?'

'No, it's OK,' said Alex. 'You're just suffering from paranoid success syndrome. If you're not achieving, you're failing. First law of the careers service.'

Laura smiled. 'That's easy for you to say. You're not the marrying type, anyway.'

'What do you mean by that?' demanded Alex, stung. 'Maybe I'm just waiting for the right person. Maybe if I wanted a big party, I'd just have a big party.'

'OK, OK,' said Laura, holding up her hands, 'I just thought . . .'

'You just thought that because I haven't had a conspicuous boyfriend, I'm a . . . bluestocking. For want of a better word.' Alex sniffed. 'Actually, *if* I get married, I intend to have a fifties wedding with the bridesmaids dressed as the Ronettes and the bride and groom departing on a motorbike.'

Rachel laughed, thinking of George perched on a Vespa in winklepickers, complaining about the long-term effect on his metatarsals.

'Anyway,' Alex went on before Rachel could let any cats out of the bag, 'it's a funny time for getting married, our generation, don't you think? I mean, on one hand, we're told to be realistic – you know, one in three marriages end in divorce, see your lover as a partner, not as a Calvin Klein advert, work out your finances in advance.' She counted off the fingers of her hand. 'But on the other, there's still all this romantic Hollywood myth,' she folded her fingers back down, 'white weddings, honeymoons, films, advertising . . .' She looked up, her eyebrows raised. 'What are we poor children of MTV meant to think?'

'Oh yeah,' said Rachel, 'it's all for the wedding photos and that's how you were for one day. It doesn't mean you'll be like that for ever. It doesn't even mean you'll be like that tomorrow, once all the corsetry's off.' She gave Alex her mock-professor look. 'And that's literally *and* metaphorically.'

'You're so cynical,' said Laura, looking sadly at a beaming mother-of-the-bride, safely dressed up in a navy suit and perky hat. If only her mother could be persuaded to wear something sensible like that. Something with neck-to-knee coverage.

'No, you're right,' said Rachel, feeling around under the sofa for her shoes. 'We *are* too cynical. What can you do, if you can't dream at twenty-five? I intend to grow old and grey with Fin, with or without a wedding ring, but certainly with a rocking chair. And Humpty's more than enough to keep us together.'

Humpty was curled up in a box by the window, with a shaft of sunlight falling directly onto his tricolour back. He snored gently, and every so often shook his head and snuffled in his sleep at dream rabbits. He had been sleeping away since lunchtime, getting up once or twice for a drink, or to pad round and round in a circle, squashing down the blanket in the box. He added a pleasantly companionable air to the afternoon. It will feel not entirely dissimilar when one of them drops a sprog, thought Alex, and brings it round for tea in a Moses basket.

'Maybe we should go out for a walk,' suggested Rachel. 'Make Humpty stretch his legs, now the heat of the day's gone.'

'I'd be on for that,' said Alex. 'I'd love to have a bit of an explore – it looks so wonderful from the window.' She got up and drained her glass. 'Aaah. Lovely.'

'Welllll,' said Laura uncertainly. 'The thing is, there's only one key and if the boys come back . . .'

'They can sit in the garden and wait,' Rachel finished for her, crawling over on her hands and knees to Humpty's basket. 'Walkies!' she trilled. Humpty opened one sleepy eye and looked unimpressed. Rachel attached his lead anyway.

'Come on, Laura,' said Alex, picking up a pair of sunglasses from the table and slipping them on to the top of her head. 'You can tell us about honeymoon destinations.'

Laura fiddled with the lever on her lever arch file.

'We won't be long,' said Rachel. 'I can't stay out for more than an hour in this weather anyway. We'll just walk up the road a bit and sit down by the lake.' She was rubbing suncream into her shoulders.

'Mind you get the bit on your back that you can't normally reach,' said Laura, getting up. 'I had terrible peeling sunburn last month. This Batman shape on my back just peeled and peeled. It looked like I had an unsightly disease.' She gathered her things together and put them in a tidy pile on the sofa. 'OK, but we'll have to go by the shop. The boys finished all the milk having cereal last thing before bed last night. After all that food I cooked, too. You know, John was eating out of a *trifle* bowl?'

Laura tutted and pulled a sunhat on. She wasn't risking freckles.

'Should we leave a note?'

Rachel considered. 'No, I don't think we'll be that long, will we?'

With Humpty dragging reluctantly on his lead, and after Laura had duly checked that all the plugs were switched off, the three of them went outside, where the heat seemed to scorch their faces on impact. All three wore sunhats at Laura's insistence, and making their way along the rocky path, they headed for the shade of the lakeside, where Laura intended to broach the topic of Rachel getting her something out of press stock for going away in, and where Caroline's absence continued to hang over them like Banquo's ghost.

chapter twenty-five

Around teatime – time seemed to drift by without a mark in the mountain air – Mike, George and John arrived back at the foot of the hill, sweating profusely but with Lads' Camaraderie fully restored. John had filmed some great footage of Mike's 'Wide-Mouthed Frog' joke and also some top comedy moments with a very patient sheep, which had subsequently chased Mike into a stone wall.

They jumped over the stile separating the hill from the garden of Hawk Cottage. John went over first and knelt by the wall, getting worm's-eye views of Mike and George's feet flying over.

'Gor,' said John, 'I'm parched. I wonder if the girls have got any cold drinks going?' He walked round to the back door, jiggling the camera in the style of an investigative documentary.

Mike bobbed up and down in front of him. 'Here we are, at Hawk Cottage, where we have heard reports that there is a crack kitchen operating. We're going to go in and see if we can catch the head cook, Miss Laura Parker, at work.' He banged on the door. 'Open up! This is Mike Craig of Channel Five! We know you're in there!'

There was a deafening silence. Mike grinned at the camera. 'Playing hard to get, eh?' The camera nodded up and down.

Mike banged again on the back door, which shook but was clearly locked.

He looked back at John, putting his head on one side. 'Hmm. Shall we try round the front? They might be in the garden. Come, come.' He beckoned the camera with his hand and John followed him to the front of the cottage.

The garden was empty. John panned around to demonstrate how empty it was. He picked up George coming round the side of the house with an irate expression on his face.

'I don't know where they've gone, but they've taken my car!' he yelled. He furrowed his brow. 'Alex can't drive on her own and Rachel claims she doesn't know which is the go pedal and which is the stop.' He looked at Mike. 'Be honest with me, Mike. Would Laura have taken my new Audi?'

Mike shook his head. 'Why would she? She's got a perfectly good hire Fiat Punto. Or mine, for that matter. And she prefers a little car. I doubt if she could reach the pedals on yours.'

John walked round the side of the cottage and zoomed in on the drive. The Fiat was still parked outside the house, while fresh tyre tracks ran down the drive and out on to the road. For good measure, John walked down the drive, which curved behind some trees, hiding the cottage from the road on one side. Once out on the road, he caught sight of the girls walking back from the lake.

He waved and pointed at the camcorder.

'Oh God, there's John with that bloody camera,' said Alex.

She gave John a half-hearted wave, but didn't take off her shades.

'He doesn't stop, does he?' said Rachel, screwing up her eyes against the light. Humpty waddled along by her side. His coat was spiky from splashing in the cool water of the lake and he had managed to find a small amount of something smelly to roll in while the girls had sat talking on a rock, their bare legs paddling in the water and sliding over the cool stones.

'You know, I'm a bit worried about that tape he's making,' said Laura. 'I suppose he'll have us all on from last night when Caroline arrived. I don't really want to have to watch that at the reception, or whenever it gets its première.'

Alex blushed beneath her sunglasses. She had been the one wielding the camcorder at that point and the shock of Caroline's big entrance hadn't stopped her from getting a good pan shot of the whole group, from Laura's frozen smile to Mike's cheesy grin.

'I wouldn't worry, Laura,' she said. 'The stuff he has from the journey up with me and George is enough to make your toes curl.'

They crested the bank up on to the road in time to see George running up to meet them. His face was beetroot.

'Someone's stolen my car!' he yelled. 'It's got a security system that sounds like a Nuclear Air Attack siren and some country bumpkin has hot-wired it! Oh my God!' He stood on the side of the road with his hands stuck up in his hair and looked utterly bereft.

Alex carefully blocked John's lens with her hand and pushed the camcorder away. He protested and she kicked his shins.

'Come on, George,' she said, putting her arm around him.

'We would have heard the alarm go off if someone had tried to break in. And the cottage isn't on the road; you can't see the cars unless you walk up the drive.'

'Well, was it there when you came out?' he said desperately.

Alex thought. 'I can't actually . . .'

'We came out of the old front door,' said Rachel. 'The one that leads on to the garden and down to the lake? It's normally locked – I don't think it's used very often. So no, we didn't see.'

'Wait a minute,' said Alex. 'Is Caroline with you?'

'No,' said George, looking surprised. 'Of course not, we've been up Yewbarrow.' He gestured up the hill, where several distant spots of colour now moved at intervals along the winding path.

'Well, there you go,' said Alex. 'She's not with us. She said she was going to try to catch you up, we went into the sitting room to look at Laura's wedding planner, put some music on – she must have taken your car. The keys were in the dish in the hall, weren't they?'

George nodded dumbly.

'I didn't think she was dressed for a hike,' said Rachel. 'Mind you, if Wordsworth were around today, I suppose he'd prefer to do his lonely cloud-like wandering from the leather seats of an air-conditioned Audi.'

George was holding chunks of his hair in his hands, as though he were about to rip it out. And he's not got much to play with, thought Alex.

She renewed her squeeze on his shoulders. 'Look, George, wherever she's gone, she'll be back soon, OK? Why don't we have a walk down to the shop and get some ice-creams or cold drinks and sit in the garden and wait for her? I'm sure there'll be a reason for her going off like that,' – she whispered in his ear – 'and at least Mike was with you the whole time.' A series of emotions, none happy, trooped across George's face.

Meanwhile Laura had walked up the drive to the cottage with Mike and John, who was ostentatiously limping and scowling at Alex. She jogged back now, jangling her house keys.

'The keys have gone from the dish,' she panted. 'It can only be Caroline who's taken it. Don't worry,' she said to George, who didn't look particularly consoled by this news, 'she's a perfectly competent driver. And she's used to sports cars.'

Alex steered George on to the road, with Rachel taking the other side. 'We're going for ice-creams,' she said. 'And then we're going to come back, make a big Caesar salad and get drunk in the garden.'

The door of Lewthwaite's Stores jangled as they trooped in and headed for the ice-cream cabinet. Mrs Lewthwaite gave them a nod of recognition as they shuffled past the till and remarked to her pony-tailed assistant, 'I told you, Leanne.'

What Mrs Lewthwaite had told her lovely assistant was not immediately apparent, but as they leaned over the chill cabinet, Alex could hear a whispered commentary, punctuated by sharp intakes of breath. Sadly, individual words were not distinguishable.

There was a large selection of ice-creams and it took the girls a while to make up their minds. John and Mike decided immediately, opting for the cheapest and the one with the crap joke on the stick respectively, and loitered about, sniggering at the community messages board. Rachel, suffering from the heat, leaned with her arms almost in the freezer, while Laura dithered about the various calorie contents, secretly hankering after a double chocolate Magnum and ending up with some frozen yoghurt that didn't look as if it were worth the effort of eating.

A couple of coughs from the direction of the till hurried them along and with a heap of ice-creams in the basket, George got out his wallet to pay.

'That'll be your car parked up on t'fell, then,' said Mrs Lewthwaite disapprovingly as she rang the prices through. It was another statement, framed as a question. Leanne put the ice-creams in a plastic bag and backed up the disapproval.

'What?' said George. 'Have you found it? A blue Audi coupé?' He looked as though he were about to fall on his knees in front of the counter.

Mrs Lewthwaite sniffed. 'I don't know about that, but it were an offcomer's registration. We're RM or AO round here.'

'It's parked in front of Tyson Moore's field,' added Leanne helpfully. She smiled. 'He'll be wanting to get his cows out for milking soon.'

George looked white and, thrusting a ten-pound note at Mrs Lewthwaite, he rushed outside. John pocketed the change with a cheerful nod and followed him out.

chapter twenty-six

It took three gin and tonics to restore George to his usual good humour. Four if you counted the time it took to get him to talk without taking sideways glances at the drive between sentences.

After Rachel and Alex had pleaded their northern backgrounds all the way back to the Wars of the Roses to convince George that you couldn't grow cows on the side of a grass-free mountain, he had insisted on driving round the surrounding area in Laura's Punto until they found the Audi parked in front of a flimsy-looking gate, which was indeed next to a field full of sheep, halfway up another pass. George did not appreciate local humour and after his close encounter the previous evening was already wary of sheep the size of Shetland ponies. Fortunately, he had a spare set of keys and had managed, after four ear-splitting minutes, to deactivate the alarm and drive the car back, irked beyond speech all the way by Caroline's very strong perfume, which lingered in the car, even with all the windows and the sunroof open.

He was sitting now on a stripy deckchair in the long garden. Under the shade of one of the trees, Alex and Rachel were doing the crossword together – or rather, Rachel was trying to teach Alex how to work out the clues, while they half-listened to George agonising over what damage Caroline might have inflicted on the new gearbox he had had fitted when he bought the car.

'. . . and I don't care if she *is* stuck up a mountain,' he said. 'She's got a phone. She can ring us up, apologise for taking the car and someone can go and get her. Not me. This is one liberty too far.' George took a long drink from his tumbler.

'She's been out a long time,' observed Alex. 'When do you think we should start worrying?'

'When the Mountain Rescue ring up and say they've got a reverse-charge-call victim who demands to be brought down Business Class?' Rachel filled in a clue and crossed it off the list.

'Won't she call us first?'

'Not necessarily.'

'Well, I must say this is the ideal weekend away with Caroline,' said Rachel. 'She turns up, snaffles the best of the nail varnishes I bring up for Laura –' she tipped her sunglasses on to the edge of her nose and looked over them at Alex 'yes, I *did* notice – and then buggers off after a couple of hours. I haven't even had to bite my tongue.'

'Or indeed, had to bite *hers*,' said George. 'As for Mike, though, I couldn't possibly . . .'

'George,' said Alex in a warning tone. Laura was coming across the grass, tea towel flung over one shoulder, looking flustered. She sat down with a thump next to Alex and Rachel and poured herself a stiff gin and tonic, adding plenty of ice from the bucket.

'Ahhhh,' she sighed. 'I suppose I shouldn't be drinking when I'm cooking but I *so* need this.' She almost drained her glass.

'Steady on, Laura,' said George in surprise.

'Oh, let her,' said Rachel. 'So what if she's drunk in charge of an Aga? She can't leave it halfway up a mountain with a field full of sheep.'

Laura finished her drink and looked penitently at George. 'Is it OK if we just have a big salad tonight?' she asked. 'Only it's so much hotter than yesterday and I just can't stand being in front of that hot stove. I'll make you something special tomorrow?'

'I'd love a salad,' said Rachel. 'It's about time the boys had some nutrition anyway.'

'Yeah,' said Alex. 'And anyway, why should you spend the weekend cooking? You'll be doing that for the rest of your life once you're married.'

Laura opened her mouth to say something. Alex held up her hands and said, 'Joke! Joke!'

'And with the salad, I suppose we can just wait until Caroline comes back, can't we?' said Laura, checking her watch. 'It's not going to spoil. She's been gone ages. I hope she's not hurt herself in those shoes.'

'She'll be fine, Laura,' said Alex, squinting at the crossword, which Rachel had now almost completed.

'I know how Mike picks at things.' Laura looked up at the house. 'I left him making his special garlic dressing. I hope he's not going to overdo it. It's the only healthy eating thing he knows: garlic clears out your cholesterol.'

Rachel nodded towards the kitchen. 'They are washing up, aren't they?'

'Yes, though I'm not sure you had to *make* them do it,

Rachel,' said Laura, reproachfully. Despite what she privately wished about Mike, she still didn't feel *right* about making male guests wash up.

'Oh, come on, there was hardly anything!' protested Rachel. 'Some tea things, the salad chopping stuff and one or two glasses from this morning.'

'Er, well, that'll be just the one glass now then,' said George. 'When I went in for the ice . . .' He decided to miss out the bit about Mike and John's cocktail barmen impression. 'Well, these things happen.'

A cloud of worry floated across Laura's face.

'Ah, you see, that's the trouble with your stone floor kitchens,' said Alex. 'Very unforgiving on the old glassware.'

'We'll get some new ones!' said George. 'I know where they're from – the stickers were still on some of them.' He decided to miss out the price bit too.

Rachel rolled her eyes. 'Sometimes I think men just do this so we can't trust you to do anything unsupervised.'

'That's the plan,' said George, shutting his eyes and leaning back in his chair. He felt pleasantly sleepy with the sun and the gin; his legs were heavy after the walk up the hill and he had changed out of his shorts into loose linen trousers and a white polo shirt. The kind of clothes he'd worn all the time in the days before dress-down Fridays and security tags. He stretched out his bare feet on the grass. Summer clothes, for lounging out in the sun . . .

Rachel leaned over him teasingly, reaching for the tonic water by his side. 'Ah, yes, but as I tell Finlay, practice makes perfect . . .'

George swallowed as Rachel's suddenly familiar perfume of roses and musk floated dangerously close to his nose. I won't open my eyes, he thought, she must be so close to me, her breasts must be right above my face. He held his breath, all the morning's memories now vivid with the forgotten smell of Rachel on a hot summer day.

George heard Laura stifle a giggle, but couldn't bring himself to open his eyes. He could hear a sheep baaing on the hillside as if it were right by his ear and through his velvety eyelids could see Rachel leaning over him on the Backs, feeding him strawberries, her soft smile framed by the wide straw brim of her sun hat.

Suddenly he heard a shriek right above him and the musky shadow that had been hanging over his closed eyes was replaced by the bright light of the afternoon sun. A white dart of cold shot through his chest and George's eyes snapped open. Alex was standing behind his chair, laughing, with a handful of ice cubes in her hands and Rachel, also laughing hysterically, was wriggling up and down, trying to extricate an ice cube from the back of her long blue sundress. The shocking coldness was turning into a spreading dampness and, putting his hand to his chest, George frantically tried to locate the ice cube down his shirt without making the deckchair snap him up like a stripy Venus Fly Trap.

Laura squealed in delight and zoomed in on George's writhings with the camcorder.

'Ooooh, you pigs!' shrieked Rachel delightedly, hopping up and down. 'You had this all planned, didn't you! Where did you hide the camcorder, Alex? Oh my God, I think the ice cube's got lodged in my pants!' and she went off into hysterical giggles again.

'Is there a problem with your trousers, George?' asked Laura demurely. George looked down in panic and saw the ice cube's melting trail spreading in what Mike would have called a top comedy manner. Staring right into the lens, he said, 'Ah, Laura, you asked for this!' and standing up, removed his trousers to the whoops and shrieks of the girls and walked barefoot up the garden to the cottage door in his boxer shorts, soggy trousers slung over his shoulder.

Alex shut her eyes and thanked God for crisp white cotton boxers.

Rather than walk all the way round to the back, and unable to open the locked front door, George climbed in carefully through the open kitchen window. The kitchen was alive with the smell of garlic and there were still bowls everywhere. Mike and John were standing by the sink, flicking foam at each other with washing-up brushes. George stood on the window seat and looked at them critically. It would be fair to say that they had not changed very much since he had first met them. Mike flicked a whole brush-head of froth at John and showered him with spray, at which John lunged at Mike with a warlike grunt and took him in a playful head-lock. Or at least it began as a playful headlock.

George was weighing up whether to separate this almost classical grappling when the front door opened and Caroline waltzed in carrying a small hamper. Mike and John sprang apart immediately and coughed.

'Oooh, George,' said Caroline recklessly. 'That brings back memories!'

The boys stared at her. They had never heard anyone refer directly to Caroline and George. Much hinting and alluding had lent it a taboo quality. George flushed and stepped down from the window seat, suddenly very self-conscious. He couldn't think of anything to say, which annoyed him, and he walked through to the staircase, acutely aware that her words were hanging in the air behind him. Once out of her sight, he bounded up the stairs as quickly as he could and didn't feel comfortable again until he had pulled on another pair of trousers.

Mike and John stood awkwardly in the kitchen. Mike knew he should say something witty and Georgesque at this point but was hopelessly lost for words. Caroline looked at them both from behind her shades and laughed cattishly.

'Everyone in the garden?' she enquired.

Mike nodded. 'They're all out there with the gin and tonic.'

John was staring at the wicker hamper she was dangling from her fingers like Little Red Riding Hood. 'Been shopping?' he said.

'Oh, this?' said Caroline, looking down at the hamper as if seeing it for the first time. 'Oh, I, er, brought this up yesterday, but forgot to give it to Laura. I'll go round and give it to her now.' She smiled again, turned and left.

'I don't remember that,' said Mike, as he watched her glide past the window. 'I think I'd have remembered her packing a Fortnum and Mason hamper into the boot.'

'Maybe she arranged for Whatsisname, the bloke who owns the cottage, to have it sent up?' suggested John. 'Fortnum and Mason – there'll be some decent stuff in there.'

They looked at the big bowl of salad that Laura had prepared on the table. Freshly torn lettuce, glossy local-grown tomatoes, plump radishes, transparent shavings of cucumber, wedges of boiled egg and anchovies, garnished with a generous rash of flowers, rosettes, anemones and carved balls. Beside it stood Mike's glass jug of sludgy-looking dressing.

They followed Caroline and her hamper into the back garden.

chapter twenty-seven

Fin and Dan were parked on top of Hardknott Pass, waiting. They had already spent the best part of an hour playing with the radio handsets and listening to Dan's dreadful MOR tapes, which he collected, at extortionate prices, from motorway service stations. As far as Fin was concerned, evening couldn't come quickly enough. Dan, on the other hand, was wearing a mask of Zen-like tranquillity, which Fin knew from experience to be misleading.

Once Dan had decided to give Marvin up for the day, Fin had driven around and done some cursory stock shots of the Lakes, in case he ever needed them for a feature, but the novelty of driving the narrow roads behind a stream of Sunday drivers had worn off after about an hour.

Fin had mentally divided the majority of Cumbrian traffic into two separate categories: bobble-hat drivers and flat-cap drivers. Bobble-hat drivers were erratic, took straights as well as corners in the middle of the road and seemed to follow the dotted lines down the middle as some kind of navigation aid. Flat-cap drivers, who all seemed to be hunched over the wheel, had a minimum of three passengers, average age usually seventy-one, all related by marriage, and would not go over thirty miles an hour, presumably to avoid setting off any pacemakers. They drove their large four-door saloons as though they were unpredictable and potentially frisky carthorses.

At one point, crawling along near Windermere nose to tail with a Morris Minor in remarkably good nick, Fin had come to the conclusion that there must be some major series of roadworks ahead, until he came to a bend in the road, from which vantage point he could see an Allegro in the far distance, doggedly following a bicycle. The bicycle kept pulling in to the side of the road to allow the car to pass, but it wouldn't, and eventually the cyclist gave up and just carried on cycling. Confident that he would never see London traffic in the same light again (if he ever saw London traffic again), Fin turned off at the first side road he came to, even though it meant going down a farm track.

That had eventually brought him back to Dan, who had spent his afternoon recceing various different places he thought Marvin might be that evening, and arranging, rearranging and checking his equipment. And 'talking to people'. Fin didn't ask who.

The two Golfs were parked up at the top of the pass, well out of the way. Fin was lying on the grass, fiddling with one of the phones, and swigging thirstily out of a chilled bottle of water. Whereas his car was like a toaster, Dan's was filled with cool boxes. Fin had found his missing Mars bar down the side of his chair. In liquid form, all over his atlas, and, on closer inspection, his jeans.

Dan looked at his diver's watch. It was nearly seven o'clock.

'Do you fancy a run round to Marvin's, see if he's back yet?'

Fin took a screwdriver out of his bag and adjusted a tiny screw on the side of the radio. 'I think you'll find that'll stop it cutting out now.' He passed the handset back up to Dan, who took it with a wry smile.

'I don't think it *did* cut out until you took it for that job in Scotland,' he said. 'And ran over it.'

'Er, hello?' said Fin indignantly. 'Who set off with both the radios in the car? And whose idea was it to drop one off *in the middle of the road* so I could pick it up? You're lucky I got it at all.'

'You're lucky we got the pictures at all,' said Dan, testing the battery.

'I'm learning,' said Fin.

Dan looked at him. 'Finlay, you are not a paparazzo. You are a classic portrait photographer. I can't imagine Cecil Beaton desperately trying to steer his Bentley with his knees while snapping away at Margot Fonteyn coming out of the back entrance of Simpsons. On a hot date with George Formby.'

'It's different. That's all.'

'It's not photography.'

Fin grunted dismissively.

'It's not,' said Dan. 'What you do is photography. It's showing a subject's personality through their eyes, their expression. A lifetime in one picture. What *I* do is . . .'

'Just as revealing,' said Fin defensively. 'But you get one second to show someone's soul before they can put up the pose, the defence. I only get to see what they want to show me.'

'Don't,' said Dan. He thought of Fin's portraits, the shades of character caught between the shadows of black and white. Fin took pictures of familiar, famous faces and stripped them of the prepared smile, unveiled them as people with the perception of his lens. If his own pictures were full-colour shock exposés, Fin's were black and white X-rays of their inner selves. The silent dialogue between photographer and subject, as telling as the interview itself. Rachel had once told him that she thought Fin's photographs were illustrated by the interview and not the other way around. Dan had agreed with her.

Fin was moodily staring out at the valley beneath and Dan guessed that he was thinking about Rachel. Where she was, what she was doing. Whether she minded what they were doing. Usually Fin talked about her constantly when they were apart – there must be something up for him to be so quiet.

'If we can get Marvin tonight, some good clean pictures, we can wire them back on the Mac and you can spend the rest of the weekend with Rachel,' he said, trying to be light. It wasn't the time to get into another debate about the ethics of photography. Particularly if it meant he was going to have to give Fin another lecture about staying with his art. Dan grimaced internally. Fin was the most gifted photographer he knew but as far as hanging on to the back of ski lifts with a long lens went, he wasn't much of an Action Man.

But he tried, thought Dan, he really tried. He tousled Fin's thick brown hair affectionately.

Fin looked up, his brows knitted in offence.

'Oi! What's the plan, then?'

'We'll drive over to Marvin's place, see if his car's back. If it is, presumably Margery's there with him. We can wait a bit, see if they come out, see if we can get a clear shot of them together. Fine. If his car isn't there, we could wait out of sight, see if we can catch them coming back together later this evening. The light should still be OK. Apparently they're not at the place I was looking at this morning.'

Fin gave him a suspicious look. 'How do you know?'

'The network stretches,' said Dan. 'There is one other place they might be, but I don't want to hang around in case someone's got it wrong. And we still haven't found Margery's red MG.'

'I still can't believe it's him,' said Fin, a hundred childhood TV memories running through his mind. 'I won't believe it until I see him.'

'You're too sweet for this game,' said Dan, shaking his head and flicking through his bulging black Filofax. 'I saw our man this afternoon while you were having your cream tea or whatever in Windermere and believe me, it's all perfectly believable once he's on the other end of an 800 mil and walking into focus, with bloody Lady Madonna on his arm.'

'Dan! You didn't say you'd seen them! Why didn't you phone me?'

'Well, there was nothing to see, really, the shots I got. Just a bit of shopping, out in his car. She had shades on and he was looking knackered. Not surprising, I suppose. I'd be knackered too, a weekend away with a bird like that.' Dan stretched out his legs and flexed his back. 'Come on, let's see what we can do before the light goes.'

Fin got up reluctantly. Even with all the doors left open, his car was still radiating heat.

'Are we taking both cars?' he asked. 'Won't it look a bit suspicious?'

Dan pondered. 'Yeah, you've got a point there. Why don't you follow me, we'll find a car park to leave your car in and then you can drive up to Marvin's place. I can't see us need-ing both cars, now I know Margery's in position.'

Fin opened the boot and started to load his equipment into the matt black interior of Dan's car.

chapter twenty-eight

Once the rabbit food was supplemented by the various delicacies from Caroline's hamper, supper had been pretty good after all, in John's opinion. Salad and stuff was fine for the girls, even if he had caught Rachel tipping Mike's garlic dressing down the kitchen sink, but you couldn't beat game pie and smoked salmon. Unless, he thought with a chuckle, you just happened to have a pot of caviar and some mini blinis . . .

The evening had been very warm – 'close', according to Rachel, whatever that meant – and supper was carried out on to the lawn. Now the light was beginning to fade as evening drew on and John wanted to try to capture the drowsy, dusky mood that had settled over the party. He would have called it mellow if he didn't think that Alex would pull him up on his vocabulary.

He panned his camera round the lounging figures, finally coming to rest on the two empty Pimms bottles and an empty jug, festooned with washed-up pieces of oranges and cucumbers, all tinged a dirty brown. In a washing-up bowl of melting ice cubes, next to George's deckchair, there were a further two bottles of lemonade, a bottle of gin and some tonic and three untouched bottles of mineral water.

'Much has been drunk,' John slurred into the camcorder. He walked over to where Alex and Rachel were lying on their own, some distance from the others, talking, only a slight wobble belying the ferocious cocktails he'd been quaffing.

Rachel was plaiting Alex's long hair into a loose Red Indian squaw braid. '. . . no, I hope Laura won't notice. I did try to unblock it, but I'm not kidding, he'd actually used *whole* cloves of garlic. I found four . . . Oh John, piss off.' She put her hand up to the lens in a practised way.

Alex smiled up lazily at the camera, feeling quite at peace after a tense supper. By her third official Pimms with the meal – and who was counting the ones this afternoon? – she had stopped worrying about Mike and Laura, Caroline and Rachel, deciding that George looked far too good in white cotton to waste her time looking at anything else. So what if his attitudes to women were antediluvian and he had shocking taste in music? She had forgotten how much better fizzy alcohol tasted outside in the summer. How could she have forgotten so quickly?

John zoomed in on a suspicious round red mark on the base of her neck, discreetly placed by George so as not to show with a shirt on, John had no doubt, but revealed by her vest top.

'You should have some music on this tape, John,' she said.

'What, and miss the conversations?'

'Exactly.'

Alex closed her eyes and relaxed again as Rachel's

soothing hands stroked her hair into unusual neatness. They began talking about Divinyl and what they could do with the muffin counter when Alex won the Lottery.

John wandered off to the deckchairs where Laura was listening agog to Caroline telling her about the New York flat and the fabulous opportunities that were coming up for her. She was also dropping yet more hints about the mysterious new man in her life. George was wearing his cocktail-party look of polite but noncommittal interest and Mike was mixing yet another round of drinks.

'So, do you think you'll be bringing this bloke of yours over to meet us?' asked Laura, thinking for the millionth time how wonderful it must be to be able to leave one's partner quite legitimately for a month or two without any subsequent fallout. She loved Mike totally but sometimes it would be nice . . . Mike was fine to leave, just as long as there were enough pizza delivery leaflets on the kitchen pinboard. Then the ghostly suspicion of Mike and Caroline's drive up to the cottage marched across her mind and she bit her lip.

Caroline paused in her story and smiled. Ah, that's nice, thought Laura, immediately touched, as she always was, by signs of need in Caroline. She misses him. It was reassuring that even the gorgeous Caroline was susceptible to the same worries and anxieties as she was herself.

'Well, he's a babe,' said Caroline, smiling in a suggestive way. 'More than that, I cannot say, I'm afraid. Anyway, enough about me, I want to hear all about the wedding. Have you had some lovely engagement presents?'

'Well, there's my ring . . .' said Laura coyly, stretching out her hand so Caroline could admire the elegant diamond solitaire. Caroline cooed and took Laura's hand in hers to inspect it more closely. Laura tried not to notice the flashy gold and ruby ring Caroline had had reset from her grandmother's for her eighteenth birthday, which she wore on her right hand. But to her surprise, Laura saw that on Caroline's engagement finger was another ring – a Russian wedding ring in three coloured gold bands, set with tiny diamonds. She gasped involuntarily.

'What?' said Caroline, then, seeing Laura's face, covered her mouth slightly with her free hand – which just happened to be the one with the ring on it – and said, 'Ooops, eagle eyes! I wasn't going to show anyone that.'

'Who gave you that?' asked George, his interest now piqued.

'Ooooh, what can I say?' said Caroline coquettishly. 'Let's just say that it's from an admirer.' She held up the hand to stop any more questions, giving Laura another flash of diamond. 'I won't be drawn on this. Now,' she said, satisfied that they were all well and truly intrigued, 'what did everyone bring you for the weekend?'

'Well, George brought a case of that lovely red wine, as you know, John brought, um, a game of Twister, Rachel brought up some gorgeous nail varnish and stuff and,' Laura blushed slightly, 'and those beautiful roses in the kitchen . . .'

'And,' George said reproachfully, 'if you'd been here this afternoon, you would have had some of Alex's biscuits and Rachel's muffins and tea.'

'Sorry,' said Caroline, hanging her head in an attempt at schoolgirl contrition. 'Sorry for missing the big girlie chat. But did you like the hamper?'

'Oh, definitely,' said Mike, coming round with another tray of icy tumblers. 'We *loved* the hamper.'

'Mike,' murmured Laura, 'steady on with these drinks. I

feel as though I've been drinking all day!' The first breeze of the evening ruffled through the trees but brought no refreshing cool air, only the distant shivering sound in the leaves.

'Oh, what the hell,' said Mike. 'If we were in London, we'd only be in some stuffy wine bar somewhere, spending a fortune on jugs of watered-down rubbish. And there's no work tomorrow, is there?' Laura carefully lifted a brimming gin and tonic off the tray.

'You still make these the way you used to when you were on the Student Union,' observed George.

'What? Very quickly?'

'No, using a paper cup as a measure.'

'Ah yes,' said Mike, settling into a deckchair next to Laura, his drinks distributed. 'Those were the days. Two-fifty to get into a dance, then four-fifty for three cocktails, shake it all about a bit and Bob's your uncle. Not the same now,' he said, slightly glumly.

Laura gave him a sideways look.

'Prices! Prices!' said Mike quickly.

John tried to sit down and take a drink at the same time. 'Talking about getting out of your head for very little money, do you remember the weekend of nutmeg?' he said, focusing on Mike and George simultaneously so he could catch the guarded looks that duly scampered across their faces.

'Mmm,' said Mike. George said nothing, but flapped his hand at the lens.

'The what?' said Laura.

'Did you know,' said John, still behind the camera, 'and this will appeal to you, Laura, being a cook, *did you know* that if you grind up a lot of fresh nutmeg, about twenty whole ones, and, say, brew it like tea, it can act as a hallucinogenic? And in certain extreme cases, a morphine-like sedative? Or that in even *more* extreme cases, it can make even the most serious subject talk in strange Jim Morrison-like prophecies of Armageddon?'

George got up quickly and walked down the garden to Rachel and Alex, flicking a V-sign at John as he went past. John cackled uproariously and took George's deckchair.

Rachel had finished braiding Alex's hair and was sticking daisies into the plait. They looked rather beautiful together, thought George as he walked over: Rachel, fair and curving in her blue halterneck dress, Alex tanned and slender in vest and shorts. Very different girls, though. Rachel was talking with a serious expression, and Alex's head was bent to listen. George couldn't catch the words. As he came closer, George saw Alex look up at Rachel tenderly and push a blond curl back behind her ear with a comforting smile. He felt a pang of jealousy that both of them should be closer to the other than he was, then remembering his Damascean self-examination of the afternoon, realised that that was probably his own fault. His conscience stung with the shame of a recently discovered truism.

Rachel looked up as he approached and, smiling, beckoned him to join them.

'You're sure I'm not interrupting?' he asked politely.

'Oh, that's just what I was saying to Alex,' said Rachel. 'I was hoping that we weren't looking standoffish.'

George raised his eyebrows. 'Don't tell me. You're longing to be joining in the conversation about Caroline's auditions in NY but don't know how to ask? It's very easy – you just go up and say, "Enough about everyone else, Caroline, let's talk about you! No, go on, don't be shy!"'

Alex laughed and put her finger on her chin. 'If Caroline Cox fell in a forest, would there be a sound or would she not bother for trees?'

'There's a joke in there about wooden performers, but I'm not going to make it,' said Rachel, her eyes sparkling. 'Look, George, as the official grown-up amongst us, I want you to note for future reference that I did not make that comment.' She wagged a finger at Alex. 'She's taking all my lines, that one. Have you not noticed my top polite behaviour? Am I not being the perfect guest with a grudge?'

'You are indeed,' said George. He added more seriously, 'I am amazed though, Rachel. You're being very . . . stoic.'

Rachel shrugged. She wasn't, really. She didn't know if it was seeing George again like this and seeing him curiously vulnerable with Alex, though he was trying to hide it, or perhaps seeing Caroline and noticing for the first time how needy she was, all that attention-seeking, but Rachel felt more of an observer than a participant. She kept remembering fragments to repeat to Fin, things that she was sure would have wounded her into silence last year. Things that only made her ache now.

She and Alex had been dissecting the dinner conversation when George had come over, and were trying to think of a topic of conversation that Caroline had brought up that hadn't, in some way, led back to her within five minutes. Rachel had noticed this phenomenon after an hour or so of (macrobiotic) diets, the pressures of (having to be thin all the time for) work and the difficulties of buying a flat (in New York), and had started signalling with her eyebrows to Alex, while politely introducing topics as apparently diverse as body piercing, shortbread and trout farming. How could she be emotionally terrorised by someone who claimed that

Transcendental Meditation had cleared up her Irritable Bowel Syndrome?

But then all nightmares are ridiculous in the daylight, she thought, catching a tiny gesture of intimacy between George and Alex out of the corner of her eye. He had tucked the label of her vest back inside, to stop her advertising her shopping habits to the world. Alex, Rachel knew, didn't care much for clothes, but when George bought things, he bought the best. So they'd got as far as buying clothes for each other. With George it was usually an anti-embarrassment precaution rather than anything else. Alex had flashed a quick but significant smile up at him. Maybe there *was* more to it this time. Oh, get it together, thought Rachel affectionately. But she said nothing.

'I particularly liked Caroline's one comment aimed directly at you,' said Alex. 'She was economical, just gave herself the one chance for the bull's-eye and she got it.'

Rachel smacked Alex's hand playfully.

'What was that? I missed it,' said George.

Alex looked at Rachel, who was smiling. 'Can I?'

'Oh, I don't care,' said Rachel. 'Even though I'm wounded to the quick and am packing my bags for Loserville as we speak.'

'Caroline turned to Rachel as Rachel was handing round the salad and said, "Rachel, what a *very* flattering dress that is! It's amazing what they can do with Lycra, isn't it?"'

George who, unlike Mike and John, had a woman's sensibility, pulled a face. 'And you said?'

'I said nothing,' said Rachel, taking a sip of her drink. 'As is my wont these days. Oh, apart from "Thank you", in my most civil tone. She looked most disappointed.'

'Sometimes, as I get drunker, I really want to say

something to her,' said Alex. 'But I never can. It pops up in my head, but won't come out. I wanted to say something to her about taking George's car without asking . . .'

'Tell me about it,' said George.

'But when it came to it, what happened? We all just looked at her and said, "Did you have a nice afternoon?" and Laura said something about putting the kettle on. I can't believe that. How does she do it?'

'Did anyone ask her how she got back?' asked Rachel, touching her lip with a daisy.

'No, they didn't.' George picked a stray blade of grass out of his tumbler.

They sat thinking. It was getting darker, and the lights inside the house were throwing shadows on to the drive. George wondered whether Inigo Aikin-Rose had some outdoor flares stashed away somewhere and whether he could be bothered to break the moment to get up and find them. He decided not.

'Well, at least Mike and Laura seem to be OK,' he said, looking over to the deckchairs. Caroline was holding forth straight into camera for John, and Laura and Mike were holding hands, but not looking at each other. Mike kept stealing surreptitious glances at Caroline, and Laura, when she wasn't talking or listening, had the slightly grim look of a prison warder with an armed robber handcuffed to her.

'She's been rather up and down all day,' observed Rachel. 'I think the strain of being suspicious is proving a bit much for her. You know, having to reconcile a previously undiscovered facet of Mike's character with the three facets he's got already.'

George clawed the air with his hand.

'No, she's right,' said Alex. 'She's been fine most of the

time and then that funny, twitchy look comes over her. I can't work out what's going on at all. Did she tell Mike about the Radio Cumbria triumph?'

'No,' said Rachel. 'Maybe she's saving it as a surprise.'

'I think John might have put his foot in it though,' said George, eyeing Mike and Laura's entwined hands. For the last hour, he had been feeling a bit like a prison warder himself, sitting poised between Mike, Caroline and Laura, ready to pour oil on troubled waters at the first sign of any friction.

'Oh, for God's sake! Trust the lads to botch things up!' said Alex. 'What did he say?'

'Just that if something wasn't going on with Caroline, he ought to ask himself why not, since she was so on for it. Or words to that effect.'

'And you said nothing to deflect this subtle hint?'

'I just said he would be stupid to let anything come between him and Laura. Which he would be. Is.'

'You know, I reckon Laura's a lot tougher than you give her credit for,' said Rachel, chewing a strand of hair thoughtfully.

Alex and George looked at her in surprise.

'What? Mrs Little Piggie?'

'I really don't see Laura letting go of her big white wedding and happy ever after, just because Caroline crosses her legs. Or doesn't cross her legs, whatever.' Rachel looked across the garden at Laura, noting the neat bob like a helmet, the knees purposefully clamped together, the hand that wasn't clutching Mike's supporting her chin as she leaned on her elbow to talk to Caroline. Lots of eye contact. She was, to Rachel, now well-schooled in magazine-type pop psychology after daily scanning the glossies for press cuttings, a lesson in combative body language, even if the fragments of conversation floating across were the usual drivel about wedding lists and Peter Jones's superior selection of goosefeather duvets.

George and Alex, on the other hand, saw a woman with a hygiene fixation who seemed to want to live in 'I Love Lucy' land.

'Do you think she would have hung on to Mike all these years if she wasn't the determined sort?' said Rachel. 'You're just used to seeing her as Mrs Little Piggie . . . No! Can this be true?'

Caroline had abandoned her monologue into John's camcorder and, leaving Mike to Laura's full attention, was walking over the grass towards them.

'I suppose it was too much to hope for,' murmured Rachel. *Be polite but distant! Don't say anything she can repeat in a conversation about you! Pretend that she's as nervous as you are!* I think it's getting to the stage, thought Rachel, over the torrent of self-help catchphrases, where I can only deal with prepared situations.

George and Alex exchanged an anxious look. There couldn't be any hiding in a group this small and although Rachel had been keeping a brave face uppermost all afternoon, this would be the first proper conversation she had had with Caroline since their big row.

Rachel was only too aware of this. She put a hand to her forehead, which was damp with sweat. Her head was throbbing with one too many Pimms – she had been unable to water them down much with Mike wielding the lemonade – and she really was tired. She had had no idea how tired she would be, especially in this heat. *Smile! Look just past her ear! Look at how close together her eyes are! Remember how she used to cut labels out of Top Shop clothes and pretend they were from Jigsaw!*

'Hello everyone!' said Caroline. Everyone looked up and smiled politely. 'What's the gossip here then?'

'Oh, we're just talking about, um, the old photo albums,' said Alex breezily. 'How young we all look.'

'Oh, yes,' agreed Caroline. 'Although I like to think we've all changed a little since then. I mean, I'm sure *I've* lost weight.' She looked pointedly at Rachel, who was staring at her glass. Getting no response, she went on, 'I think it's so sweet, all those parties we used to go to, every Friday.'

George thought that the conversation was on reasonably safe ground, and didn't see the harm in punting the ball in Rachel's direction. 'Did you see those lovely pictures from Rachel's birthday in the first year? The surprise Pancake Day party we threw in Alex's kitchen?'

Rachel smiled down at the grass at the memory. It had been one of the happiest days of her first year – she had felt for the first time that she was accepted into a crowd of friends. Strange as it seemed now, to have the remarkably suave George Warner gravely ask her whether she liked her pancake with or without lemon had been a real high point. Little did she know then that the pancakes had an ulterior motive . . .

'Ah, that was a really great evening,' said Alex. 'Who was it whose mother had sent them to college with maple syrup?'

Caroline stiffened. 'I don't know. I don't think I was invited to that one. It must have been before I knew you all.' She forced a hard smile but her words had been sulky.

A short silence fell. Rachel's head throbbed.

'This is just like being back at college,' said George, a fall-back observation that could be made at every opportunity: when Laura produced strawberries, when the sun came out, when the breeze hovered through the trees. Rachel thought the evening, heavy and quiet, with a strangely brindled sky, was just like one she had experienced before. It made her shiver.

'Oh, is it?' said Caroline, sharpened into nastiness by the mention of the albums. She had been reminded as she flicked through them, alone in the sitting room the previous night, of the times she had missed out on. She hadn't seen the cute group hugs on the river side, nor the late-night ice creams near Magdalene Bridge. When Rachel, in her curly white subtitles, had been 'Hanging Out with My Girl Friends' on the steps of the University Library, Caroline had not been one of them. All right, so she had probably been at some party at the Union or at a first night at the ADC. But . . . But. Well, things were afoot in her career. Soon, she would be 'hanging out with' more than just Alex and Laura.

George was looking at her, startled by her unusually sharp response. Lately she had been cultivating an unvarying bored drawl. 'I remember having *far* more fun than just sitting around like this. Don't you, George?' Caroline gave him an arch look and he blushed and cast his eyes down to the grass.

Alex glared at Caroline, who was preening, running a hand through that body-permed hair. How could she be so outrageously rude? It was breathtaking, absolutely breathtaking. She cast an anxious glance at Rachel, who looked exhausted. Oh God, Alex wished she could say something, but yet again, she just couldn't bring herself to be rude. It was so frustrating! Caroline seemed to know exactly how to play on their nice middle-class sensibilities and they just let her, every time. Alex glared at George instead. It was his call, his insult.

Rachel got to her feet. 'I hope you'll all excuse me if I head in for the night? I'm not so good in this weather – as you know.' She smiled apologetically at Alex, averting her eyes from Caroline. Part of her longed to be able to stay out and snipe back at Caroline, but the heat, the sickness, the strain, the drinks, the drive up with Fin, the sheer effort of keeping everything under the surface was making her head ring. She knew that this would be interpreted the wrong way, but she just *couldn't*. Getting up and going might be letting Caroline win, but maybe it was a tactical loss. All in all, Rachel felt sick.

Alex put out her hand worriedly. 'Are you OK, Rach? Can I do anything?'

Rachel smiled. 'No, I'm just tired. Been a long day. I need a few quiet moments. On my own.' She put out a hand to Alex's shoulder. 'See you in bed, hey?'

George got to his feet and kissed her on the cheek. 'Night, Rachel. Sleep well.' As she turned away, he aimed a poisonous look at Caroline, who simply shrugged.

'I was just joking, George,' she said, loud enough to carry to Rachel's retreating back. 'Some people have no sense of humour.'

'And some people have no sense,' said George feelingly, and made himself leave it at that.

Caroline looked offended and got up.

'Oh God,' sighed Alex. 'Is this going to go on all weekend?' She watched Rachel walk up to the house, dropping kisses on Mike and Laura's head, Humpty trotting at her heels. She saw concern flit across Laura's face and then, once Rachel was safely up the drive, cast her eyes over to them with a questioning expression. Alex raised her eyebrows and nodded in the direction of Caroline, who was now gazing at the lake at the bottom of the garden. They both raised their hands in despair. Although Alex felt that Laura was probably more despairing of Rachel than Caroline.

Alex sank into the grass. 'George,' she murmured, 'you really have to take my mind off this.'

'My mind is on little else,' replied George in a knee-wobbling tone. 'But we'd better join Mr and Mrs Craig before anyone else guesses what I have in mind for you later.'

Alex's spine tingled and she followed him reluctantly up the garden, allowing herself just one glance at his neat arse before returning to the more persistent concern for her best friend, who was probably crying herself to sleep as they spoke.

chapter twenty-nine

Half-asleep by two o'clock and sliding into a dream about The Mini-Pops, Alex felt a movement of cold air on her legs and realised that her duvet was being lifted up at the corner. A second later she felt George's cold foot and the roughness of George's hairy leg on hers.

At least she hoped it was George.

'Rachel!' she hissed. The leg hesitated.

'Er, is there something you want to tell me, Alex?' George hissed back at her.

'No, I meant, is Rachel there? Or, alternatively, help me, Rachel, the Yeti is trying to get into my bed.'

George slid under the covers and Alex lay on her side with her back to the cold wall to make room for him.

'Well, Rachel isn't there, for your information. I'm not a pervert. I heard her tiptoe downstairs about ten minutes ago. If I hear her coming back, I'll say I came in because you were talking in your sleep. And anyway, would you prefer to sleep with a man who *shaves* his legs? Or doesn't have any hair to shave? Stop wriggling, you'll wake everyone up.'

The bed squeaked accusingly. They both froze.

'Don't get huffy with me, George,' whispered Alex into George's armpit. 'I sometimes wonder whether all this sneaking around is worth it. I mean, I'm sure they all know.'

'We've been through all this.'

'I know.'

They wriggled tentatively in Alex's warm bed until they had reached a position with no squashed arms for either party. George curled himself around Alex's back, with his arm underneath her neck and the other resting in the curve of her waist. They were not normally so cuddly, but needs must in single beds.

It was so good, thought Alex, luxuriously, to be in *bed* at last with George after all the frustration of the last few days. His body, subtly muscly from the gym, felt gorgeous against her back. She sighed and snuggled backwards, closer into him. His arms slid further round her and began exploring. She let out a contented, if discreetly muted, sigh.

'Alex?'

'Yes?'

'Is that nice?'

Alex wondered yet again whether or not to tell George that what he thought he was stroking was in fact something else, albeit in roughly the right area. It would involve an explanation and, with George, she imagined that nothing less than a full examination of the relevant parts would suffice. She tutted inside at herself and at the stumbling block of their otherwise very promising sex life. What was it about him that rendered her suddenly unable to say the word 'clitoris'? She had no problem using it in conversation with Rachel, writing it (should such an occasion arise in her correspondence) and she read it without blushing at least ten times every time she opened a magazine – though probably not the ones George read. He was slowly but surely turning her into a girlie and no mistake. Brain rot was definitely setting in.

But before Alex could think up an alternative, her attention was distracted by the sound of a smashing plate. Her body went rigid and George, who had his head mostly muffled in a pillow, smiled to himself.

'George! Did you hear that?' she whispered urgently.

'No, you were very quiet,' he said. 'I don't think anyone heard.'

Alex sat up in bed and strained her ears. 'I thought I heard something downstairs.'

George sat up next to her and nearly pushed her off the edge of the bed. They listened in silence for a few moments, and then, again, the unmistakable sound of shattering china came from downstairs.

Alex winced as her bare feet came into contact with the prickly seagrass and pulled on her pyjamas. 'It sounds as though it's coming from the kitchen.' She looked across at the empty bed where Rachel should have been. The duvet was ruffled but it was clearly empty and the heap of clothes on the chair had gone.

'Oh, shit,' said Alex, looking at George with wide eyes.

'No. No,' George reassured her automatically, but then concern creased his brow. 'Rachel wouldn't. Not in someone else's house.'

'Not with someone else's crockery,' added Alex hopefully. 'She *loves* Denbyware.'

There was another, louder smash, as though a large bowl had been hurled with some force at the Aga. This time there was an indecipherable hiss of invective accompanying it.

George looked at Alex. 'You go first. I'll follow in a couple of minutes.'

'Oh for God's sake, George, no one's going to notice which bedroom you're coming out of with World War Three erupting downstairs,' hissed Alex. She wondered why she was bothering to keep her voice down. 'There's only Mike and Laura up here – don't wake them up. It's the last thing they need.'

She padded out on to the landing. The plates were getting more frequent. This would be costing someone a fortune, thought George, pulling on his dressing-gown. Still, very good theatrical practice for Caroline, plate-hurling.

Alex tiptoed downstairs, feeling cautiously for the edge of each stone-flagged step with her feet. A light was shining from underneath the kitchen door and there was a disembodied snoring coming from somewhere, to which the crashes from the kitchen ran as a violent counterpoint. She peered under the stairs and saw John heavily asleep by the wine racks outside the kitchen, a pillow pressed around his head. He looked strangely cherubic and utterly peaceful. Typical.

Alex decided that it was probably best to leap in before one of them got hurt. She could hardly believe that neither Rachel, erstwhile netball player, nor Caroline, expert drama queen, had managed to land one direct hit in ten or so plates. She offered up a quick prayer that there wouldn't be any need for her rusty first-aid skills. She'd always been useless at bandages with broken bits sticking out. And Rachel invariably threw up at the sight of blood. Gingerly, Alex pushed open the door, using it partly as a shield, and stuck her hand round it.

'Both of you, stop it! I'm sure we can sort this out before—'

There was no response from the kitchen and Alex peered round.

To her amazement, Mike and Laura were facing each other off across the pine table, spitting hysterically and unintelligibly at each other, swaying slightly as they did so. Alex noted with dismay two empty bottles of George's wine on the side of the work surface. The glasses, it seemed, had long since bitten the dust. Mike was sporting a long red mark on one cheek in the shape of Laura's hand. Laura's mascara had run down her face and her eyes were red with tears and anger.

Oh, thought Alex: Plan B.

They didn't seem to have noticed Alex's arrival and continued their muted argument, now punctuated by stabbing fingers and brandished plates. She noted, impressed, that such were the powers of ingrained manners that they were still bothering to curse and swear in a polite hiss, presumably so as not to wake the sleeping guests, notwithstanding the crockery shards all over the floor.

'You know, I have always *loathed* hysterical women!' spat Mike, the 'New Man' mantle Laura had tried to pin on him for so long obviously shattered somewhere amongst the plates.

Laura ran a hand through her tangled bob, which Alex had never seen looking anything other than glass-smooth. Now it looked like something that had been washed up on a beach. Her fringe was sticking up in chunks, clumped with sweat. Her mouth twisted in an ugly snarl and she unconsciously weighed the plate in her hand like a discus. They didn't break their glare lock. In any case Mike was busy twisting a tea towel and snapping it between his hands like a garrotte.

'Well, you could have fooled me! She's about as hysterical as it gets!'

'Well, you should know!'

Laura let out a muffled yelp of outrage and, holding Mike's stare, she hurled the blue plate at the stripped pine wall cupboard. He didn't flinch as it broke with a crash behind his head. Laura gave another agonised squeal and stamped her foot in frustration. Mike just stared back, his lip curled in disdain.

Alex, who could barely believe what she was seeing, was somehow reassured by this. At least Laura wasn't flinging them at Mike too accurately. Plate throwing equalled wronged woman, perhaps. Deliberate wounding of fiancé was a little uncouth.

'What in the name of God is going on?' whispered a voice at her shoulder.

Alex shut the door and turned to George. 'Tell me I'm dreaming,' she said. 'We *did* leave them at this very table last night behaving like King and Queen of Cuddleland, didn't we?'

'Right,' said George, with his hand on the doorknob. 'This has gone on long enough. Someone's going to get hurt.' He moved to push open the door with his shoulder.

Unfortunately, Laura chose that moment to kick the door shut and hiss, 'You'll wake everyone up with your fucking Neanderthal shrieking!' at an unrepentant Mike. But in fact it was George's howl of pain as the slamming door made contact with his nose that brought the scene to a standstill, leaving Alex to barge the door open and help George to a chair.

Laura immediately started to flap as George dripped blood on to the tiles and had wiped up the evidence before

Alex could get a tea towel to him. It was hard to maintain a stern presence with his head between his knees, but to give George credit, he still managed to bring Laura and Mike to an almost shamefaced silence. Laura replaced her pasta bowl on the rack as if she had just dried it up. Mike wound the towel around his knuckles.

'OK,' said George, 'why don't the pair of you sit down? Sit *down*, Mike. Right, who's going to tell me what's going on?' He looked from one to the other. Won't he be marvellous with children! thought Alex, and pushed the thought out of her mind with a shudder.

There was a long silence, broken only by John's muffled snores outside, in which Mike glared mutinously at Laura and Laura turned white and red.

'Come on,' said George, in his best Jeremy Paxman, 'I'm waiting.' Mind you, continued the disobedient voice in Alex's head, he's probably the sort to time piano practice with an alarm clock. *Shut up! Shut up!*

Mike seemed to decide that it would be better to get his side of the story in first – you can practically hear the cogs ticking, thought George – and drew in a deep breath. Laura looked away, out into the navy blue of the night sky.

'My wife,' Mike began, looking between George and Alex for emphasis, 'my wife—'

'Not yet, Mike, not *yet!*' interrupted Laura querulously, and turned her head again, this time blinking rapidly.

Mike looked even more enraged and yelled, 'My *fiancée*, it would seem, is a *bloody dyke!*'

The words hung in the air like smoke.

Alex swallowed. 'Mike. That's very . . . Are you sure you haven't—'

'No,' hissed Mike. 'It came out of her own mouth. She

"thought I ought to know". She "thought marriages have to be founded on complete trust and knowledge of the other party".' He mimicked Laura's crystalline vowels cruelly. 'And I suppose you're another one?' He narrowed his eyes at Alex.

'How dare you!' said George as Alex brought her hand to her mouth, unable to work out what on earth was going on, what had got into the normally sweet-tempered Mike. She barely noticed the implication of his jibe, she was so flummoxed by the unreality of it all. George, his protective instincts aroused, looked thunderous, as though some marauder had attempted to steal his oxen.

'I should slap you for that,' she said, 'but I see someone else has made a pretty good job of that already.'

A brief smile flickered on Laura's lips and promptly disappeared.

Alex turned to Laura and put her hand on her shoulder. 'Laura? Why don't you tell us what's happened? I'm sure there's been some . . .' Her voice trailed away. Given the advanced state of plate-hurling, perhaps there was no reasonable explanation. And anyway, she thought suddenly, why should there be?

Laura pulled in a shuddering breath and turned her shoulders to face Alex and George. She looked up at the ceiling for a few moments, seemingly formulating her response and then let out the hiccuping breath, as if in a dreadful relaxation exercise.

'Alex,' said Laura.

Oh God, thought Alex, she's got her newsreader voice on.

'Alex, you have always advised me to be honest and open. And I like to think that on the whole, I *have* always been honest with my friends. But obviously there are some things that are private and it's best that they remain so. However, as everyone has said to me over the past few weeks, there can be no secrets between a man and his wife.'

She paused again. It sounded like a rehearsed speech, as though she was hiding behind proper sentences, gaining time as she calmed down and regained control. Mike had obviously thrown her on to rockier improvisational ground. For once, he had not been following the script. George racked his brains to think what she might be on about, but could come up with nothing. Alex, on the other hand, was beginning to put two and two together. Mike snorted again.

'Tonight I thought it was the best time to confess all my secrets to Mike, before we get married and for all the . . . *revulsion* it has apparently caused him, I'm glad I did it because I had no idea that the man I *thought* I loved was such an unreconstructed *bigot!*' Alex had never, in all the time she had known Laura, seen her so – for want of a better word – unLauralike. It was shocking – like watching Snow White light up a fag, whip out her air rifle and take a pot-shot at Bambi's mother.

'Not to mention a raving hypocrite!' finished Laura, her hard-won calmness vanished. Alex put her hand on Laura's, more as a restraining gesture than a comforting one.

'Go on,' goaded Mike, 'tell them what you told me – if they don't know already.'

Laura fixed her eyes on Mike's and held his gaze. 'If you knew *anything* about the world outside your own stupid little circle of rugby and cricket and beer, you'd realise that you have no *right* to take the moral high ground here, you cheating *bastard*.' Her voice built up to a squeaky crescendo and she calmed herself down with some more deep breaths.

Alex squeezed her hand for moral support. Behind the chair, George squeezed Alex's shoulder.

Laura looked at George and Alex, her eyes full of brave tears now. 'In our second year, while I was sharing the set in Newton Court with Caroline—' she swallowed again— 'we had a brief . . . relationship, I suppose is the word. It was something that felt right at the time and it just happened. It didn't last long. About a fortnight. It was nothing to do with Mike, either now or then. I've never wanted to repeat the experience. It's just a part of my life that has always been private and I wanted Mike to know the whole of me, as a gesture of the trust I've put in him.'

Mike snorted yet again.

'Oh for God's sake, Mike, can't you make a different noise?' snapped Alex. 'Is that all you can say, when Laura's being so honest with you?' This was a conversation quite out of the realms of her experience with these people. Snapping was as high as disapproval went usually. George was silent – Alex could imagine how casual lesbianism fitted in with his traditional views on womanhood. My God, he didn't even like her to wear trousers to restaurants.

'No,' said Mike, 'let her tell you *why* she was so open and honest. Go on, Laura. Explain why you were so keen to get your story in first. About your *best friend*.' He folded his arms and leaned back in his chair.

Laura glared again. 'Oh, how naïve I was,' she spat. 'If only I'd known—'

'Look, you've had your row already,' George cut in. 'Why don't you let the rest of us catch up?'

More mutual death looks. Laura and Mike mutely challenged each other to speak first. John's snoring continued incongruously in the hall.

Eventually, Laura said in a rush, 'I thought Caroline might tell Mike and I wanted it to come from me.' She pressed her lips tightly together until they turned white. She looked like a frightened version of her mother.

'Laura thought Caroline might blackmail her with the information if she wasn't picked as a bridesmaid and that's why she didn't ask Rachel. And when I arrived with Caroline – which was meant as a surprise for you, as a matter of fact, you selfish cow! – Little Miss . . . *Lesbigay* here thought we'd been having a leading conversation in the car,' crowed Mike.

Laura smacked the table. 'Instead of which it turns out that you were leading her somewhere else entirely! As if she needed to be led!'

'Well, she didn't seem to be displaying any lesbian tendencies with me!'

'She is *not* a lesbian! *I* am not a lesbian!'

'Too right she's not!'

Laura let out an agonised howl. 'You cheating scum! Whatever happened to all that "I understand women" shit? Was that just a technique you had for pulling? Who else did it work on?'

Alex sunk her head on her hands. This was worse than anything she had ever imagined. Not that something had happened between Laura and Caroline – she had wondered about that for years. In fact it was Rachel, with her intuitive guesses about people, who had mentioned it first; they had both put it down to one of those growing up things and Caroline's flamboyant nature. Neither expected to be 'told' about it.

So that was that bit. And the second bit just confirmed what they all knew about Caroline and Mike. So the actual revelations weren't all that shocking in themselves. But as for

Laura, descending rapidly from 'a confession I prepared earlier' into obscenity and then into wordless howls, or Mike,
swinging from *Guardian* liberal to *Mirror* queerbasher . . .
You think you know folk, thought Alex.

'Mike,' said George, 'what's going on with you and
Caroline? Really?'

'Tell me she made you do it!' pleaded Laura in a sudden
change of tack. 'She can be so persuasive when she wants
something – tell me you didn't mean it.'

Mike just looked smug, folded his arms and said nothing.
Alex wanted to slap him.

'Oh, for God's sake, Mike, that's not what you were saying
to me this afternoon!' exploded George.

'*What* were you saying this afternoon?' snapped Alex and
Laura simultaneously. Laura, relieved to have a different
target for her wrath, followed up with, 'I knew you boys
would be a bad influence on him. He's not like you lot! Can't
you see that?'

There was an immediate cacophony of shouting and
punching the table. Even Alex lost her temper at this,
though she wasn't sure who to yell at first. The problem was
solved for them by the belated arrival of the traditional
scapegoat, John, who was finally awoken by the shriek of
high-velocity chair leg on floor tile as Mike leapt up to
punch George, the only member of the company he felt per-
mitted to punch.

John stood in the doorway, Eeyorish in an old dressing
gown.

'Wha's going on in here?' he mumbled, screwing his eyes
up against the light. Alex grabbed him by the arm, dragged
him in and pushed him into a vacant chair. 'Now come in
and shut up!' she said, a little unnecessarily.

Four pairs of eyes were trained on him.

'Tell Laura what you said to Mike this afternoon,' said George.

'What is this, detention?' whined John.

'Go on!'

John looked from white-faced Laura to red-faced Mike. 'What are you on about?'

George let out a controlled breath. 'About Caroline.'

John giggled. 'I can't say that . . . Oh. Er, OK. I, er . . . You're not making this very easy for me, George. It was a Lads' Chat. Confidential.'

'It's all right, John,' said Laura primly. 'I think we're all grown-ups here.'

'Even if some of us aren't ladies,' muttered Mike.

'You are pushing your luck, Mike,' said Alex through gritted teeth. Mike shut up. He'd seen the bruises on John's shins administered earlier.

'Look, I just said to Mike, that . . . that I thought that . . . as you do . . . at least, I got the impression that . . . well, Caroline seemed to be, you know, *on for it* this weekend.' John looked round the table, his hands spread in innocence. Laura had shut her eyes and seemed to be praying. Mike was looking like a fish that had narrowly avoided a very cunning bait. Alex had her head back in her hands.

Encouraged by this apparently calm response, John went on, 'I mean, what else was I meant to think? She was giving it all the signs, you told me you'd been in touch recently—'

'We were arranging this weekend!' bellowed Mike, smacking his hands on the table. He turned back to Laura, a flash of his usual, more placatory personality emerging, 'We wanted— I wanted it to be a surprise for you! Caroline suggested it and—'

'Oh, I *bet* she did!' roared Laura, shockingly unladylike.

There is a certain lack of logic to arguments, thought Alex, watching Mike and Laura all but lock horns; no one really listened to the actual words the other was saying. It didn't seem to make a difference. Poor John thought he was off the hook altogether and had begun to relax, enjoying a ringside seat as Laura and Mike resumed where they had left off. He really should have seen the dual attack coming.

Laura wheeled round to face him. 'Why do you hate me so much that you try to sabotage my marriage before it's even begun?' she wailed, her distress somewhat undercut by the never-before-seen glint of Valkyrie in her eye. 'You always *were* jealous of anyone with a stable relationship, even at college!'

This was matched by Mike yelling, 'You total bastard! You total fucking stirring bastard!' in the other ear.

John, all six feet five of him, cowered in his chair ('Was it because I told that girl from New Hall about your bloody "Chilean" crabs? Because you told everyone else!') and silently appealed to George ('I'm going to black your other fucking eye, you mixing little shit!'). Alex and George stared back at him, stony-faced.

'Better out than in,' said Alex.

George let the screaming carry on for another ten blood-curdling minutes, until Laura literally ran out of breath. It said something for her manic aerobics sessions that she could last for ten minutes. Mike was reduced to pointing and stamping after five.

'So, let me get this straight,' said George slowly. 'Mike isn't actually—' he hesitated over the right word, not wanting to inflame either Laura or Mike— 'having an affair with Caroline—'

'Although, to be accurate, he did say this afternoon that it might be—' John added unwisely.

Alex trod on his bare foot hard. John, his eyes popping, thought he could hear the bones crunch.

'Mike *isn't* having an affair with Caroline and Laura *isn't* a lesbian, even though she has admitted that, in the past, she and Caroline had a . . . relationship,' finished George.

The kitchen went silent. The clock ticked on the chimneypiece. These are the first seconds, thought Alex. The first seconds in which my friends have abandoned almost every recognisable personality trait that I would have given them in a basic *Cosmo* questionnaire and stand here, all new. Or is this what they've been like all the time, underneath?

Laura started to cry quietly. Big hopeless tears slid down her face and her mouth opened wide in a grimace of agony. Lucy from 'Peanuts', bawling her head off with a big black rectangle for her mouth, popped into her mind, but she didn't care. She didn't care what she looked like any more. How? How had the itchy feeling that had begun yesterday afternoon, of things slipping under her feet like marbles on the floor, moved so quickly to this? How had she gone from happy fiancée with a happy wedding planner to abandoned girlfriend in the space of forty-eight hours? She thought of her wedding planner, still lying open at the 'Bridesmaids' Dresses' section on the sofa, and a fresh wave of misery swept through her.

George had his gaze fixed on the roses on the table but he wasn't seeing them. Out of the corner of his eye, he noticed one of Laura's tears splash on the table and, as subtly as he could, he pulled a white cotton handkerchief out of his dressing gown pocket and put it on her lap. She took it silently.

'So,' said Alex, into the silence, 'all roads lead to Caroline.'

Laura's soundless tears turned into proper sobbing. 'I thought she was my friend,' she hiccuped. 'It was so wonderful and now you've made it all cheap and sordid!' She raised her streaming eyes to Mike, who looked disgusted.

'That's because it *is* sordid,' he said. Laura buried her eyes in George's hanky again. Alex got up from her seat and, squatting by Laura's chair, embraced her as well as she could.

'That was completely unnecessary, Mike,' said Alex, her voice acid with contempt. She caught his eye and made him feel the anger running through her. 'She has had the courage to admit something very brave, while you . . . I don't care what you say, but I don't believe your . . . protestations about Caroline. There *is* something going on, isn't there?'

George opened his mouth to stop her, but realised that there was no point. Someone would say it and Alex would no doubt say it better than he could.

'You've been with her in town, creeping around. She's not been where she says she has. Phone calls at strange times.' Alex felt Laura's sobbing increase, her rib cage rising and falling erratically under her embrace. Alex leaned her head on Laura's side. 'I'm sorry, Laura, I'm really sorry to be saying this, but I don't want this pig to talk to you like this. Caroline's been leading him by the bloody nose.'

Alex tried to breathe deeply to calm down. Adrenalin was coursing through her. All the years of staying out of arguments, suppressing opinions, seemed to be exploding in the room, like a box of fireworks chucked wholesale on to a bonfire. But she could carry on. Nothing was stopping her from saying the thoughts appearing in her head. It was strangely intoxicating.

'We've all been too bloody soft on Caroline. She's got

away with murder and we've just carried on as though nothing has happened, every time. We invite her for dinner, she's snide about the food, still we invite her. She makes no effort to keep in touch until she wants something, we just give it to her, she pisses off. "She's temperamental" or "She's idiosyncratic" or "She's had a difficult upbringing".' Alex took a deep breath. 'She screws Rachel's boyfriend, for Christ's sake, and what happens? Suddenly Rachel is a paranoid depressive with an alleged STD and no one notices that she hasn't eaten in Hall for three months!'

To her horror, Alex realised that she was crying too. She felt as though she had no control over her body or her tongue and yet she was supremely powerful. The tears were rolling down her face and it seemed to be having no effect on her voice. Brilliant. Soap-opera crying.

Laura had stopped crying and was looking at her, open-mouthed. So were Mike and George and John. The only sound in the room was now Alex's heavy breathing and Laura's less glamorous hiccuping sobs. A mobile phone rang once in the sitting room.

'Oh for God's sake, can't you see?' said Alex, more quietly but still as passionately. 'Can't you see what we've done, between us?'

Laura suddenly moaned and broke into fresh peals of sobbing.

'What is it, Laura?' said Alex, renewing her hug. 'Poor Laura. It can only be better now, now there's nothing for anyone to come out with.'

'It's not that,' Laura snuffled into Alex's chest, wishing she could fight down the sobs long enough to get a whole sentence out. She hated her voice sounding hole-punched and quite so much like a disconsolate toddler. With an effort she lifted her head and looked into Alex's eyes. Alex smiled encouragingly.

'I've just realised . . . Caroline and . . . me,' Laura began.

'Go on,' said Alex.

Laura's face crumpled. 'It was just after my Dad got his sodding BAFTA!' And she burst into tearing sobs of anger and misery.

Mike put his head in his hands, his belligerence dissipated at the sight of Laura's anguish.

'The utter . . .' began George, and realised that he didn't have a word in his vocabulary to finish the sentence.

As he was groping for a word, the kitchen door swung open and, for what felt like the millionth time, Caroline stood framed in the doorway. She was apparently incapable of making any other entrance. She had taken care to switch on the hall light, so she was backlit, and her long legs were clearly visible through the sheer nightdress and dressing gown she was wearing. Lady Macbeth dressed by La Perla, thought Alex.

'If you're going to discuss me,' she said, sounding pained but brave, 'you might at least do it to my face.'

A self-conscious silence fell. Caroline pushed her hair off her face and aimed her profile at the light. Her skin was looking suspiciously even-toned and her lashes suspiciously sooty for someone who had just awoken from deep slumber.

Alex wondered how long she had been listening. She wouldn't have had much of a choice in the sitting room. Adrenalin still pounded through her, but she was aware that this was not her fight. Come on, Laura, she thought desperately, don't go all middle class and polite on us now. George was looking magisterial again and Mike – Mike was looking plainly embarrassed.

The difficulty of Mike's situation had not escaped Alex. If he were having an affair with Caroline, then he would have to admit it now and either incur her wrath by finishing it in front of everyone, or he would have to incur the wrath of everyone else by standing by her. And if he *wasn't* having an affair with Caroline and had been fantasising the whole thing, and Laura accused Caroline of home-wrecking . . . Alex looked at Mike, squirming, and thought that he now looked much more like the Mike she knew.

Caroline was a supreme judge of dramatic tension. The expensive private drama classes had not been for nothing. She pulled herself up to full height and bit her lip bravely, like a tragic heroine.

'I can't believe the way you've treated me,' she began, sweeping her eyes over the assembled audience. Only Alex looked her in the eye. 'I organise all this for you, I fly all the way over from America so I can see you, oh,' her voice caught and she put a hand to her mouth. 'I just can't believe it,' she finished in a whisper. There was a pause – in which the audience could admire her performance, Alex thought cynically. But before she could go on, George lifted his chin and coughed.

'Tell me something, Caroline,' he said, as casually as if they'd been in a bar.

Alex swivelled her head. How could he seem so cool? Her heart started thumping in her chest.

'Maybe you can settle a discussion here.' He held Caroline's inquisitive gaze steadily. 'Are you, or are you not, having an affair with Mike?' He gestured towards a quivering Mike.

Caroline looked at George and then at Mike and threw her head back and laughed. Her laugh rattled round the kitchen and had no trace of humour in it whatsoever. Alex narrowed her eyes at her, but it was Laura who suddenly pushed back her chair in anger.

'I'm pleased you find that funny, because you've come very close to breaking up my marriage before it's even begun, you little tart!' She jutted her sharp little chin. Caroline had not been anticipating an attack from this quarter and looked appropriately taken aback.

'Laura!' she said, hurt. 'I can't think what you mean.'

'Oh, yes, you can,' snapped Laura. 'Mike might be easily led but he's not stupid. How dare you laugh at him? I love him and we have a relationship you can't even imagine. As far as I'm concerned, there is no one who can come between me and Mike, no matter how low that other person is prepared to stoop.'

George thought privately that, in the light of what they had just heard, this might be gilding the lily somewhat.

'Laura, hon, I have no idea what you're talking about. Do you really think I would want to steal your fiancé?' Caroline tried to look appealing.

'I wouldn't put it past you.'

Caroline gasped and then her face darkened. 'Oh, come on, Laura, Mike? And me? I don't think so. He's not . . . *my type*.'

Mike looked outraged, but not as outraged as Laura.

'What do you mean, he's not your type?' she snapped.

Caroline did her annoying tinkly laugh. 'I think we just agreed that the deal was off, Laura – there's no use trying to persuade me. Mike's a *friend*. He's very sweet, but, well . . .' She smiled dismissively and shook her head.

Laura's face, which had gone through more emotions in the last hour than anyone had ever thought possible, flushed with anger. She screwed up her eyes, as if everything might vanish, including her newfound Wagnerian personality. But it didn't. Caroline still stood in the doorway, looking triumphant. Everyone held their breath.

'How *dare* you treat me as though I'm just someone you can push over? Someone you can use? Someone you can patronise?' Laura snarled, getting into her stride. She was leaning forward on the table now, her hands curled into fists.

'I can't believe you're saying this,' gasped Caroline. She spread her hands and looked around the table, much as John had done earlier but with even less of a result. 'Give me one instance of my patronising you.'

'All right.' Laura drew a deep breath and seemed to elevate herself way beyond her official five feet four. 'All right, what about the tea service? Did that ever cross your mind?'

'What tea service?' said Mike.

'The tea service that Caroline gave Laura in the second year,' muttered Alex.

'It was a gift!' cried Caroline. 'You couldn't afford the rest so I bought it for you!'

'And how do you think that made me feel?' yelled Laura, thumping her chest. 'Eh? How do you think that made me feel? Especially when you suggested having everyone round for tea to look at it and then spent two hours telling everyone you'd bought it and how much it cost and what splendid taste you had!'

Mike was looking thoroughly puzzled. 'I don't get it. It was a present, right?'

Caroline seized on this. '*Thank* you, Mike. *Thank* you for pointing out how ridiculous this argument is.'

Mike looked pleased and then remembered that he couldn't possibly be considered Caroline's type and re-knitted his brows.

'You think you can just buy into everything,' yelled Laura. 'Well, I gave you my friendship *free* for all those years. I have always been there when you've needed a shoulder to cry on. I was the one walking you up and down the river – *the night before my Finals* – when Simon Hargreves dumped you—'

'He did not dump me!' hissed Caroline. 'I was having a mild nervous breakdown. As you well know.'

Laura ignored her. 'You've interrupted countless dinners with your "urgent" phone calls, you've had me running around London for you all the time you've been in America, you've practically *never* returned supper invitations, but, no, I've never made a big thing about any of that because you were my friend. Even when all I got in return was cast-off clothing and the odd tearful tribute to my patience when you were pissed,' she said, clenching and unclenching her fists.

'Oh my God, I can't believe that you can view our friendship like that,' said Caroline, taking advantage of Laura's pausing for breath. But Laura, who was erupting with years of suppressed thoughts and bitten tongues, could not be stopped by mere words.

'And what do you do now?' she yelled rhetorically. 'You come up here, disrupt my plans, create friction between me and Mike, act in what I can only call a furtive manner and generally behave like Lady bloody Muck! On *my* weekend! Caroline, I am not a friendship supermarket!'

'And I am not Florence Nightingale!' yelled Caroline. 'I really thought you cared about me, deep down. If there is anything deep down in you!'

George cringed internally, sensing that the deeper waters they had now entered would mean more mud-slinging. But the storm he was braced for didn't come.

Laura had sunk into her chair, the force of her passion spent. The words were still ringing in her ears and she was amazed that she'd actually said them: until they'd come tumbling out, she'd only ever been half aware of the feelings in her heart. Now she felt horribly alone, as though she were standing on an upturned canoe in a very big lake. She also felt very tired.

Mike reached across the table and took her hand in his. Laura managed a weak smile, more from habit than feeling. She couldn't work out how she should be feeling about Mike now. Her mind was numb, unable to take in what was happening, let alone process it, but there at least was something familiar in the gesture. That was, in a small way, comforting.

George looked at Alex. He had a feeling that everyone except Caroline had run out of lines. Alex was looking out of the window, an expression of concern on her face. Caroline, though, had only just begun and apparently suffered from none of the shock the others were feeling at the sudden torrent of harsh words flooding like spring water from the most unlikely sources.

'Oh, that's right, look sorry for yourself,' she sneered. Her eyes narrowed. 'Well, come on, it's about time you were honest with each other. For God's sake, Mike, I can't believe you didn't know that about me and Laura. Yes, I heard you screaming in here. So what? We had a thing – most women do at some point. We don't have your stupid hang-ups about sexuality. If I were you, I'd be more worried about the fact that she's never had the balls to tell you – if you pardon the expression.'

Laura and Mike sat frozen at the end of the table. Alex had turned away from the window and now sat glowering at Caroline. Before she could say anything, Caroline had turned to her, obviously disappointed in Laura and Mike's lack of fight.

'And don't you look so fucking superior, Alex! It's exactly what you're thinking but you just don't know who to say it to. Because bitching is fine but saying things to people's faces is simply not the done thing, isn't that right? I suppose that's the way George prefers you to do things.'

Caroline crossed her arms and revelled in the shocked silence. This was going almost as well as her analyst had said it would. She felt purer already. And, since she'd started . . .

'Right, we're in business.' Dan put down the binoculars he'd had trained on the cottage for the last hour and a half and picked up his camera. His hands ran over the long lenses in the bag on his knee and he twisted in the appropriate one. Suddenly he was buzzing with barely suppressed tension.

Fin's concentration, which had been itching away in a circular fashion at the Rachel problem, snapped back to the scene in front of him. The valley in which Marvin's cottage nestled was dark but the black Porsche could just be made out in the drive. Marvin had come home as predicted by Dan at about eight o'clock and nothing had happened since; they had parked up the road in a spot Dan had found that afternoon and hadn't left the car, except for snatched pees.

The lights were still on in Marvin's cottage, but without Dan's surveillance binoculars, Fin could only detect some movement. A few moments later, the door opened. About bloody time, thought Fin. He squinted but couldn't make out the face. And surely *he* wouldn't be wearing those jeans and a polo neck . . . Fin leaned forward, unable and unwilling to believe his eyes. Talk about mutton dressed as lamb.

Dan turned to him. 'Right. I want you to follow him at a

close-ish distance but not too close – I don't want him making off at high speed. I know where he's going anyway.' He lifted the camera and fired off a few frames of Marvin looking about, satisfying himself that the coast was clear, throwing something into the car and getting in.

'What was that?' asked Fin. 'What did he just throw in the back?'

Dan gave a dirty laugh. 'That was what is commonly known as a travel rug. Sheep shit is a real passion killer, or so I'm told.' He rewound the film and reloaded without taking his eyes off the Porsche and said, 'OK, let's go.'

Fin did a textbook-perfect hill start and drove up to the main road.

'It's so *unhealthy*,' said Caroline, looking down her nose at Mike and Laura. 'My analyst says that it's not surprising that I have poor self-image, given the repressive atmosphere I had to experience at university, when I should have been at my most creative.' She ran a hand through her hair.

This was too much for Alex, who saw that Laura's moment of rebellion had passed and that Mike, George and John were practically quavering.

'Oh come on, Caroline,' she said, matching Caroline's sarcasm with what she hoped was an equally sardonic adult arguing tone. One that suggested that actually the subject is far too boring to be discussing. She pitched it around the drawls she used to hear regularly in English supervisions. 'I don't think poor self-image is ever something that you've suffered from, is it?'

'Are you a psychologist, Alex?' replied Caroline witheringly. 'Do you have any idea of the damaging effects of low self-esteem?'

Alex tried a dry laugh and was surprised at how good it sounded. 'Oh dear. And I always thought the whole *point* of your sharing with Laura was so that every time you wanted an ego boost you could pop your head round the door and get her to tell you how nice your hair was.'

'You wouldn't understand.'

'Why not?'

'Because you're so . . . bland.'

Alex recoiled at this. 'Is there a punchline to all this, Caroline? Because it sounds like the banal ramblings of a spoilt brat to me. Did you always mean to come up to Laura's party so you could insult us all? Or is this just spur of the moment stuff? *Impro*?'

Caroline glared at her and massaged the small of her back. Her very short nightdress rode up at the side, but she didn't seem to notice. She milked the pause and then put her head on one side.

'The problem with you is that you're so small.' She let this sink in and looked round the faces at the table, which were rapidly resembling a *Titanic* Reunion Party. Caroline allowed herself a smile.

'You thought you were all so clever at college – The Gang.' She did the inverted commas in the air with her fingers. 'You were a *bit* clever, a *bit* sporty, a *bit* trendy, a *bit* funny . . . But never enough to actually be anything *special*. Just the Bland Gang. And you're all just like that now. A bit successful, a bit married, a bit clubby. Nothing that might be different. Or new.' She curled her lip, but only succeeded in looking like Posh Spice.

George found his voice at last. He couldn't understand what had brought this on at all, only that he was being personally attacked in a way he hadn't experienced since prep school. Had he really *slept* with this woman?

'I seem to remember you being in that gang, though, Caroline,' he said. 'I seem to remember you in all the photographs.'

Caroline waved her hand dismissively. 'Just because you have someone's photograph doesn't mean you really know them. I never wanted to end up like you. Euch! Accountancy! Where's your sense of ambition? Oh God, I mean, you all *travel*, but you never go anywhere.'

'That is not true!' exclaimed John, who obviously felt that the argument had come round to him. Caroline did not dignify him with a response and he subsided quickly.

'Well, as this is the time to air grievances,' said Alex, 'let me say that I can *never* forgive you for what you did to Rachel. I think that was about as small-minded as it gets. And, let's face it, someone else's man is hardly breaking new ground, is it? Doesn't look like low self-esteem to me. I'd call that arrogance.' Her face hardened and she felt the light-headedness again. Caroline's expression didn't change. 'You were a bitch to steal her boyfriend and just . . . malicious to spread those rumours afterwards. I'm only ashamed that I didn't come round and have it out with you at the time, but Rachel begged me not to.' And how she wished she'd done it anyway.

'Oh, but *how* convenient,' sneered Caroline. 'She *begged* you to ignore it. So for the sake of poor Rachel, you all pretended that it didn't happen.' She turned to George, who was colouring with either embarrassment or rage. 'And you, you just pretended it didn't happen too, didn't you? Just crawled out of bed, went for a run, had a shower and spent the rest of the day in the library. Hoping I'd have gone when you came back. And then that polite silence for the rest of term.' She sneered again. 'Well, it wasn't an experience I ever wanted to talk about again anyway. So much for the erotic charge of forbidden fruit.'

'You nearly destroyed Rachel!' Alex could barely put enough emotion into her voice, wondering if anything could shatter the hard shell of Caroline's self-centredness. She was fighting a passionate impulse to punch her, boiling with frustration at the uselessness of words. 'Do you honestly not realise that? She was a wreck for weeks after what happened with you and George. I don't think she's ever been able to trust anyone properly again, despite all that surface stuff. Does that not mean *anything* to you?'

Caroline flushed. 'Oh, spare me. Poor Rachel, the victim. Poor Rachel, the abandoned girlfriend. I didn't see George rushing to her side, did you? And despite what you might like to think, I don't remember forcing him to do anything he didn't want to. She's traded on this for *years* and you just tacitly encourage her, rather than talk about something that embarrasses you. You and your pathetic girlie sisterhood.' She tossed her head. 'Clever women don't need excuses.'

'Was it that you never had a proper friend at university, Caroline?' came a voice from the open door. 'Or are you a natural cow, just for fun?'

Fin had never had so much fun in a car, and he had never felt so incredibly aware of his own skill. Dan's car was like no other Golf he had ever driven and it practically demanded its own soundtrack. Powerful, responsive, it clung to the roads like a skate. Following the weaving red tail lights of the Carrera round the lanes, frequently with his headlights off, was like being in a very, very fast virtual reality game. Doom, but without the chainsaws.

They had kept a safe distance to begin with, Dan worrying that the throaty roar of the tweaked engine would alert Marvin to their nearness, but about ten minutes into the chase, there had been a low rumble of thunder, booming through the heavy night air and echoing round the valley.

'Shit!' swore Dan. 'The lightning! Kill the lights!' Fin had switched off the lights, relying on Marvin's tail lights, Dan's rally-style navigation and his own instinct to follow the twisting road. He had no idea where they were, what road they were on, where they were going. All he could think of was not losing Marvin and not scaring him away.

But there was really no need to drive without the round headlights, as the forked lightning cracked through the sky far off behind the lowering presence of the Scawfells, and Marvin had shown no sign of slowing or indeed acknowledging their presence. He was driving like a man possessed. A man on a mission. A man used to driving responsibly through London streets with a child seat in the back.

Fin saw the tail lights slow and realised that they were coming to a fork in the road.

'Which way?'

Marvin was turning left without indicating – bad driver, thought Fin automatically, before realising that if he was unaware of other road users it was probably a good sign.

'Right! Go right!'

'But he's going—'

'Trust me, go right!'

Fin accordingly veered off to the right. Marvin's tail lights disappeared into the blackness. 'I hope you know what you're doing.'

'Look, what do you think I was doing all afternoon? The road he's on only goes part way round the lake. This one cuts him off.' Dan was grappling with his camera. He looked up and gave Fin the cheeky smile that made waitresses give him extra coffee. 'I'll tell you when we get there, OK?'

Rachel stood in the doorway with Humpty at her feet. She was still wearing her blue dress with a soft angora cardigan over it, the colour of wheat. That's what was missing from the kitchen, Alex thought abstractedly. The dog. No smell.

'Where have you been?' asked George. 'Aren't you freezing?'

Rachel shook herself, as if waking up from a sleepwalk. 'I felt sick, so I got up and went down to the lake,' she said politely. 'The Screes look wonderful in the moonlight, but I think there's a storm coming on.'

Caroline shifted slightly, temporarily upstaged. She opened her mouth to speak, but Rachel cut in first, her voice calm and conversational.

'No, don't, Caroline. I know what you're going to say already and it's so *dull*. The same old melodramatic "Nobody loves me" actress shit. I've heard all Laura's excuses for you over the last few years and I don't think yours are going to be anything new. Look, forgive me for my famous small-town way of seeing things, but what it all comes down to is the fact that you're just jealous.'

Caroline's mouth closed into a hard line. She no longer looked like a transatlantic actress. Signs of the old, pre-gloss Caroline were showing through.

'Jealous of my friendship with Alex, jealous of Laura and Mike, jealous of my old relationship with George . . . whatever,' went on Rachel. 'It's all very sad. But I'm sure you'll get counselling for it.'

No one spoke or moved. Even Caroline was silenced by Rachel's eerily measured composure.

'I suppose you're wondering why I'm not in hysterics. I wondered too – I mean, it's not exactly my idea of a fun weekend, spending it in close contact with the woman who nearly drove me to a breakdown – but it occurred to me last night that having hysterics was what everyone expected me to do,' said Rachel coolly, as if she were breaking down a poem into literary criticism themes. 'Including me. And then it occurred to me that a *lot* of my behaviour is based on what you all expect me to do. Sort of easier than working out what I really want to do, isn't it?'

Caroline seized the moment and tutted sarcastically. But Rachel turned to her with a smile on her face.

'You know, and this is the great irony – we're all so keen on irony, aren't we? The irony for today is that Caroline, despite all that self-deluding psycho bollocks, is absolutely right about something after all.'

Laura swallowed and gripped Mike's hand. This was scary, she thought. She wondered if Rachel had changed the habits of a lifetime and had been taking drugs outside. Maybe she was in some kind of a trance. This kind of calmness wasn't normal. It almost made the earlier screaming reassuring.

'You know, we've never had a row in all this time. That's not normal, for God's sake, is it? And I wish we had done. I wish I'd been able to let go and smack your smug little face and get it all out of my system at the time, instead of hiding it all away and letting it fester like this. Turning away from it in my mind. Shows what kind of trust I had in you lot, that I was so afraid that you'd take her side. Now *that's* low self-esteem,' she said, fixing Caroline with a cool stare. 'Not just having to go to a colour consultant to find out whether you look good in green or not.'

'Life goes on,' said Caroline nastily.

Rachel put her head on one side and considered. 'Well, that's it, isn't it? Life does go on, but you don't. You hang around in the past, still fretting away at the old resentments. And you don't bother to update your friendships, because you're afraid of actually talking to people properly and maybe having to discuss all these sensitive things, so you stick with the cardboard cut-outs, which still do pretty well, I've found. But they don't grow. They're like having plastic flowers in your house instead of real ones. They get dusty but they won't die on you.'

'But,' said Alex softly, 'you know they're fake when you look closely.'

Rachel's familiar smile appeared behind her grave expression, as though a gauzy scarf of composure was hiding her face. 'Exactly. I only thought of that this evening. Although it didn't sound quite so pretentious when it was an image in my head.'

'So all this time, I've been a cardboard cut-out?' George broke in, wounded. A feeling was expanding in his chest that he had lost more than he realised and it hurt his pride, his feeling of possession. Rachel had put into words the vague awareness that he'd had all weekend: that she was actually a completely different person from the filecard reference of her he kept in his head. She hadn't always been 'Neurotic, Creative, Emotional', she had been a lot more. And now it was too late to find out again: he had turned back and the old Rachel had gone.

'Not always,' she said gently.

Caroline was beginning to feel isolated again, feeling the bands of loyalties slowly recovering around her, shutting her out of their little cliques, and she still hadn't said all she wanted to say. She looked at the door and then looked at Rachel.

'Oh, well, you can tell who the English students were,' she said sarcastically. 'But I don't see how you can justify calling *me* melodramatic when you were the one who had everyone scouring the Cam to see if you'd thrown yourself in. Who did you think you were, bloody Ophelia? Then all the hiding away and not talking to anyone except Alex – you're the drama queen, Rachel. If you'd only had the guts to face up to the problem, then at least I could have respected you for it.' She stood aggressively, her hands on her bony hips. The fishwife buried deep in Caroline's shiny family tree had finally emerged.

'Turn right now!' yelled Dan, his camera ready in his hand, another round his neck.

Fin hauled the wheel round into a narrower lane. They were right up by the lake now. The tyres screeched on the road and then scuffed through some loose stones. His heart was hammering. Ahead on the road he could see the black Carrera, parked up on the verge, facing in the opposite direction, next to a concealed entrance. The car was empty.

'Pull up here and block him in,' said Dan, his hand already on the door handle. Fin slowed down and before he could come to a halt, Dan was out of the car and running up the drive. There was a tremendous crack of lightning and up the driveway he could see Dan only a hundred metres behind another figure, which was certainly Marvin. It was a good walk up to the cottage and he was sauntering casually, oblivious to Dan following him, like a cat stalking a three-legged mouse. It was in the unreal white flash of the lightning that Fin suddenly realised where they were.

Yanking open the door, he threw himself out of the car and yelled, 'Dan! Stop! For fuck's sake, stop!' But the thunder was rumbling too loudly and Dan had the scent of blood in his nostrils. He was already lining up his camera for a long shot. Fin grabbed his cameras and scrambled across the road after him.

Rachel blinked and twisted the ring on her finger, running her finger over the emerald. She stood at the edge of a cliff and knew that if she jumped she would not fall. She had imagined this moment for years, and now it was here, she was so calm that it seemed as though the words were flowing out of her, so she could listen too.

'I've learned you can't move on when there are secrets chaining you to something that isn't relevant any more,' she said. 'And part of me can't move on until you all understand properly. Well, I don't care if you don't understand, but at least I can stop blaming myself for not telling you. It's holding me back, all this pretending it hasn't happened, just because none of it fitted in with what I had imagined should happen. Perhaps the whole story *is* melodramatic.' She paused and looked up at the expectant faces round the table. 'When I went away for the weekend up to Manchester, before . . . Well, it wasn't because my granny was in hospital. It was because I was pregnant.'

George went very pale, feeling the second shock fall on the first like a barely noticed bruise. Alex hung her head, and thought of all the things she had nearly said at the time.

'I needed some time to think about what I should do. It's such a different thing when it's actually happening to you.' She looked at George and gave him a weak smile. An expression of miserable dread weighed down on his face and he looked at her as though he wanted her to stop but couldn't deny the truth from coming out.

'Don't worry, George,' she said tenderly. 'I hadn't decided what to do when I came back. I was going to tell you, talk to you about it. That wasn't easy either – I knew once I'd said it, I couldn't unsay the words, deny the reality of what was happening to me, but you had to know. I was coming back that morning to tell you. I did love you. I hoped we'd work out what to do together.'

He put his head in his hands and listened to the voice that was now speaking to him from three years ago, from the bedroom of his set, the room murky with morning light filtered through the rough blue curtains. He could feel the sheen of summer sweat on his skin again – a sickening mixture of hangover, old sex and guilt.

'But when I found you with Caroline . . . oh, I'm not going through all that again. If you can't imagine what I felt then, there's no point.' Rachel closed her eyes and fought back the lump closing up her throat. 'But, oh God, I felt as though all my senses had ended. That I was in a well, with all life passing above me, miles above my head. I can't remember much about it.' She opened her eyes and looked at George. His eyes were brimming with tears.

'I lost the baby,' she said simply.

Laura drew in her breath and murmured something, remembering. Mike put his arms round her and she laid her head on his shoulder. He gazed at Rachel, still standing by the door like a visiting monarch, her dog lying guard at her feet. It was like he'd never seen her before.

Alex put her arm around George, his head sunk in his hands, and looked up at Rachel, her eyes filling up too.

Rachel wrapped her cardigan tightly round her, tucking

her arms under her armpits and looked at no one. She was almost talking to herself. 'It was easier not to think. Easier just to go on as if nothing had happened. So I did; I had no choice. By the time I saw you all again, it was like I'd never even been out with George. But there's no *point* in the end, because it just holds you to something you refuse to face.'

She stood silently for a moment and turned to Caroline. 'I mean, I've made you a symbol of all this, half of which you didn't even know about. How ridiculous is that? I didn't want to admit to myself that my friends had let me down – that I'd let myself down by running away. Even that terrible feeling of loss I had, for something I'd only just acknowledged, was my fault. You can't imagine how . . . how it was. You were the obvious scapegoat, so I transferred it all on to you. How can I blame *you* for me not sorting myself out and getting a proper job? How can I blame *you* for me being too scared to trust Fin enough to marry him or not? You're nothing, Caroline. Really nothing at all.'

Caroline had no reply. She had never expected this and, like Laura, was not prepared for ad lib. There were one or two parting lines she had in reserve but she didn't quite know when to deliver them, being in the unenviable position of being on stage and not knowing when the curtain was to fall. George, on the verge of tears, looked as though he were about to begin a big speech and she really didn't think she could be bothered with that.

But George was immediately upstaged by a doorbell.

The surreal suburban chimes rang politely through into the kitchen, and were followed by a rumble of thunder. Everyone stared stupidly at each other. Laura felt the effects of the red wine wearing off and a dull headache setting in.

'Where's that coming from?' said Alex.

The doorbell rang again above the sounds of the approaching thunderstorm outside.

'It's the other door!' said Laura in a flash of inspiration. She winced as her head lurched. 'You know, the front door.'

Everyone looked blank.

'Oh, you know the one I mean! The locked door next to the sitting room. I don't think it's used very often.' Amidst all the turmoil, Laura was troubled by a disorientated sense of hospitality. The kitchen was a mess. Who could it be and what could they offer them to drink?

'Where's the key?' snapped Caroline. 'Oh, come on, Laura, where've you put the key?' She held her hand out impatiently.

'I think it's in the lock,' said Laura as Caroline rushed out. 'But shouldn't we find out who it is first?' she shouted as Alex followed Caroline out in to the hall. George was slumped in his chair, tears running down his face, wanting Rachel to come over and take his hand, anything to make the implications breaking in on him real.

'Can I get you an aspirin, piggie?' Mike asked Laura solicitously, really wanting one for himself and not knowing where they were.

At the front door Caroline fiddled with the key, her fingers all clumsy in panic. Alex jostled behind her. Who would come to the front? None of the locals would think of using it. Had Laura invited someone else? Or had Fin come to take Rachel away?

Alex was most intrigued by Caroline's taking charge of the situation. She realised that Caroline needed to make some kind of sweeping exit, but she could hardly have called for a minicab round here. Could she?

Caroline was swearing under her breath as she tugged at the door, which was indeed warped. It was evidently rarely used and despite her nightie, she hardly presented a picture of elegance. With a final tug at the handle, the door swung open.

'I threw stones at your window, darling, but you weren't— Who the hell are these people, Caroline? You said you were staying here on your own!'

Alex stood gaping in amazement behind Caroline, who was radiant with smug pride at displaying her clandestine lover so dramatically and at last effecting the grand departure she had been anticipating for the last twenty minutes.

George stumbled like a sleepwalker to the door and wondered stupidly if a red book was about to be produced – then remembered that that was Michael Aspel. Alex, on the other hand, suddenly understood the display of sheer nightwear and matching negligées. She might have known it wasn't for Mike's benefit. But this was straying into the realms of David Lynch. Who else was going to turn up? The Nolan Sisters?

Caroline flung herself into his arms, nightie riding up saucily, and closing her eyes and lifting her face up to be kissed, she declared, 'Take me away from all this!' She had waited a lifetime to say it and now, even if her audience was only George and Alex . . .

As if by divine approval, the great lighting man in the sky illuminated the moment with another bolt of forked lightning, the instant that she felt his arms tightening round her (and one hand, she noticed, fixing itself lecherously on her left buttock). This is the pinnacle of my life so far, thought Caroline happily. Even better than the week in New York with all his charge cards.

It was a brief moment, for as soon as the thought had appeared in her mind, the arms loosened and she heard her lover say, most unromantically, 'Fucking hell! Oh my God! Oh my God! Come here, you bastard!'

Dan was standing in a bush about fifty metres from the back door, flicking a cheery finger to the enraged Marvin. Fin came charging down to the end of the drive just in time to hear Dan's camera rewinding. He doubled over to try to get his breath back, gasping and staring at his knees.

'No, no, Dan,' he panted, 'you can't . . .' He looked up and saw the startled scene at the door; Alex and George transfixed on the doorstep like passers-by caught on an outside broadcast, Marvin swearing and sweating and Caroline leaning against the door frame for support, her clothes in *News of the World* disarray, watching her best-laid plans unravel and frantically thinking how she might still salvage them. She was looking at Dan and his cameras with a somewhat ambiguous expression.

'Too late, mate,' said Dan, a broad grin on his face. It was not clear whether he was talking to Marvin or Fin.

'What's going on?' Rachel's voice floated out as she, Mike, Laura and John came to the door to see what all the shrieking was in aid of. John, inevitably, had his camcorder to his eye.

As Rachel appeared on the doorstep behind Alex, Fin saw an expression of disbelief cross her face and his heart sank. She looked so serene, so beautiful. In an instant he knew that he would give it all up tomorrow as long as he could keep her. Nothing else mattered. Just being with Rachel and making her happy.

He held his breath, hardly daring to look at her. But suddenly Rachel broke into a dazzling smile, as though she had seen the funniest thing in the world. Fin could see what she must have looked like when she was seven years old.

Rachel leaned forward between George and Alex's rigid shoulders and held out her hand. 'Marvin, I presume? I'm a great fan of yours. My mum thinks you're such a dish! Can we invite you in for a cup of tea? Or perhaps something stronger?'

The absurdity of the situation had thrown a strange kind of suspension over proceedings, after the frantic succession of Laura's revelations, Mike's fall from grace, Rachel's shattering admissions and now the discovery of a displaced celebrity on their front doorstep. But the spell was suddenly broken, as though the pause button had been released again.

Laura pushed her way to the front of the crowd at the door, her forehead furrowed unbecomingly. Marvin's expression changed from pure rage to horrified rage.

'Laura?' he stuttered. Caroline instinctively released her arms from his neck and swivelled round, her eyes narrowed.

'What the hell are you doing here – with her?' snapped Laura, ignoring everyone else. 'What about Fiona? And Charlie and Rosie?' She moved to slap him and Mike had to restrain her.

Caroline turned back, outraged that her final scene was being stolen, and by *Laura*, of all people. 'How do you know Laura?' she asked him icily. She knew all too well who Fiona, Charlie and Rosie were.

'Because he's my bloody godfather,' answered Laura, a grim smile playing briefly on her face before disappearing into a thunderous frown. Mike looked to the sky for some help. 'He's my dad's best mate and has been since they were at the BBC together.'

'Oh my God, I've been set up!' bellowed Marvin, who

had clearly taken Rachel's greeting as evidence of a plot, given the unlikelihood of her not recognising him. 'Give me that film!' he roared at Dan, who simply took the rewound film out of the camera and dropped it in the top pocket of his combat trousers. 'How much money do you want for that film?' he roared again.

'You can discuss that with tomorrow's papers,' said Dan, turning to go.

'Double it!' roared Marvin, the famously smooth Northern tones strangled in rage.

'Er, you can triple it,' said John boldly, pointing at the camcorder, which was still rolling. This seemed to convince Marvin that the Ides of March were nigh and, displaying none of the easy charm that had made him such a well-loved household name, he rattled off a string of expletives, turned on his heel and began running down the drive towards his car, presumably to get on the phone to his lawyers.

'I hope he's going to ring his wife,' observed Alex, glaring at the back of Caroline's neck.

'What about me?' wailed Caroline, flinging her arms out. She didn't care about the pictures – she knew she looked good, she could only get publicity from it and although she wasn't naïve enough to think that he would leave his wife, Caroline knew a thing or two about *her* that would make a good four-page spread. Health-giving properties of porridge, my arse. That wasn't what she'd been in that clinic for.

But this wasn't looking good. Worst case scenario: being stuck here in the cottage having well and truly burned her bridges and with Rachel well up in the sympathy stakes, George on full-on guilt-trip mode and Alex being sarcastic for England. And as for Laura . . .

Caroline shivered. 'Oh God, what about me?' she yelled at Marvin's retreating back. 'What about this afternoon? The ring?'

Marvin didn't bother to answer and down the drive she heard the Porsche's engine roar – the Porsche! The Porsche that she was going to have for running around in when they got back to London, to the gorgeous secret flat in Knightsbridge!

'Don't leave me!' she yelled into the darkness. There was no reply. She hesitated, knowing that she had maybe half a minute to act before she would start looking pathetic. The lovely weekends together in town while his wife looked after the brats in Sussex, the jetting off to New York pretending to be his PA, the sexy sneaking around – all flashed before her eyes. Her cynical assertions that, OK, they were using each other and she didn't care, left a nasty taste in her mouth and she suddenly felt sick. With a heaving sob, Caroline ran upstairs and in place of her triumphant exit with her famous, rich, married lover in a sportscar she had to make do with slamming the door of Rachel and Alex's room and locking herself in, emitting wracking sobs that hurt her to make.

'Well, there's another thing to hold against us,' said Alex to George. He put his arm around her and led her inside.

'I can't believe it, I just can't believe it,' Laura was hissing to Mike, who was trying to calm her down. Her fists banged impotently on his chest. 'Wait till I phone Dad. God, my family . . . and you wonder why I went to boarding school? You know I'm godmother to his little boy? Oh, I just can't . . . I can't believe she's done this – I can't believe *he's* done this! Oh my God . . . It's all just so horrendous, it proves everything I've always said about bloody actors, it'll be all over the papers . . .'

Rachel walked out into the garden where Fin was still standing, stunned. She stretched out her hand and he could see that she was wearing his ring on her finger. Everything else faded away. With a murmur of joy, he wrapped her up in his arms and nuzzled his nose into her hair.

'Don't ever let me go,' she said into his chest.

'Oh, I'll never let you go,' said Fin. 'Never.' They swayed in their hug, Fin not knowing what to say to express the happiness and relief he felt and Rachel knowing that words would only be half of what she wanted to say. It was a very healthy silence.

'Can I take you away?' he asked.

Rachel giggled into his jumper. 'That's a very Caroline thing to say.'

'Go in and get your bags and the dog and we'll go,' said Fin. 'I don't want you spending another night in there with them.'

'What, and miss all the gossip?'

'You can catch up when you get back to London. Dan's booked into a hotel somewhere – we can get a room. I think the drinks are on him, after tonight.' Fin unwrapped Rachel from his bear hug and held her at arm's length. 'Are you all right? About . . . you know, Marvin?' The codename seemed stupid afterwards. 'You don't mind?'

Rachel shook her head. 'No. Not in the least. But do I want to go to bed. It's been a very long night.' She thought of the baby. It was definitely a baby now.

epilogue

John, smartly turned out in a sharply cut navy suit, zoomed in on the sign outside the church which proclaimed, amongst other things, that the white tiered spire of St Bride's, Fleet Street, was the largest built by Sir Christopher Wren and had inspired the modern wedding cake. He then raised his camera and panned up the entire length of said spire, which was gleaming white against a clear blue sky.

Background detail thus established, he moved his focus back to the matter in hand and panned round the crowd of folk assembled by the church door. He didn't know very many people, although experience told him that they looked quite 'media', and after picking out some rather smart girls in summery dresses and large feathery hats for special treatment and lingering panning shots, he walked over to where he could see a familiar face.

Or rather two familiar faces. Laura, dressed in a neat pink

suit and cream straw hat, was busy giving Mike a lecture on something. Although Laura's usual placid smile was much in evidence, her eyes were boring into Mike's forehead and Mike was looking glumly at his shoes, occasionally shooting a sideways glance at a long-legged redhead John thought he recognised from college. Laura put her hand on Mike's arm, effectively blocking that line of vision.

'. . . you won't forget about my mother's birthday, will you, Mike? I just want you to be at home for the evening on Monday and I'll cook something for her and my dad. They've not been round since we got back from Venice, have they? Mike, darling, are you listening?'

The hand on his arm tightened its grip. Mike looked down at the wedding band on her pink-polished finger, the rose gold still as shiny as the day they had picked it up from Hatton Garden. Mike's was a perfect match, slightly thicker, which he suspected was to accommodate the tracking device Laura had had planted in it.

'Yes, darling, of course I'm listening. Monday night.' Monday night was rugby. This would have to be handled cunningly nearer the time. But not now. He patted her hand and gave her what he hoped was an uxorious beam.

Laura smiled up at him. Excellent. She had got her request in before rugby had been mentioned. She would have a word with John, make sure any conniving at excuses was headed off at the pass. She slipped her arm through Mike's in a happy, wifely way. There had been some bumps along the way to the altar, but as her mother had said, once you have the invitations printed, it's in the hands of a higher authority. Whether she had meant God or the Court and Circular column, Laura did not know. But she did know that Mike was on a bloody tight rein from now on. And he knew that too. And they both knew that, apart from anything else, she knew some very good divorce lawyers.

John caught the smiles but not the dialogue and, happy that they had not looked up and spoiled the effect of his unobtrusive fly-on-the-wall style, he turned back to the gate.

'Sharp suit, John, my man!' said a voice behind him, just as a hand clapped itself on his shoulder. John wheeled round and almost fell over George and Alex.

'Oh, for God's sake, George!' snapped John, giving up and pausing his recording. He shook George heartily by the hand, clapping the other on his shoulder in the Lads' Society Greeting, and kissed Alex on both cheeks. 'Oh, er, the suit, yes, courtesy of Caroline's friend, actually. Sold him the tape at a bargain price. Well, a copy of the tape, anyway.' He picked an invisible piece of fluff off a lapel. 'Handmade, this is. Great lining, look.' He swung his jacket open to reveal a flash of bright cerise silk.

George flinched. 'Er, great.'

George's suit on the other hand, thought Alex, made him look like something from a very expensive car advert. And now, at last, she could show him off. She squeezed him with the arm she had around his waist. The funny thing was that now she could openly phone him, meet him, snog him in public and make arrangements that implicitly included him, all her earlier doubts about his suitability had vanished. It turned out that he wasn't actually as anal as she had feared. He had recently come into Divinyl, put his AMEX on the counter and told her to pick out the fifteen albums she really needed to listen to. He had offered to give her a hand in the new shop on Saturdays, when Rachel couldn't come in. He had made his peace with Otis and now could, with a few hints, be brought to open up a tin of the old Science Diet. To

Alex's amazement, he had even begun talking tentatively about 'love'. And what it might mean after all.

Alex sighed happily and looked up to catch George giving her a proprietorial smile.

I'm so glad I persuaded her to try on that dress, George thought proudly. Her legs look *so* long. Alex was wearing a short yellow shift dress, her dark hair in soft curls pinned up by a red silk poppy. She had drawn the line at a hat, although he had marched her round all the stores he had chargecards for. Not even Rachel could persuade her. After a lifetime of jeans, leggings and shorts, Alex in dresses, it was generally agreed, was a revelation. George thought she was just a revelation in general.

There was no point hiding something so good, he thought. He had missed enough already, losing sight of what was important, trying to work out what he *should* be doing instead of what he wanted. George looked at Alex, almost the same height as him in her high heels – another discovery – and made a mental promise to send her some flowers or something as soon as Divinyl opened on Monday.

'Oh, look, John, quick, they're coming!' said Alex, pointing to the door of the little church. John hastily put his camera to his eye and zoomed in on the doorway.

Fin and Rachel emerged with the vicar to cheers of delight from the crowd. Some threw rose petals, which fell in a pink shower around the happy couple. Fin, looking positively distinguished in a suit, but with his brown hair tousled as ever, had his arm around a beaming, blooming Rachel. Both looked as though they were about to burst with pride. Rachel, wearing a wide-skirted sundress and deep-brimmed hat, had the air of a Dior New Look Madonna, her blond hair in a mass of curls around her neck. Cradled in her arms was a tiny baby, with a halo of dark fluff and big green eyes.

'Aaaaah,' said Alex emotionally. 'He was so good all the way through. I didn't hear him make a sound. He just gurgled. It made me feel all—'

'Don't say it,' said George. 'Not while that thing's on.' He gestured towards John. 'You might live to regret it.'

They walked through the gathered friends and relations, murmuring hellos and exchanging nods of approval at the very happy family. Alex recognised some faces: Harriet Blythe from Rachel's office, who was kitted out in an almost-Chanel suit, her eyes darting here and there, hoping for a sighting of Dan Wingate; some picture editor friends of Fin that she'd met at parties, all of whom seemed to wear rectangular glasses with thick black frames; Rachel's mum and dad, he peering fascinatedly at the architectural details of the church and she peering at some of the more flamboyantly dressed guests with Rachel's quizzical eye.

Alex reached Rachel and leaned over to kiss her cheek, then bent down to touch a gentle kiss on the baby's forehead. His skin was like, well, a peach. Despite all her best intentions of being a cool godmother, she could feel tears begin to prick at her eyes.

'Thank you for the present, Alex,' said Fin as they exchanged kisses.

'Ah, well, it's really from George and me,' she said. 'A joint godparental present.'

Rachel raised her eyebrows. 'Oooh,' she said. 'Sounds pretty permanent. A bottle of port a year for what? Twenty-one years? I hope you've talked all this through?'

'I know,' said Alex. 'I was hoping you'd have a girl. I had it all planned – a charm bracelet and then a charm every birthday.' She rolled her eyes in George's direction.

'*Originally*, I was going to give him the classic backlist of one essential artist each year, starting with the Beatles, but I was talked out of it. Still, George knows his port.'

She glanced over to where George was chatting to Laura and Mike. Laura had her head cocked on one side in her old manner, and was obviously relishing her marital status. Mike just looked glad to see George.

'What did they send? Pretty cunning, by the way, transferring your wedding list to the christening.'

'Laura and Mike sent a pushchair. Deluxe. And it made sense, you know – we've already got all the stuff we want at home, like toasters and things. What we don't have lying around are nappies and liquidisers and baby alarms. Don't worry, you can have the whole lot when you produce,' said Rachel, jiggling her baby in her arms. He was falling asleep and beginning to glow.

Every time she looked at little Tom, she felt her heart swell up alarmingly with love. He looked so like Finlay, even down to the black eyebrows that knitted with concentration as he fed. A tiny finger fastened itself around hers, her wedding ring finger. Mrs Moran smiled to herself. Rachel and Finlay had turned the christening into a big gathering, since the October wedding that had satisfied Rachel's lingering need for order had been in Ireland last year, in the small Galway village where Finlay's family came from. Only their parents, all with hankies happily at the ready, Alex, holding the white roses of Rachel's bouquet, and George, standing in for Dan as best man, after an emergency call to EuroDisney had rendered him unavailable, had watched as they spoke aloud promises they had already made to each other. The priest had been only too glad to arrange the quiet ceremony for one of Joseph Moran's boys and they had spent a honeymoon week walking hand in hand along the deserted beaches of Carraroe and Gorumna Island, collecting seashells in empty Pringles tubes from the white-gold sand and taking photos of the frothy tide washing around their boots at the water's edge.

By the time they got back, the money from the Marvin story had come through from Dan's account, and Fin, in a fit of guilt, had given it all to Rachel and told her to leave Dunleary & Bright and do something proper with her life. It was a pretty substantial amount, even after Dan's dubious 50/50 split, which Rachel reckoned was more likely to be 60/40, but still enough to tweak Fin's sense of propriety, if not Rachel's.

After careful, detailed discussion over many, many cups of tea, it was decided that Rachel would become an investor in the new improved Divinyl, now with added muffin and coffee extension and relocated to a more desirable Upper Street address. Rachel found she could fit in her baking with the PR she did for the shop, look after the place while Alex went off to record fairs, and still have time to catch up on her sleep; Fin, whose broad shoulders and generous stomach came into their own with the arrival of the papoose, took care of his wife and child like a big bear, rushing home from assignments to preside happily over bathtime and playtime. She had never been so contented.

'Do you want to hold him?' Rachel asked Alex, who was looking lovingly at her godson. 'I have to go and get those ridiculous flowers out of the church before the next family come in at three.'

Alex held out her arms tentatively and Rachel decanted Thomas Hartley Moran into the crook of her arms. Alex laughed involuntarily. 'He's so warm!'

'I know,' said Rachel, tucking the christening robe under the baby's feet. 'Fin uses him like a hot-water bottle on his knee in the evenings. Watch out, he snores like me. Apparently.'

Alex stroked the appley cheek with her little finger and was delighted to see a tiny curve appear on Tom's lips. 'How did she know which church to send the flowers to?'

'Oh, I suppose Laura must have told her,' said Rachel, straightening her hat. 'That's what's so funny – it's so typically Caroline: "Sorry, darlings, can't be with you since I'm filming but here's an enormous bouquet of extra pungent lilies to make my presence felt." And we didn't even *invite* her.'

On the strength of the *News of the World* spread – four colour pages featuring Top TV Star In Northern Nookienest Snaps Shock and a centrespread of a scantily clad Caroline claiming mistily that she had been led astray – Caroline had gained a certain notoriety and been offered a part in a new Channel 4 sitcom. Partly thanks to John, she was also a regular on a variety of Channel Five game shows, all featuring tanned young things who were famous for being famous and not a lot else. Marvin meanwhile had retaliated by appearing on everything that would have him with his lovely wife, who had also brought out a gluten-free cookbook. And John had got a tidy amount from Laura's dad for the videotape of the night in question, but not before it had been lasciviously described in *Private Eye*.

Laura had continued to express disapproval – touched with a fair amount of resentment at the ruining of her weekend, according to Alex – that remorse had not yet been forthcoming from Caroline. Not even a note of apology, let alone divine come-uppance. She hadn't appeared at Laura and Mike's wedding, but mainly because she was in New York, auditioning. And this time, of course, she hadn't had a secret assignation to fly back for. Rachel knew that remorse probably never would come. There were a lot of polite people in the world. But thankfully not too many in the world Caroline was aiming at.

'Aren't you having any photographs?' Alex asked Fin.

Fin grinned. 'Oh, but we are.'

'Well, they've missed a lot. You don't want to be left with just John's video as the only memento, believe me.' She juggled Tom carefully in her arms. Fin tucked a stray baby leg, pinkly plump with a bare foot, expertly back into her cradled arms.

'Look over by the white building,' he said without looking up.

Alex looked. There was scaffolding all over the building, where workmen in bright yellow hard hats were busy converting an old print works into luxury flats. None of them had a camera as far as she could see.

'I can't see anything.'

'Damn,' said Fin. He finished fiddling with his baby and looked up, squinting against the sharp autumn sunshine. They both stared until Fin laughed and deliberately turned away to watch Rachel coming out of the church with a huge bouquet of long-stemmed lilies and twigs hiding most of her face.

'We have an arrangement with the photographer. If we can spot him doing our covert photos, we get them free as a christening present. If we *don't* see him, we have to take him out for a meal at the Anglesea. But he's up there, in that building. We gave him a bit of a handicap in that he had to look after Humpty during the service, but I'm pretty sure he'll be up there.' Fin pointed and waved. Alex still couldn't see what they were meant to be looking at. Eventually, returning little Tom to his father, she shrugged, giving Dan a superb photo opportunity, and joined George in admiring Laura's hat. As she did so, Dan appeared from round the back of the St Bride's Institute, nowhere near where Fin had anticipated, counting a handful of film canisters and just about keeping a barking Humpty under control.

Fin walked over to his wife and held out his free hand to her. He had taken thousands of pictures of Rachel in the time they had been together but had never seen her look as beautiful as she did today. She could have been anywhere between eighteen or thirty, radiating the peaceful serenity of a woman who finally knows who she is and what she is doing.

'So, Mrs Moran, do you feel grown up now?'

'No,' said Rachel, as Fin put his arms around her and they held their soft and gently snoring baby between them. With marriage and motherhood suddenly entwining her, she felt dizzyingly alive and acutely aware of everything. Every possibility, every hope, every challenge, every moment. Nothing was impossible any more. Rachel kissed Fin's soft mouth and whispered into his ear, 'And nor do I ever *want* to be grown up.'

GETTING HOME

Celia Brayfield

THERE IS ONLY ONE RULE IN A SUBURB –
NEVER TRUST YOUR NEIGHBOURS

Westwick, the ultimate suburb. Nothing ever happens in
Westwick; that's why people live there. Nice people, like
Stephanie Sands. Loving husband, adorable son, dream job
– life is just about perfect for Stephanie until the day her
husband is kidnapped.

Big mistake, losing your husband in the suburbs. The
neighbours turn nasty. The TV totty sees Stephanie as a
media victim and the totty's husband sees Stephanie as
'lonely' – codeword for desperate. Suddenly it's a jungle
out there – adultery, blackmail, sleaze in high places and
lust on the lawns, until Westwick scrambles the helicopters
and takes to the streets with an army of eco-warriors in the
hilarious live-TV climax.

Getting Home has outraged upholders of Volvo culture
everywhere. It's the funniest and wickedest novel yet from
one of our most modern and gifted storytellers.

'I couldn't be wrested away from it though they tried'
Fay Weldon

Other bestselling Warner titles available by mail:

☐ Getting Home	Celia Brayfield	£5.99
☐ A Peculiar Chemistry	Kitty Ray	£5.99
☐ All That She Wants	Maeve Haran	£5.99
☐ The Actresses	Babara Ewing	£5.99

The prices shown above are correct at time of going to press. However, the publishers reserve the right to increase prices on covers from those previously advertised without prior notice.

W

WARNER BOOKS

WARNER BOOKS
Cash Sales Department, P.O. Box 11, Falmouth, Cornwall, TR10 9EN
Tel: +44 (0) 1326 372400, Fax: +44 (0) 1326 374888
Email: books@barni.avel.co.uk.

POST AND PACKING:
Payments can be made as follows: cheque, postal order (payable to Warner Books) or by credit cards. Do not send cash or currency.

All U.K. Orders	**FREE OF CHARGE**
E.E.C. & Overseas	25% of order value

Name (Block Letters) _____

Address_____

_____

Post/zip code:_____

☐ Please keep me in touch with future Warner publications

☐ I enclose my remittance £_____

☐ I wish to pay by Visa/Access/Mastercard/Eurocard

Card Expiry Date

_____